THE MONASTERY.

By SIR WALTER SCOTT, BART.

Oh ay! the monks, the monks, they did the mischief!
Theirs all the grossness, all the superstition
Of a most gross and superstitious age.
                              —*Old Play.*

A. L. BURT COMPANY, PUBLISHERS
NEW YORK

THE MONASTERY.

CHAPTER I.

Oh ay! the monks, the monks,they did the mischief
Theirs all the grossness, all the superstition
Of a most gross and superstitious age.
May He be praised that sent the healthful tempest
And scatter'd all these pestilential vapours!
But that we owed them *all* to yonder harlot
Throned on the seven hills with her cup of gold,
I will as soon believe, with kind Sir Roger,
That old Moll White took wing with cat and broomstick
And raised the last night's thunder.

Old Play.

THE village described in the Benedictine's manuscript by
the name of Kennaquhair bears the same Celtic termination
which occurs in Traquhair, Caquhair, and other compounds.
The learned Chalmers derives this word "quhair" from the
winding course of a stream; a definition which coincides, in
a remarkable degree, with the serpentine turns of the river
Tweed near the village of which we speak. It has been long
famous for the splendid Monastery of St. Mary, founded by
David the First of Scotland, in whose reign were formed, in
the same county, the no less splendid establishments of Melrose, Jedburgh, and Kelso. The donations of land with which
the King endowed these wealthy fraternities procured him
from the monkish historians the epithet of Saint, and from
one of his impoverished descendants the splenetic censure,
"that he had been a sore saint for the crown."

It seems probable, notwithstanding, that David, who was a
wise as well as a pious monarch, was not moved solely by religious motives to those great acts of munificence to the church,
but annexed political views to his pious generosity. His pos-

sessions in Northumberland and Cumberland became precarious after the loss of the Battle of the Standard; and since the comparatively fertile valley of Teviotdale was likely to become the frontier of his kingdom, it is probable he wished to secure at least a part of these valuable possessions by placing them in the hands of the monks, whose property was for a long time respected, even amidst the rage of a frontier war. In this manner alone had the King some chance of ensuring protection and security to the cultivators of the soil; and, in fact, for several ages the possessions of these abbeys were each a sort of Goshen, enjoying the calm light of peace and immunity, while the rest of the country, occupied by wild clans and marauding barons, was one dark scene of confusion, blood, and unremitted outrage.

But these immunities did not continue down to the union of the crowns. Long before that period the wars betwixt England and Scotland had lost their original character of international hostilities, and had become on the part of the English a struggle for subjugation, on that of the Scots a desperate and infuriated defence of their liberties. This introduced on both sides a degree of fury and animosity unknown to the earlier period of their history; and as religious scruples soon gave way to national hatred, spurred by a love of plunder, the patrimony of the church was no longer sacred from incursions on either side. Still, however, the tenants and vassals of the great abbeys had many advantages over those of the lay barons, who were harassed by constant military duty, until they became desperate, and lost all relish for the arts of peace. The vassals of the church, on the other hand, were only liable to be called to arms on general occasions, and at other times were permitted in comparative quiet to possess their farms and feus.[1] They, of course, exhibited superior skill in everything that related to the cultivation of the soil, and were therefore both wealthier and better informed than the military retainers of the restless chiefs and nobles in their neighbourhood.

The residence of these church vassals was usually in ⌃ small

[1] See Church Tenants. Note 1.

village or hamlet, where, for the sake of mutual aid and protection, some thirty or forty families dwelt together. This was called the town, and the land belonging to the various families by whom the town was inhabited was called the township. They usually possessed the land in common, though in various proportions, according to their several grants. The part of the township properly arable, and kept as such continually under the plough, was called *in-field*. Here the use of quantities of manure supplied in some degree the exhaustion of the soil, and the feuars raised tolerable oats and bear, usually sowed on alternate ridges, on which the labour of the whole community was bestowed without distinction, the produce being divided after harvest, agreeably to their respective interests.

There was, besides, *out-field* land, from which it was thought possible to extract a crop now and then, after which it was abandoned to the "skyey influences," until the exhausted powers of vegetation were restored. These out-field spots were selected by any feuar at his own choice, amongst the sheep-walks and hills which were always annexed to the township, to serve as pasturage to the community. The trouble of cultivating these patches of out-field, and the precarious chance that the crop would pay the labour, were considered as giving a right to any feuar who chose to undertake the adventure to the produce which might result from it.

There remained the pasturage of extensive moors, where the valleys often afforded good grass, and upon which the whole cattle belonging to the community fed indiscriminately during the summer, under the charge of the town-herd, who regularly drove them out to pasture in the morning, and brought them back at night, without which precaution they would have fallen a speedy prey to some of the snatchers in the neighbourhood. These are things to make modern agriculturists hold up their hands and stare; but the same mode of cultivation is not yet entirely in desuetude in some distant parts of North Britain, and may be witnessed in full force and exercise in the Zetland Archipelago.

The habitations of the church feuars were not less primitive than their agriculture. In each village or town were several small towers, having battlements projecting over the side walls, and usually an advanced angle or two with shot-holes for flanking the doorway, which was always defended by a strong door of oak, studded with nails, and often by an exterior grated door of iron. These small peel-houses were ordinarily inhabited by the principal feuars and their families; but, upon the alarm of approaching danger, the whole inhabitants thronged from their own miserable cottages, which were situated around, to garrison these points of defence. It was then no easy matter for a hostile party to penetrate into the village, for the men were habituated to the use of bows and firearms, and the towers being generally so placed that the discharge from one crossed that of another, it was impossible to assault any of them individually.

The interior of these houses was usually sufficiently wretched, for it would have been folly to have furnished them in a manner which could excite the avarice of their lawless neighbours. Yet the families themselves exhibited in their appearance a degree of comfort, information, and independence which could hardly have been expected. Their in-field supplied them with bread and home-brewed ale, their herds and flocks with beef and mutton (the extravagance of killing lambs or calves was never thought of). Each family killed a mart, or fat bullock, in November, which was salted up for winter use, to which the goodwife could, upon great occasions, add a dish of pigeons or a fat capon; the ill-cultivated garden afforded "lang-cale"; and the river gave salmon to serve as a relish during the season of Lent.

Of fuel they had plenty, for the bogs afforded turf; and the remains of the abused woods continued to give them logs for burning, as well as timber for the usual domestic purposes. In addition to these comforts, the goodman would now and then sally forth to the greenwood, and mark down a buck of season with his gun or his cross-bow; and the father confessor seldom refused him absolution for the trespass, if duly invited to take his share of the smoking haunch. Some, still bolder, made, either with their own domestics or by associating themselves with the moss-troopers, in the language of shepherds, "a start and overloup"; and the golden ornaments and silken headgear worn by the females of one or two families of note were invidiously traced by their neighbours to such successful excursions. This, however, was a more inexpiable crime in the eyes of the abbot and community of St. Mary's than the borrowing one of the "gude king's deer"; and they failed not to discountenance and punish, by every means in their power, offences which were sure to lead to severe retaliation upon the property of the church, and which tended to alter the character of their peaceful vassalage.

As for the information possessed by those dependants of the abbacies, they might have been truly said to be better fed than taught, even though their fare had been worse than it was. Still, however, they enjoyed opportunities of knowledge from which others were excluded. The monks were in general well acquainted with their vassals and tenants, and familiar in the families of the better class among them, where they were sure to be received with the respect due to their twofold character of spiritual father and secular landlord. Thus it often happened, when a boy displayed talents and inclination for study, one of the brethren, with a view to his being bred to the church, or out of good-nature, in order to pass away his own idle time, if he had no better motive, initiated him into the mysteries of reading and writing, and imparted to him such other knowledge as he himself possessed. And the heads of these allied families, having more time for reflection, and more skill, as well as stronger motives for improving their small properties, bore amongst their neighbours the character of shrewd, intelligent men, who claimed respect on account of their comparative wealth, even while they were despised for a less warlike and enterprising turn than the other Borderers. They lived as much as they well could amongst themselves, avoiding the company of others, and dreading nothing more than to be involved in the deadly feuds and ceaseless contentions of the secular landholders.

Such is a general picture of these communities. During the fatal wars in the commencement of Queen Mary's reign they had suffered dreadfully by the hostile invasions. For

the English, now a Protestant people, were so far from sparing the church lands, that they forayed them with more unrelenting severity than even the possessions of the laity. But
the peace of 1550 had restored some degree of tranquillity to
these distracted and harassed regions, and matters began again
gradually to settle upon the former footing. The monks re-
paired their ravaged shrines; the feuar again roofed his small
fortalice which the enemy had ruined; the poor labourer re-
built his cottage—an easy task, where a few sods, stones, and a
few pieces of wood from the next copse furnished all the materials necessary. The cattle, lastly, were driven out of the
wastes and thickets in which the remnant of them had been
secreted; and the mighty bull moved at the head of his sera-
glio and their followers, to take possession of their wonted pastures. There ensued peace and quiet, the state of the age and
nation considered, to the Monastery of St. Mary and its de-
pendencies for several tranquil years.

CHAPTER II.

In yon lone vale his early youth was ored,
Not solitary then ; the bugle-horn
Of fell Alecto often waked its windings,
From where the brook joins the majestic river
To the wild northern bog, the curlew's haunt,
Where oozes forth its first and feeble streamlet.
                                             Old Play.

WE have said that most of the feuars dwelt in the village
belonging to their township. This was not, however, universally the case. A lonely tower, to which the reader must now
be introduced, was at least one exception to the general rule.
  It was of small dimensions, yet larger than those which occurred in the village, as intimating that, in case of assault, the
proprietor would have to rely upon his own unassisted strength.
Two or three miserable huts, at the foot of the fortalice, held
the bondsmen and tenants of the feuar. The site was a beautiful green knoll, which started up suddenly in the very throat
of a wild and narrow glen, and which, being surrounded, ex-

cept on one side, by the winding of a small stream, afforded a position of considerable strength.

But the great security of Glendearg, for so the place was called, lay in its secluded and almost hidden situation. To reach the tower, it was necessary to travel three miles up the glen, crossing about twenty times the little stream, which, winding through the narrow valley, encountered at every hundred yards the opposition of a rock or precipitous bank on the one side, which altered its course, and caused it to shoot off in an oblique direction to the other. The hills which ascend on each side of this glen are very steep, and rise boldly over the stream, which is thus imprisoned within their barriers. The sides of the glen are impracticable for horse, and are only to be traversed by means of the sheep-paths which lie along their sides. It would not be readily supposed that a road so hopeless and so difficult could lead to any habitation more important than the summer shealing of a shepherd.

Yet the glen, though lonely, nearly inaccessible, and sterile, was not then absolutely void of beauty. The turf which covered the small portion of level ground on the sides of the stream was as close and verdant as if it had occupied the scythes of a hundred gardeners once a fortnight; and it was garnished with an embroidery of daisies and wild-flowers which the scythes would certainly have destroyed. The little brook, now confined betwixt closer limits, now left at large to choose its course through the narrow valley, danced carelessly on from stream to pool, light and unturbid, as that better class of spirits who pass their way through life, yielding to insurmountable obstacles, but as far from being subdued by them as the sailor who meets by chance with an unfavourable wind, and shapes his course so as to be driven back as little as possible.

The mountains, as they would have been called in England, *Scotticé* the steep braes, rose abruptly over the little glen, here presenting the grey face of a rock, from which the turf had been peeled by the torrents, and there displaying patches of wood and copse, which had escaped the waste of the cattle and the sheep of the feuars, and which, feathering naturally

5

up the beds of empty torrents, or occupying the concave recesses of the bank, gave at once beauty and variety to the landscape. Above these scattered woods rose the hill in barren but purple majesty; the dark rich hue, particularly in autumn, contrasting beautifully with the thickets of oak and birch, the mountain-ashes and thorns, the alders and quivering aspens, which chequered and varied the descent, and not less with the dark green and velvet turf, which composed the level part of the narrow glen.

Yet, though thus embellished, the scene could neither be strictly termed sublime or beautiful, and scarcely even picturesque or striking. But its extreme solitude pressed on the heart; the traveller felt that uncertainty whither he was going, or in what so wild a path was to terminate, which at times strikes more on the imagination than the grand features of a show-scene, when you know the exact distance of the inn where your dinner is bespoke, and at the moment preparing. These are ideas, however, of a far later age; for at the time we treat of, the picturesque, the beautiful, the sublime, and all their intermediate shades were ideas absolutely unknown to the inhabitants and occasional visitors of Glendearg.

These had, however, attached to the scene feelings fitting the time. Its name, signifying the Red Valley, seems to have been derived not only from the purple colour of the heath, with which the upper part of the rising banks was profusely clothed, but also from the dark red colour of the rocks, and of the precipitous earthen banks, which in that country are called "scaurs." Another glen, about the head of Ettrick, has acquired the same name from similar circumstances; and there are probably more in Scotland to which it has been given.

As our Glendearg did not abound in mortal visitants, superstition, that it might not be absolutely destitute of inhabitants, had peopled its recesses with beings belonging to another world. The savage and capricious Brown Man of the Moors, a being which seems the genuine descendant of the Northern dwarfs, was supposed to be seen there frequently, especially after the autumnal equinox, when the fogs were thick and objects not easily distinguished.   The Scottish fairies, too, a whimsical, irritable, and mischievous tribe, who, though at times capriciously benevolent, were more frequently adverse to mortals, were also supposed to have formed a residence in a particularly wild recess of the glen, of which the real name was, in allusion to that circumstance, Corrie-nan-Shian, which, in corrupted Celtic, signifies the Hollow of the Fairies.   But the neighbours were more cautious in speaking about this place, and avoided giving it a name, from an idea common then throughout all the British and Celtic provinces of Scotland, and still retained in many places, that to speak either good or ill of this capricious race of imaginary beings is to provoke their resentment, and that secrecy and silence is what they chiefly desire from those who may intrude upon their revels or discover their haunts.

A mysterious terror was thus attached to the dale, which afforded access from the broad valley of the Tweed, up the little glen we have described, to the fortalice called the Tower of Glendearg.   Beyond the knoll, where, as we have said, the tower was situated, the hills grew more steep, and narrowed on the slender brook, so as scarce to leave a footpath; and there the glen terminated in a wild waterfall, where a slender thread of water dashed in a precipitous line of foam over two or three precipices.   Yet farther in the same direction, and above these successive cataracts, lay a wild and extensive morass, frequented only by water-fowl—wide, waste, apparently almost interminable, and serving in a great measure to separate the inhabitants of the glen from those who lived to the northward.

To restless and indefatigable moss-troopers, indeed, these morasses were well known and sometimes afforded a retreat. They often rode down the glen, called at this tower, asked and received hospitality, but still with a sort of reserve on the part of its more peaceful inhabitants, who entertained them as a party of North American Indians might be received by a new European settler, as much out of fear as hospitality, while the uppermost wish of the landlord is the speedy departure of the savage guests.

This had not always been the current of feeling in the little valley and its tower. Simon Glendinning, its former inhabitant, boasted his connexion by blood to that ancient family of Glendonwyne, on the western border. He used to narrate at his fireside, in the autumn evenings, the feats of the family to which he belonged, one of whom fell by the side of the brave Earl of Douglas at Otterbourne. On these occasions Simon usually held upon his knee an ancient broadsword, which had belonged to his ancestors before any of the family had consented to accept a fief under the peaceful dominion of the monks of St. Mary's. In modern days, Simon might have lived at ease on his own estate, and quietly murmured against the fate that had doomed him to dwell there, and cut off his access to martial renown. But so many opportunities, nay, so many calls, there were for him who in those days spoke big to make good his words by his actions, that Simon Glendinning was soon under the necessity of marching with the men of the halidome, as it was called, of St. Mary's in that disastrous campaign which was concluded by the battle of Pinkie.

The Catholic clergy were deeply interested in that national quarrel, the principal object of which was to prevent the union of the infant Queen Mary with the son of the heretical Henry VIII. The monks had called out their vassals, under an experienced leader. Many of themselves had taken arms, and marched to the field, under a banner representing a female, supposed to personify the Scottish Church, kneeling in the attitude of prayer, with the legend, *Afflictæ sponsæ ne obliviscaris*.

The Scots, however, in all their wars, had more occasion for good and cautious generals than for excitation, whether political or enthusiastic. Their headlong and impatient courage uniformly induced them to rush into action without duly weighing either their own situation or that of their enemies, and the inevitable consequence was frequent defeat. With the dolorous slaughter of Pinkie we have nothing to do, excepting that, among ten thousand men of low and high degree, Simon Glendinning, of the Tower of Glendearg, bit the dust, no way disparaging in his death that ancient race from which he claimed his descent.

When the doleful news, which spread terror and mourning through the whole of Scotland, reached the Tower of Glendearg, the widow of Simon, Elspeth Brydone by her family name, was alone in that desolate habitation, excepting a hind or two, alike past martial and agricultural labour, and the helpless widows and families of those who had fallen with their master. The feeling of desolation was universal; but what availed it? The monks, their patrons and protectors, were driven from their abbey by the English forces, who now overran the country, and compelled at least an appearance of submission on the part of the inhabitants. The Protector, Somerset, formed a strong camp among the ruins of the ancient castle of Roxburgh, and compelled the neighbouring country to come in, pay tribute, and take assurance from him, as the phrase then went. Indeed, there was no power of resistance remaining; and the few barons, whose high spirit disdained even the appearance of surrender, could only retreat into the wildest fastnesses of the country, leaving their houses and property to the wrath of the English, who detached parties everywhere to distress, by military exaction, those whose chiefs had not made their submission. The abbot and his community having retreated beyond the Forth, their lands were severely forayed, as their sentiments were held peculiarly inimical to the alliance with England.

Amongst the troops detached on this service was a small party commanded by Stawarth Bolton, a captain in the English army, and full of the blunt and unpretending gallantry and generosity which have so often distinguished that nation. Resistance was in vain. Elspeth Brydone, when she descried a dozen of horsemen threading their way up the glen, with a man at their head whose scarlet cloak, bright armour, and dancing plume proclaimed him a leader, saw no better protection for herself than to issue from the iron gate, covered with a long mourning veil, and holding one of her two sons in each hand, to meet the Englishman, state her deserted condition, place the little tower at his command, and beg for his mercy. She stated, in a few brief words, her intention, and added, "I submit, because I have nae means of resistance."

"And I do not ask your submission, mistress, for the same reason," replied the Englishman. "To be satisfied of your peaceful intentions is all I ask; and, from what you tell me, there is no reason to doubt them."

"At least, sir," said Elspeth Brydone, "take share of what our spence and our garners afford. Your horses are tired; your folk want refreshment."

"Not a whit—not a whit," answered the honest Englishman; "it shall never be said we disturbed by carousal the widow of a brave soldier, while she was mourning for her husband. Comrades, face about. Yet stay," he added, checking his war-horse, "my parties are out in every direction; they must have some token that your family are under my assurance of safety. Here, my little fellow," said he, speaking to the eldest boy, who might be about nine or ten years old, "lend me thy bonnet."

The child reddened, looked sulky, and hesitated, while the mother, with many a "fye" and "nay pshaw," and such sarsenet chidings as tender mothers give to spoiled children, at length succeeded in snatching the bonnet from him, and handing it to the English leader.

Stawarth Bolton took his embroidered red cross from his barret-cap, and putting it into the loop of the boy's bonnet, said to the mistress, for the title of lady was not given to dames of her degree, "By this token, which all my people will respect, you will be freed from any importunity on the part of our forayers." [1] He placed it on the boy's head; but it was no sooner there than the little fellow, his veins swelling and his eyes shooting fire through tears, snatched the bonnet from his head, and, ere his mother could interfere, skimmed it into the brook. The other boy ran instantly to fish it out again, threw it back to his brother, first taking out the cross, which, with great veneration, he kissed and put into his bosom. The Englishman was half-diverted, half-surprised with the scene.

"What mean ye by throwing away St. George's red cross?" said he to the elder boy, in a tone betwixt jest and earnest.

[1] See Gallantry. Note 2.

'Because St. George is a Southern saint," said the child, sulkily.

"Good!" said Stawarth Bolton. "And what did you mean by taking it out of the brook again, my little fellow?" he demanded of the younger.

"Because the priest says it is the common sign of salvation to all good Christians."

"Why, good again!" said the honest soldier. "I protest unto you, mistress, I envy you these boys. Are they both yours?"

Stawarth Bolton had reason to put the question, for Halbert Glendinning, the elder of the two, had hair as dark as the raven's plumage, black eyes, large, bold, and sparkling, that glittered under eyebrows of the same complexion, a skin deep embrowned, though it could not be termed swarthy, and an air of activity, frankness, and determination far beyond his age. On the other hand, Edward, the younger brother, was light-haired, blue-eyed, and of fair complexion, in countenance rather pale, and not exhibiting that rosy hue which colours the sanguine cheek of robust health. Yet the boy had nothing sickly or ill-conditioned in his look, but was, on the contrary, a fair and handsome child, with a smiling face and mild yet cheerful eye.

The mother glanced a proud motherly glance, first at the one and then at the other, ere she answered the Englishman— "Surely, sir, they are both my children."

"And by the same father, mistress?" said Stawarth; but, seeing a blush of displeasure arise on her brow, he instantly added: "Nay, I mean no offence; I would have asked the same question at any of my gossips in merry Lincoln. Well, dame, you have two fair boys; I would I could borrow one, for Dame Bolton and I live childless in our old hall. Come, little fellows, which of you will go with me?"

The trembling mother, half-fearing as he spoke, drew the children towards her, one with either hand, while they both answered the stranger. "I will not go with you," said Halbert, boldly, "for you are a false-hearted Southern, and the Southerns killed my father; and I will war on you to the death, when I can draw my father's sword."

"God-a-mercy, my little levin-bolt," said Stawarth, "the goodly custom of deadly feud will never go down in thy day, I presume. And you, my fine white-head, will you not go with me, to ride a cock-horse?"

"No," said Edward, demurely, "for you are a heretic."

"Why, God-a-mercy still!" said Stawarth Bolton. "Well, dame, I see I shall find no recruits for my troop from you; and yet I do envy you these two little chubby knaves." He sighed a moment, as was visible, in spite of gorget and corslet, and then added, "And yet my dame and I would but quarrel which of the knaves we should like best; for J should wish for the black-eyed rogue, and she, I warrant me, for that blue-eyed, fair-haired darling. Natheless, we must brook our solitary wedlock, and wish joy to those that are more fortunate. Sergeant Brittson, do thou remain here till recalled; protect this family, as under assurance; do them no wrong, and suffer no wrong to be done to them, as thou wilt answer it. Dame, Brittson is a married man, old and steady; feed him on what you will, but give him not over much liquor."

Dame Glendinning again offered refreshments, but with a faltering voice, and an obvious desire her invitation should not be accepted. The fact was, that, supposing her boys as precious in the eyes of the Englishman as in her own (the most ordinary of parental errors), she was half afraid that the admiration he expressed of them in his blunt manner might end in his actually carrying off one or other of the little darlings whom he appeared to covet so much. She kept hold of their hands, therefore, as if her feeble strength could have been of service had any violence been intended, and saw with joy she could not disguise the little party of horse countermarch, in order to descend the glen. Her feelings did not escape Stawarth Bolton. "I forgive you, dame," he said, "for being suspicious that an English falcon was hovering over your Scottish moor-brood. But fear not—those who have fewest children have fewest cares; nor does a wise man covet those of another household. Adieu, dame; when the black-eyed rogue is able to drive a foray from England, teach him to spare women and children, even for the sake of Stawarth Bolton."

"God be with you, gallant Southern!" said Elspeth Glendinning, but not till he was out of hearing, spurring on his good horse to regain the head of his party, whose plumage and armour were now glancing and gradually disappearing in the distance, as they winded down the glen.

"Mother," said the elder boy, "I will not say 'amen' to a prayer for a Southern."

"Mother," said the younger, more reverentially, "is it right to pray for a heretic?"

"The God to whom I pray only knows," answered poor Elspeth; "but these two words, 'Southern' and 'heretic,' have already cost Scotland ten thousand of her best and bravest, and me a husband and you a father; and, whether blessing or banning, I never wish to hear them more. Follow me to the place, sir," she said to Brittson, "and such as we have to offer you shall be at your disposal."

CHAPTER III.

They lighted down on Tweed water,
    And blew their coals sae het,
And fired the March and Teviotdale,
    All in an evening late.
                              Auld Maitland.

THE report soon spread through the patrimony of St. Mary's and its vicinity that the mistress of Glendearg had received assurance from the English captain, and that her cattle were not to be driven off, or her corn burnt. Among others who heard this report, it reached the ears of a lady who, once much higher in rank than Elspeth Glendinning, was now by the same calamity reduced to even greater misfortune.

She was the widow of a brave soldier, Walter Avenel, descended of a very ancient Border family, who once possessed immense estates in Eskdale. These had long since passed from them into other hands, but they still enjoyed an ancient barony of considerable extent, not very far from the patrimony of St. Mary's, and lying upon the same side of the river with the narrow vale of Glendearg, at the head of which was the little tower of the Glendinnings. Here they had lived, bearing a respectable rank amongst the gentry of their province, though neither wealthy nor powerful. This general regard had been much augmented by the skill, courage, and enterprise which had been displayed by Walter Avenel, the last baron.

When Scotland began to recover from the dreadful shock she had sustained after the battle of Pinkie Cleuch, Avenel was one of the first who, assembling a small force, set an example in those bloody and unsparing skirmishes which showed that a nation, though conquered and overrun by invaders, may yet wage against them such a war of detail as shall in the end become fatal to the foreigners. In one of these, however, Walter Avenel fell, and the news which came to the house of his fathers was followed by the distracting intelligence that a party of Englishmen were coming to plunder the mansion and lands of his widow, in order, by this act of terror, to prevent others from following the example of the deceased.

The unfortunate lady had no better refuge than the miserable cottage of a shepherd among the hills, to which she was hastily removed, scarce conscious where or for what purpose her terrified attendants were removing her and her infant daughter from her own house. Here she was tended with all the duteous service of ancient times by the shepherd's wife, Tibb Tacket, who in better days had been her own bower-woman. For a time the lady was unconscious of her misery; but when the first stunning effect of grief was so far passed away that she could form an estimate of her own situation, the widow of Avenel had cause to envy the lot of her husband in his dark and silent abode. The domestics who had guided her to her place of refuge were presently obliged to disperse for their own safety, or to seek for necessary subsistence; and the shepherd and his wife, whose poor cottage she shared, were soon after deprived of the means of affording their late mistress even that coarse sustenance which they had gladly shared with her. Some of the English forayers had discovered and driven off the few sheep which had escaped the first researches of their avarice. Two cows shared the fate of the remnant of their stock; they had afforded the family almost their sole support, and now famine appeared to stare them in the face.

"We are broken and beggared now, out and out," said old Martin, the shepherd, and he wrung his hands in the bitterness of agony; "the thieves—the harrying thieves! not a cloot left of the haill hirsel!"

"And to see poor Grizzy and Crummie," said his wife, "turning back their necks to the byre, and routing while the stony-hearted villains were brogging them on wi' their lances!"

"There were but four of them," said Martin, "and I have seen the day forty wad not have ventured this length. But our strength and manhood is gane with our puir maister!"

"For the sake of the holy rood, whisht, man!" said the good wife; "our leddy is half gane already, as ye may see by that fleightering of the ee-lid—a word mair and she's dead outright."

"I could almost wish," said Martin, "we were a' gane, for what to do passes my puir wit. I care little for mysell, or you, Tibb; we can make a fend—work or want—we can do baith, but she can do neither."

They canvassed their situation thus openly before the lady, convinced by the paleness of her look, her quivering lip, and dead-set eye that she neither heard nor understood what they were saying.

"There is a way," said the shepherd, "but I kenna if she could bring her heart to it: there's Simon Glendinning's widow of the glen yonder has had assurance from the Southern loons, and nae soldier to steer them for one cause or other. Now, if the leddy could bow her mind to take quarters with Elspeth Glendinning till better days cast up, nae doubt it wad be doing an honour to the like of her, but——"

"An honour!" answered Tibb; "ay, by my word, sic an honour as wad be pride to her kin mony a lang year after her banes were in the mould. Oh! gudeman, to hear ye even the Lady of Avenel to seeking quarters wi' a kirk-vassal's widow!"

"Loth should I be to wish her to it," said Martin; "but what may we do? To stay here is mere starvation; and where to go, I'm sure I ken nae mair than ony tup I ever herded."

"Speak no more of it," said the widow of Avenel, suddenly joining in the conversation, "I will go to the tower. Dame Elspeth is of good folk, a widow, and the mother of orphans; she will give us house-room until something be thought upon. These evil showers make the low bush better than no bield."

"See there—see there," said Martin, "you see the leddy has twice our sense."

"And natural it is," said Tibb, "seeing that she is convent bred, and can lay silk broidery, forbye white-seam and shell-work."

"Do you not think," said the lady to Martin, still clasping her child to her bosom, and making it clear from what motives she desired the refuge, "that Dame Glendinning will make us welcome?"

"Blythely welcome—blythely welcome, my leddy," answered Martin, cheerily, "and we shall deserve a welcome at her hand. Men are scarce now, my leddy, with these wars; and gie me a thought of time to it, I can do as gude a day's darg as ever I did in my life, and Tibb can sort cows with ony living woman."

"And muckle mair could I do," said Tibb, "were it in ony feasible house; but there will be neither pearlins to mend nor pinners to busk up in Elspeth Glendinning's."

"Whisht wi' your pride, woman," said the shepherd; "eneugh ye can do, baith outside and inside, an ye set your mind to it; and hard it is if we twa canna work for three folks' meat, forbye my dainty wee leddy there. Come awa' —come awa,' nae use in staying here langer; we have five Scots miles over moss and muir, and that is nae easy walk for a leddy born and bred."

Household stuff there was little or none to remove or care for; an old pony which had escaped the plunderers, owing partly to its pitiful appearance, partly for the reluctance which it showed to be caught by strangers, was employed to carry the few blankets and other trifles which they possessed. When Shagram came to his master's well-known whistle, he was surprised to find the poor thing had been wounded, though slightly, by an arrow, which one of the forayers had shot off in anger after he had long chased it in vain.

"Ay, Shagram," said the old man, as he applied something to the wound, "must you rue the lang-bow as weel as all of us?"

"What corner in Scotland rues it not?" said the Lady of Avenel.

"Ay, ay, madam," said Martin, "God keep the kindly Scot from the cloth-yard shaft, and he will keep himself from the handy stroke. But let us go our way; the trash that is left I can come back for. There is nae ane to stir it but the good neighbours, and they——"

"For the love of God, goodman," said his wife, in a remonstrating tone, "haud your peace! Think what ye're saying, and we hae sae muckle wild land to go over before we win to the girth gate."

The husband nodded acquiescence; for it was deemed highly imprudent to speak of the fairies either by their title of *good neighbours* [1] or by any other, especially when about to pass the places which they were supposed to haunt.

They set forward on their pilgrimage on the last day of October. "This is thy birthday, my sweet Mary," said the mother, as a sting of bitter recollection crossed her mind. "Oh, who could have believed that the head which, a few years since, was cradled amongst so many rejoicing friends, may perhaps this night seek a cover in vain!"

The exiled family then set forward—Mary Avenel, a lovely girl between five and six years old, riding gipsy fashion upon Shagram, betwixt two bundles of bedding; the Lady of Avenel walking by the animal's side; Tibb leading the bridle;

[1] See Note 3.

and old Martin walking a little before, looking anxious
around him to explore the way.

Martin's task as guide, after two or three miles' walking,
became more difficult than he himself had expected, or than
he was willing to avow. It happened that the extensive
range of pasturage with which he was conversant lay to the
west, and to get into the little valley of Glendearg he had to
proceed easterly. In the wilder districts of Scotland, the
passage fom one vale to another, otherwise than by descending that which you leave and reascending the other, is often
very difficult. Heights and hollows, mosses and rocks, intervene, and all those local impediments which throw a traveller
out of his course. So that Martin, however sure of his general direction, became conscious, and at length was forced reluctantly to admit, that he had missed the direct road to Glendearg, though he insisted they must be very near it. "If we
can but win across this wide bog," he said, "I shall warrant
we are on the top of the tower."

But to get across the bog was a point of no small difficulty.
The farther they ventured into it, though proceeding with all
the caution which Martin's experience recommended, the more
unsound the ground became, until, after they had passed some
places of great peril, their best argument for going forward
came to be that they had to encounter equal danger in returning.

The Lady of Avenel had been tenderly nurtured, but what
will not a woman endure when her child is in danger? Com-
plaining less of the dangers of the road than her attendants,
who had been inured to such from their infancy, she kept
herself close by the side of the pony, watching its every foot-
step, and ready, if it should flounder in the morass, to snatch
her little Mary from its back.

At length they came to a place where the guide greatly
hesitated, for all around him was broken lumps of heath, divided from each other by deep sloughs of black tenacious
mire. After great consideration, Martin, selecting what he
thought the safest path, began himself to lead forward Shagram, in order to afford greater security to the child. But

Shagram snorted, laid his ears back, stretched his two feet forward, and drew his hind feet under him, so as to adopt the best possible posture for obstinate resistance, and refused to move one yard in the direction indicated. Old Martin, much puzzled, now hesitated whether to exert his absolute authority, or to defer to the contumacious obstinacy of Shagram, and was not greatly comforted by his wife's observation, who, seeing Shagram stare with his eyes, distend his nostrils, and tremble with terror, hinted that "He surely saw more than they could see."

In this dilemma, the child suddenly exclaimed, "Bonny leddy signs to us to come yon gate." They all looked in the direction where the child pointed, but saw nothing, save a wreath of rising mist, which fancy might form into a human figure; but which afforded to Martin only the sorrowful conviction that the danger of their situation was about to be increased by a heavy fog. He once more essayed to lead forward Shagram; but the animal was inflexible in its determination not to move in the direction Martin recommended. "Take your awn way for it, then," said Martin, "and let us see what you can do for us."

Shagram, abandoned to the direction of his own free will, set off boldly in the direction the child had pointed. There was nothing wonderful in this, nor in its bringing them safe to the other side of the dangerous morass; for the instinct of these animals in traversing bogs is one of the most curious parts of their nature, and is a fact generally established. But it was remarkable that the child more than once mentioned the beautiful lady and her signals, and that Shagram seemed to be in the secret, always moving in the same direction which she indicated. The Lady of Avenel took little notice at the time, her mind being probably occupied by the instant danger; but her attendants exchanged expressive looks with each other more than once.

"All-Hallow eve!" said Tibb, in a whisper to Martin.

"For the mercy of Our Lady, not a word of that now!" said Martin in reply. "Tell your beads, woman, if you cannot be silent."

When they got once more on firm ground, Martin recognised certain landmarks, or cairns, on the tops of the neighbouring hills, by which he was enabled to guide his course, and ere long they arrived at the Tower of Glendearg.

It was at the sight of this fortalice that the misery of her lot pressed hard on the poor Lady Avenel. When by any accident they had met at church, market, or place of public resort, she remembered the distant and respectful air with which the wife of the warlike baron was addressed by the spouse of the humble feuar. And now, so much was her pride humbled, that she was to ask to share the precarious safety of the same feuar's widow, and her pittance of food, which might perhaps be yet more precarious. Martin probably guessed what was passing in her mind, for he looked at her with a wistful glance, as if to deprecate any change of resolution; and answering to his looks rather than his words, she said, while the sparkle of subdued pride once more glanced from her eye, "If it were for myself alone, I could but die; but for this infant, the last pledge of Avenel——"

"True, my lady," said Martin, hastily; and, as if to prevent the possibility of her retracting, he added: "I will step on and see Dame Elspeth. I kenn'd her husband weel, and have bought and sold with him, for as great a man as he was."

Martin's tale was soon told, and met all acceptance from her companion in misfortune. The Lady of Avenel had been meek and courteous in her prosperity; in adversity, therefore, she met with the greater sympathy. Besides, there was a point of pride in sheltering and supporting a woman of such superior birth and rank; and, not to do Elspeth Glendinning injustice, she felt sympathy for a woman whose fate resembled her own in so many points, yet was so much more severe. Every species of hospitality was gladly and respectfully extended to the distressed travellers, and they were kindly requested to stay as long at Glendearg as their circumstances rendered necessary or their inclination prompted.

CHAPTER IV.

Ne'er be I found by thee unawed,
On that thrice hallow'd eve abroad,
When goblins haunt from flood and fen,
The steps of men.
COLLIN's *Ode to Fear.*

As the country became more settled, the Lady of Avenel would have willingly returned to her husband's mansion. But that was no longer in her power. It was a reign of minority, when the strongest had the best right, and when acts of usurpation were frequent amongst those who had much power and little conscience.

Julian Avenel, the younger brother of the deceased Walter, was a person of this description. He hesitated not to seize upon his brother's house and lands so soon as the retreat of the English permitted him. At first he occupied the property in the name of his niece; but when the lady proposed to return with her child to the mansion of its fathers, he gave her to understand that Avenel, being a male fief, descended to the brother, instead of the daughter, of the last possessor. The ancient philosopher declined a dispute with the emperor who commanded twenty legions, and the widow of Walter Avenel was in no condition to maintain a contest with the leader of twenty moss-troopers. Julian was also a man of service, who could back a friend in case of need, and was sure, therefore, to find protectors among the ruling powers. In short, however clear the little Mary's right to the possessions of her father, her mother saw the necessity of giving way, at least for the time, to the usurpation of her uncle.

Her patience and forbearance were so far attended with advantage, that Julian, for very shame's sake, could no longer suffer her to be absolutely dependent on the charity of Elspeth Glendinning. A drove of cattle and a bull, which were probably missed by some English farmer, were driven to the pastures of Glendearg; presents of raiment and household stuff were sent liberally, and some little money, though with a

6

more sparing han ; for those in the situation of Julian Ave
nel could come more easily by the goods than the representing
medium of value, and made their payments chiefly in kind.

In the mean time, the widows of Walter Avenel and Simon
Glendinning had become habituated to each other's society,
and were unwilling to part. The lady could hope no more
secret and secure residence than in the Tower of Glendearg, and
she was now in a condition to support her share of the mutual
housekeeping. Elspeth, on the other hand, felt pride, as well
as pleasure, in the society of a guest of such distinction, and
was at all times willing to pay much greater deference than
the Lady of Walter Avenel could be prevailed on to accept.

Martin and his wife diligently served the united family in
their several vocations, and yielded obedience to both mis-
tresses, though always considering themselves as the especial
servants of the Lady of Avenel. This distinction sometimes
occasioned a slight degree of difference between Dame Elspeth
and Tibb; the former being jealous of her own consequence,
and the latter apt to lay too much stress upon the rank and
family of her mistress. But both were alike desirous to conceal such petty squabbles from the lady, her hostess scarce
yielding to her old domestic in respect for her person.
Neither did the difference exist in such a degree as to interrupt the general harmony of the family, for the one wisely
gave way as she saw the other become warm; and Tibb,
though she often gave the first provocation, had generally the
sense to be the first in relinquishing the argument.

The world which lay beyond was gradually forgotten by the
inhabitants of this sequestered glen, and unless when she attended mass at the monastery church upon some high holiday,
Alice of Avenel almost forgot that she once held an equal rank
with the proud wives of the neighbouring barons and nobles
who on such occasions crowded to the solemnity. The recollection gave her little pain. She loved her husband for himself, and in his inestimable loss all lesser subjects of regret
had ceased to interest her. At times, indeed, she thought of
claiming the protection of the Queen Regent (Mary of Guise)
for her little orphan, but the fear of Julian Avenel always

came between. She was sensible that he would have neither scruple nor difficulty in spiriting away the child (if he did not proceed farther), should he once consider its existence as formidable to his interest. Besides, he led a wild and unsettled life, mingling in all feuds and forays, wherever there was a spear to be broken; he evinced no purpose of marrying, and the fate which he continually was braving might at length remove him from his usurped inheritance. Alice of Avenel, therefore, judged it wise to check all ambitious thoughts for the present, and remain quiet in the rude but peaceable retreat to which Providence had conducted her.

It was upon an All-Hallow's eve, when the family had resided together for the space of three years, that the domestic circle was assembled round the blazing turf-fire, in the old narrow hall of the Tower of Glendearg. The idea of the master or mistress of the mansion feeding or living apart from their domestics was at this period never entertained. The highest end of the board, the most commodious settle by the fire—these were the only marks of distinction; and the servants mingled, with deference indeed, but unreproved and with freedom, in whatever conversation was going forward. But the two or three domestics, kept merely for agricultural purposes, had retired to their own cottages without, and with them a couple of wenches, usually employed within doors, the daughters of one of the hinds.

After their departure, Martin locked first the iron grate, and secondly the inner door, of the tower, when the domestic circle was thus arranged. Dame Elspeth sate pulling the thread from her distaff; Tibb watched the progress of scalding the whey, which hung in a large pot upon the "crook," a chain terminated by a hook, which was suspended in the chimney to serve the purpose of the modern crane. Martin, while busied in repairing some of the household articles—for every man in those days was his own carpenter and smith, as well as his own tailor and shoemaker—kept from time to time a watchful eye upon the three children.

They were allowed, however, to exercise their juvenile restlessness by running up and down the hall, behind the seats of the elder members of the family, with the privilege of occasionally making excursions into one or two small apartments which opened from it, and gave excellent opportunity to play at hide-and-seek. This night, however, the children seemed not disposed to avail themselves of their privilege of visiting these dark regions, but preferred carrying on their gambols in the vicinity of the light.

In the mean while, Alice of Avenel, sitting close to an iron candlestick, which supported a misshapen torch of domestic manufacture, read small detached passages from a thick clasped volume, which she preserved with the greatest care. The art of reading the lady had acquired by her residence in a nunnery during her youth, but she seldom of late years put it to any other use than perusing this little volume, which formed her whole library. The family listened to the portions which she selected, as to some good thing which there was a merit in hearing with respect, whether it was fully understood or no. To her daughter Alice of Avenel had determined to impart their mystery more fully, but the knowledge was at that period attended with personal danger, and was not rashly to be trusted to a child.

The noise of the romping children interrupted, from time to time, the voice of the lady, and drew on the noisy culprits the rebuke of Elspeth.

"Could they not go farther a-field, if they behoved to make such a din, and disturb the lady's good words?" And this command was backed with the threat of sending the whole party to bed if it was not attended to punctually. Acting under the injunction, the children first played at a greater distance from the party, and more quietly, and then began to stray into the adjacent apartments, as they became impatient of the restraint to which they were subjected. But all at once the two boys came open-mouthed into the hall, to tell that there was an armed man in the spence.

"It must be Christie of Clinthill," said Martin, rising; "what can have brought him here at this time?"

"Or how came he in?" said Elspeth.

"Alas! what can he seek?" said the Lady of Avenel, to

whom this man, a retainer of her husband's brother, and who sometimes executed his commissions at Glendearg, was an object of secret apprehension and suspicion. "Gracious Heavens!" she added, rising up, "where is my child?" All rushed to the spence, Halbert Glendinning first arming himself with a rusty sword, and the younger seizing upon the lady's book. They hastened to the spence, and were relieved of a part of their anxiety by meeting Mary at the door of the apartment. She did not seem in the slightest degree alarmed or disturbed. They rushed into the spence, a sort of interior apartment in which the family ate their victuals in the summer season; but there was no one there.

"Where is Christie of Clinthill?" said Martin.

"I do not know," said little Mary; "I never saw him."

"And what made you, ye misleard loons," said Dame Elspeth to her two boys, "come yon gate into the ha', roaring like bullseggs, to frighten the leddy, and her far frae strong?" The boys looked at each other in silence and confusion, and their mother proceeded with her lecture. "Could ye find nae night for daffin but Hallowe'en, and nae time but when the leddy was reading to us about the holy saints? May—ne'er be in my fingers, if I dinna sort ye baith for it!" The eldest boy bent his eyes on the ground, the younger began to weep, but neither spoke; and the mother would have proceeded to extremities, but for the interposition of the little maiden.

"Dame Elspeth, it was *my* fault; I did say to them that I saw a man in the spence."

"And what made you do so, child," said her mother, "to startle us all thus?"

"Because," said Mary, lowering her voice, "I could not help it."

"Not help it, Mary!—you occasioned all this idle noise, and you could not help it? How mean you by that, minion?"

"There really was an armed man in the spence," said Mary; "and because I was surprised to see him, I cried out to Halbert and Edward——"

"She has told it herself," said Halbert Glendinning, "or it had never been told by me."

"Nor by me neither," said Edward, emulously.

"Mistress Mary," said Elspeth, "you never told us anything before that was not true; tell us if this was a Hallowe'en cantrip, and make an end of it." The Lady of Avenel looked as if she would have interfered, but knew not how; and Elspeth, who was too eagerly curious to regard any distant hint, persevered in her inquiries. "Was it Christie of the Clinthill? I would not for a mark that he were about the house, and a body no ken whare."

"It was not Christie," said Mary; "it was—it was a gentleman—a gentleman with a bright breastplate, like what I hae seen langsyne, when we dwelt at Avenel——"

"What like was he?" continued Tibb, who now took share in the investigation.

"Black-haired, black-eyed, with a peaked black beard," said the child, "and many a fold of pearling round his neck, and hanging down his breast ower his breastplate; and he had a beautiful hawk, with silver bells, standing on his left hand, with a crimson silk hood upon its head——"

"Ask her no more questions, for the love of God," said the anxious menial to Elspeth, "but look to my leddy!" But the Lady of Avenel, taking Mary in her hand, turned hastily away, and, walking into the hall, gave them no opportunity of remarking in what manner she received the child's communication, which she thus cut short. What Tibb thought of it appeared from her crossing herself repeatedly, and whispering into Elspeth's ear, "St. Mary preserve us! the lassie has seen her father!"

When they reached the hall, they found the lady holding her daughter on her knee, and kissing her repeatedly. When they entered, she again rose, as if to shun observation, and retired to the little apartment where her child and she occupied the same bed.

The boys were also sent to their cabin, and no one remained by the hall fire save the faithful Tibb and Dame Elspeth, excellent persons both, and as thorough gossips as ever wagged a tongue.

It was but natural that they should instantly resume the

subject of the supernatural appearance, for such they deemed it, which had this night alarmed the family.

"I could hae wished it had been the deil himself—be good to and preserve us!—rather than Christie o' the Clinthill," said the matron of the mansion, "for the word runs rife in the country that he is ane of the maist masterfu' thieves ever lap on horse."

"Hout tout, Dame Elspeth," said Tibb, "fear ye naething frae Christie; tods keep their ain holes clean. You kirk-folk make sic a fasherie about men shifting a wee bit for their living! Our Border lairds would ride with few men at their back, if a' the light-handed lads were out o' gate."

"Better they rade wi' nane than distress the country-side the gate they do," said Dame Elspeth.

"But wha is to haud back the Southron, then," said Tibb, "if ye take away the lances and broadswords? I trow we auld wives couldna do that wi' rock and wheel, and as little the monks wi' bell and book."

"And sae weel as the lances and broadswords hae kept them back, I trow! I was mair beholden to ae Southron, and that was Stawarth Bolton, than to a' the Border-riders ever wore St. Andrew's cross. I reckon their skelping back and forward, and lifting honest men's gear, has been a main cause of a' the breach between us and England, and I am sure that cost me a kind goodman. They spoke about the wedding of the Prince and our Queen, but it's as like to be the driving of the Cumberland folks' stocking that brought them down on us like dragons."

Tibb would not have failed in other circumstances to answer what she thought reflections disparaging to her country folk; but she recollected that Dame Elspeth was mistress of the family, curbed her own zealous patriotism, and hastened to change the subject.

"And is it not strange," she said, "that the heiress of Avenel should have seen her father this blessed night.?"

"And ye think it was her father, then?" said Elspeth Glendinning.

"What else can I think?" said Tibb.

"It may hae been something waur, in his likeness," said Dame Glendinning.

"I ken naething about that," said Tibb; "but his likeness it was, that I will be sworn to, just as he used to ride out a-hawking; for having enemies in the country, he seldom laid off the breastplate; and for my part," added Tibb, "I dinna think a man looks like a man unless he has steel on his breast and by his side too."

"I have no skill of your harness on breast or side either," said Dame Glendinning; "but I ken there is little luck in Hallowe'en sights, for I have had ane mysell."

"Indeed, Dame Elspeth?" said old Tibb, edging her stool closer to the huge elbow-chair occupied by her friend, "I should like to hear about that."

"Ye maun ken then, Tibb," said Dame Glendinning, "that, when I was a hempie of nineteen or twenty, it wasna my fault if I wasna at a' the merry-makings time about."

"That was very natural," said Tibb; "but ye hae sobered since that, or ye wadna haud our braw gallants sae lightly."

"I have had that wad sober me or ony ane," said the matron. "Aweel, Tibb, a lass like me wasna to lack wooers, for I wasna sae ill-favoured that the tykes wad bark after me."

"How should that be," said Tibb, "and you sic a weel-favoured woman to this day?"

"Fie, fie, cummer," said the matron of Glendearg, hitching her seat of honour, in her turn, a little nearer to the cuttiestool no which Tibb was seated; "weel-favoured is past my time of day; but I might pass then, for I wasna sae tocherless but what I had a bit land at my breast-lace. My father was portioner of Littledearg."

"Ye hae tell'd me that before," said Tibb; "but anent the Hallowe'en?"

"Aweel—aweel, I had mair joes than ane, but I favoured nane o' them; and sae, at Hallowe'en, Father Nicolas, the cellarer—he was cellarer before this father, Father Clement, that now is—was cracking his nuts and drinking his brown beer with us, and as blythe as might be, and they would have me try a cantrip to ken wha suld wed me; and the monk said

there was nae ill in it, and if there was, he would assoil me
for it.   And wha but I into the barn to winnow my three
weights o' naething?   Sair, sair my mind misgave me for fear
of wrang-doing and wrang-suffering baith; but I had aye a
bauld spirit.   I had not winnowed the last weight clean out,
and the moon was shining bright upon the floor, when in
stalked the presence of my dear Simon Glendinning, that is
now happy.   I never saw him plainer in my life than I did
that moment; he held up an arrow as he passed me, and I
swarf'd awa' wi' fright.   Muckle wark there was to bring me
to mysell again, and sair they tried to make me believe it was
a trick of Father Nicolas and Simon between them, and that
the arrow was to signify Cupid's shaft, as the father called
it; and mony a time Simon wad threep it to me after I was
married—gude man, he liked not it should be said that he
was seen out o' the body!   But mark the end o' it, Tibb: we
were married, and the grey-goose wing was the death o' him
after a'!"

"As it has been of ower mony brave men," said Tibb; "I
wish there wasna sic a bird as a goose in the wide warld, forbye the clecking that we hae at the burn-side."

"But tell me, Tibb," said Dame Glendinning, "what does
your leddy aye do reading out o' that thick black book wi'
the silver clasps?   there are ower mony gude words in it to
come frae ony body but a priest.   An it were about Robin
Hood, or some o' David Lindsay's ballants, ane wad ken better what to say to it.   I am no misdoubting your mistress
nae way, but I wad like ill to hae a decent house haunted
wi' ghaists and gyre-carlines."

"Ye hae nae reason to doubt my leddy, or ony thing she
says or does, Dame Glendinning," said the faithful Tibb,
something offended; "and touching the bairn, it's weel
kenn'd she was born on Hallowe'en was nine years gane, and
they that are born on Hallowe'en whiles see mair than ither
folk."

"And that wad be the cause, then, that the bairn didna
mak muckle din about what it saw?   If it had been my Halbert himself, forbye Edward, who is of softer nature, he wad

hae yammered the haill night of a constancy. But it's like
Mistress Mary has sic sights mair natural to her."

"That may weel be," said Tibb; "for on Hallowe'en she
was born, as I tell ye, and our auld parish priest wad fain hae
had the night ower, and All-Hallow day begun. But for a'
that the sweet bairn is just like ither bairns, as ye may see
yoursell; and except this blessed night, and ance before when
we were in that weary bog on the road here, I kenna that it
saw mair than ither folk."

"But what saw she in the bog, then," said Dame Glendinning, "forbye moor-cocks and heather-blutters?"

"The wean saw something like a white leddy that weised
us the gate," said Tibb, "when we were like to hae perished
in the moss-hags: certain it was that Shagram reisted, and I
ken Martin thinks he saw something."

"And what might the white leddy be?" said Elspeth;
"have ye ony guess o' that?"

"It's weel kenn'd that, Dame Elspeth," said Tibb; "if ye
had lived under grit folk, as I hae dune, ye wadna be to seek
in that matter."

"I hae aye keepit my ain ha' house abune my head," said
Elspeth, not without emphasis, "and if I havena lived wi'
grit folk, grit folk have lived wi' me."

"Weel—weel, dame," said Tibb, "your pardon's prayed,
there was nae offence meant. But ye maun ken the great
ancient families canna be just served wi' the ordinary saunts
—praise to them!—like Saunt Anthony, Saunt Cuthbert, and
the like, that come and gang at every sinner's bidding, but
they hae a sort of saunts or angels, or what not, to themsells;
and as for the White Maiden of Avenel, she is kenn'd ower
the haill country. And she is aye seen to yammer and wail
before ony o' that family dies, as was weel kenn'd by twenty
folk before the death of Walter Avenel, haly be his cast!"

"If she can do nae mair than that," said Elspeth, somewhat
scornfully, "they needna make mony vows to her, I trow.
Can she make nae better fend for them than that, and has naething better to do than wait on them?"

"Mony braw services can the White Maiden do for them to

the boo. of that, and has dune in the auld histories," said
Tibb; "but I mind o' naething in my day, except it was her
that the bairn saw in the bog."

"Aweel—aweel, Tibb," said Dame Glendinning, rising and
lighting the iron lamp, "these are great privileges of your
grand folk. But Our Lady and Saunt Paul are good eneugh
saunts for me, and I'se warrant them never leave me in a bog
that they can help me out a', seeing I send four waxen candles
to their chapels every Candlemas; and if they are not seen to
weep at my death, I'se warrant them smile at my joyful rising again, whilk Heaven send to all of us, Amen."

"Amen," answered Tibb, devoutly; "and now it's time I
should hap up the wee bit gathering turf, as the fire is ower
low."

Busily she set herself to perform this duty. The relic of
Simon Glendinning did but pause a moment to cast a heedful
and cautious glance all around the hall, to see that nothing
was out of its proper place; then, wishing Tibb good-night,
she retired to repose.

"The deil's in the carline," said Tibb to herself; "because
she was the wife of a cock-laird, she thinks herself grander,
I trow, than the bower-woman of a lady of that ilk!" Having given vent to her suppressed spleen in this little ejaculation, Tibb also betook herself to slumber.

CHAPTER V.

A priest, ye cry, a priest!—lame shepherds they,
How shall they gather in the straggling flock?
Dumb dogs which bark not—how shall they compel
The loitering vagrants to the Master's fold?
Fitter to bask before the blazing fire,
And snuff the mess neat-handed Phillis dresses,
Than on the snow-wreath battle with the wolf.
                                        The Reformation.

THE health of the Lady of Avenel had been gradually decaying ever since her disaster. It seemed as if the few years
which followed her husband's death had done on her the work

of half a century. She lost the fresh elasticity of form, the colour and the mien of health, and became wasted, wan, and feeble. She appeared to have no formed complaint; yet it was evident to those who looked on her that her strength waned daily. Her lips at length became blenched and her eye dim; yet she spoke not of any desire to see a priest, until Elspeth Glendinning in her zeal could not refrain from touching upon a point which she deemed essential to salvation. Alice of Avenel received her hint kindly, and thanked her for it.

"If any good priest would take the trouble of such a journey," she said, "he should be welcome; for the prayers and lessons of the good must be at all times advantageous."

This quiet acquiescence was not quite what Elspeth Glendinning wished or expected. She made up, however, by her own enthusiasm, for the lady's want of eagerness to avail herself of ghostly counsel, and Martin was despatched with such haste as Shagram would make, to pray one of the religious men of St. Mary's to come up to administer the last consolations to the widow of Walter de Avenel.

When the sacristan had announced to the lord abbot that the lady of the umquhile Walter de Avenel was in very weak health in the Tower of Glendearg, and desired the assistance of a father confessor, the lordly monk paused on the request.

"We do remember Walter de Avenel," he said—"a good knight and a valiant; he was dispossessed of his lands, and slain by the Southron. May not the lady come hither to the sacrament of confession? The road is distant, and painful to travel."

"The lady is unwell, holy father," answered the sacristan, "and unable to bear the journey."

"True—ay—yes—then must one of our brethren go to her. Knowest thou if she hath aught of a jointure from this Walter de Avenel."

"Very little, holy father," said the sacristan; "she hath resided at Glendearg since her husband's death, wellnigh on the charity of a poor widow, called Elspeth Glendinning."

"Why, thou knowest all the widows in the country-side?"

said the abbot. "Ho! ho! ho!" and he shook his portly sides at his own jest.

"Ho! ho! ho!" echoed the sacristan, in the tone and tune in which an inferior applauds the jest of his superior; then added, with a hypocritical snuffle and a sly twinkle of his eye, "It is our duty, most holy father, to comfort the widow. He! he! he! he!"

This last laugh was more moderate, until the abbot should put his sanction on the jest.

"Ho! ho!" said the abbot; "then, to leave jesting, Father Philip, take thou thy riding-gear, and go to confess this Dame Avenel."

"But," said the sacristan——

"Give me no 'buts'; neither 'but' nor 'if' pass between monk and abbot, Father Philip; the bands of discipline must not be relaxed; heresy gathers force like a snowball; the multitude expect confessions and preachings from the Benedictine as they would from so many beggarly friars, and we may not desert the vineyard, though the toil be grievous unto us."

"And with so little advantage to the holy monastery," said the sacristan.

"True, Father Philip; but wot you not that what preventeth harm doeth good? This Julian de Avenel lives a light and evil life, and should we neglect the widow of his brother, he might foray our lands, and we never able to show who hurt us; moreover, it is our duty to an ancient family, who, in their day, have been benefactors to the abbey. Away with thee instantly, brother; ride night and day, an it be necessary, and let men see how diligent Abbot Boniface and his faithful children are in the execution of their spiritual duty; toil not deterring them, for the glen is five miles in length; fear not withholding them, for it is said to be haunted of spectres; nothing moving them from pursuit of their spiritual calling, to the confusion of calumnious heretics, and the comfort and edification of all true and faithful sons of the Catholic Church. I wonder what our brother Eustace will say to this?"

Breathless with his own picture of the dangers and toil which he was to encounter, and the fame which he was to acquire (both by proxy), the abbot moved slowly to finish his luncheon in the refectory; and the sacristan, with no very good will, accompan.ed Old Martin in his return to Glendearg; the greatest impediment in the journey being the trouble of restraining his pampered mule, that she might tread in something like an equal pace with poor Shagram.

After remaining an hour in private with his penitent, the monk returned, moody and full of thought. Dame Elspeth, who had placed for the honoured guest some refreshment in the hall, was struck with the embarrassment which appeared in his countenance. Elspeth watched him with great anxiety. She observed there was that on his brow which rather resembled a person come from hearing a confession of some enormous crime than the look of a confessor who resigns a reconciled penitent, not to earth, but to Heaven. After long hesitating, she could not at length refrain from hazarding a question. "She was sure," she said, "the leddy had made an easy shrift. Five years had they resided together, and she could safely say no woman lived better."

"Woman," said the sacristan, sternly, "thou speakest thou knowest not what. What avails clearing the outside of the platter, if the inside be foul with heresy?"

"Our dishes and trenchers are not so clean as they could be wished, holy father," said Elspeth, but half understanding what he said, and beginning with her apron to wipe the dust from the plates, of which she supposed him to complain.

"Forbear, Dame Elspeth," said the monk; "your plates are as clean as wooden trenchers and pewter flagons can well be; the foulness of which I speak is that of pestilential heresy, which is daily becoming ingrained in this our Holy Church of Scotland, and as a canker-worm in the rose-garland of the Spouse."

"Holy Mother of Heaven!" said Dame Elspeth, crossing herself, "have I kept house with a heretic?"

"No, Elspeth—no," replied the monk; "it were too strong a speech for me to make of this unhappy lady, but I would I could say she is free from heretical opinions. Alas! they fly about like the pestilence by noonday, and infect even the first

and fairest of the flock! For it is easy to see of this dame
that she hath been high in judgment as in rank."

"And she can write and read, I had almost said as weel as
your reverence," said Elspeth.

"Whom doth she write to, and what doth she read?" said
the monk, eagerly.

"Nay," replied Elspeth, "I cannot say I ever saw her write
at all, but her maiden that was—she now serves the family—
says she can write. And for reading, she has often read to
us good things out of a thick black volume with silver
clasps."

"Let me see it," said the monk, hastily—"on your allegiance as a true vassal—on your faith as a Catholic Christian
—instantly—instantly, let me see it!"

The good woman hesitated, alarmed at the tone in which
the confessor took up her information; and being, moreover,
of opinion that what so good a woman as the Lady of Avenel
studied so devoutly could not be of a tendency actually evil.
But, borne down by the clamour, exclamations, and something
like threats, used by Father Philip, she at length brought him
the fatal volume. It was easy to do this without suspicion
on the part of the owner, as she lay on her bed exhausted with
the fatigue of a long conference with her confessor, and as the
small "round," or turret closet, in which was the book and her
other trifling property, was accessible by another door. Of
all her effects, the book was the last she would have thought
of securing, for of what use or interest could it be in a family
who neither read themselves nor were in the habit of seeing
any who did? So that Dame Elspeth had no difficulty in possessing herself of the volume, although her heart all the while
accused her of an ungenerous and an inhospitable part towards
her friend and inmate. The double power of a landlord and
a feudal superior was before her eyes; and, to say truth, the
boldness with which she might otherwise have resisted this
double authority was, I grieve to say it, much qualified by the
curiosity she entertained, as a daughter of Eve, to have some
explanation respecting the mysterious volume which the lady
cherished with so much care, yet whose contents she imparted

with such caution. For never had Alice of Avenel read them any passage from the book in question until the iron door of the tower was locked, and all possibility of intrusion prevented. Even then she had shown, by the selection of particular passages, that she was more anxious to impress on their minds the principles which the volume contained than to introduce them to it as a new rule of faith.

When Elspeth, half-curious, half-remorseful, had placed the book in the monk's hands, he exclaimed, after turning over the leaves, "Now, by mine order, it is as I suspected! My mule— my mule! I will abide no longer here. Well hast thou done, dame, in placing in my hands this perilous volume."

"Is it then witchcraft or devil's work?" said Dame Elspeth, in great agitation.

"Nay, God forbid," said the monk, signing himself with the cross, "it is the Holy Scripture. But it is rendered into the vulgar tongue, and therefore, by the order of the Holy Catholic Church, unfit to be in the hands of any lay person."

"And yet is the Holy Scripture communicated for our common salvation," said Elspeth. "Good father, you must instruct mine ignorance better; but lack of wit cannot be a deadly sin, and truly, to my poor thinking, I should be glad to read the Holy Scripture."

"I dare say thou wouldst," said the monk; "and even thus did our mother Eve seek to have knowledge of good and evil, and thus sin came into the world, and death by sin."

"I am sure, and that's true!" said Elspeth. "Oh, if she had dealt by the counsel of St. Peter and St. Paul!"

"If she had reverenced the command of Heaven," said the monk, "which, as it gave her birth, life, and happiness, fixed upon the grant such conditions as best corresponded with its holy pleasure. I tell thee, Elspeth, *the Word slayeth*: that is, the text alone, read with unskilled eye and unhallowed lips, is like those strong medicines which sick men take by the advice of the learned. Such patients recover and thrive; while those dealing in them at their own hand shall perish by their own deed."

"Nae doubt—nae doubt," said the poor woman, "your reverence knows best."

"Not I," said Father Philip, in a tone as deferential as he thought could possibly become the sacristan of St. Mary's—"not I, but the Holy Father of Christendom, and our own holy father the lord abbot, know best. I, the poor sacristan of St. Mary's, can but repeat what I hear from others my superiors. Yet of this, good woman, be assured—the Word—the mere Word, slayeth. But the church hath her ministers to gloze and to expound the same unto her faithful congregation; and this I say not so much, my beloved brethren—I mean, my beloved sister (for the sacristan had got into the end of one of his old sermons)—this I speak not so much of the rectors, curates, and secular clergy, so called because they live after the fashion of the *seculum* or age, unbound by those ties which sequestrate us from the world; neither do I speak this of the mendicant friars, whether black or grey, whether crossed or uncrossed; but of the monks, and especially of the monks Benedictine, reformed on the rule of St. Bernard of Clairvaux, thence called Cistercian, of which monks, Christian brethren—sister, I would say—great is the happiness and glory of the country in possessing the holy ministers of St. Mary's, whereof I, though an unworthy brother, may say it hath produced more saints, more bishops, more popes—may our patrons make us thankful!—than any holy foundation in Scotland. Wherefore—— But I see Martin hath my mule in readiness, and I will but salute you with the kiss of sisterhood, which maketh not ashamed, and so betake me to my toilsome return, for the glen is of bad reputation for the evil spirits which haunt it. Moreover, I may arrive too late at the bridge, whereby I may be obliged to take the river, which I observed to be somewhat waxen."

Accordingly, he took his leave of Dame Elspeth, who was confounded by the rapidity of his assurance, and the doctrine he gave forth, and by no means easy on the subject of the book, which her conscience told her she should not have communicated to any one without the knowledge of its owner.

Notwithstanding the haste which the monk as well as his

7

mule made to return to better quarters than they had left at the head of Glendearg; notwithstanding the eager desire Father Philip had to be the very first who should acquaint the abbot that a copy of the book they most dreaded had been found within the halidome, or patrimony, of the abbey; notwithstanding, moreover, certain feelings which induced him to hurry as fast as possible through the gloomy and evil-reputed glen, still the difficulties of the road, and the rider's want of habitude of quick motion, were such that twilight came upon him ere he had nearly cleared the narrow valley.

It was indeed a gloomy ride. The two sides of the valley were so near that at every double of the river the shadows from the western sky fell upon, and totally obscured, the eastern bank; the thickets of copsewood seemed to wave with a portentous agitation of boughs and leaves, and the very crags and scaurs seemed higher and grimmer than they had appeared to the monk while he was travelling in daylight and in company. Father Philip was heartily rejoiced when, emerging from the narrow glen, he gained the open valley of the Tweed, which held on its majestic course from current to pool, and from pool stretched away to other currents, with a dignity peculiar to itself amongst the Scottish rivers; for, whatever may have been the drought of the season, the Tweed usually fills up the space between its banks, seldom leaving those extensive sheets of shingle which deform the margins of many of the celebrated Scottish streams.

The monk, insensible to beauties which the age had not regarded as deserving of notice, was, nevertheless, like a prudent general, pleased to find himself out of the narrow glen in which the enemy might have stolen upon him unperceived. He drew up his bridle, reduced his mule to her natural and luxurious amble, instead of the agitating and broken trot at which, to his no small inconvenience, she had hitherto proceeded, and, wiping his brow, gazed forth at leisure on the broad moon, which, now mingling with the lights of evening, was rising over field and forest, village and fortalice, and, above all, over the stately monastery, seen far and dim amid the yellow light.

The worst part of this magnificent view, in the monk's apprehension, was that the monastery stood on the opposite side of the river, and that, of the many fine bridges which have since been built across that classical stream, not one then existed. There was, however, in recompense, a bridge then standing which has since disappeared, although its ruins may be still traced by the curious.

It was of a very peculiar form. Two strong abutments were built on either side of the river, at a part where the stream was peculiarly contracted. Upon a rock in the centre of the current was built a solid piece of masonry, constructed like the pier of a bridge, and presenting, like a pier, an angle to the current of the stream. The masonry continued solid until the pier rose to a level with the two abutments upon either side, and from thence the building rose in the form of a tower. The lower story of this tower consisted only of an archway or passage through the building, over either entrance to which hung a drawbridge with counterpoises, either of which, when dropped, connected the archway with the opposite abutment, where the further end of the drawbridge rested. When both bridges were tnus lowered, the passage over the river was complete.

The bridge-keeper, who was the dependant of a neighbouring baron, resided with his family in the second and third stories of the tower, which, when both drawbridges were raised, formed an insulated fortalice in the midst of the river. He was entitled to a small toll or custom for the passage, concerning the amount of which disputes sometimes arose between him and the passengers. It is needless to say that the bridge-ward had usually the better in these questions, since he could at pleasure detain the traveller on the opposite side; or, suffering him to pass half-way, might keep him prisoner in his tower till they were agreed on the rate of pontage.[1]

But it was most frequently with the monks of St. Mary's that the warder had to dispute his perquisites. These holy men insisted for, and at length obtained, a right of gratuitous passage to themselves, greatly to the discontent of the bridge-

[1] See Drawbridge at Bridge-end. Note 4.

keeper. But when they demanded the same immunity for the numerous pilgrims who visited the shrine, the bridge-keeper waxed restive, and was supported by his lord in his resistance. The controversy grew animated on both sides: the abbot menaced excommunication, and the keeper of the bridge, though unable to retaliate in kind, yet made each individual monk who had to cross and recross the river endure a sort of purgatory ere he would accommodate them with a passage. This was a great inconvenience, and would have proved a more serious one, but that the river was fordable for man and horse in ordinary weather.

It was a fine moonlight night, as we have already said, when Father Philip approached this bridge, the singular construction of which gives a curious idea of the insecurity of the times. The river was not in flood, but it was above its ordinary level—"a heavy water," as it is called in that country, through which the monk had no particular inclination to ride, if he could manage the matter better.

"Peter, my good friend," cried the sacristan, raising his voice—"my very excellent friend, Peter, be so kind as to lower the drawbridge. Peter, I say, dost thou not hear? it is thy gossip, Father Philip, who calls thee."

Peter heard him perfectly well, and saw him into the bargain; but, as he had considered the sacristan as peculiarly his enemy in his dispute with the convent, he went quietly to bed, after reconnoitring the monk through his loophole, observing to his wife, that "riding the water in a moonlight night would do the sacristan no harm, and would teach him the value of a brig the neist time, on whilk a man might pass high and dry, winter and summer, flood and ebb."

After exhausting his voice in entreaties and threats, which were equally unattended to by Peter of the Brig, as he was called, Father Philip at length moved down the river to take the ordinary ford at the head of the next stream. Cursing the rustic obstinacy of Peter, he began, nevertheless, to persuade himself that the passage of the river by the ford was not only safe, but pleasant. The banks and scattered trees were so beautifully reflected from the bosom of the dark stream, the whole cool and delicious picture formed so pleasing a contrast to his late agitation, to the warmth occasioned by his vain endeavours to move the relentless porter of the bridge, that the result was rather agreeable than otherwise.

As Father Philip came close to the water's edge, at the spot where he was to enter it, there sat a female under a large broken, scathed oak-tree, or rather under the remains of such a tree, weeping, wringing her hands, and looking earnestly on the current of the river. The monk was struck with astonishment to see a female there at that time of night. But he was in all honest service—and if a step farther, I put it upon his own conscience—a devoted squire of dames. After observing the maiden for a moment, although she seemed to take no notice of his presence, he was moved by her distress, and willing to offer his assistance. "Damsel," said he, "thou seemest in no ordinary distress; peradventure, like myself, thou hast been refused passage at the bridge by the churlish keeper, and thy crossing may concern thee either for performance of a vow or some other weighty charge."

The maiden uttered some inarticulate sounds, looked at the river, and then in the face of the sacristan. It struck Father Philip at that instant that a Highland chief of distinction had been for some time expected to pay his vows at the shrine of St. Mary's; and that possibly this fair maiden might be one of his family, travelling alone for accomplishment of a vow, or left behind by some accident, to whom, therefore, it would be but right and prudent to use every civility in his power, especially as she seemed unacquainted with the Lowland tongue. Such at least was the only motive the sacristan was ever known to assign for his courtesy; if there was any other, I once more refer it to his own conscience.

To express himself by signs, the common language of all nations, the cautious sacristan first pointed to the river, then to his mule's crupper, and then made, as gracefully as he could, a sign to induce the fair solitary to mount behind him. She seemed to understand his meaning, for she rose up as if to accept his offer; and while the good monk, who, as we have hinted, was no great cavalier, laboured with the pressure of the right leg and the use of the left rein to place his mule with her side to the bank in such a position that the lady might mount with ease, she rose from the ground with rather portentous activity, and at one bound sate behind the monk upon the animal, the much firmer rider of the two. The mule by no means seemed to approve of this double burden; she bounded, bolted, and would soon have thrown Father Philip over her head, had not the maiden with a firm hand detained him in the saddle.

At length the restive brute changed her humour; and, from refusing to budge off the spot, suddenly stretched her nose homeward, and dashed into the ford as fast as she could scamper. A new terror now invaded the monk's mind: the ford seemed unusually deep, the water eddied off in strong ripple from the counter of the mule, and began to rise upon her side. Philip lost his presence of mind, which was at no time his most ready attribute; the mule yielded to the weight of the current, and as the rider was not attentive to keep her head turned up the river, she drifted downward, lost the ford and her footing at once, and began to swim with her head down the stream. And what was sufficiently strange, at the same moment, notwithstanding the extreme peril, the damsel began to sing, thereby increasing, if anything could increase, the bodily fear of the worthy sacristan.

> Merrily swim we, the moon shines bright,
> Both current and ripple are dancing in light.
> We have roused the night raven, I heard him croak,
> As we plashed along beneath the oak
> That flings its broad branches so far and so wide,
> Their shadows are dancing in midst of the tide.
> " Who wakens my nestlings," the raven he said,
> " My beak shall ere morn in his blood be red.
> For a blue swoln corpse is a dainty meal,
> And I'll have my share with the pike and the eel."
>
> Merrily swim we, the moon shines bright,
> There's a golden gleam on the distant height:
> There's a silver shower on the alders dank,
> And the drooping willows that wave on the bank
> I see the abbey, both turret and tower,
> It is all astir for the vesper hour ;

The monks for the chapel are leaving each cell,
But where's Father Philip, should toll the bell?

Merrily swim we, the moon shines bright,
Downward we drift through shadow and light,
Under yon rock the eddies sleep,
Calm and silent, dark and deep.
The Kelpy has risen from the fathomless pool,
He has lighted his candle of death and of dool.
Look, father, look, and you'll laugh to see
How he gapes and glares with his eyes on thee!

Good luck to your fishing, whom watch ye to-night?
A man of mean or a man of might?
Is it layman or priest that must float in your cove,
Or lover who crosses to visit his love?
Hark! heard ye the Kelpy reply as we pass'd—
"God's blessing on the warder, he lock'd the bridge fast!
All that come to my cove are sunk,
Priest or layman, lover or monk."

How long the damsel might have continued to sing, or where
the terrified monk's journey might have ended, is uncertain.
As she sung the last stanza, they arrived at, or rather in, a
broad tranquil sheet of water, caused by a strong wear or
dam-head, running across the river, which dashed in a broad
cataract over the barrier. The mule, whether from choice or
influenced by the suction of the current, made towards the cut
intended to supply the convent mills, and entered it half swimming, half wading, and pitching the unlucky monk to and fro
in the saddle at a fearful rate.

As his person flew hither and thither, his garment became
loose, and in an effort to retain it, his hand lighted on the
volume of the Lady of Avenel which was in his bosom. No
sooner had he grasped it than his companion pitched him out
of the saddle into the stream, where, still keeping her hand
on his collar, she gave him two or three good souses in the
watery fluid, so as to ensure that every part of him had its
share of wetting, and then quitted her hold when he was so
near the side that by a slight effort—of a great one he was
incapable—he might scramble on shore. This accordingly he
accomplished, and turning his eyes to see what had become of
his extraordinary companion, she was nowhere to be seen; but
still he heard, as if from the surface of the river, and mixing

with the noise of the water breaking over the dam-head, a
fragment of her wild song, which seemed to run thus:

> Landed—landed ! the black book hath won,
> Else had you seen Berwick with morning sun !
> Sain ye, and save ye, and blythe mot ye be,
> For seldom they land that go swimming with me.

The ecstasy of the monk's terror could be endured no longer;
his head grew dizzy, and, after staggering a few steps onward,
and running himself against a wall, he sunk down in a state of
insensibility.

CHAPTER VI.

> Now let us sit in conclave. That these weeds
> Be rooted from the vineyard of the church,
> That these foul tares be sever'd from the wheat,
> We are, I trust, agreed. Yet how to do this,
> Nor hurt the wholesome crop and tender vine-plants,
> Craves good advisement.
>
> _The Reformation._

THE vesper service in the monastery church of St. Mary's
was now over.   The abbot had disrobed himself of his magnificent vestures of ceremony, and resumed his ordinary habit,
which was a black gown, worn over a white cassock, with a
narrow scapulary; a decent and venerable dress, which was
well calculated to set off to advantage the portly mien of
Abbot Boniface.

In quiet times no one could have filled the state of a mitred
abbot, for such was his dignity, more respectably than this
worthy prelate.   He had, no doubt, many of those habits of
self-indulgence which men are apt to acquire who live for
themselves alone.   He was vain, moreover; and, when boldly
confronted, had sometimes shown symptoms of timidity not
very consistent with the high claims which he preferred as an
eminent member of the church, or with the punctual deference which he exacted from his religious brethren, and all
who were placed under his command.   But he was hospitable,
charitable, and by no means of himself disposed to proceed

with severity against any one. In short, he would in other times have slumbered out his term of preferment with as much credit as any other "purple abbot," who lived easily, but at the same time decorously, slept soundly, and did not disquiet himself with dreams.

But the wide alarm spread through the whole Church of Rome by the progress of the reformed doctrines sorely disturbed the repose of Abbot Boniface, and opened to him a wide field of duties and cares which he had never so much as dreamed of. There were opinions to be combated and refuted, practices to be inquired into, heretics to be detected and punished, the fallen off to be reclaimed, the wavering to be confirmed, scandal to be removed from the clergy, and the vigour of discipline to be re-established. Post upon post arrived at the Monastery of St. Mary's—horses reeking and riders exhausted—this from the privy council, that from the Primate of Scotland, and this other again from the Queen Mother, exhorting, approving, condemning, requesting advice upon this subject and requiring information upon that.

These missives Abbot Boniface received with an important air of helplessness, or a helpless air of importance, whichever the reader may please to term it, evincing at once gratified vanity and profound trouble of mind.

The sharp-witted Primate of St. Andrews had foreseen the deficiencies of the abbot of St. Mary's, and endeavoured to provide for them by getting admitted into his monastery, as sub-prior, a brother Cistercian, a man of parts and knowledge, devoted to the service of the Catholic Church, and very capable not only to advise the abbot on occasions of difficulty, but to make him sensible of his duty in case he should, from good-nature or timidity, be disposed to shrink from it.

Father Eustace played the same part in the monastery as the old general who, in foreign armies, is placed at the elbow of the prince of the blood, who nominally commands in chief, on condition of attempting nothing without the advice of his dry-nurse; and he shared the fate of all such dry-nurses, being heartily disliked as well as feared by his principal. Still, however, the Primate's intention was fully answered.

Father Eustace became the constant theme and often the bug-bear of the worthy abbot, who hardly dared to turn himself in his bed without considering what Father Eustace would think of it. In every case of difficulty, Father Eustace was summoned, and his opinion asked; and no sooner was the embarrassment removed than the abbot's next thought was how to get rid of his adviser. In every letter which he wrote to those in power, he recommended Father Eustace to some high church preferment—a bishopric or an abbey; and as they dropped one after another, and were otherwise conferred, he began to think, as he confessed to the sacristan in the bit-terness of his spirit, that the Monastery of St. Mary's had got a life-rent lease of their sub-prior.

Yet more indulgent he would have been had he suspected that Father Eustace's ambition was fixed upon his own mitre, which, from some attacks of an apoplectic nature, deemed by the abbot's friends to be more serious than by himself, it was supposed might be shortly vacant. But the confidence which, like other dignitaries, he reposed in his own health, prevented Abbot Boniface from imagining that it held any concatenation with the motions of Father Eustace.

The necessity under which he found himself of consulting with his grand adviser, in cases of real difficulty, rendered the worthy abbot particularly desirous of doing without him in all ordinary cases of administration, though not without considering what Father Eustace would have said of the mat-ter. He scorned, therefore, to give a hint to the sub-prior of the bold stroke by which he had despatched Brother Philip to Glendearg; but when the vespers came without his reap-pearance he became a little uneasy, the more as other matters weighed upon his mind. The feud with the warder or keeper of the bridge threatened to be attended with bad consequences, as the man's quarrel was taken up by the martial baron under whom he served; and pressing letters of an unpleasant ten-dency had just arrived from the Primate. Like a gouty man who catches hold of his crutch while he curses the infirmity that reduces him to use it, the abbot, however reluctant, found himself obliged to require Eustace's presence, after the service was over, in his house, or rather palace, which was attached to, and made part of, the monastery.

Abbot Boniface was seated in his high-backed chair, the grotesque carved back of which terminated in a mitre, before a fire where two or three large logs were reduced to one red glowing mass of charcoal. At his elbow, on an oaken stand, stood the remains of a roasted capon, on which his reverence had made his evening meal, flanked by a goodly stoup of Bourdeaux of excellent flavour. He was gazing indolently on the fire, partly engaged in meditation on his past and present fortunes, partly occupied by endeavouring to trace towers and steeples in the red embers.

" Yes," thought the abbot to himself, " in that red perspective I could fancy to myself the peaceful towers of Dundrennan, where I passed my life ere I was called to pomp and to trouble. A quiet brotherhood we were, regular in our domestic duties; and when the frailties of humanity prevailed over us we confessed, and were absolved by each other, and the most formidable part of the penance was the jest of the convent on the culprit. I can almost fancy that I see the cloister garden and the pear-trees which I grafted with my own hands. And for what have I changed all this, but to be overwhelmed with business which concerns me not, to be called 'My Lord Abbot,' and to be tutored by Father Eustace? I would these towers were the Abbey of Aberbrothwick, and Father Eustace the abbot; or I would he were in the fire on any terms, so I were rid of him! The Primate says our Holy Father the Pope hath an adviser; I am sure he could not live a week with such a one as mine. Then there is no learning what Father Eustace thinks till you confess your own difficulties. No hint will bring forth his opinion: he is like a miser, who will not unbuckle his purse to bestow a farthing, until the wretch who needs it has owned his excess of poverty, and wrung out the boon by importunity. And thus I am dishonoured in the eyes of my religious brethren, who behold me treated like a child which hath no sense of its own. I will bear it no longer! Brother Bennet (a lay brother answered to his call), tell Father Eustace that I need not his presence."

"I came to say to your reverence that the holy father is entering even now from the cloisters."

"Be it so," said the abbot, "he is welcome; remove these things—or rather, place a trencher, the holy father may be a little hungry; yet no, remove them, for there is no good fellowship in him. Let the stoup of wine remain, however, and place another cup."

The lay brother obeyed these contradictory commands in the way he judged most seemly: he removed the carcass of the half-sacked capon, and placed two goblets beside the stoup of Bourdeaux. At the same instant entered Father Eustace.

He was a thin, sharp-faced, slight-made little man, whose keen grey eyes seemed almost to look through the person to whom he addressed himself. His body was emaciated not only with the fasts which he observed with rigid punctuality, but also by the active and unwearied exercise of his sharp and piercing intellect:

> A fiery soul, which, working out its way,
> Fretted the puny body to decay,
> And o'er-inform'd the tenement of clay.

He turned with conventual reverence to the lord abbot; and as they stood together it was scarce possible to see a more complete difference of form and expression. The good-natured rosy face and laughing eye of the abbot, which even his present anxiety could not greatly ruffle, was a wonderful contrast to the thin, pallid cheek and quick, penetrating glance of the monk, in which an eager and keen spirit glanced through eyes to which it seemed to give supernatural lustre.

The abbot opened the conversation by motioning to the monk to take a stool, and inviting him to a cup of wine. The courtesy was declined with respect, yet not without a remark that the vesper-service was past.

"For the stomach's sake, brother," said the abbot, colouring a little—"you know the text."

"It is a dangerous one," answered the monk, "to handle alone, or at late hours. Cut off from human society—the juice of the grape becomes a perilous companion of solitude, and therefore I ever shun it."

Abbot Boniface had poured himself out a goblet which might hold about half an English pint; but, either struck with the truth of the observation, or ashamed to act in direct opposition to it, he suffered it to remain untasted before him, and immediately changed the subject.

"The Primate hath written to us," said he, "to make strict search within our bounds after the heretical persons denounced in this list, who have withdrawn themselves from the justice which their opinions deserve. It is deemed probable that they will attempt to retire to England by our borders, and the Primate requireth me to watch with vigilance, and what not."

"Assuredly," said the monk, "the magistrate should not bear the sword in vain—those be they that turn the world upside down—and doubtless your reverend wisdom will with due diligence second the exertions of the right reverend father in God, being in the peremptory defence of the Holy Church."

"Ay, but how is this to be done?" answered the abbot. "St. Mary aid us! The Primate writes to me as if I were a temporal baron—a man under command, having soldiers under him! He says, send forth—scour the country—guard the passes. Truly these men do not travel as those who would give their lives for nothing: the last who went south passed the Dry March at the Riding Burn with an escort of thirty spears, as our reverend brother the abbot of Kelso did write unto us. How are cowls and scapularies to stop the way?"

"Your bailiff is accounted a good man-at-arms, holy father," said Eustace; "your vassals are obliged to rise for the defence of the Holy Kirk—it is the tenure on which they hold their lands; if they will not come forth for the church which gives them bread, let their possessions be given to others."

"We shall not be wanting," said the abbot, collecting himself with importance, "to do whatever may advantage Holy Kirk—thyself shall hear the charge to our bailiff and our officials; but here again is our controversy with the warden of the bridge and the Baron of Meigallot. St. Mary! vexations do so multiply upon the house, and upon the generation, that a man wots not where to turn to! Thou didst say, Father Eustace, thou wouldst look into our evidents touching this free passage for the pilgrims?"

"I have looked into the chartulary of the house, holy father," said Eustace, "and therein I find a written and formal grant of all duties and customs payable at the drawbridge of Brigton, not only by ecclesiastics of this foundation, but by every pilgrim truly designed to accomplish his vows at this house, to the Abbot Ailford, and the monks of the house of St. Mary in Kennaquhair, from that time and for ever. The deed is dated on St. Bridget's Even, in the year of Redemption 1137, and bears the sign and seal of the granter, Charles of Meigallot, great-great-grandfather of this baron, and purports to be granted for the safety of his own soul, and for the weal of the souls of his father and mother, and of all his predecessors and successors, being Baron of Meigallot."

"But he alleges," said the abbot, "that the bridge-wards have been in possession of these dues, and have rendered them available, for more than fifty years, and the baron threatens violence; meanwhile, the journey of the pilgrims is interrupted, to the prejudice of their own souls, and the diminution of the revenues of St. Mary. The sacristan advised us to put on a boat; but the warden, whom thou knowest to be a godless man, has sworn the devil tear him, but that, if they put on a boat on the laird's stream, he will rive her board from board. And then some say we should compound the claim for a small sum in silver." Here the abbot paused a moment for a reply, but receiving none, he added, "But what thinkest thou, Father Eustace? why art thou silent?"

"Beause I am surprised at the question which the lord abbot of St. Mary's asks at the youngest of his brethren."

"Youngest in time of your abode with us, Brother Eustace," said the abbot, "not youngest in years, or, I think, in experience—sub-prior also of this convent."

"I am astonished," continued Eustace, "that the abbot of this venerable house should ask of any one whether he can alienate the patrimony of our holy and divine patroness, or

give up to an unconscientious, and perhaps a heretic, baron
the rights conferred on this church by his devout progenitor.
Popes and councils alike prohibit it; the honour of the living
and the weal of departed souls alike forbid it: it may not be.
To force, if he dare use it, we must surrender; but never by
our consent should we see the goods of the church plundered,
with as little scruple as he would drive off a herd of English
beeves. Rouse yourself, reverend father, and doubt nothing
but that the good cause shall prevail. Whet the spiritual
sword, and direct it against the wicked who would usurp our
holy rights. Whet the temporal sword if it be necessary, and
stir up the courage and zeal of your loyal vassals."

The abbot sighed deeply. "All this," he said, "is soon
spoken by him who hath to act it not; but——" He was interrupted by the entrance of Bennet rather hastily. "The
mule on which the sacristan had set out in the morning had
returned," he said, "to the convent stable all over wet, and
with the saddle turned round beneath her belly."

"Sancta Maria!" said the abbot, "our dear brother hath
perished by the way!"

"It may not be," said Eustace, hastily; "let the bell be
tolled—cause the brethren to get torches—alarm the village—
hurry down to the river—I myself will be the foremost."

The real abbot stood astonished and agape when at once he
beheld his office filled, and saw all which he ought to have
ordered going forward at the dictates of the youngest monk
in the convent. But ere the orders of Eustace, which nobody
dreamed of disputing, were carried into execution, the necessity was prevented by the sudden apparition of the sacristan,
whose supposed danger excited all the alarm.

CHAPTER VII.

Erase the written troubles of the brain,
Cleanse the foul bosom of the perilous stuff
That weighs upon the heart.

Macbeth.

WHAT betwixt cold and fright, the afflicted sacristan stood before his superior, propped on the friendly arm of the convent miller, drenched with water, and scarce able to utter a syllable.

After various attempts to speak, the first words he uttered were

" Swim we merrily, the moon shines bright."

" Swim we merrily!" retorted the abbot, indignantly; " a merry night have ye chosen for swimming, and a becoming salutation to your superior!"

" Our brother is bewildered," said Eustace; " speak, Father Philip, how is it with you?"

" Good luck to your fishing,"

continued the sacristan, making a most dolorous attempt at the tune of his strange companion.

" Good luck to your fishing!" repeated the abbot, still more surprised and displeased; " by my halidome, he is drunken with wine, and comes to our presence with his jolly catches in his throat! If bread and water can cure this folly——"

" With your pardon, venerable father," said the sub-prior, " of water our brother has had enough; and methinks the confusion of his eye is rather that of terror than of aught unbecoming his profession. Where did you find him, Hob Miller?"

" An it please your reverence, I did but go to shut the sluice of the mill, and as I was going to shut the sluice, I heard something groan near to me; but judging it was one of Giles Fletcher's hogs—for so please you, he never shuts his gate—I caught up my lever, and was about—St. Mary forgive me!—to strike where I heard the sound, when, as the saints would have it, I heard the second groan just like that of a living man. So I called up my knaves, and found the father sacristan lying wet and senseless under the wall of our kiln. So soon as we brought him to himself a bit, he prayed to be brought to your reverence, but I doubt me his wits have gone a bell-wavering by the road. It was but now that he spoke in somewhat better form."

"Well!" said Brother Eustace, "thou hast done well, Hob Miller; only begone now, and remember a second time to pause ere you strike in the dark."

"Please your reverence, it shall be a lesson to me," said the miller, "not to mistake a holy man for a hog again, so long as I live." And, making a bow with profound humility, the miller withdrew.

"And now that this churl is gone, Father Philip," said Eustace, "wilt thou tell our venerable superior what ails thee? Art thou *vino gravatus*, man? If so, we will have thee to thy cell."

"Water!—water! not wine," muttered the exhausted sacristan.

"Nay," said the monk, "if that be thy complaint, wine may perhaps cure thee"; and he reached him a cup, which the patient drank off to his great benefit.

"And now," said the abbot, "let his garments be changed, or rather let him be carried to the infirmary; for it will prejudice our health, should we hear his narrative while he stands there, steaming like a rising hoar-frost."

"I will hear his adventure," said Eustace, "and report it to your reverence." And, accordingly, he attended the sacristan to his cell. In about half an hour he returned to the abbot.

"How is it with Father Philip?" said the abbot; "and through what came he into such a state?"

"He comes from Glendearg, reverend sir," said Eustace; "and for the rest, he telleth such a legend as hath not been heard in this monastery for many a long day." He then gave the abbot the outline of the sacristan's adventures in the homeward journey, and added, that for some time he was inclined to think his brain was infirm, seeing he had sung, laughed, and wept all in the same breath.

"A wonderful thing it is to us," said the abbot, "that Satan has been permitted to put forth his hand thus far on one of our sacred brethren!"

"True," said Father Eustace; "but for every text there is a paraphrase; and I have my suspici ns that, if the drenching of Father Philip cometh f the Ev l One, yet it may not have been altogether without his own personal fault."

"How!" said the father abbot; "I will not believe that thou makest doubt that Satan, in former days, hath been permitted to afflict saints and holy men even as he afflicted the pious Job?"

"God forbid I should make question of it," said the monk, crossing himself; "yet, where there is an exposition of the sacristan's tale which is less than miraculous, I hold it safe to consider it at least, if not to abide by it. Now, this Hob the Miller hath a buxom daughter. Suppose—I say only suppose—that our sacristan met her at the ford on her return from her uncle's on the other side, for there she hath this evening been; suppose that, in courtesy, and to save her stripping hose and shoon, the sacristan brought her across behind him; suppose he carried his familiarities farther than the maiden was willing to admit; and we may easily suppose, father, that this wetting was the result of it."

"And this legend invented to deceive us!" said the superior, reddening with wrath; "but most strictly shall it be sifted and inquired into; it is not upon us that Father Philip must hope to pass the result of his own evil practices for doings of Satan. To-morrow cite the wench to appear before us; we will examine, and we will punish."

"Under your reverence's favour," said Eustace, "that were but poor policy. As things now stand with us, the heretics catch hold of each flying report which tends to the scandal of our clergy. We must abate the evil, not only by strengthening discipline, but also by suppressing and stifling the voice of scandal. If my conjectures are true, the miller's daughter will be silent for her own sake; and your reverence's authority may also impose silence on her father and on the sacristan. If he is again found to afford room for throwing dishonour on his order, he can be punished with severity, but at the same time with secrecy. For what say the Decretals? *Facinora ostendi dum punientur, flagitia autem abscondi debent.*"

A sentence of Latin, as Eustace had before observed, had often much influence on the abbot, because he understood it not fluently, and was ashamed to acknowledge his ignorance. On these terms they parted for the night.

The next day, Abbot Boniface strictly interrogated Philip on the real cause of his disaster of the previous night. But the sacristan stood firm to his story; nor was he found to vary from any point of it, although the answers he returned were in some degree incoherent, owing to his intermingling with them ever and anon snatches of the strange damsel's song, which had made such deep impression on his imagination that he could not prevent himself from imitating it repeatedly in the course of his examination. The abbot had compassion with the sacristan's involuntary frailty, to which something supernatural seemed annexed, and finally became of opinion that Father Eustace's more natural explanation was rather plausible than just. And, indeed, although we have recorded the adventure as we find it written down, we cannot forbear to add that there was a schism on the subject in the convent, and that several of the brethren pretended to have good reason for thinking that the miller's black-eyed daughter was at the bottom of the affair after all. Whichever way it might be interpreted, all agreed that it had too ludicrous a sound to be permitted to get abroad, and therefore the sacristan was charged, on his vow of obedience, to say no more of his ducking—an injunction which, having once eased his mind by telling his story, it may be well conjectured that he joyfully obeyed.

The attention of Father Eustace was much less forcibly arrested by the marvellous tale of the sacristan's danger and his escape than by the mention of the volume which he had brought with him from the Tower of Glendearg. A copy of the Scriptures, translated into the vulgar tongue, had found its way even into the proper territory of the church, and had been discovered in one of the most hidden and sequestered recesses of the halidome of St. Mary's!

He anxiously requested to see the volume. In this the sacristan was unable to gratify him, for he had lost it, as far as he recollected, when the supernatural being, as he conceived her to be, took her departure from him. Father Eustace went down to the spot in person, and searched all around it, in hopes of recovering the volume in question; but his labour was in vain. He returned to the abbot, and reported that it must have fallen into the river or the mill-stream; "For I will hardly believe," he said, "that Father Philip's musical friend would fly off with a copy of the Holy Scriptures."

"Being," said the abbot, "as it is, an heretical translation, it may be thought that Satan may have power over it."

"Ay," said Father Eustace, "it is indeed his chiefest magazine of artillery, when he inspireth presumptuous and daring men to set forth their own opinions and expositions of Holy Writ. But though thus abused, the Scriptures are the source of our salvation, and are no more to be reckoned unholy, because of these rash men's proceedings, than a powerful medicine is to be contemned, or held poisonous, because bold and evil leeches have employed it to the prejudice of their patients. With the permission of your reverence, I would that this matter were looked into more closely. I will myself visit the Tower of Glendearg ere I am many hours older, and we shall see if any spectre or white woman of the wild will venture to interrupt my journey or return. Have I your reverend permission and your blessing?" he added, but in a tone that appeared to set no great store by either.

"Thou hast both, my brother," said the abbot; but no sooner had Eustace left the apartment than Boniface could not help breaking on the willing ear of the sacristan his sincere wish that any spirit, black, white, or grey, would read the adviser such a lesson as to cure him of his presumption in esteeming himself wiser than the whole community.

"I wish him no worse lesson," said the sacristan, "than to go swimming merrily down the river with a ghost behind, and

kelpies, night-crows, and mud-eels all waiting to have a snatch
at him.

> Merrily swim we, the moon shines bright!
> Good luck to your fishing, whom watch you to-night?"

"Brother Philip," said the abbot, "we exhort thee to say
thy prayers, compose thyself, and banish that foolish chant
from thy mind; it is but a deception of the devil's."

"I will essay, reverend father," said the sacristan, "but
the tune hangs by my memory like a burr in a beggar's rags:
it mingles with the psalter; the very bells of the convent
seem to repeat the words, and jingle to the tune; and were
you to put me to death at this very moment, it is my belief I
should die singing it, 'Now swim we merrily': it is as it
were a spell upon me."

He then again began to warble

> "Good luck to your fishing."

And checking himself in the strain with difficulty, he exclaimed: "It is too certain—I am but a lost priest! 'Swim
we merrily'—I shall sing it at the very mass. Woe is me!
I shall sing all the remainder of my life, and yet never be
able to change the tune."

The honest abbot replied, "He knew many a good fellow
in the same condition"; and concluded the remark with "ho!
ho! ho!" for his reverence, as the reader may partly have observed, was one of those dull folks who love a quiet joke.

The sacristan, well acquainted with his superior's humour,
endeavoured to join in the laugh, but his unfortunate canticle
came again across his imagination, and interrupted the hilarity of his customary echo.

"By the rood, Brother Philip," said the abbot, much moved,
"you become altogether intolerable! and I am convinced that
such a spell could not subsist over a person of religion, and
in a religious house, unless he were under mortal sin. Wherefore, say the seven penitentiary psalms—make diligent use
of thy scourge and hair-cloth—refrain for three days from all
food, save bread and water—I myself will shrive thee, and we
will see if this singing devil may be driven out of thee; at

least I think Father Eustace himself could devise no better exorcism."

The sacristan sighed deeply, but knew remonstrance was vain. He retired therefore to his cell, to try how far psalmody might be able to drive off the sounds of the siren tune which haunted his memory.

Meanwhile, Father Eustace proceeded to the drawbridge, in his way to the lonely valley of Glendearg. In a brief conversation with the churlish warder, he had the address to render him more tractable in the controversy betwixt him and the convent. He reminded him that his father had been a vassal under the community; that his brother was childless; and that their possession would revert to the church on his death, and might be either granted to himself the warder, or to some greater favourite of the abbot, as matters chanced to stand betwixt them at the time. The sub-prior suggested to him, also, the necessary connexion of interests betwixt the monastery and the office which this man enjoyed. He listened with temper to his rude and churlish answers; and by keeping his own interest firm pitched in his view, he had the satisfaction to find that Peter gradually softened his tone, and consented to let every pilgrim who travelled upon foot pass free of exaction until Pentecost next; they who travelled on horseback or otherwise consenting to pay the ordinary custom. Having thus accommodated a matter in which the weal of the convent was so deeply interested, Father Eustace proceeded on his journey.

CHAPTER VIII.

> ay, dally not with time, the wise man's treasure.
> Though fools are lavish on't; the fatal Fisher
> Hooks souls, while we waste moments.
> *Old Play.*

A NOVEMBER mist overspread the little valley, up which slowly but steadily rode the monk Eustace. He was not insensible to the feeling of melancholy inspired by the scene and by the season. The stream seemed to murmur with deep and oppressed note, as if bewailing the departure of autumn. Among the scattered copses which here and there fringed its banks, the oak-trees only retained that pallid green that precedes their russet hue. The leaves of the willows were most of them stripped from the branches, lay rustling at each breath, and disturbed by every step of the mule; while the foliage of other trees, totally withered, kept still precarious possession of the boughs, waiting the first wind to scatter them.

The monk dropped into the natural train of pensive thought which these autumnal emblems of mortal hopes are peculiarly calculated to inspire. "There," he said, looking at the leaves which lay strewed around, "lie the hopes of early youth, first formed that they may soonest wither, and loveliest in spring to become most contemptible in winter; but you, ye lingerers," he added, looking to a knot of beeches which still bore their withered leaves—"you are the proud plants of adventurous manhood, formed later, and still clinging to the mind of age, although it acknowledges their inanity! None lasts—none endures, save the foliage of the hardy oak, which only begins to show itself when that of the rest of the forest has enjoyed half its existence. A pale and decayed hue is all it possesses, but still it retains that symptom of vitality to the last. So be it with Father Eustace! The fairy hopes of my youth I have trodden under foot like those neglected rustlers; to the prouder dreams of my manhood I look back as to lofty chimeras, of which the pith and essence have long since faded; but my religious vows, the faithful profession which I have made in my maturer age, shall retain life while aught of Eustace lives. Dangerous it may be—feeble it must be—yet live it shall, the proud determination to serve the church of which I am a member, and to combat the heresies by which she is assailed." Thus spoke, at least thus thought, a man zealous acccording to his imperfect knowledge, confounding the vital interests of Christianity with the extravagant and usurped claims of the Church of Rome, and defending his cause with ardour worthy of a better.

While moving onward in this contemplative mood, he could not help thinking more than once that he saw in his path the form of a female dressed in white, who appeared in the attitude of lamentation. But the impression was only momentary, and whenever he looked steadily to the point where he conceived the figure appeared, it always proved that he had mistaken some natural object—a white crag, or the trunk of a decayed birch-tree with its silver bark—for the appearance in question.

Father Eustace had dwelt too long in Rome to partake the superstitious feelings of the more ignorant Scottish clergy; yet he certainly thought it extraordinary that so strong an impression should have been made on his mind by the legend of the sacristan. "It is strange," he said to himself, "that this story, which doubtless was the invention of Brother Philip to cover his own impropriety of conduct, should run so much in my head, and disturb my more serious thoughts: I am wont, I think, to have more command over my senses. I will repeat my prayers, and banish such folly from my recollection."

The monk accordingly began with devotion to tell his beads, in pursuance of the prescribed rule of his order, and was not again disturbed by any wanderings of the imagination, until he found himself beneath the little fortalice of Glendearg.

Dame Glendinning, who stood at the gate, set up a shout of surprise and joy at seeing the good father. "Martin," she said—"Jasper, where be a' the folk? Help the right reverend sub-prior to dismount, and take his mule from him. O father! God has sent you in our need. I was just going to send man and horse to the convent, though I ought to be ashamed to give so much trouble to your reverences."

"Our trouble matters not, good dame," said Father Eustace; "in what can I pleasure you? I came hither to visit the Lady of Avenel."

"Well-a-day!" said Dame Elspeth, "and it was on her part that I had the boldness to think of summoning you, for the good lady will never be able to wear over the day! Would it please you to go to her chamber?"

"Hath she not been shriven by Father Philip?" said the monk.

"Shriven she was," said the Dame of Glendearg, "and by Father Philip, as your reverence truly says; but—I wish it may have a clean shrift. Methought Father Philip looked but moody upon it; and there was a book which he took away with him, that——" She paused, as if unwilling to proceed.

"Speak out, Dame Glendinning," said the father; "with us it is your duty to have no secrets."

"Nay, if it please your reverence, it is not that I would keep anything from your reverence's knowledge, but I fear I should prejudice the lady in your opinion; for she is an excellent lady—months and years has she dwelt in this tower, and none more exemplary than she; but this matter, doubtless she will explain it herself to your reverence."

"I desire first to know it from you, Dame Glendinning," said the monk; "and I again repeat, it is your duty to tell it to me."

"This book, if it please your reverence, which Father Philip removed from Glendearg, was this morning returned to us in a strange manner," said the good widow.

"Returned!" said the monk. "How mean you?"

"I mean," answered Dame Glendinning, "that it was brought back to the Tower of Glendearg, the saints best know how—that same book which Father Philip carried with him but yesterday. Old Martin, that is my tasker and the lady's servant, was driving out the cows to the pasture—for we have three good milk-cows, reverend father, blessed be St. Waldhave, and thanks to the holy monastery——"

The monk groaned with impatience; but he remembered that a woman of the good dame's condition was like a top, which, if you let it spin on untouched, must at last come to a pause; but, if you interrupt it by flogging, there is no end to its gyrations. "But to speak no more of the cows, your reverence, though they are likely cattle as ever were tied to a stake, the tasker was driving them out, and the lads, that is my Halbert and my Edward, that your reverence has seen at church on holidays, and especially Halbert—for you patted him on the head, and gave him a brooch of St. Cuthbert, which he wears in his bonnet—and little Mary Avenel, that is the lady's daughter, they ran all after the cattle, and began to play up and down the pasture as young folk will, your reverence. And at length they lost sight of Martin and the cows; and they began to run up a little cleuch which we call Corrienan-Shian, where there is a wee bit stripe of a burn, and they saw there—God guide us!—a white woman sitting on the burn-side wringing her hands; so the bairns were frightened to see a strange woman sitting there—all but Halbert, who will be sixteen come Whitsuntide—and, besides, he never feared ony thing—and when they went up to her—behold she was passed away!"

"For shame, good woman!" said Father Eustace; "a woman of your sense to listen to a tale so idle! The young folk told you a lie, and that was all."

"Nay, sir, it was more than that," said the old dame; "for, besides that they never told me a lie in their lives, I must warn you that on the very ground where the white woman was sitting they found the Lady of Avenel's book, and brought it with them to the tower."

"That is worthy of mark at least," said the monk. "Know you no other copy of this volume within these bounds?"

"None, your reverence," returned Elspeth; "why should there? no one could read it were there twenty."

"Then you are sure it is the very same volume which you gave to Father Philip?" said the monk.

"As sure as that I now speak with your reverence."

"It is most singular!" said the monk; and he walked across the room in a musing posture.

"I have been upon nettles to hear what your reverence would say," continued Dame Glendinning, "respecting this matter. There is nothing I would not do for the Lady of Avenel and her family, and that has been proved, and for her servants to boot, both Martin and Tibb, although Tibb is not so civil sometimes as altogether I have a right to expect; but I cannot think it beseeming to have angels, or ghosts, or fairies, or the like, waiting upon a leddy when she is in another woman's house, in respect it is no ways creditable. Ony thing she had to do was always done to her hand, without costing her either pains or pence, as a country body says; and, besides the discredit, I cannot but think that there is no safety in having such unchancy creatures about me. But I have tied red thread round the bairns' throats (so her fondness still called them), and given ilk ane of them a riding-wand of rowan-tree, forbye sewing up a slip of witch-elm into their doublets; and I wish to know of your reverence if there by ony thing mair that a lone woman can do in the matter of ghosts and fairies? —— be here! that I should have named their unlucky names twice ower!"

"Dame Glendinning," answered the monk, somewhat abruptly, when the good woman had finished her narrative, "I pray you, do you know the miller's daughter?"

"Did I know Kate Happer?" replied the widow; "as weel as the beggar knows his dish—a canty quean was Kate, and a special cummer of my ain may be twenty years syne."

"She cannot be the wench I mean," said Father Eustace: "she after whom I inquire is scarce fifteen, a black-eyed girl; you may have seen her at the kirk."

"Your reverence must be in the right; and she is my cummer's niece, doubtless, that you are pleased to speak of. But I thank God I have always been too duteous in attention to the mass to know whether young wenches have black eyes or green ones."

The good father had so much of the world about him that he was unable to avoid smiling when the dame boasted her absolute resistance to a temptation which was not quite so liable to beset her as those of the other sex.

"Perhaps, then," he said, "you know her usual dress, Dame Glendinning?"

"Ay, ay, father," answered the dame readily enough, "a white kirtle the wench wears, to hide the dust of the mill no doubt; and a blue hood, that might weel be spared, for pridefulness."

"Then, may it not be she," said the father, "who has brought back this book, and stepped out of the way when the children came near her?"

The dame paused, was unwilling to combat the solution suggested by the monk, but was at a loss to conceive why the lass of the mill should come so far from home into so wild a corner, merely to leave an old book with three children, from whose observation she wished to conceal herself. Above all, she could not understand why, since she had acquaintances in the family, and since the Dame Glendinning had always paid her multure and knaveship duly, the said lass of the mill had not come in to rest herself and eat a morsel, and tell her the current news of the water.

These very objections satisfied the monk that his conjectures were right. "Dame," he said, "you must be cautious in what you say. This is an instance—I would it were the sole one—of the power of the Enemy in these days. The matter must be sifted with a curious and careful hand."

"Indeed," said Elspeth, trying to catch and chime in with the ideas of the sub-prior, "I have often thought the miller's folk at the monastery mill were far over careless in sifting our melder, and in bolting it too; some folk say they will not stick at whiles to put in a handful of ashes amongst Christian folks' corn-meal."

"That shall be looked after also, dame," said the sub-prior, not displeased to see that the good old woman went off on a false scent; "and now, by your leave, I will see this lady; do you go before, and prepare her to see me."

Dame Glendinning left the lower apartment accordingly, which the monk paced in anxious reflection, considering how he might best discharge, with humanity as well as with effect, the important duty imposed on him. He resolved to approach the bedside of the sick person with reprimands, mitigated only by a feeling for her weak condition; he determined, in case of her reply, to which late examples of hardened heretics might encourage her, to be prepared with answers to their customary scruples. High fraught, also, with zeal against her unauthorised intrusion into the priestly function, by study of the Sacred Scriptures, he imagined to himself the answers which one of the modern school of heresy might return to him; the victorious refutation which should lay the disputant prostrate at the confessor's mercy; and the healing, yet awful exhortation, which, under pain of refusing the last consolations of religion, he designed to make to the penitent, conjuring her, as she loved her own soul's welfare, to disclose to him what she knew of the dark mystery of iniquity by which heresies were introduced into the most secluded spots of the very patrimony of the church herself; what agents they had who could thus glide, as it were unseen, from place to place, bring back the volume which the church had interdicted to the spots from which it had been removed under her express auspices; and who, by encouraging the daring and profane thirst after knowledge forbidden and useless to the laity, had encouraged the Fisher of souls to use with effect his old bait of ambition and vainglory.

Much of this premeditated disputation escaped the good father when Elspeth returned, her tears flowing faster than her apron could dry them, and made him a signal to follow her. "How," said the monk, "is she then so near her end? Nay, the church must not break or bruise, when comfort is yet possible"; and, forgetting his polemics, the good sub-prior hastened to the little apartment where, on the wretched bed which she had occupied since her misfortunes had driven her to the Tower of Glendearg, the widow of Walter Avenel had rendered up her spirit to her Creator. "My God!" said the sub-prior, "and has my unfortunate dallying suffered her to depart without the church's consolation! Look to her, dame," he exclaimed with eager impatience; "is there not yet a sparkle of the life left? may she not be recalled—recalled but for a moment? Oh! would that she could express, but by the most imperfect word, but by the most feeble motion, her acquiescence in the needful task of penitential prayer! Does she not breathe? Art thou sure she doth not?"

"She will never breathe more," said the matron. "Oh! the poor fatherless girl—now motherless also! Oh, the kind companion I have had these many years, whom I shall never see again! But she is in Heaven for certain, if ever woman went there; for a woman of better life——"

"Woe to me," said the good monk, "if indeed she went not

hence in good assurance; woe to the reckless shepherd, who suffered the wolf to carry a choice one from the flock, while he busied himself with trimming his sling and his staff to give the monster battle! Oh! if in the long Hereafter aught but weal should that poor spirit share, what has my delay cost? the value of an immortal soul!"

He then approached the body, full of the deep remorse natural to a good man of his persuasion, who devoutly believed the doctrines of the Catholic Church. "Ay," said he, gazing on the pallid corpse, from which the spirit had parted so placidly as to leave a smile upon the thin blue lips, which had been so long wasted by decay that they had parted with the last breath of animation without the slightest convulsive tremor—"ay," said Father Eustace, "there lies the faded tree, and as it fell so it lies—awful thought for me, should my neglect have left it to descend in an evil direction!" He then again and again conjured Dame Glendinning to tell him what she knew of the demeanour and ordinary walk of the deceased.

All tended to the high honour of the deceased lady; for her companion, who admired her sufficiently while alive, notwithstanding some trifling points of jealousy, now idolised her after her death, and could think of no attribute of praise with which she did not adorn her memory.

Indeed, the Lady of Avenel, however she might privately doubt some of the doctrines announced by the Church of Rome, and although she had probably tacitly appealed from that corrupted system of Christianity to the volume on which Christianity itself is founded, had nevertheless been regular in her attendance on the worship of the church, not, perhaps, extending her scruples so far as to break off communion. Such, indeed, was the first sentiment of the earlier reformers, who seem to have studied, for a time at least, to avoid a schism, until the violence of the Pope rendered it inevitable.

Father Eustace, on the present occasion, listened with eagerness to everything which could lead to assure him of the lady's orthodoxy in the main points of belief; for his conscience reproached him sorely that, instead of protracting conversation with the Dame of Glendearg, he had not instantly hastened where his presence was so necessary. "If," he said, addressing the dead body, "thou art yet free from the utmost penalty due to the followers of false doctrine; if thou dost but suffer for a time, to expiate faults done in the body, but partaking of mortal frailty more than of deadly sin, fear not that thy abode shall be long in the penal regions to which thou mayest be doomed—if vigils, if masses, if penance, if maceration of my body till it resembles that extenuated form which the soul hath abandoned, may assure thy deliverance. The Holy Church, the godly foundation, our blessed patroness herself, shall intercede for one whose errors were counterbalanced by so many virtues. Leave me, dame; here, and by her bedside, will I perform those duties which this piteous case demands!"

Elspeth left the monk, who employed himself in fervent and sincere, though erroneous, prayers for the weal of the departed spirit. For an hour he remained in the apartment of death, and then returned to the hall, where he found the still weeping friend of the deceased.

But it would be injustice to Mrs. Elspeth Glendinning's hospitality if we suppose her to have been weeping during this long interval, or rather, if we suppose her so entirely absorbed by the tribute of sorrow which she paid frankly and plentifully to her deceased friend, as to be incapable of attending to the rites of hospitality due to the holy visitor, who was confessor at once and sub-prior, mighty in all religious and secular considerations, so far as the vassals of the monastery were interested.

Her barley-bread had been toasted, her choicest cask of home-brewed ale had been broached, her best butter had been placed on the hall table, along with her most savoury ham and her choicest cheese, ere she abandoned herself to the extremity of sorrow; and it was not till she had arranged her little repast neatly on the board that she sat down in the chimney-corner, threw her checked apron over her head, and gave way to the current of tears and sobs. In this there was no grimace or affectation. The good dame held the honours of her house to be as essential a duty, especially when a monk was her visitant, as any other pressing call upon her conscience; nor until these were suitably attended to did she find herself at liberty to indulge her sorrow for her departed friend.

When she was conscious of the sub-prior's presence, she rose with the same attention to his reception; but he declined all the offers of hospitality with which she endeavoured to tempt him. Not her butter, as yellow as gold, and the best, she assured him, that was made in the patrimony of St. Mary; not the barley-scones, which "the departed saint, God sain her! used to say were so good"; not the ale, nor any other cates which poor Elspeth's stores afforded, could prevail on the sub-prior to break his fast.

"This day," he said, "I must not taste food until the sun go down—happy if, in so doing, I can expiate my own negligence; happier still, if my sufferings of this trifling nature, undertaken in pure faith and singleness of heart, may benefit the soul of the deceased. Yet, dame," he added, "I may not so far forget the living in my cares for the dead as to leave behind me that book, which is to the ignorant what to our first parents the tree of Knowledge of Good and Evil unhappily proved—excellent indeed in itself, but fatal because used by those to whom it is prohibited."

"Oh, blythely, reverend father," said the widow of Simon Glendinning, "will I give you the book, if so be I can wile it from the bairns; and indeed, poor things, as the case stands with them even now, you might take the heart out of their bodies, and they never find it out, they are sae begrutten."

"Give them this missal instead, good dame," said the father, drawing from his pocket one which was curiously illuminated with paintings, "and I will come myself, or send one at a fitting time, and teach them the meaning of these pictures."

"The bonny images!" said Dame Glendinning, forgetting for an instant her grief in her admiration; "and weel I wot," added she, "it is another sort of a book than the poor Lady of Avenel's; and blessed might we have been this day if your reverence had found the way up the glen instead of Father Philip, though the sacristan is a powerful man too, and speaks as if he would gar the house fly abroad, save that the walls are gey thick. Simon's forbears—may he and they be blessed!—took care of that."

The monk ordered his mule, and was about to take his leave; and the good dame was still delaying him with questions about the funeral, when a horseman, armed and accoutred, rode into the little courtyard which surrounded the keep.

CHAPTER IX.

> For since they rode among our doors
> With splent on spauld and rusty spurs,
> There grows no fruit into our furs;
>   Thus said John Up-on-land.
>   *Bannatyne MS.*

THE Scottish laws, which were as wisely and judiciously made as they were carelessly and ineffectually executed, had in vain endeavoured to restrain the damage done to agriculture by the chiefs and landed proprietors retaining in their service what were called jack-men, from the "jack," or doublet quilted with iron, which they wore as defensive armour. These military retainers conducted themselves with great insolence towards the industrious part of the community, lived in a great measure by plunder, and were ready to execute any commands of their master, however unlawful. In adopting this mode of life, men resigned the quiet hopes and regular labours of industry for an unsettled, precarious, and dangerous trade, which yet had such charms for those once accustomed to it that they became incapable of following any other. Hence the complaint of John Upland, a fictitious character, representing a countryman, into whose mouth the poets of the day put their general satires upon men and manners:

> They ride about in such a rage
> By forest, firth, and field,
>   With buckler, bow, and brand.
> Lo! where they ride out through the rye!
> The Devil mot save the company,
>   Quoth John Up-on-land.

Christie of the Clinthill, the horseman who now arrived at the little Tower of Glendearg, was one of the hopeful company of whom the poet complains, as was indicated by his "splent on spauld" (iron-plates on his shoulder), his rusted spurs, and his long lance. An iron skull-cap, none of the brightest, bore for distinction a sprig of the holly, which was Avenel's badge. A long two-edged straight sword, having a handle made of polished oak, hung down by his side. The meagre condition of his horse, and the wild and emaciated look of the rider, showed their occupation could not be accounted an easy or a thriving one. He saluted Dame Glendinning with little courtesy, and the monk with less; for the growing disrespect to the religious orders had not failed to extend itself among a class of men of such disorderly habits, although it may be supposed they were tolerably indifferent alike to the new or the ancient doctrines.

"So, our lady is dead, Dame Glendinning?" said the jackman. "My master has sent you even now a fat bullock for her mart; it may serve for her funeral. I have left him in the upper cleuch, as he is somewhat kenspeckle, and is marked both with cut and birn; the sooner the skin is off, and he is in sault-fat, the less like you are to have trouble—you understand me? Let me have a peck of corn for my horse, and beef and beer for myself, for I must go on to the monastery—though I think this monk here might do mine errand."

"Thine errand, rude man!" said the sub-prior, knitting his brows——

"For God's sake!" cried poor Dame Glendinning, terrified at the idea of a quarrel between them. "Oh, Christie! it is the sub-prior—oh, reverend sir, it is Christie of the Clinthill, the laird's chief jack-man; ye know that little havings can be expected from the like o' them."

"Are you a retainer of the Laird of Avenel?" said the monk, addressing himself to the horseman, "and do you speak thus rudely to a brother of St. Mary's, to whom thy master is so much beholden?"

"He means to be yet more beholden to your house, sir monk," answered the fellow; "for, hearing his sister-in-law, the widow of Walter of Avenel, was on her death-bed, he sent me to say to the father abbot and the brethren that he will hold the funeral-feast at their convent, and invites himself thereto, with a score of horse, and some friends, and to abide there for three days and three nights, having horse-meat and men's-meat at the charge of the community; of which his intention he sends due notice, that fitting preparation may be timeously made."

"Friend," said the sub-prior, "believe not that I will do to the father abbot the indignity of delivering such an errand. Think'st thou the goods of the church were bestowed upon her by holy princes and pious nobles, now dead and gone, to be consumed in revelry by every profligate layman who numbers in his train more followers than he can support by honest means, or by his own incomings? Tell thy master, from the sub-prior of St. Mary's, that the Primate hath issued his commands to us that we submit no longer to this compulsory exaction of hospitality on slight or false pretences. Our lands and goods were given to relieve pilgrims and pious persons, not to feast bands of rude soldiers."

"This to me!" said the angry spearman—"this to me and to my master! Look to yourself then, sir priest, and try if *ave* and *credo* will keep bullocks from wandering and haystacks from burning."

"Dost thou menace the Holy Church's patrimony with waste and fire-raising," said the sub-prior, "and that in the face of the sun? I call on all who hear me to bear witness to the words this ruffian has spoken. Remember how the Lord James drowned such as you by scores in the black pool at Jeddart. To him and to the Primate will I complain." The soldier shifted the position of his lance, and brought it down to a level with the monk's body.

Dame Glendinning began to shriek for assistance. "Tibb Tacket! Martin! where be ye all? Christie, for the love of God, consider he is a man of Holy Kirk!"

"I care not for his spear," said the sub-prior; "if I am slain in defending the rights and privileges of my community, the Primate will know how to take vengeance."

"Let him look to himself," said Christie, but at the same time depositing his lance against the wall of the tower; "if the Fife men spoke true who came hither with the governor in the last raid, Norman Leslie has him at feud, and is like to set him hard. We know Norman a true bloodhound, who will never quit the slot. But I had no design to offend the holy father," he added, thinking perhaps he had gone a little too far: "I am a rude man, bred to lance and stirrup, and not used to deal with book-learned men and priests; and I am willing to ask his forgiveness and his blessing if I have said aught amiss."

"For God's sake, your reverence," said the widow of Glendearg apart to the sub-prior, "bestow on him your forgiveness; how shall we poor folk sleep in security in the dark nights, if the convent is at feud with such men as he is?"

"You are right, dame," said the sub-prior, "your safety should, and must, be in the first instance consulted. Soldier, I forgive thee, and may God bless thee, and send thee honesty!"

Christie of the Clinthill made an unwilling inclination with his head, and muttered apart, "That is as much as to say, 'God send thee starvation.' But now to my master's demand, sir priest? What answer am I to return?"

"That the body of the widow of Walter of Avenel," answered the father, "shall be interred as becomes her rank, and in the tomb of her valiant husband. For your master's proffered visit of three days, with such a company and retinue, I have no authority to reply to it; you must intimate your chief's purpose to the reverend lord abbot."

"That will cost me a farther ride," said the man, "but it is all in the day's work. How now, my lad," said he to Halbert, who was handling the long lance which he had laid aside; "how do you like such a plaything? Will you go with me, and be a moss-trooper?"

"The saints in their mercy forbid!" said the poor mother; and then, afraid of having displeased Christie by the vivacity of her exclamation, she followed it up by explaining that since Simon's death she could not look on a spear or a bow, or any implement of destruction, without trembling.

"Pshaw!" answered Christie, "thou shouldst take another husband, dame, and drive such follies out of thy thoughts; what says thou to such a strapping lad as I? Why, this old tower of thine is fencible enough, and there is no want of cleuchs, and crags, and bogs, and thickets, if one was set hard; a man might bide here, and keep his half-score of lads, and as many geldings, and live on what he could lay his hand on, and be kind to thee, old wench."

"Alas! Master Christie," said the matron, "that you should talk to a lone woman in such a fashion, and death in the house besides!"

"Lone woman! why, that is the very reason thou shouldst take a mate. Thy old friend is dead, why, good—choose thou another of somewhat tougher frame, and that will not die of the pip like a young chicken. Better still—— Come, dame, let me have something to eat, and we will talk more of this."

Dame Elspeth, though she well knew the character of the man, whom in fact she both disliked and feared, could not help simpering at the personal address which he thought proper to make to her. She whispered to the sub-prior, "Ony thing just to keep him quiet," and went into the tower to set before the soldier the food he desired, trusting, betwixt good cheer and the power of her own charms, to keep Christie of the Clinthill so well amused that the altercation betwixt him and the holy father should not be renewed.

The sub-prior was equally unwilling to hazard any unnecessary rupture between the community and such a person as Julian of Avenel. He was sensible that moderation, as well as firmness, was necessary to support the tottering cause of the Church of Rome; and that, contrary to former times, the quarrels betwixt the clergy and laity had, in the present, usually terminated to the advantage of the latter. He resolved, therefore, to avoid further strife by withdrawing, but failed not, in the first place, to possess nimself of the volume which the sacristan carried off the evening before, and which had been returned to the glen in such a marvellous manner.

Edward, the younger of Dame Elspeth's boys, made great objections to the book being removed, in which Mary would probably have joined, but that she was now in her little sleeping-chamber with Tibb, who was exerting her simple skill to console the young lady for her mother's death. But the younger Glendinning stood up in defence of her property, and, with a positiveness which had hitherto made no part of his character, declared, that now the kind lady was dead, the book was Mary's, and no one but Mary should have it.

"But if it is not a fit book for Mary to read, my dear boy," said the father, gently, "you would not wish it to remain with her?"

"The lady read it," answered the young champion of property, "and so it could not be wrong; it shall not be taken away, I wonder where Halbert is? listening to the bravading tales of gay Christie, I reckon! He is always wishing for fighting, and now he is out of the way!"

"Why, Edward, you would not fight with me, who am both a priest and an old man?"

"If you were as good a priest as the Pope," said the boy, "and as old as the hills to boot, you shall not carry away Mary's book without her leave. I will do battle for it."

"But see you, my love," said the monk, amused with the resolute friendship manifested by the boy, "I do not take it; I only borrow it; and I leave in its place my own gay missal, as a pledge I will bring it back again."

Edward opened the missal with eager curiosity, and glanced at the pictures with which it was illustrated. "St. George and the dragon—Halbert will like that; and St. Michael brandishing his sword over the head of the Wicked One—and that will do for Halbert too. And see the St. John leading his lamb in the wilderness, with his little cross made of reeds, and his scrip and staff—that shall be my favourite; and where shall we find one for poor Mary?—here is a beautiful woman weeping and lamenting herself."

"That is St. Mary Magdalen repenting of her sins, my dear boy," said the father.

"That will not suit *our* Mary; for she commits no faults, and is never angry with us but when we do something wrong."

"Then," said the father, "I will show you a Mary who will protect her and you and all good children. See how fairly she is represented, with her gown covered with golden stars."

The boy was lost in wonder at the portrait of the Virgin which the sub-prior turned up to him.

"This," he said, "is really like our sweet Mary; and I think I will let you take away the black book, that has no such goodly shows in it, and leave this for Mary instead. But you must promise to bring back the book, good father; for now I think upon it, Mary may like that best which was her mother's."

"I will certainly return," said the monk, evading his answer, "and perhaps I may teach you to write and read such beautiful letters as you see there written, and to paint them blue, green, and yellow, and to blazon them with gold."

"Ay, and to make such figures as those blessed saints, and especially these two Marys?" said the boy.

"With their blessing," said the sub-prior, "I can teach you that art too, so far as I am myself capable of showing and you of learning it."

"Then," said Edward, "will I paint Mary's picture; and remember you are to bring back the black book, that you must promise me."

The sub-prior, anxious to get rid of the boy's pertinacity, and to set forward on his return to the convent, without having any farther interview with Christie the galloper, answered by giving the promise Edward required, mounted his mule, and set forth on his return homeward.

The November day was well spent ere the sub-prior resumed his journey; for the difficulty of the road, and the various delays which he had met with at the tower, had detained him longer than he proposed. A chill easterly wind was sighing among the withered leaves, and stripping them from the hold they had yet retained on the parent trees.

"Even so," said the monk, "our prospects in this vale of time grow more disconsolate as the stream of years passes on. Little have I gained by my journey, saving the certainty that heresy is busy among us with more than his usual activity, and that the spirit of insulting religious orders and plundering the church's property, so general in the eastern districts of Scotland, has now come nearer home."

The tread of a horse which came up behind him interrupted his reverie, and he soon saw he was mounted by the same wild rider whom he had left at the tower.

"Good even, my son, and *benedicite*," said the sub-prior as he passed. But the rude soldier scarce acknowledged the greeting by bending his head; and dashing the spurs into his horse, went on at a pace which soon left the monk and his mule far behind. "And there," thought the sub-prior, "goes another plague of the times—a fellow whose birth designed him to cultivate the earth, but who is perverted, by the unhallowed and unchristian divisions of the country, into a daring, dissolute robber. The barons of Scotland are now turned masterful thieves and ruffians, oppressing the poor by violence, and wasting the church, by extorting free quarters from abbeys and priories, without either shame or reason. I fear me I shall be too late to counsel the abbot to make a stand against these daring sorners [1]—I must make haste." He struck his mule with his riding-wand accordingly; but, instead of mending her pace, the animal suddenly started from the path, and the rider's utmost efforts could not force her forward.

"Art thou, too, infected with the spirit of the times?" said the sub-prior; "thou wert wont to be ready and serviceable, and art now as restive as any wild jack-man or stubborn heretic of them all."

While he was contending with the startled animal, a voice, like that of a female, chanted in his ear, or at least very close to it:

> "Good evening, sir priest, and so late as you ride,
> With your mule so fair, and your mantle so wide;
> But ride you through valley, or ride you o'er hill,
> There is one that has warrant to wait on you still.
>   Back, back,
>   The volume black!
> I have a warrant to carry it back."

The sub-prior looked around, but either bush or brake was near which could conceal an ambushed songstress. "May Our

[1] See To Sorne. Note 5.

Lady have mercy on me!" he said; "I trust my senses have not forsaken me; yet how my thoughts should arrange themselves into rhymes which I despise, and music which I care not for, or why there should be the sound of a female voice in ears to which its melody has been so long indifferent, baffles my comprehension, and almost realises the vision of Philip the sacristan. Come, good mule, betake thee to the path, and let us hence while our judgment serves us."

But the mule stood as if it had been rooted to the spot, backed from the point to which it was pressed by its rider, and by her ears laid close into her neck, and her eyes almost starting from their sockets, testified that she was under great terror.

While the sub-prior, by alternate threats and soothing, endeavoured to reclaim the wayward animal to her duty, the wild musical voice was again heard close beside him:

> " What ho! sub-prior, and came you but here
> To conjure a book from a dead woman's bier?
> Sain you, and save you, be wary and wise,
> Ride back with the book, or you'll pay for your prize.
> > Back, back,
> > There's death in the track!
> In the name of my master, I bid thee bear back."

"In the name of MY Master," said the astonished monk, "that name before which all things created tremble, I conjure thee to say what thou art that hauntest me thus?"

The same voice replied:

> " That which is neither ill nor well,
> That which belongs not to Heaven nor to hell,
> A wreath of the mist, a bubble of the stream,
> 'Twixt a waking thought and a sleeping dream;
> > A form that men spy
> > With the half-shut eye,
> In the beams of the setting sun, am I."

"This is more than simple fantasy," said the sub-prior, rousing himself; though, notwithstanding the natural hardihood of his temper, the sensible presence of a supernatural being so near him failed not to make his blood run cold and his hair bristle. "I charge thee," he said, aloud, "be thine

errand what it will, to depart and trouble me no more! False
spirit, thou canst not appal any save those who do the work
negligently."

The voice immediately answered:

> " Vainly, sir, wouldst thou bar me my right?
> Like the star when it shoots, I can dart through the night;
> I can dance on the torrent and ride on the air,
> And travel the world with the bonny nightmare.
>   Again, again,
>   At the crook of the glen,
> Where bickers the burnie, I'll meet thee again."

The road was now apparently left open; for the mule collected herself, and changed from her posture of terror to one
which promised advance, although a profuse perspiration and
general trembling of the joints indicated the bodily terror she
had undergone.

"I used to doubt the existence of Cabalists and Rosicru-
cians," thought the sub-prior, "but, by my holy order, I know
no longer what to say! My pulse beats temperately, my hand
is cool, I am fasting from everything but sin, and possessed
of my ordinary faculties. Either some fiend is permitted to
bewilder me, or the tales of Cornelius Agrippa, Paracelsus,
and others who treat of occult philosophy art not without
foundation. At the crook of the glen? I could have desired
to avoid a second meeting, but I am on the service of the
church, and the gates of hell shall not prevail against me."

He moved forward accordingly, but with precaution, and
not without fear; for he neither knew the manner in which,
or the place where, his journey might be next interrupted by
his invisible attendant. He descended the glen without interruption for about a mile farther, when, just at the spot where
the brook approached the steep hill, with a winding so abrupt
as to leave scarcely room for a horse to pass, the mule was
again visited with the same symptoms of terror which had before interrupted her course. Better acquainted than before
with the cause of her restiveness, the priest employed no
effort to make her proceed, but addressed himself to the object, which he doubted not was the same that had formerly

interrupted him, in the words of solemn exorcism prescribed
by the Church of Rome on such occasions.

In reply to his demand, the voice again sung:

> " Men of good are bold as sackless,
> Men of rude are wild and reckless.
> Lie thou still
> In the nook of the hill,
> For those be before thee that wish thee ill."

While the sub-prior listened, with his head turned in the
direction from which the sounds seemed to come, he felt as if
something rushed against him; and ere he could discover the
cause, he was pushed from his saddle with gentle but irresistible force.   Before he reached the ground his senses were gone,
and he lay long in a state of insensibility; for the sunset had
not ceased to gild the top of the distant hill when he fell, and
when he again became conscious of existence the pale moon
was gleaming on the landscape.   He awakened in a state of
terror, from which, for a few minutes, he found it difficult to
shake himself free.   At length he sate up on the grass, and
became sensible, by repeated exertion, that the only personal
injury which he had sustained was the numbness arising from
extreme cold.   The motion of something near him made the
blood again run to his heart, and by a sudden effort he started
up, and, looking around, saw to his relief that the noise was
occasioned by the footsteps of his own mule.   The peaceable
animal had remained quietly beside her master during his
trance, browsing on the grass which grew plentifully in that
sequestered nook.

With some exertion he collected himself, remounted the animal, and, meditating upon his wild adventure, descended the
glen till its junction with the broader valley through which
the Tweed winds.   The drawbridge was readily dropped at
his first summons; and so much had he won upon the heart
of the churlish warden, that Peter appeared himself with a
lantern to show the sub-prior his way over the perilous pass.

" By my sooth, sir," he said, holding the light up to Father
Eustace's face, "you look sorely travelled and deadly pale;
but a little matter serves to weary out you men of the cell.   I

now who speak to you—I have ridden, before I was perched up here on this pillar betwixt wind and water, it may be thirty Scots miles before I broke my fast, and have had the red of a bramble rose in my cheek all the while. But will you taste some food, or a cup of distilled waters?"

"I may not," said Father Eustace, "being under a vow; but I thank you for your kindness, and I pray you to give what I may not accept to the next poor pilgrim who comes hither pale and fainting, for so it shall be the better both with him here and with you hereafter."

"By my faith, and I will do so," said Peter Bridge-Ward, "even for thy sake. It is strange how, how this sub-prior gets round one's heart more than the rest of these cowled gentry, that think of nothing but quaffing and stuffing! Wife, I say—wife, we will give a cup of distilled waters and a crust of bread unto the next pilgrim that comes over; and ye may keep for the purpose the grunds of the last greybeard, and the ill-baked bannock which the bairns couldna eat."

While Peter issued these charitable, and at the same time prudent, injunctions, the sub-prior, whose mild interference had awakened the bridge-ward to such an act of unwonted generosity, was pacing onward to the monastery. In the way, he had to commune with and subdue his own rebellious heart, an enemy, he was sensible, more formidable than any which the external powers of Satan could place in his way.

Father Eustace had indeed strong temptation to suppress the extraordinary incident which had befallen him, which he was the more reluctant to confess, because he had passed so severe a judgment upon Father Philip, who, as he was now not unwilling to allow, had, on his return from Glendearg, encountered obstacles somewhat similar to his own. Of this the sub-prior was the more convinced when, feeling in his bosom for the book which he had brought off from the Tower of Glendearg, he found it was amissing, which he could only account for by supposing it had been stolen from him during his trance.

"If I confess this strange visitation," thought the sub-prior, "I become the ridicule of all my brethren—I whom the

Primate sent hither to be a watch, as it were, and a check upon their follies. I give the abbot an advantage over me which I shall never again recover, and Heaven only knows how he may abuse it, in his foolish simplicity, to the dishonour and loss of Holy Kirk. But then, if I make not true confession of my shame, with what face can I again presume to admonish or restrain others? Avow, proud heart," continued he, addressing himself, "that the weal of Holy Church interests thee less in this matter than thine own humiliation. Yes, Heaven has punished thee even in that point in which thou didst deem thyself most strong, in thy spiritual pride and thy carnal wisdom. Thou hast laughed at and derided the inexperience of thy brethren; stoop thyself in turn to their derision; tell what they may not believe; affirm that which they will ascribe to idle fear, or perhaps to idle falsehood; sustain the disgrace of a silly visionary or a wilful deceiver. Be it so; I will do my duty, and make ample confession to my superior. If the discharge of this duty destroys my usefulness in this house, God and Our Lady will send me where I can better serve them."

There was no little merit in the resolution thus piously and generously formed by Father Eustace. To men of any rank the esteem of their order is naturally most dear; but in the monastic establishment, cut off, as the brethren are, from other objects of ambition, as well as from all exterior friendship and relationship, the place which they hold in the opinion of each other is all in all.

But the consciousness how much he should rejoice the abbot and most of the other monks of St. Mary's, who were impatient of the unauthorised yet irresistible control which he was wont to exercise in the affairs of the convent, by a confession which would put him in a ludicrous, or perhaps even in a criminal, point of view could not weigh with Father Eustace in comparison with the task which his belief enjoined.

As, strong in his feelings of duty, he approached the exterior gate of the monastery, he was surprised to see torches gleaming, and men assembled around it, some on horseback, some on foot, while several of the monks, distinguished through the night by their white scapularies, were making themselves busy among the crowd. The sub-prior was received with a unanimous shout of joy, which at once made him sensible that he had himself been the object of their anxiety.

"There he is!—there he is! God be thanked—there he is, hale and feir!" exclaimed the vassals; while the monks exclaimed: " *Te Deum laudamus;* the blood of Thy servants is precious in Thy sight!"

"What is the matter, children?—what is the matter, my brethren?" said Father Eustace, dismounting at the gate.

"Nay, brother, if thou know'st not, we will not tell thee till thou art in the refectory," answered the monks. "Suffice it that the lord abbot had ordered these, our zealous and faithful vassals, instantly to set forth to guard thee from imminent peril. Ye may ungirth your horses, children, and dismiss; and to-morrow each who was at this rendezvous may send to the convent kitchen for a quarter of a yard of roast-beef [1] and a black-jack full of double ale."

The vassals dispersed with joyful acclamation, and the monks, with equal jubilee, conducted the sub-prior into the refectory.

CHAPTER X.

Here we stand
Woundless and well, may Heaven's high name be bless'd for't!
As erst, ere treason couch'd a lance against us.

DECKER.

No sooner was the sub-prior hurried into the refectory by his rejoicing companions, than the first person on whom he fixed his eye proved to be Christie of the Clinthill. He was seated in the chimney-corner, fettered and guarded, his features drawn into that air of sulky and turbid resolution with which those hardened in guilt are accustomed to view the approach of punishment. But as the sub-prior drew near to him

[1] See Note 6.

his face assumed a more wild and startled expression, while he exclaimed: "The devil—the devil himself brings the dead back upon the living!"

"Nay," said a monk to him, "say rather, that Our Lady foils the attempts of the wicked on her faithful servants: our dear brother lives and moves."

"Lives and moves!" said the ruffian, rising and shuffling towards the sub-prior as well as his chains would permit; "nay, then I will never trust ashen shaft and steel point more. It is even so," he added, as he gazed on the sub-prior with astonishment; "neither wem nor wound—not as much as a rent in his frock!"

"And whence should my wound have come?" said Father Eustace.

"From the good lance that never failed me before," replied Christie of the Clinthill.

"Heaven absolve thee for thy purpose!" said the sub-prior; "wouldst thou have slain a servant of the altar?"

"To choose!" answered Christie. "The Fifemen say, an the whole pack of ye were slain, there were more lost at Flodden."

"Villain! art thou heretic as well as murderer?"

"Not I, by St. Giles," replied the rider; "I listened blythely enough to the Laird of Monance, when he told me ye were all cheats and knaves; but when he would have had me go hear one Wiseheart, a gospeller, as they called him, he might as well have persuaded the wild colt that had flung one rider to kneel down and help another into the saddle."

"There is some goodness about him yet," said the sacristan to the abbot, who at that moment entered. "He refused to hear a heretic preacher."

"The better for him in the next world," answered the abbot. "Prepare for death, my son: we deliver thee over to the secular arm of our bailie, for execution on the gallow-hill by peep of light."

"Amen!" said the ruffian; "'tis the end I must have come by sooner or later; and what care I whether I feed the crows at St. Mary's or at Carlisle?"

"Let me implore your reverend patience for an instant," said the sub-prior; "until I shall inquire——"

"What!" exclaimed the abbot, observing him for the first time. "Our dear brother restored to us when his life was unhoped for!—nay, kneel not to a sinner like me—stand up—thou hast my blessing. When this villain came to the gate, accused by his own evil conscience, and crying out he had murdered thee, I thought that the pillar of our main aisle had fallen; no more shall a life so precious be exposed to such risks as occurred in this Border country; no longer shall one beloved and rescued of Heaven hold so low a station in the church as that of a poor sub-prior: I will write by express to the Primate for thy speedy removal and advancement."

"Nay, but let me understand," said the sub-prior; "did this soldier say that he had slain me?"

"That he had transfixed you," answered the abbot, "in full career with his lance; but it seems he had taken an indifferent aim. But no sooner didst thou fall to the ground mortally gored, as he deemed, with his weapon, than our blessed patroness appeared to him, as he averred——"

"I averred no such thing," said the prisoner; "I said a woman in white interrupted me, as I was about to examine the priest's cassock, for they are usually well lined; she had a bulrush in her hand, with one touch of which she struck me from my horse, as I might strike down a child of four years old with an iron mace; and then, like a singing fiend as she was, she sung to me:

> 'Thank the holly-bush
>   That nods on thy brow;
> Or with this slender rush
>   I had strangled thee now.'

I gathered myself up with fear and difficulty, threw myself on my horse, and came hither like a fool to get myself hanged for a rogue."

"Thou seest, honoured brother," said the abbot to the sub-prior, "in what favour thou art with our blessed patroness, that she herself becomes the guardian of thy paths. Not since the days of our blessed founder hath she shown such grace to any one. All unworthy were we to hold spiritual superiority over thee, and we pray thee to prepare for thy speedy removal to Aberbrothwick."

"Alas! my lord and father," said the sub-prior, "your words pierce my very soul. Under the seal of confession will I presently tell thee why I conceive myself rather the baffled sport of a spirit of another sort than the protected favourite of the heavenly powers. But first let me ask this unhappy man a question or two."

"Do as ye list," replied the abbot; "but you shall not convince me that it is fitting you remain in this inferior office in the convent of St. Mary."

"I would ask of this poor man," said Father Eustace, "for what purpose he nourished the thought of putting to death one who never did him evil?"

"Ay! but thou didst menace me with evil," said the ruffian, "and no one but a fool is menaced twice. Dost thou not remember what you said touching the Primate and Lord James, and the black pool of Jedwood? Didst thou think me fool enough to wait till thou hadst betrayed me to the sack and the fork? There were small wisdom in that, methinks—as little as in coming hither to tell my own misdeeds: I think the devil was in me when I took this road. I might have remembered the proverb: 'Never friar forgot feud.'"

"And it was solely for that—for that only hasty word of mine, uttered in a moment of impatience, and forgotten ere it was well spoken?" said Father Eustace.

"Ay! for that, and—for the love of thy gold crucifix," said Christie of the Clinthill.

"Gracious Heaven! and could the yellow metal—the glittering earth—so far overcome every sense of what is thereby represented? Father abbot, I pray, as a dear boon, you will deliver this guilty person to my mercy."

"Nay, brother," interposed the sacristan, "to your doom if you will, not to your mercy. Remember, we are not all equally favoured by our blessed Lady, nor is it likely that every frock in the convent will serve as a coat of proof when a lance is couched against it."

10

"For that very reason," said the sub-prior, "I would not that for my worthless self the community were to fall at feud with Julian of Avenel, this man's master."

"Our Lady forbid!" said the sacristan; "he is a second Julian the Apostate."

"With our reverend father the abbot's permission, then," said Father Eustace, "I desire this man may be freed from his chains and suffered to depart uninjured. And here, friend," he added, giving him the golden crucifix, "is the image for which thou wert willing to stain thy hands with murder. View it well, and may it inspire thee with other and better thoughts than those which referred to it as a piece of bullion. Part with it, nevertheless, if thy necessities require, and get thee one of such coarse substance that mammon shall have no share in any of the reflections to which it gives rise. It was the bequest of a dear friend to me; but dearer service can it never do than that of winning a soul to Heaven."

The Borderer, now freed from his chains, stood gazing alternately on the sub-prior and on the golden crucifix. "By St. Giles," said he, "I understand ye not! An ye give me gold for couching my lance at thee, what would you give me to level it at a heretic?"

'The church," said the sub-prior, "will try the effect of her spiritual censures to bring these stray sheep into the fold ere she employ the edge of the sword of St. Peter."

"Ay, but," said the ruffian, "they say the Primate recommends a little strangling and burning in aid both of censure and of sword. But fare ye well! I owe you a life, and it may be I will not forget my debt."

The bailie now came bustling in, dressed in his blue coat and bandaliers, and attended by two or three halberdiers. "I have been a thought too late in waiting upon your reverend lordship. I am grown somewhat fatter since the field of Pinkie, and my leathern coat slips not on so soon as it was wont; but the dungeon is ready, and though, as I said, I have been somewhat late——"

Here his intended prisoner walked gravely up to the officer's nose, to his great amazement.

"You have been indeed somewhat late, bailie," said he, "and I am greatly obliged to your buff-coat, and to the time you took to put it on. If the secular arm had arrived some quarter of an hour sooner, I had been out of the reach of spiritual grace; but as it is, I wish you good even, and a safe riddance out of your garment of durance, in which you have much the air of a hog in armour."

Wroth was the bailie with this comparison, and exclaimed in ire: "An it were not for the presence of the venerable lord abbot, thou knave——"

"Nay, an thou wouldst try conclusions," said Christie of the Clinthill, "I will meet thee at daybreak by St. Mary's well."

"Hardened wretch!" said Father Eustace, "art thou but this instant delivered from death, and dost thou so soon nurse thoughts of slaughter?"

"I will meet with thee ere it be long, thou knave," said the bailie, "and teach thee thine *oremus*."

"I will meet thy cattle in a moonlight night before that day," said he of the Clinthill.

"I will have thee by the neck one misty morning, thou strong thief," answered the secular officer of the church.

"Thou art thyself as strong a thief as ever rode," retorted Christie; "and if the worms were once feasting on that fat carcass of thine, I might well hope to have thine office, by favour of these reverend men."

"A cast of their office, and a cast of mine," answered the bailie; "a cord and a confessor, that is all thou wilt have from us."

"Sirs," said the sub-prior, observing that his brethren began to take more interest than was exactly decorous in this wrangling betwixt justice and iniquity, "I pray you both to depart. Master bailie, retire with your halberdiers, and trouble not the man whom we have dismissed. And thou, Christie, or whatever be thy name, take thy departure, and remember thou owest thy life to the lord abbot's clemency."

"Nay, as to that," answered Christie, "I judge that I owe it to your own; but impute it to whom ye list, I owe a life among ye, and there is an end." And, whistling as he went, he left the apartment, seeming as if he held the life which he had forfeited not worth farther thanks.

"Obstinate even to brutality!" said Father Eustace; "and yet, who knows but some better ore may lie under so rude an exterior?"

"'Save a thief from the gallows,'" said the sacristan— "you know the rest of the proverb; and admitting, as may Heaven grant, that our lives and limbs are safe from this outrageous knave, who shall ensure our meal and our malt, our herds and our flocks?"

"Marry, that will I, my brethren," said an aged monk. "Ah, brethren, you little know what may be made of a repentant robber. In Abbot Ingelram's days—ay, and I remember them as it were yesterday—the freebooters were the best welcome men that came to St. Mary's. Ay, they paid tithe of every drove that they brought over from the South; and because they were something lightly come by, I have known them make the tithe a seventh—that is, if their confessor knew his business. Ay, when we saw from the tower a score of fat bullocks or a drove of sheep coming down the valley, with two or three stout men-at-arms behind them, with their glittering steel caps, and their black-jacks, and their long lances, the good Lord Abbot Ingelram was wont to say—he was a merry man: "There come the tithes of the spoilers of the Egyptians!" Ay, and I have seen the famous John the Armstrang—a fair man he was and a goodly, the more pity that hemp was ever heckled for him—I have seen him come into the abbey church with nine tassels of gold in his bonnet, and every tassel made of nine English nobles, and he would go from chapel to chapel, and from image to image, and from altar to altar, on his knees—and leave here a tassel, and there a noble, till there was as little gold on his bonnet as on my hood: you will find no such Border thieves now!"

"No, truly, Brother Nicolas," answered the abbot; "they are more apt to take any gold the church has left than to bequeath or bestow any; and for cattle, beshrew me if I think

they care whether beeves have fed on the meadows of Laner-
cost Abbey or of St. Mary's!"

"There is no good thing left in them," said Father Nicolas;
"they are clean naught. Ah, the thieves that I have seen!—
such proper men! and as pitiful as proper, and as pious as
pitiful!"

"It skills not talking of it, Brother Nicolas," said the abbot;
"and I will now dismiss you, my brethren, holding your meeting upon this our inquisition concerning the danger of our
reverend sub-prior instead of the attendance on the lauds this
evening. Yet let the bells be duly rung for the edification of
the laymen without, and also that the novices may give due
reverence. And now, *benedicite*, brethren! The cellarer will
bestow on each a grace-cup and a morsel as ye pass the buttery, for ye have been turmoiled and anxious, and dangerous
it is to fall asleep in such case with empty stomach."

"*Gratias agimus quam maximas, domine reverendissime!*"
replied the brethren, departing in their due order.

But the sub-prior remained behind, and falling on his knees
before the abbot, as he was about to withdraw, craved him to
hear under the seal of confession the adventures of the day.
The reverend lord abbot yawned, and would have alleged
fatigue; but to Father Eustace, of all men, he was ashamed
to show indifference in his religious duties. The confession
therefore proceeded, in which Father Eustace told all the extraordinary circumstances which had befallen him during the
journey. And being questioned by the abbot, whether he
was not conscious of any secret sin, through which he might
have been subjected for a time to the delusions of evil spirits, the sub-prior admitted with frank avowal that he thought
he might have deserved such penance for having judged
with unfraternal rigour of the report of Father Philip, the
sacristan.

"Heaven," said the penitent, "may have been willing to
convince me, not only that He can at pleasure open a communication betwixt us and beings of a different and, as we word
it, supernatural class, but also to punish our pride of superior
wisdom, or superior courage, or superior learning."

It is well said that virtue is its own reward; and I question if duty was ever more completely recompensed than by the audience which the reverend abbot so unwillingly yielded to the confession of the sub-prior. To find the object of his fear, shall we say, or of his envy, or of both, accusing himself of the very error with which he had so tacitly charged him, was at once a corroboration of the abbot's judgment, a soothing of his pride, and an allaying of his fears. The sense of triumph, however, rather increased than diminished his natural good-humour; and so far was Abbot Boniface from being disposed to tyrannise over his sub-prior in consequence of this discovery, that in his exhortation he hovered somewhat ludicrously betwixt the natural expression of his own gratified vanity and his timid reluctance to hurt the feelings of Father Eustace.

"My, brother," said he, *ex cathedrâ*, "it cannot have escaped your judicious observation that we have often declined our own judgment in favour of your opinion, even about those matters which most nearly concerned the community. Nevertheless, grieved would we be could you think that we did this either because we deemed our own opinion less pregnant, or our wit more shallow, than that of our other brethren. For it was done exclusively to give our younger brethren, such as your much-esteemed self, my dearest brother, that courage which is necessary to a free deliverance of your opinion; we ofttimes setting apart our proper judgment, that our inferiors, and especially our dear brother the sub-prior, may be comforted and encouraged in proposing valiantly his own thoughts. Which our deference and humility may, in some sort, have produced in your mind, most reverend brother, that self-opinion of parts and knowledge which hath led unfortunately to your over-estimating your own faculties, and thereby subjecting yourself, as is but too visible, to the japes and mockeries of evil spirits. For it is assured that Heaven always holdeth us in the least esteem when we deem of ourselves most highly; and also, on the other hand, it may be that we have somewhat departed from what became our high seat in this abbey, in suffering ourselves to be too much guided, and even, as it were, controlled, by the voice of our inferior. Wherefore," continued the lord abbot, "in both of us such faults shall and must be amended—you hereafter presuming less upon your gifts and carnal wisdom, and I taking heed not so easily to relinquish mine own opinion for that of one lower in place and in office. Nevertheless, we would not that we should thereby lose the high advantage which we have derived, and may yet derive, from your wise counsel, which hath been so often recommended to us by our most reverend Primate. Wherefore, on affairs of high moment, we will call you to our presence in private, and listen to your opinion, which, if it shall agree with our own, we will deliver to the chapter as emanating directly from ourselves; thus sparing you, dearest brother, that seeming victory which is so apt to engender spiritual pride, and avoiding ourselves the temptation of falling into that modest facility of opinion whereby our office is lessened and our person—were that of consequence—rendered less important in the eyes of the community over which we preside."

Notwithstanding the high notions which, as a rigid Catholic, Father Eustace entertained of the sacrament of confession, as his church calls it, there was some danger that a sense of the ridiculous might have stolen on him, when he heard his superior, with such simple cunning, lay out a little plan for availing himself of the sub-prior's wisdom and experience, while he should take the whole credit to himself. Yet his conscience immediately told him that he was right.

"I should have thought more," he reflected, "of the spiritual superior and less of the individual. I should have spread my mantle over the frailties of my spiritual father, and done what I might to support his character, and, of course, to extend his utility among the brethren, as well as with others. The abbot cannot be humbled but what the community must be humbled in his person. Her boast is, that all over her children, especially over those called to places of distinction, she can diffuse those gifts which are necessary to render them illustrious."

Actuated by these sentiments, Father Eustace frankly assented to the charge which his superior, even in that moment of authority, had rather intimated than made, and signified his humble acquiescence in any mode of communicating his counsel which might be most agreeable to the lord abbot, and might best remove from himself all temptation to glory in his own wisdom. He then prayed the reverend father to assign him such penance as might best suit his offence, intimating, at the same time, that he had already fasted the whole day.

"And it is that I complain of," answered the abbot, instead of giving him credit for his abstinence—"it is these very penances, fasts, and vigils of which we complain, as tending only to generate air and fumes of vanity, which, ascending from the stomach into the head, do but puff us up with vainglory and self-opinion. It is meet and beseeming that novices should undergo fast and vigils; for some part of every community must fast, and young stomachs may best endure it. Besides, in them it abates wicked thoughts, and the desire of worldly delights. But, reverend brother, for those to fast who are dead and mortified to the world, as I and thou, is work of supererogation, and is but the matter of spiritual pride. Wherefore, I enjoin thee, most reverend brother, go to the buttery, and drink two cups at least of good wine, eating withal a comfortable morsel, such as may best suit thy taste and stomach. And in respect that thine opinion of thy own wisdom hath at times made thee less conformable to, and companionable with, the weaker and less learned brethren, I enjoin thee, during the said repast, to choose for thy companion our reverend brother Nicolas, and, without interruption or impatience, to listen for a stricken hour to his narration concerning those things which befell in the times of our venerable predecessor, Abbot Ingelram, on whose soul may Heaven have mercy! And for such holy exercises as may further advantage your soul, and expiate the faults whereof you have contritely and humbly avowed yourself guilty, we will ponder upon that matter, and announce our will unto you the next morning."

It was remarkable that, after this memorable evening, the feelings of the worthy abbot towards his adviser were much more kindly and friendly than when he deemed the sub-prior

the impeccable and infallible person in whose garment of vir-
ture and wisdom no flaw was to be discerned. It seemed as
if this avowal of his own imperfections had recommended
Father Eustace to the friendship of the superior, although at
the same time this increase of benevolence was attended with
some circumstances, which, to a man of the sub-prior's natural elevation of mind and temper, were more grievous than
ever undergoing the legends of the dull and verbose Father
Nicolas. For instance, the abbot seldom mentioned him to
the other monks without designing him " our beloved Brother
Eustace, poor man!" and now and then he used to warn the
younger brethren against the snares of vainglory and spiritual
pride, which Satan sets for the more rigidly righteous, with
such looks and demonstrations as did all but expressly desig-
nate the sub-prior as one who had fallen at one time under
such delusions. Upon these occasions it required all the vo-
tive obedience of a monk, all the philosophical discipline of the
schools, and all the patience of a Christian, to enable Father
Eustace to endure the pompous and patronising parade of his
honest but somewhat thick-headed superior. He began himself to be desirous of leaving the monastery, or at least he
manifestly declined to interfere with its affairs in that marked
and authoritative manner which he had at first practised.

CHAPTER XI.

> You call this education, do you not?
> Why, 'tis the forced march of a herd of bullocks
> Before a shouting drover. The glad van
> Move on at ease, and pause a while to snatch
> A passing morsel from the dewy greensward;
> While all the blows, the oaths, the indignation,
> Fall on the croupe of the ill-fated laggard
> That cripples in the rear.
>
> *Old Play.*

Two or three years glided on, during which the storm of
the approaching alteration in church government became each
day louder and more perilous. Owing to the circumstances

which we have intimated in the end of the last chapter, the Sub-Prior Eustace appeared to have altered considerably his habits of life. He afforded, on all extraordinary occasions, to the abbot, whether privately or in the assembled chapter, the support of his wisdom and experience; but in his ordinary habits he seemed now to live more for himself, and less for the community, than had been his former practice.

He often absented himself for whole days from the convent; and as the adventure of Glendearg dwelt deeply on his memory, he was repeatedly induced to visit that lonely tower, and to take an interest in the orphans who had their shelter under its roof. Besides, he felt a deep anxiety to know whether the volume which he had lost, when so strangely preserved from the lance of the murderer, had again found its way back to the Tower of Glendearg. "It was strange," he thought, "that a spirit," for such he could not help judging the being whose voice he had heard, "should on one side seek the advancement of heresy, and on the other interpose to save the life of a zealous Catholic priest."

But from no inquiry which he made of the various inhabitants of the Tower of Glendearg could he learn that the copy of the translated Scriptures for which he made such diligent inquiry had again been seen by any of them.

In the mean while, the good father's occasional visits were of no small consequence to Edward Glendinning and to Mary Avenel. The former displayed a power of apprehending and retaining whatever was taught him which filled Father Eustace with admiration. He was at once acute and industrious, alert and accurate—one of those rare combinations of talent and industry which are seldom united.

It was the earnest desire of Father Eustace that the excellent qualities thus early displayed by Edward should be dedicated to the service of the church, to which he thought the youth's own consent might be easily obtained, as he was of a calm, contemplative, retired habit, and seemed to consider knowledge as the principal object, and its enlargement as the greatest pleasure, in life. As to the mother, the sub-prior had little doubt that, trained as she was to view the monks of St. Mary's with such profound reverence, she would be but too happy in an opportunity of enrolling one of her sons in its honoured community.   But the good father proved to be mistaken in both these particulars.

When he spoke to Elspeth Glendinning of that which a mother best loves to hear, the proficiency and abilities of her son, she listened with a delighted ear.   But when Father Eustace hinted at the duty of dedicating to the service of the church talents which seemed fitted to defend and adorn it, the dame endeavoured always to shift the subject; and when pressed farther, enlarged on her own incapacity, as a lone woman, to manage the feu, on the advantage which her neighbours of the township were often taking of her unprotected state, and on the wish she had that Edward might fill his father's place, remain in the tower, and close her eyes.

On such occasions the sub-prior would answer that, even in a worldly point of view, the welfare of the family would be best consulted by one of the sons entering into the community of St. Mary's, as it was not to be supposed that he would fail to afford his family the important protection which he could then easily extend towards them.   What could be a more pleasing prospect than to see him high in honour? or what more sweet than to have the last duties rendered to her by a son revered for his holiness of life and exemplary manners? Besides, he endeavoured to impress upon the dame that her eldest son, Halbert, whose bold temper and headstrong indulgence of a wandering humour rendered him incapable of learning, was, for that reason, as well as that he was her eldest-born, fittest to bustle through the affairs of the world and manage the little fief.

Elspeth durst not directly dissent from what was proposed, for fear of giving displeasure, and yet she always had something to say against it.   "Halbert," she said, "was not like any of the neighbour boys: he was taller by the head, and stronger by the half, than any boy of his years within the halidome.   But he was fit for no peaceful work that could be devised.   If he liked a book ill, he liked a plough or a pattle worse.   He had scoured his father's old broadsword, suspend-

ed it by a belt round his waist, and seldom stirred without it.
He was a sweet boy and a gentle if spoken fair, but cross him
and he was a born devil.   In a word," she said, bursting into
tears, "deprive me of Edward, good father, and ye bereave
my house of prop and pillar; for my heart tells me that Halbert will take to his father's gates, and die his father's death."

When the conversation came to this crisis, the good-humoured monk was always content to drop the discussion for
the time, trusting some opportunity would occur of removing
her prejudices, for such he thought them, against Edward's
proposed destination.

When, leaving the mother, the sub-prior addressed himself to the son, animating his zeal for knowledge, and pointing out how amply it might be gratified should he agree to
take holy orders, he found the same repugnance which Dame
Elspeth had exhibited.   Edward pleaded a want of sufficient
vocation to so serious a profession, his reluctance to leave his
mother, and other objections, which the sub-prior treated as
evasive.

"I plainly perceive," he said one day, in answer to them,
"that the devil has his factors as well as Heaven, and that
they are equally, or, alas! the former are perhaps more active, in bespeaking for their master the first of the market.
I trust, young man, that neither idleness, nor licentious pleasure, nor the love of worldly gain and worldly grandeur, the
chief baits with which the great Fisher of souls conceals his
hook, are the causes of your declining the career to which I
would incite you.   But above all, I trust—above all, I hope—
that the vanity of superior knowledge, a sin with which those
who have made proficiency in learning are most frequently
beset, has not led you into the awful hazard of listening to
the dangerous doctrines which are now afloat concerning religion.   Better for you that you were as grossly ignorant as the
beasts which perish than that the pride of knowledge should
induce you to lend an ear to the voice of the heretics."   Edward Glendinning listened to the rebuke with a downcast look,
and failed not, when it was concluded, earnestly to vindicate
himself from the charge of having pushed his studies into any

subjects which the church inhibited; and so the monk was left to form vain conjectures respecting the cause of his reluctance to embrace the monastic state.

It is an old proverb, used by Chaucer, and quoted by Elizabeth, that "The greatest clerks are not the wisest men;" and it is as true as if the poet had not rhymed or the queen reasoned on it. If Father Eustace had not had his thoughts turned so much to the progress of heresy, and so little to what was passing in the tower, he might have read, in the speaking eyes of Mary Avenel, now a girl of fourteen or fifteen, reasons which might disincline her youthful companion towards the monastic vows. I have said, that she also was a promising pupil of the good father, upon whom her innocent and infantine beauty had an effect of which he was himself, perhaps, unconscious. Her rank and expectations entitled her to be taught the arts of reading and writing; and each lesson which the monk assigned her was conned over in company with Edward, and by him explained and re-explained, and again illustrated, until she became perfectly mistress of it.

In the beginning of their studies, Halbert had been their school companion. But the boldness and impatience of his disposition soon quarrelled with an occupation in which, without assiduity and unremitted attention, no progress was to be expected. The sub-prior's visits were at irregular intervals, and often weeks would intervene between them, in which case Halbert was sure to forget all that had been prescribed for him to learn, and much which he had partly acquired before. His deficiencies on these occasions gave him pain, but it was not of that sort which produces amendment.

For a time, like all who are fond of idleness, he endeavoured to detach the attention of his brother and Mary Avenel from their task, rather than to learn his own, and such dialogues as the following would ensue:

"Take your bonnet, Edward, and make haste; the Laird of Colmslie is at the head of the glen with his hounds."

"I care not, Halbert," answered the younger brother; "two brace of dogs may kill a deer without my being there to see them, and I must help Mary Avenel with her lesson."

"Ay! you will labour at the monk's lessons till you turn monk yourself," answered Halbert. "Mary, will you go with me, and I will show you the cushat's nest I told you of?"

"I cannot go with you, Halbert," answered Mary, "because I must study this lesson; it will take me long to learn it. I am sorry I am so dull, for if I could get my task as fast as Edward I should like to go with you."

"Should you, indeed?" said Halbert; "then I will wait for you; and, what is more, I will try to get my lesson also."

With a smile and a sigh he took up the primer, and began heavily to con over the task which had been assigned him. As if banished from the society of the two others, he sat sad and solitary in one of the deep window-recesses; and, after in in vain struggling with the difficulties of his task and his disinclination to learn it, he found himself involuntarily engaged in watching the movements of the other two students, instead of toiling any longer.

The picture which Halbert looked upon was delightful in itself, but somehow or other it afforded very little pleasure to him. The beautiful girl, with looks of simple yet earnest anxiety, was bent on disentangling those intricacies which obstructed her progress to knowledge, and looking ever and anon to Edward for assistance, while, seated close by her side, and watchful to remove every obstacle from her way, he seemed at once to be proud of the progress which his pupil made and of the assistance which he was able to render her. There was a bond betwixt them, a strong and interesting tie—the desire of obtaining knowledge, the pride of surmounting difficulties.

Feeling most acutely, yet ignorant of the nature and source of his own emotions, Halbert could no longer endure to look upon this quiet scene, but, starting up, dashed his book from him, and exclaimed aloud: "To the fiend I bequeath all books, and the dreamers that make them! I would a score of Southrons would come up the glen, and we should learn how little all this muttering and scribbling is worth."

Mary Avenel and his brother started, and looked at Halbert with surprise, while he went on with great animation, his features swelling, and the tears starting into his eyes as he spoke.

"Yes, Mary, I wish a score of Southrons came up the glen this very day; and you should see one good hand, and one good sword, do more to protect you than all the books that were ever opened, and all the pens that ever grew on a goose's wing."

Mary looked a little surprised and a little frightened at his vehemence, but instantly replied affectionately: "You are vexed, Halbert, because you do not get your lesson so fast as Edward can; and so am I, for I am as stupid as you. But come, and Edward shall sit betwixt us and teach us."

"He shall not teach *me*," said Halbert, in the same angry mood; "I never can teach *him* to do anything that is honourable and manly, and he shall not teach *me* any of his monkish tricks. I hate the monks, with their drawling nasal tone like so many frogs, and their long black petticoats like so many women, and their reverences, and their lordships, and their lazy vassals, that do nothing but paddle in the mire with plough and harrow, from Yule to Michaelmas. I will call none lord but him who wears a sword to make his title good; and I will call none man but him that can bear himself manlike and masterful."

"For Heaven's sake, peace, brother!" said Edward. "If such words were taken up, and reported out of the house, they would be our mother's ruin."

"Report them yourself, then, and they will be *your* making, and nobody's marring save mine own. Say that Halbert Glendinning will never be vassal to an old man with a cowl and shaven crown, while there are twenty barons who wear casque and plume that lack bold followers. Let them grant you these wretched acres, and much meal may they bear you to make your brochan!" He left the room hastily, but instantly returned, and continued to speak with the same tone of quick and irritated feeling. "And you need not think so much, neither of you, and especially you, Edward, need not think so much of your parchment book there, and your cunning in reading it. By my faith, I will soon learn to read as well as you; and—for I know a better teacher than your grim old monk, and a better book than his printed breviary—and since you like scholar-craft so well, Mary Avenel, you shall see whether Edward or I have most of it." He left the apartment, and came not again.

"What can be the matter with him?" said Mary, following Halbert with her eyes from the window, as with hasty and unequal steps he ran up the wild glen. "Where can your brother be going, Edward? what book?—what teacher does he talk of?"

"It avails not guessing," said Edward. "Halbert is angry, he knows not why, and speaks of he knows not what; let us go again to our lessons, and he will come home when he has tired himself with scrambling among the crags as usual."

But Mary's anxiety on account of Halbert seemed more deeply rooted. She declined prosecuting the task in which they had been so pleasingly engaged, under the excuse of a headache; nor could Edward prevail upon her to resume it again that morning.

Meanwhile Halbert, his head unbonneted, his features swelled with jealous anger, and the tear still in his eye, sped up the wild and upper extremity of the little valley of Glendearg with the speed of a roebuck, choosing, as if in desperate defiance of the difficulties of the way, the wildest and most dangerous paths, and voluntarily exposing himself a hundred times to dangers which he might have escaped by turning a little aside from them. It seemed as if he wished his course to be as straight as that of the arrow to its mark.

He arrived at length in a narrow and secluded cleuch, or deep ravine, which ran down into the valley, and contributed a scanty rivulet to the supply of the brook with which Glendearg is watered. Up this he sped with the same precipitate haste which had marked his departure from the tower; nor did he pause and look around until he had reached the fountain from which the rivulet had its rise.

Here Halbert stopt short, and cast a gloomy, and almost a frightened, glance around him. A huge rock rose in front, from a cleft of which grew a wild holly-tree, whose dark green branches rustled over the spring which arose beneath.

The banks on either hand rose so high, and approached each other so closely, that it was only when the sun was at its meridian height, and during the summer solstice, that its rays could reach the bottom of the chasm in which he stood. But it was now summer, and the hour was noon, so that the unwonted reflection of the sun was dancing in the pellucid fountain.

"It is the season and the hour," said Halbert to himself; "and now I—I might soon become wiser than Edward with all his pains! Mary should see whether he alone is fit to be consulted, and to sit by her side, and hang over her as she reads, and point out every word and every letter. And she loves me better than him—I am sure she does, for she comes of noble blood, and scorns sloth and cowardice. And do I myself not stand here slothful and cowardly as any priest of them all? Why should I fear to call upon this form—this shape? Already have I endured the vision, and why not again? What can it do to me, who am a man of lith and limb, and and have by my side my father's sword? Does my heart beat, do my hairs bristle, at the thought of calling up a painted shadow, and how should I face a band of Southrons in flesh and blood? By the soul of the first Glendinning, I will make proof of the charm!"

He cast the leathern brogue or buskin from his right foot, planted himself in a firm posture, unsheathed his sword, and first looking around to collect his resolution, he bowed three times deliberately towards the holly-tree, and as often to the little fountain, repeating at the same time, with a determined voice, the following rhyme:

> "Thrice to the holly brake,
>   Thrice to the well;
> I bid thee awake,
>   White Maid of Avenel!
>
> Noon gleams on the lake,
>   Noon glows on the fell;
> Wake thee, O wake,
>   White Maid of Avenel!"

These lines were hardly uttered, when there stood the figure of a female clothed in white, within three steps of Halbert Glendinning.

> I guess, 'twas frightful there to see
> A lady richly clad as she—
> Beautiful exceedingly.[2]

CHAPTER XII.

> There's something in that ancient superstition,
> Which, erring as it is, our fancy loves.
> The spring that, with its thousand crystal bubbles,
> Bursts from the bosom of some desert rock
> In secret solitude, may well be deem'd
> The haunt of something purer, more refined,
> And mightier than ourselves.
>
>   *Old Play.*

YOUNG Halbert Glendinning had scarcely pronounced the mystical rhymes, when, as we have mentioned in the conclusion of the last chapter, an appearance as of a beautiful female dressed in white stood within two yards of him. His terror for the moment overcame his natural courage, as well as the strong resolution which he had formed that the figure which he had now twice seen should not a third time daunt him. But it would seem there is something thrilling and abhorrent to flesh and blood in the consciousness that we stand in presence of a being in form like to ourselves, but so different in faculties and nature that we can neither understand its purposes nor calculate its means of pursuing them.

Halbert stood silent and gasped for breath, his hairs erecting themselves on his head, his mouth open, his eyes fixed, and, as the sole remaining sign of his late determined purpose, his sword pointed towards the apparition. At length, with a voice of ineffable sweetness, the White Lady—for by that name we shall distinguish this being—sung, or rather chanted, the following lines:

[2] Coleridge's *Christabel.*

" Youth of the dark eye, wherefore didst thou call me?
  Wherefore art thou here, if terrors can appal thee?
  He that seeks to deal with us must know nor fear nor failing :
  To coward and churl our speech is dark, our gifts are unavailing,
  The breeze that brought me hither now must sweep Egyptian ground,
  The fleecy cloud on which I ride for Araby is bound ;
  The fleecy cloud is drifting by, the breeze sighs for my stay,
  For I must sail a thousand miles before the close of day."

The astonishment of Halbert began once more to give way to his resolution, and he gained voice enough to say, though with a faltering accent, " In the name of God, what art thou?"

The answer was in melody of a different tone and measure:

" What I am I must not show,
  What I am thou couldst not know.
  Something betwixt heaven and hell,
  Something that neither stood nor fell,
  Something that through thy wit or will
  May work thee good, may work thee ill.
  Neither substance quite, nor shadow,
  Haunting lonely moor and meadow,
  Dancing by the haunted spring,
  Riding on the whirlwind's wing;
  Aping in fantastic fashion
  Every change of human passion,
  While o'er our frozen minds they pass,
  Like shadows from the mirror'd glass.
  Wayward, fickle is our mood,
  Hovering betwixt bad and good,
  Happier than brief-dated man,
  Living twenty times his span ;
  Far less happy, for we have
  Help nor hope beyond the grave !
  Man awakes to joy or sorrow ;
  Ours the sleep that knows no morrow.
  This is all that I can show,
  This is all that thou mayst know."

The White Lady paused, and appeared to await an answer; but, as Halbert hesitated how to frame his speech, the vision seemed gradually to fade, and become more and more incorporeal. Justly guessing this to be a symptom of her disappearance, Halbert compelled himself to say: " Lady, when I saw you in the glen, and when you brought back the black book of Mary of Avenel, thou didst say I should one day learn to read it."

The White Lady replied:

> ' Ay ! and I taught thee the word and the spell,
> To waken me here by the Fairies' Well.
> But thou hast loved the heron and hawk,
> More than to seek my haunted walk;
> And thou hast loved the lance and the sword,
> More than good text and holy word;
> And thou hast loved the deer to track,
> More than the lines and the letters black;
> And thou art a ranger of moss and of wood,
> And scornest the nurture of gentle blood."

"I will do so no longer, fair maiden," said Halbert. "I desire to learn, and thou didst promise me that, when I did so desire, thou wouldst be my helper; I am no longer afraid of thy presence, and I am no longer regardless of instruction." As he uttered these words, the figure of the White Maiden grew gradually as distinct as it had been at first; and what had well-nigh faded into an ill-defined and colourless shadow again assumed an appearance at least of corporeal consistency, although the hues were less vivid, and the outline of the figure less distinct and defined—so at least it seemed to Halbert— than those of an ordinary inhabitant of the earth. "Wilt thou grant my request," he said, "fair lady, and give to my keeping the holy book which Mary of Avenel has so often wept for?"

The White Lady replied:

> Thy craven fear my truth accused,
> Thine idlehood my trust abused.
> He that draws to harbour late,
> Must sleep without, or burst the gate.
> There is a star for thee which burn'd,
> Its influence wanes, its course is turn'd
> Valour and constancy alone
> Can bring thee back the chance that's flown."

"If I have been a loiterer, lady," answered young Glendinning, "thou shalt now find me willing to press forward with double speed. Other thoughts have filled my mind, other thoughts have engaged my heart, within a brief period—and by Heaven, other occupations shall henceforward fill up my time. I have lived in this day the space of years: I came hither a boy—I will return a man—a man such as may converse not only with his own kind but what whatever God permits to be visible to him. I will learn the contents of that mysterious volume; I will learn why the Lady of Avenel loved it, why the priests feared, and would have stolen, it; why thou didst twice recover it from their hands. What mystery is wrapt in it? Speak, I conjure thee!" The lady assumed an air peculiarly sad and solemn, as, drooping her head and folding her arms on her bosom, she replied:

> " Within that awful volume lies
> The mystery of mysteries!
> Happiest they of human race,
> To whom God has granted grace
> To read, to fear, to hope, to pray,
> To lift the latch, and force the way;
> And better had they ne'er been born,
> Who read to doubt, or read to scorn."

"Give me the volume, lady," said young Glendinning. "They call me idle—they call me dull; in this pursuit my industry shall not fail, nor, with God's blessing, shall my understanding. Give me the volume."

The apparition again replied:

> " Many a fathom dark and deep
> I have laid the book to sleep;
> Ethereal fires around it glowing,
> Ethereal music ever flowing,
>   The sacred pledge of Heav'n
> All things revere,
> Each in his sphere,
>   Save man, for whom 'twas giv'n.
> Lend thy hand, and thou shalt spy
> Things ne'er seen by mortal eye."

Halbert Glendinning boldly reached his hand to the White Lady.

"Fearest thou to go with me?" she said, as his hand trembled at the soft and cold touch of her own:

> " Fearest thou to go with me?
> Still it is free to thee
>   A peasant to dwell;
> Thou mayst drive the dull steer,
> And chase the king's deer,
> But never more come near
>   This haunted well."

"If what thou sayest be true," said the undaunted boy, "my destinies are higher than thine own. There shall be neither well nor wood which I dare not visit. No fear of night, natural or supernatural, shall bar my path through my natural native valley."

He had scarce uttered the words, when they both descended through the earth with a rapidity which took away Halbert's breath and every other sensation, saving that of being hurried on with the utmost velocity. At length they stopped with a shock so sudden that the mortal journeyer through this un-known space must have been thrown down with violence had he not been upheld by his supernatural companion.

It was more than a minute ere, looking around him, he be-held a grotto, or natural cavern, composed of the most splendid spars and crystals, which returned in a thousand prismatic hues the light of a brilliant flame that glowed on an altar of alabaster. This altar, with its fire, formed the central point of the grotto, which was of a round form, and very high in the roof, resembling in some respects the dome of a cathedral. Corresponding to the four points of the compass, there went off four long galleries, or arcades, constructed of the same brilliant materials with the dome itself, and the termination of which was lost in darkness.

No human imagination can conceive, or words suffice to de-scribe, the glorious radiance which, shot fiercely forth by the flame, was returned from so many hundred thousand points of reflection, afforded by the sparry pillars and their numerous angular crystals. The fire itself did not remain steady and unmoved, but rose and fell, sometimes ascending in a brilliant pyramid of condensed flame half-way up the lofty expanse, and again fading into a softer and more rosy hue, and hovering, as it were, on the surface of the altar, to collect its strength for another powerful exertion. There was no visible fuel by which it was fed, nor did it emit either smoke or vapour of any kind.

What was of all the most remarkable, the black volume so often mentioned lay not only unconsumed, but untouched in the slightest degree, amid this intensity of fire, which, while it seemed to be of force sufficient to melt adamant, had no effect whatever on the sacred book thus subjected to its utmost influence.

The White Lady, having paused long enough to let young Glendinning take a complete survey of what was around him, now said, in her usual chant:

> " Here lies the volume thou boldly hast sought;
> Touch it and take it,—'twill dearly be bought! "

Familiarised in some degree with marvels, and desperately desirous of showing the courage he had boasted, Halbert plunged his hand without hesitation into the flame, trusting to the rapidity of the motion to snatch out the volume before the fire could greatly affect it. But he was much disappointed. The flame instantly caught upon his sleeve, and though he withdrew his hand immediately, yet his arm was so dreadfully scorched that he had wellnigh screamed with pain. He suppressed the natural expression of anguish, however, and only intimated the agony which he felt by a contortion and a muttered groan. The White Lady passed her cold hand over his arm, and ere she had finished the following metrical chant his pain had entirely gone, and no mark of the scorching was visible:

> " Rash thy deed,
> Mortal weed
> To immortal flames applying;
> Rasher trust
> Has thing of dust,
> On his own weak worth relying.
> Strip thee of such fences vain,
> Strip, and prove thy luck again."

Obedient to what he understood to be the meaning of his conductress, Halbert bared his arm to the shoulder, throwing down the remains of his sleeve, which no sooner touched the floor on which he stood than it collected itself together, shrivelled itself up, and was without any visible fire reduced to light tinder, which a sudden breath of wind dispersed into empty space. The White Lady, observing the surprise of the youth, immediately repeated:

" Mortal warp and mortal woof
    Cannot brook this charmed roof:
    All that mortal art hath wrought,
    In our cell returns to nought.
    The molten gold returns to clay,
    The polish'd diamond melts away;
    All is alter'd, all is flown,
    Nought stands fast but truth alone.
    Not for that thy quest give o'er;
    Courage! prove thy chance once more."

Emboldened by her words, Halbert Glendinning made a
second effort, and, plunging his bare arm into the flame, took
out the sacred volume without feeling either heat or inconvenience of any kind.   Astonished, and almost terrified, at his
own success, he beheld the flame collect itself and shoot up
into one long and final stream, which seemed as if it would
ascend to the very roof of the cavern, and then, sinking as
suddenly, became totally extinguished.   The deepest darkness ensued; but Halbert had no time to consider his situation, for the White Lady had already caught his hand, and
they ascended to upper air with the same velocity with which
they had sunk into the earth.

They stood by the fountain in the Corrie-nan-Shian when
they emerged from the bowels of the earth; but, on casting a
bewildered glance around him, the youth was surprised to observe that the shadows had fallen far to the east, and that the
day was wellnigh spent.   He gazed on his conductress for
explanation; but her figure began to fade before his eyes: her
cheeks grew paler, her features less distinct, her form became
shadowy, and blended itself with the mist which was ascending the hollow ravine.   What had late the symmetry of form,
and the delicate yet clear hues of feminine beauty, now resembled the flitting and pale ghost of some maiden who has
died for love, as it is seen, indistinctly and by moonlight, by
her perjured lover.

"Stay, spirit!" said the youth, emboldened by his success
in the subterraneous dome, "thy kindness must not leave me,
as one encumbered with a weapon he knows not how to wield.
Thou must teach me the art to read and to understand this
volume; else, what avails it me that I possess it?"

But the figure of the White Lady still waned before his eye, until it became an outline as pale and indistinct as that of the moon, when the winter morning is afar advanced; and ere she had ended the following chant, she was entirely invisible:

> " Alas! alas!
> Not ours the grace
> These holy characters to trace:
>   Idle forms of painted air,
>   Not to us is given to share
> The boon bestow'd on Adam's race:
>   With patience bide,
>   Heaven will provide
> The fitting time, the fitting guide."

The form was already gone, and now the voice itself had melted away in melancholy cadence, softening, as if the being who spoke had been slowly wafted from the spot where she had commenced her melody.

It was at this moment that Halbert felt the extremity of the terror which he had hitherto so manfully suppressed. The very necessity of exertion had given him spirit to make it, and the presence of the mysterious being, while it was a subject of fear in itself, had nevertheless given him the sense of protection being near to him. It was when he could reflect with composure on what had passed, that a cold tremor shot across his limbs, his hair bristled, and he was afraid to look around, lest he should find at his elbow something more frightful than the first vision. A breeze arising suddenly realised the beautiful and wild idea of the most imaginative of our modern bards:[1]

> It fann'd his cheek, it raised his hair,
>   Like a meadow gale in spring;
> It mingled strangely with his fears,
>   Yet it felt like a welcoming.

The youth stood silent and astonished for a few minutes. It seemed to him that the extraordinary being he had seen, half his terror, half his protectress, was still hovering on the gale which swept past him, and that she might again make herself sensible to his organs of sight. "Speak!" he said,

[1] Coleridge.

wildly tossing his arms—"speak yet again: be once more present, lovely vision! Thrice have I now seen thee, yet the idea of thy invisible presence around or beside me makes my heart beat faster than if the earth yawned and gave up a demon." But neither sound nor appearance indicated the presence of the White Lady, and nothing preternatural beyond what he had already witnessed was again audible or visible. Halbert, in the mean while, by the very exertion of again inviting the presence of this mysterious being, had recovered his natural audacity. He looked around once more, and resumed his solitary path down the valley into whose recesses he had penetrated.

Nothing could be more strongly contrasted than the storm of passion with which he had bounded over stock and crag, in order to plunge himself into the Corrie-nan-Shian, and the sobered mood in which he now returned homeward, industriously seeking out the most practicable path, not for a wish to avoid danger, but that he might not by personal toil distract his attention, deeply fixed on the extraordinary scene which he had witnessed. In the former case he had sought by hazard and bodily exertion to indulge at once the fiery excitation of passion and to banish the cause of the excitement from his recollection; while now he studiously avoided all interruption to his contemplative walk, lest the difficulty of the way should interfere with or disturb his own deep reflections. Thus slowly pacing forth his course, with the air of a pilgrim rather than of a deer hunter, Halbert about the close of the evening regained his paternal tower.

CHAPTER XIII.

The miller was of manly make,
  To meet him was na mows ;
There durst na ten come him to take,
  Sae noited he their pows.
          Christ's Kirk on the Green.[1]

IT was after sunset, as we have already stated, when Halbert Glendinning returned to the abode of his father. The hour of dinner was at noon, and that of supper about an hour after sunset at this period of the year. The former had passed without Halbert's appearing; but this was no uncommon circumstance, for the chase, or any other pastime which occurred, made Halbert a frequent neglecter of hours; and his mother, though angry and disappointed when she saw him not at table, was so much accustomed to his occasional absence, and knew so little how to teach him more regularity, that a testy observation was almost all the censure with which such omissions were visited.

On the present occasion, however, the wrath of good Dame Elspeth soared higher than usual. It was not merely on account of the special tup's-head and trotters, the haggis and the side of mutton, with which her table was set forth, but also because of the arrival of no less a person than Hob Miller, as he was universally termed, through the man's name was Happer.

The object of the miller's visit to the Tower of Glendearg was, like the purpose of those embassies which potentates send to each other's courts, partly ostensible, partly politic. In outward show, Hob came to visit his friends of the halidome, and share the festivity common among country folk after the barnyard has been filled, and to renew old intimacies by new conviviality. But in very truth he also came to have an eye upon the contents of each stack, and to obtain such information respecting the extent of the crop reaped and gathered in by each feuar as might prevent the possibility of abstracted multures.

[1] See Motto to Chap. xiii. Note 7.

All the world knows that the cultivators of each barony or regality, temporal or spiritual, in Scotland, are obliged to bring their corn to be grinded at the mill of the territory, for which they pay a heavy charge, called the "intown multures." I could speak to the thirlage of *invecta et illata* too, but let that pass. I have said enough to intimate that I talk not without book. Those of the "sucken," or enthralled ground, were liable in penalties if, deviating from this thirlage (or thraldom), they carried their grain to another mill. Now such another mill, erected on the lands of a lay baron, lay within a tempting and convenient distance of Glendearg; and the miller was so obliging, and his charges so moderate, that it required Hob Miller's utmost vigilance to prevent evasions of his right of monopoly.

The most effectual means he could devise was this show of good fellowship and neighbourly friendship; under colour of which he made his annual cruise through the barony, numbered every cornstack, and computed its contents by the boll, so that he could give a shrewd hint afterwards whether or not the grist came to the right mill.

Dame Elspeth, like her compeers, was obliged to take these domiciliary visits in the sense of politeness; but in her case they had not occurred since her husband's death, probably because the Tower of Glendearg was distant, and there was but a trifling quantity of arable or infield land attached to it. This year there had been, upon some speculation of Old Martin's, several bolls sown in the outfield, which, the season being fine, had ripened remarkably well. Perhaps this circumstance occasioned the honest miller's including Glendearg, on this occasion, in his annual round.

Dame Glendinning received with pleasure a visit which she used formerly only to endure with patience; and she had changed her view of the matter chiefly, if not entirely, because Hob had brought with him his daughter Mysie, of whose features she could give so slight an account, but whose dress she had described so accurately, to the sub-prior.

Hitherto this girl had been an object of very trifling consideration in the eyes of the good widow; but the sub-prior's particular and somewhat mysterious inquiries had set her brains to work on the subject of Mysie of the Mill; and she had here asked a broad question, and there she had thrown out an innuendo, and there again she had gradually led on to a conversation on the subject of poor Mysie. And from all inquiries and investigations, she had collected that Mysie was a dark-eyed, laughter-loving wench, with cherry-cheeks, and a skin as white as her father's finest bolted flour, out of which was made the abbot's own wastel-bread. For her temper, she sung and laughed from morning to night; and for her fortune, a material article, besides that which the miller might have amassed by means of his proverbial golden thumb, Mysie was to inherit a good handsome lump of land, with a prospect of the mill and mill-acres descending to her husband on an easy lease, if a fair word were spoken in season to the abbot, and to the prior, and to the sub-prior, and to the sacristan, and so forth.

By turning and again turning these advantages over in her own mind, Elspeth at length came to be of opinion that the only way to save her son Halbert from a life of "spur, spear, and snaffle," as they called that of the Border riders, from the dint of a cloth-yard shaft, or the loop of an inch-cord, was, that he should marry and settle, and that Mysie Happer should be his destined bride.

As if to her wish, Hob Miller arrived on his strong-built mare, bearing on a pillion behind him the lovely Mysie, with cheeks like a peony-rose (if Dame Glendinning had ever seen one), spirits all afloat with rustic coquetry, and a profusion of hair as black as ebony. The beau-ideal which Dame Glendinning had been bodying forth in her imagination became unexpectedly realised in the buxom form of Mysie Happer, whom, in the course of half an hour, she settled upon as the maiden who was to fix the restless and untutored Halbert. True, Mysie, as the dame soon saw, was likely to love dancing round a May-pole as well as managing a domestic concern, and Halbert was likely to break more heads than he would grind stacks of corn. But then a miller should always be of manly make, and has been described so since the days of

Chaucer and James I. Indeed, to be able to outdo and bully
the whole sucken (once more we use this barbarous phrase) in
all athletic exercises was one way to render easy the collection
of dues which men would have disputed with a less formidable
champion. Then, as to the deficiencies of the miller's wife,
the dame was of opinion that they might be supplied by the
activity of the miller's mother. "I will keep house for the
young folk myself, for the tower is grown very lonely,"
thought Dame Glendinning, "and to live near the kirk will be
mair comfortable in my auld age; and then Edward may agree
with his brother about the feu, more especially as he is a favourite with the sub-prior, and then he may live in the auld
tower like his worthy father before him; and wha kens but
Mary Avenel, high-blooded as she is, may e'en draw in her
stool to the chimney-nook, and sit down here for good and a'?
It's true she has no tocher, but the like of her for beauty and
sense ne'er crossed my een, and I have kenn'd every wench
in the halidome of St. Mary's—ay, and their mothers that
bore them; ay, she is a sweet and a lovely creature as ever
tied snood over brown hair; ay, and then, though her uncle
keeps her out of her ain for the present time, yet it is to be
thought the grey-goose shaft will find a hole in his coat of
proof, as God help us! it has done in any a better man's.
And, moreover, if they should stand on their pedigree and
gentle race, Edward might say to them, that is, to her gentle
kith and kin, 'Whilk o' ye was her best friend when she came
down the glen to Glendearg in a misty evening, on a beast
mair like a cuddie than aught else?' And if they tax him
with churl's blood, Edward might say that, forbye the old
proverb, how

> Gentle deed
> Makes gentle bleid;

yet, moreover, there comes no churl's blood from Glendinning
or Brydone; for, says Edward——"

The hoarse voice of the miller at this moment recalled the
dame from her reverie, and compelled her to remember that,
if she meant to realise her airy castle, she must begin by laying
the foundation in civility to her guest and his daughter, whom

she was at that moment most strangely neglecting, though her whole plan turned on conciliating their favour and good opinion, and that, in fact, while arranging matters for so intimate a union with her company, she was suffering them to sit unnoticed, and in their riding-gear, as if about to resume their journey. "And so I say, dame," concluded the miller, for she had not marked the beginning of his speech, "an ye be so busied with your housewifeskep, or aught else, why Mysie and I will trot our way down the glen again to Johnnie Broxmouth's, who pressed us right kindly to bide with him."

Starting at once from her dream of marriages and intermarriages, mills, mill-lands, and baronies, Dame Elspeth felt for a moment like the milkmaid in the fable, when she overset the pitcher on the contents of which so many golden dreams were founded. But the foundation of Dame Glendinning's hopes was only tottering, not overthrown, and she hastened to restore its equilibrium. Instead of attempting to account for her absence of mind and want of attention to her guests, which she might have found something difficult, she assumed the offensive, like an able general when he finds it necessary, by a bold attack, to disguise his weakness.

A loud exclamation she made, and a passionate complaint she set up against the unkindness of her old friend, "who could for an instant doubt the heartiness of her welcome to him and to his hopeful daughter; and then to think of his going back to John Broxmouth's, when the auld tower stood where it did, and had room in it for a friend or two in the worst of times; and he too a neighbour that his umquhile gossip Simon, blessed be his cast! used to think the best friend he had in the halidome." And on she went, urging her complaint with so much seriousness that she had wellnigh imposed on herself as well as upon Hob Miller, who had no mind to take anything in dudgeon, and, as it suited his plans to pass the night at Glendearg, would have been equally contented to do so even had his reception been less vehemently hospitable.

To all Elspeth's expostulations on the unkindness of his proposal to leave her dwelling he answered composedly: "Nay, dame, what could I tell? ye might have had other grist to grind, for ye looked as if ye scarce saw us; or what know I? ye might bear in mind the words Martin and I had about the last barley ye sawed, for I ken dry multures will sometimes stick in the throat. A man seeks but his awn, and yet folk shall hold him for both miller and miller's man, that is, miller and knave, [1] all the country over."

"Alas, that you will say so, neighbour Hob," said Dame Elspeth, "or that Martin should have had any words with you about the mill-dues! I will chide him roundly for it, I promise you, on the faith of a true widow. You know full well that a lone woman is sore put upon by her servants."

"Nay, dame," said the miller, unbuckling the broad belt which made fast his cloak, and served, at the same time, to suspend by his side a swinging Andrew Ferrara, "bear no grudge at Martin, for I bear none. I take it on me as a thing of mine office to maintain my right of multure, lock, and goupen. [2] And reason good, for, as the old song says,

> I live by my mill, God bless her,
> She's parent, child, and wife.

The poor old slut, I am beholden to her for my living, and bound to stand by her, as I say to my mill-knaves, in right and in wrong. And so should every honest fellow stand by his bread-winner. And so, Mysie, ye may doff your cloak since our neighbour is so kindly glad to see us; why, I think, we are as blythe to see her: not one in the halidome pays their multures more duly, sequels, arriage and carriage, and mill-service, used and wont."

With that the miller hung his ample cloak without further ceremony upon a huge pair of stag's antlers, which adorned at once the naked walls of the tower and served for what we vulgarly call cloak-pins.

In the mean time, Dame Elspeth assisted to disembarrass the damsel whom she destined for her future daughter-in-law of her hood, mantle, and the rest of her riding-gear, giving her to appear as beseemed the buxom daughter of the wealthy

[1] See Note 8.   [2] See The Sequels. Note 9.

miller, gay and goodly, in a white kirtle, the seams of which were embroidered with green silken lace or fringe, entwined with some silver thread. An anxious glance did Elspeth cast upon the good-humoured face, which was now more fully shown to her, and was only obscured by a quantity of raven-black hair, which the maid of the mill had restrained by a snood of green silk, embroidered with silver, corresponding to the trimmings of her kirtle. The countenance itself was exceedingly comely—the eyes black, large, and roguishly good-humoured, the mouth was small, the lips well formed, though somewhat full, the teeth were pearly white, and the chin had a very seducing dimple in it. The form belonging to this joyous face was full and round, and firm and fair. It might become coarse and masculine some years hence, which is the common fault of Scottish beauty; but in Mysie's six-teenth year she had the shape of an Hebe. The anxious Els-peth, with all her maternal partiality, could not help admit-ting within herself that a better man than Halbert might go farther and fare worse. She looked a little giddy, and Hal-bert was not nineteen; still it was time he should be settled—for to that point the dame always returned—and here was an excellent opportunity.

The simple cunning of Dame Elspeth now exhausted itself in commendations of her fair guest, from the snood, as they say, to the single-soled shoe. Mysie listened and blushed with pleasure for the first five minutes; but ere ten had elapsed she began to view the old lady's compliments rather as subjects of mirth than of vanity, and was much more dis-posed to laugh at than to be flattered with them, for nature had mingled the good-humour with which she had endowed the damsel with no small portion of shrewdness. Even Hob himself began to tire of hearing his daughter's praises, and broke in with: "Ay, ay, she is a clever quean enough; and, were she five years older, she shall lay a loaded sack on an aver with e'er a lass in the halidome. But I have been look-ing for your two sons, dame. Men say down-bye that Hal-bert's turned a wild springald, and that we may have word of him from Westmoreland one moonlight night or another."

12

"God forbid, my good neighbour—God, in His mercy, forbid!" said Dame Glendinning, earnestly; for it was touching the very key-note of her apprehensions to hint any probability that Halbert might become one of the marauders so common in the age and country. But, fearful of having betrayed too much alarm on the subject, she immediately added, "That though, since the last rout at Pinkie Cleuch, she had been all of a tremble when a gun or a spear was named, or when men spoke of fighting, yet, thanks to God and Our Lady, her sons were like to live and die honest and peaceful tenants to the abbey, as their father might have done, but for that awful hosting which he went forth to, with mony a brave man that never returned."

"Ye need not tell me of it, dame," said the miller, "since I was there myself, and made two pair of legs—and these were not mine, but my mare's—worth one pair of hands. I judged how it would be, when I saw our host break ranks, with rushing on through that broken ploughed field, and so, as they had made a pricker of me, I e'en pricked off with myself while the play was good."

"Ay, ay, neighbour," said the dame, "ye were aye a wise and a wary man. If my Simon had had your wit, he might have been here to speak about it this day; but he was aye cracking of his good blood and his high kindred, and less would not serve him than to bide the bang to the last, with the earls, and knights, and squires, that had no wives to greet for them, or else had wives that cared not how soon they were widows; but that is not for the like of us. But touching my son Halbert, there is no fear of him; for if it should be his misfortune to be in the like case, he has the best pair of heels in the halidome, and could run almost as fast as your mare herself."

"Is this he, neighbour?" quoth the miller.

"No," replied the mother; "that is my youngest son, Edward, who can read and write like the lord abbot himself, if it were not a sin to say so."

"Ay," said the miller; "and is that the young clerk the sub-prior thinks so much of? They say he will come far ben, that lad; wha kens but he may come to be sub-prior himself? As broken a ship has come to land."

"To be a prior, neighbour miller," said Edward, "a man must first be a priest, and for that I judge I have little vocation."

"He will take to the pleugh-pettle, neighbour," said the good dame; "and so will Halbert too, I trust. I wish you saw Halbert. Edward, where is your brother?"

"Hunting, I think," replied Edward; "at least he left us this morning to join the Laird of Colmslie and his hounds. I have heard them baying in the glen all day."

"And if I had heard that music," said the miller, "it would have done my heart good, ay, and maybe taken me two or three miles out of my road. When I was the miller of Morebattle's knave, I have followed the hounds from Eckford to the foot of Hounam Law—followed them on foot, Dame Glendinning, ay, and led the chase when the Laird of Cessford and his gay riders were all thrown out by the mosses and gills. I brought the stag on my back to Hounam Cross, when the dogs had pulled him down. I think I see the old grey knight, as he sate so upright on his strong war-horse, all white with foam; and 'Miller,' said he to me, 'an thou wilt turn thy back on the mill, and wend with me, I will make a man of thee.' But I chose rather to abide by clap and happer, and the better luck was mine; for the proud Percy caused hang five of the laird's henchmen at Alnwick for burning a rickle of houses some gate beyond Fowberry, and it might have been my luck as well as another man's."

"Ah, neighbour, neighbour," said Dame Glendinning, "you were aye wise and wary; but if you like hunting, I must say Halbert's the lad to please you. He hath all those fair holiday terms of hawk and hound as ready in his mouth as Tom with the tod's-tail, that is, the lord abbot's ranger."

"Ranges he not homeward at dinner-time, dame," demanded the miller; "for we call noon the dinner-hour at Kennaquhair?"

The widow was forced to admit that, even at this important period of the day, Halbert was frequently absent; at which the miller shook his head, intimating, at the same time, some allusion to the proverb of MacFarlane's geese,[2] which "liked their play better than their meat."

That the delay of dinner might not increase the miller's disposition to prejudge Halbert, Dame Glendinning called hastily on Mary Avenel to take the task of entertaining Mysie Happer, while she herself rushed to the kitchen, and, entering at once into the province of Tibb Tacket, rummaged among trenchers and dishes, snatched pots from the fire, and placed pans and gridirons on it, accompanying her own feats of personal activity with such a continued list of injunctions to Tibb that Tibb at length lost patience, and said, "Here was as muckle wark about meating an auld miller as if they had been to banquet the blood of Bruce." But this, as it was supposed to be spoken aside, Dame Glendinning did not think it convenient to hear.

CHAPTER XIV.

> Nay, let me have the friends who eat my victuals
> As various as my dishes. The feast's naught
> Where one huge plate prodominates. John Plaintext,
> He shall be mighty beef, our English staple;
> The worthy alderman, a butter'd dumpling;
> Yon pair of whisker'd cornets, ruffs and rees;
> Their friend the dandy, a green goose in sippets.
> And so the board is spread at once and fill'd
> On the same principle—variety.
>
> *New Play.*

"AND what brave lass is this?" said Hob Miller, as Mary Avenel entered the apartment to supply the absence of Dame Elspeth Glendinning.

"The young Lady of Avenel, father," said the Maid of the Mill, dropping as low a courtesy as her rustic manners enabled her to make. The miller, her father, doffed his bonnet and made his reverence, not altogether so low perhaps as if the young lady had appeared in the pride of rank and riches, yet so as to give high birth the due homage which the Scotch for a length of time scrupulously rendered to it.

[1] See Note 10.

Indeed, from having had her mother's example before her for so many years, and from a native sense of propriety and even of dignity, Mary Avenel had acquired a demeanour which marked her title to consideration, and effectually checked any attempt at familiarity on the part of those who might be her associates in her present situation, but could not be well termed her equals. She was by nature mild, pensive, and contemplative, gentle in disposition, and most placable when accidentally offended; but still she was of a retired and reserved habit, and shunned to mix in ordinary sports, even when the rare occurrence of a fair or wake gave her an opportunity of mingling with companions of her own age. If at such scenes she was seen for an instant, she appeared to behold them with the composed indifference of one to whom their gaiety was a matter of no interest, and who seemed only desirous to glide away from the scene as soon as she possibly could. Something also had transpired concerning her being born on All-Hallow Eve, and the powers with which that circumstances was supposed to invest her over the invisible world. And from all these particulars combined, the young men and women of the halidome used to distinguish Mary among themselves by the name of the Spirit of Avenel, as if the fair but fragile form, the beautiful but rather colourless cheek, the dark blue eye, and the shady hair, had belonged rather to the immaterial than the substantial world. The general tradition of the White Lady, who was supposed to wait on the fortunes of the family of Avenel, gave a sort of zest to this piece of rural wit. It gave great offence, however, to the two sons of Simon Glendinning; and when the expression was in their presence applied to the young lady, Edward was wont to check the petulance of those who used it by strength of argument, and Halbert by strength of arm. In such cases Halbert had this advantage, that, although he could render no aid to his brother's argument, yet, when circumstances required it, he was sure to have that of Edward, who never indeed himself commenced a fray, but, on the other hand, did not testify any reluctance to enter into combat in Halbert's behalf, or in his rescue.

But the zealous attachment of the two youths, being themselves, from the retired situation in which they dwelt, comparative strangers in the halidome, did not serve in any degree to alter the feelings of the inhabitants towards the young lady, who seemed to have dropped amongst them from another sphere of life. Still, however, she was regarded with respect, if not with fondness: and the attention of the sub-prior to the family, not to mention the formidable name of Julian Avenel, which every new incident of those tumultuous times tended to render more famous, attached to his niece a certain importance. Thus some aspired to her acquaintance out of pride, while the more timid of the feuars were anxious to inculcate upon their children the necessity of being respectful to the noble orphan. So that Mary Avenel, little loved because little known, was regarded with a mysterous awe, partly derived from fear of her uncle's moss-troopers, and partly from her own retired and distant habits, enhanced by the superstitious opinions of the time and country.

It was not without some portion of this awe that Mysie felt herself left alone in company with a young person so distant in rank, and so different in bearing, from herself; for her worthy father had taken the first opportunity to step out unobserved, in order to mark how the barn-yard was filled, and what prospect it afforded of grist to the mill. In youth, however, there is a sort of freemasonry, which, without much conversation, teaches young persons to estimate each other's character, and places them at ease on the shortest acquaintance. It is only when taught deceit by the commerce of the world that we learn to shroud our character from observation, and to disguise our real sentiments from those with whom we are placed in communion.

Accordingly, the two young women were soon engaged in such objects of interest as best became their age. They visited Mary Avenel's pigeons, which she nursed with the tenderness of a mother; they turned over her slender stores of finery, which yet contained some articles that excited the respect of her companion, though Mysie was too good-humoured to nourish envy. A golden rosary, and some female ornaments marking superior rank, had been rescued in the moment of their utmost adversity, more by Tibb Tacket's presence of mind than by the care of their owner, who was at that sad period too much sunk in grief to pay any attention to such circumstances. They struck Mysie with a deep impression of veneration; for, excepting what the lord abbot and the convent might possess, she did not believe there was so much real gold in the world as was exhibited in these few trinkets, and Mary, however sage and serious, was not above being pleased with the admiration of her rustic companion.

Nothing, indeed, could exhibit a stronger contrast than the appearance of the two girls—the good-humoured, laughter-loving countenance of the Maid of the Mill, who stood gazing with unrepressed astonishment on whatever was in her unexperienced eye rare and costly, and with a humble, and at the same time cheerful, acquiescence in her inferiority, asking all the little queries about the use and value of the ornaments, while Mary Avenel, with her quiet, composed dignity and placidity of manner, produced them one after another for the amusement of her companion.

As they became gradually more familiar, Mysie of the Mill was just venturing to ask why Mary Avenel never appeared at the May-pole, and to express her wonder when the young lady said she disliked dancing, when a trampling of horses at the gate of the tower interrupted their conversation.

Mysie flew to the shot-window in the full ardour of unrestrained female curiosity. "St. Mary! sweet lady, here come two well-mounted gallants; will you step this way to look at them?"

"No," said Mary Avenel, "you shall tell me who they are."

"Well, if you like it better," said Mysie; "but how shall I know them? Stay, I do know one of them, and so do you, lady; he is a blythe man, somewhat light of hand they say, but the gallants of these days think no great harm of that. He is your uncle's henchman, that they call Christie of the Clinthill; and he has not his old green jerkin and the rusty black-jack over it, but a scarlet cloak, laid down with silver lace three inches broad, and a breastplate you might see to dress your hair in, as well as in that keeking-glass in the ivory frame that you showed me even now. Come, dear lady —come to the shot-window and see him."

"If it be the man you mean, Mysie," replied the orphan of Avenel, "I shall see him soon enough, considering either the pleasure or comfort the sight will give me."

"Nay, but if you will not come to see gay Christie," replied the Maid of the Mill, her face flushed with eager curiosity, ' come and tell me who the gallant is that is with him, the handsomest, the very lovesomest young man I ever saw with sight."

"It is my foster-brother, Halbert Glendinning," said Mary, with apparent indifference; for she had been accustomed to call the sons of Elspeth her foster-brethren, and to live with them as if they had been her brothers in earnest.

"Nay, by Our Lady, that it is not," said Mysie; "I know the favour of both the Glendinnings well, and I think this rider be not of our country. He has a crimson velvet bonnet, and long brown hair falling down under it, and a beard on his upper lip, and his chin clean and close shaved, save a small patch on the point of it, and a sky-blue jerkin, slashed and lined with white satin, and trunk-hose to suit, and no weapon but a rapier and dagger. Well, if I was a man, I would never wear weapon but the rapier! it is so slender and becoming, instead of having a cart-load of iron at my back, like my father's broadsword, with its great rusty basket-hilt. Do you not delight in the rapier and poniard, lady?"

"The best sword," answered Mary, "if I must needs answer a question of the sort, is that which is drawn in the best cause, and which is best used when it is out of the scabbard."

"But can you not guess who this stranger should be?" said Mysie.

"Indeed, I cannot even attempt it; but, to judge by his companion, it is no matter how little he is known," replied Mary.

"My benison on his bonny face," said Mysie, "if he is not going to alight here! Now, I am as much pleased as if my father had given me the silver ear-rings he has promised me so often; nay, you had as well come to the window, for you must see him by and by, whether you will or not."

I do not know how much sooner Mary Avenel might have sought the point of observation, if she had not been scared from it by the unrestrained curiosity expressed by her buxom friend; but at length the same feeling prevailed over her sense of dignity, and satisfied with having displayed all the indifference that was necessary in point of decorum, she no longer thought herself bound to restrain her curiosity.

From the out-shot or projecting window she could perceive that Christie of the Clinthill was attended on the present occasion by a very gay and gallant cavalier, who, from the nobleness of his countenance and manner, his rich and handsome dress, and the showy appearance of his horse and furniture, must, she agreed with her new friend, be a person of some consequence.

Christie also seemed conscious of something, which made him call out with more than his usual insolence of manner: "What, ho! so ho! the house! Churl peasants, will no one answer when I call? Ho! Martin—Tibb—Dame Glendinning!—a murrain on you, must we stand keeping our horses in the cold here, and they steaming with heat, when we have ridden so sharply?"

At length he was obeyed, and Old Martin made his appearance. "'Ha!'" said Christie, "'art thou there, old true-penny?' Here, stable me these steeds, and see them well bedded, and stretch thine old limbs by rubbing them down; and see thou quit not the stable till there is not a turned hair on either of them."

Martin took the horses to the stable as commanded, but suppressed not his indignation a moment after he could vent it with safety. "Would not any one think," he said to Jasper, an old ploughman, who, in coming to his assistance, had heard Christie's imperious injunctions, "that this loon, this Christie of the Clinthill, was laird or lord at least of him? No such thing, man! I remember him a little dirty turnspit boy in the house of Avenel, that everybody in a frosty morning like this warmed his fingers by kicking or cuffing! and now he is a gentleman, and swears, 'd—n him' and 'renounce him,' as if the gentlemen could not so much as keep their own wickedness to themselves, without the like of him going to hell in their very company, and by the same road. I have as much a mind as ever I had to my dinner to go back and tell him to sort his horse himself, since he is as able as I am."

"Hout tout, man!" answered Jasper, "keep a calm sough; better to fleech a fool than fight with him."

Martin acknowledged the truth of the proverb, and, much comforted therewith, betook himself to cleaning the stranger's horse with great assiduity, remarking, it was a pleasure to handle a handsome nag, and turned over the other to the charge of Jasper. Nor was it until Christie's commands were literally complied with, that he deemed it proper, after fitting ablutions, to join the party in the spence; not for the purpose of waiting upon them, as a mere modern reader might possibly expect, but that he might have his share of dinner in their company.

In the mean while, Christie had presented his companion to Dame Glendinning as Sir Piercie Shafton, a friend of his and of his master, come to spend three or four days with little din in the tower. The good dame could not conceive how she was entitled to such an honour, and would fain have pleaded her want of every sort of convenience to entertain a guest of that quality. But, indeed, the visitor, when he cast his eyes round the bare walls, eyed the huge black chimney, scrutinised the meagre and broken furniture of the apartment, and beheld the embarrassment of the mistress of the family, intimated great reluctance to intrude upon Dame Glendinning a visit which could scarce, from all appearances, prove otherwise than an inconvenience to her and a penance to himself.

But the reluctant hostess and her guest had to do with an inexorable man, who silenced all expostulation with, "Such was his master's pleasure. And, moreover," he continued, "though the Baron of Avenel's will must and ought to prove law to all within ten miles around him, yet here, dame," he said, "is a letter from your petticoated baron, the lord-priest yonder, who enjoins you, as you regard his pleasure, that you afford to this good knight such decent accommodation as is in your power, suffering him to live as privately as he shall desire. And for you, Sir Piercie Shafton," continued Christie, "you will judge for yourself whether secrecy and safety is not more your object even now than soft beds and high cheer. And do not judge of the dame's goods by the semblance of her cottage; for you will see by the dinner she is about to spread for us that the vassal of the kirk is seldom found with her basket bare." To Mary Avenel Christie presented the stranger, after the best fashion he could, as to the niece of his master the baron.

While he thus laboured to reconcile Sir Piercie Shafton to his fate, the widow, having consulted her son Edward on the real import of the lord abbot's injunction, and having found that Christie had given a true exposition, saw nothing else left for her but to make that fate as easy as she could to the stranger. He himself also seemed reconciled to his lot, by some feeling probably of strong necessity, and accepted with a good grace the hospitality which the dame offered with a very indifferent one.

In fact, the dinner, which soon smoked before the assembled guests, was of that substantial kind which warrants plenty and comfort. Dame Glendinning had cooked it after her best manner; and, delighted with the handsome appearance which her good cheer made when placed on the table, forgot both her plans and the vexations which interrupted them, in the hospitable duty of pressing her assembled visitors to eat and drink, watching every trencher as it waxed empty, and loading it with fresh supplies ere the guest could utter a negative.

In the mean while, the company attentively regarded each other's motions, and seemed endeavouring to form a judgment of each other's character. Sir Piercie Shafton condescended to speak to no one but to Mary Avenel, and on her he conferred exactly the same familiar and compassionate, though somewhat scornful, sort of attention which a pretty fellow of these days will sometimes condescend to bestow on a country miss when there is no prettier or more fashionable woman present. The manner, indeed, was different, for the etiquette of those times did not permit Sir Piercie Shafton to pick his teeth, or to yawn, or to gabble like the beggar whose tongue (as he says) was cut out by the Turks, or to affect deafness or blindness, or any other infirmity of the organs. But though the embroidery of his conversation was different, the groundwork was the same, and the high-flown and ornate compliments with which the gallant knight of the sixteenth century interlarded his conversation were as much the offspring of egotism and self-conceit as the jargon of the coxcombs of our own days.

The English knight was, however, something daunted at finding that Mary Avenel listened with an air of indifference, and answered with wonderful brevity, to all the fine things which ought, as he conceived, to have dazzled her with their brilliancy, and puzzled her by their obscurity. But if he was disappointed in making the desired, or rather the expected, impression upon her whom he addressed, Sir Piercie Shafton's discourse was marvellous in the ears of Mysie, the miller's daughter, and not the less so that she did not comprehend the meaning of a single word which he uttered. Indeed, the gallant knight's language was far too courtly to be understood by persons of much greater acuteness than Mysie's.

It was about this period that the "only rare poet of his time, the witty, comical, facetiously quick, and quickly facetious John Lyly—he that sate at Apollo's table, and to whom Phœbus gave a wreath of his own bays without snatching"[1] —he, in short, who wrote that singularly coxcomical work, called *Euphues and his England*, was in the very zenith of his absurdity and reputation. The quaint, forced, and unnatural style which he introduced by his *Anatomy of Wit* had a fashion as rapid as it was momentary: all the court ladies were his scholars, and to *parler Euphuisme* was as necessary a qualification to a courtly gallant as those of understanding how to use his rapier or to dance a measure.

It was no wonder that the Maid of the Mill was soon as

[1] See John Lyly. Note 11.

effectually blinded by the intricacies of this erudite and court-ly style of conversation as she had ever been by the dust of her father's own meal-sacks. But there she sate with her mouth and eyes as open as the mill-door and the two win-dows, showing teeth as white as her father's bolted flour, and endeavouring to secure a word or two for her own future use out of the pearls of rhetoric which Sir Piercie Shafton scat-tered around him with such bounteous profusion.

For the male part of the company, Edward felt ashamed of his own manner and slowness of speech, when he observed the handsome young courtier, with an ease and volubility of which he had no conception, run over all the commonplace topics of high-flown gallantry. It is true, the good sense and natural taste of young Glendinning soon informed him that the gallant cavalier was speaking nonsense. But, alas! where is the man of modest merit and real talent who has not suf-fered from being outshone in conversation, and outstripped in the race of life, by men of less reserve, and of qualities more showy, though less substantial? And well constituted must the mind be that can yield up the prize without envy to competitors more worthy than himself.

Edward Glendinning had no such philosophy. While he despised the jargon of the gay cavalier, he envied the facility with which he could run on, as well as the courtly grace of his tone and expression, and the perfect ease and elegance with which he offered all the little acts of politeness to which the duties of the table gave opportunity. And if I am to speak truth, I must own that he envied those qualities the more as they were all exercised in Mary Avenel's service, and although only so far accepted as they could not be refused, intimated a wish on the stranger's part to place himself in her good graces, as the only person in the room to whom he thought it worth while to recommend himself. His title, rank, and very hand-some figure, together with some sparks of wit and spirit which flashed across the cloud of nonsense which he uttered, ren-dered him, as the words of the old song say, "a lad for a lady's viewing"; so that poor Edward, with all his real worth and acquired knowledge, in his homespun doublet, blue cap, and deerskin trowsers, looked like a clown beside the courtier, and, feeling the full inferiority, nourished no good-will to him by whom he was eclipsed.

Christie, on the other hand, so soon as he had satisfied to the full a commodious appetite, by means of which persons of his profession could, like the wolf and eagle, gorge themselves with as much food at one meal as might serve them for several days, began also to feel himself more in the background than he liked to be. This worthy had, amongst his other good qualities, an excellent opinion of himself; and, being of a bold and forward disposition, had no mind to be thrown into the shade by any one. With that impudent familiarity which such persons mistake for graceful ease, he broke in upon the knight's finest speeches with as little remorse as he would have driven the point of his lance through a laced doublet.

Sir Piercie Shafton, a man of rank and high birth, by no means encouraged or endured this familiarity, and requited the intruder either with total neglect or such laconic replies as intimated a sovereign contempt for the rude spearman who affected to converse with him upon terms of equality.

The miller held his peace; for, as his usual conversation turned chiefly on his clapper and toll-dish, he had no mind to brag of his wealth in presence of Christie of the Clinthill, or to intrude his discourse on the English cavalier.

A little specimen of the conversation may not be out of place, were it but to show young ladies what fine things they have lost by living when Euphuism is out of fashion.

"Credit me, fairest lady," said the knight, "that such is the cunning of our English courtiers of the hodiernal strain, that, as they have infinitely refined upon the plain and rusticial discourse of our fathers, which, as I may say, more beseemed the mouths of country roisterers in a May-game than that of courtly gallants in a galliard, so I hold it ineffably and unutterably impossible that those who may succeed us in that garden of wit and courtesy shall alter or amend it. Venus delighteth but in the language of Mercury, Bucephalus will stoop to no one but Alexander, none can sound Apollo's pipe but Orpheus."

"Valiant sir," said Mary, who could scarce help laughing, "we have but to rejoice in the chance which hath honoured this solitude with a glimpse of the sun of courtesy, though it rather blinds than enlightens us."

"Pretty and quaint, fairest lady," answered the Euphuist. "Ah, that I had with me my *Anatomy of Wit*—that all-to-be-unparalleled volume—that quintessence of human wit—that treasury of quaint invention—that exquisitely-pleasant-to-read, and inevitably-necessary-to-be-remembered manual of all that is worthy to be known—which indoctrines the rude in civility, the dull in intellectuality, the heavy in jocosity, the blunt in gentility, the vulgar in nobility, and all of them in that unutterable perfection of human utterance, that eloquence which no other eloquence is sufficient to praise, that art which, when we call it by its own name of Euphuism, we bestow on it its richest panegyric."

"By St. Mary," said Christie of the Clinthill, "if your worship had told me that you had left such stores of wealth as you talk of at Prudhoe Castle, Long Dickie and I would have had them off with us if man and horse could have carried them; but you told us of no treasure I wot of, save the silver tongs for turning up your mustachios."

The knight treated this intruder's mistake—for certainly Christie had no idea that all these epithets, which sounded so rich and splendid, were lavished upon a small quarto volume—with a stare, and then turning again to Mary Avenel, the only person whom he thought worthy to address, he proceeded in his strain of high-flown oratory. "Even thus," said he, "do hogs contemn the splendour of Oriental pearls; even thus are the delicacies of a choice repast in vain offered to the long-eared grazer of the common, who turneth from them to devour a thistle. Surely as idle is it to pour forth the treasures of oratory before the eyes of the ignorant, and to spread the dainties of the intellectual banquet before those who are, morally and metaphysically speaking, no better than asses."

"Sir knight, since that is your quality," said Edward, "we cannot strive with you in loftiness of language; but I pray you in fair courtesy, while you honour my father's house with your presence, to spare us such vile comparisons."

"Peace, good villagio," said the knight, gracefully waving his hand—"I prithee peace, kind rustic; and you, my guide, whom I may scarce call honest, let me prevail upon you to imitate the laudable taciturnity of that honest yeoman, who sits as mute as a mill-post, and of that comely damsel, who seems as with her ears she drank in what she did not altogether comprehend, even as a palfrey listeneth to a lute, whereof, howsoever, he knoweth not the gamut."

"Marvellous fine words," at length said Dame Glendinning, who began to be tired of sitting so long silent—"marvellous fine words, neighbour Happer, are they not?"

"Brave words—very brave words—very exceeding pyet words," answered the miller; "nevertheless, to speak my mind, a lippy of bran were worth a bushel o' them."

"I think so too, under his worship's favour," answered Christie of the Clinthill. "I well remember that at the race of Morham, as we called it, near Berwick, I took a young Southern fellow out of saddle with my lance, and cast him, it might be, a gad's length from his nag; and so, as he had some gold on his laced doublet, I deemed he might ha' the like on it in his pocket too, though that is a rule that does not aye hold good. So I was speaking to him of ransom, and out he comes with a handful of such terms as his honour there hath gleaned up, and craved me for mercy, as I was a true son of Mars, and such-like."

"And obtained no mercy at thy hand, I dare be sworn," said the knight, who deigned not to speak Euphuism excepting to the fair sex.

"By my troggs," replied Christie, "I would have thrust my lance down his throat, but just then they flung open that accursed postern gate, and forth pricked old Hunsdon, and Henry Carey, and as many fellows at their heels as turned the chase northward again. So I e'en pricked Bayard with the spur, and went off with the rest; for a man should ride when he may not wrestle, as they say in Tynedale."

"Trust me," said the knight, again turning to Mary Avenel, "if I do not pity you, lady, who, being of noble blood, are thus in a manner compelled to abide in the cottage of the ignorant, like the precious stone in the head of a toad, or like a precious garland on the brow of an ass. But soft, what gallant have we here, whose garb savoureth more of the rustic than doth his demeanour, and whose looks seem more lofty than his habit, even as——?"

"I pray you, sir knight," said Mary, "to spare your courtly similitudes for refined ears, and give me leave to name unto you my foster-brother, Halbert Glendinning."

"The son of the good dame of the cottage, as I opine," answered the English knight; "for by some such name did my guide discriminate the mistress of this mansion, which you, madam, enrich with your presence. And yet, touching this juvenal, he hath that about him which belongeth to higher birth, for all are not black who dig coals——"

"Nor all white who are millers," said honest Happer, glad to get in a word, as they say, edgeways.

Halbert, who had sustained the glance of the Englishman with some impatience, and knew not what to make of his manner and language, replied with some asperity: "Sir knight, we have in this land of Scotland an ancient saying, 'Scorn not the bush that bields you': you are a guest in my father's house to shelter you from danger, if I am rightly informed by the domestics. Scoff not its homeliness or that of its inmates; ye might long have bidden at the court of England ere we had sought your favour or cumbered you with our society. Since your fate has sent you hither amongst us, be contented with such fare and such converse as we can afford you, and scorn us not for our kindness; for the Scots wear short patience and long daggers."

All eyes were turned on Halbert while he was thus speaking, and there was a general feeling that his countenance had an expression of intelligence, and his person an air of dignity, which they had never before observed. Whether it were that the wonderful being with whom he had so lately held communication had bestowed on him a grace and dignity of look and bearing which he had not before, or whether the being con-

13

versant in high matters, and called to a destiny beyond that
of other men, had a natural effect in giving becoming confidence to his language and manner, we pretend not to determine. But it was evident to all that, from this day, young
Halbert was an altered man; that he acted with the steadiness, promptitude, and determination which belonged to riper
years, and bore himself with a manner which appertained to
higher rank.

The knight took the rebuke with good-humour. "By
mine honour," he said, "thou hast reason on thy side, good
juvenal; nevertheless, I spoke not as in ridicule of the roof
which relieves me, but rather in your own praise, to whom, if
this roof be native, thou mayest nevertheless rise from its
lowliness; even as the lark, which maketh its humble nest
in the furrow, ascendeth towards the sun, as well as the eagle
which buildeth her eyrie in the cliff."

This high-flown discourse was interrupted by Dame Glendinning, who, with all the busy anxiety of a mother, was
loading her son's trencher with food, and dinning in his ear
her reproaches on account of his prolonged absence. "And
see," she said, "that you do not one day get such a sight,
while you are walking about among the haunts of them that
are not of our flesh and bone, as befell Mungo Murray when
he slept on the greensward ring of the Auld Kirkhill at sunset, and wakened at daybreak in the wild hills of Breadal-
bane. And see that, when you are looking for deer, the red
stag does not gaul you as he did Diccon Thorburn, who never
overcast the wound that he took from a buck's horn. And
see, when you go swaggering about with a long broadsword
by your side, whilk it becomes no peaceful man to do, that
you dinna meet with them that have broadsword and lance
both: there are enow of rank riders in this land, that neither
fear God nor regard man."

Here her eye, "in a fine frenzy rolling," fell full upon that
of Christie of the Clinthill, and at once her fears for having given offence interrupted the current of maternal rebuke,
which, like rebuke matrimonial, may be often better meant
than timed. There was something of sly and watchful sig-

nificance in Christie's eye—an eye grey, keen, fierce, yet wily, formed to express at once cunning and malice—which made the dame instantly conjecture she had said too much, while she saw in imagination her twelve goodly cows go lowing down the glen in a moonlight night, with half a score of Border spearmen at their heels.

Her voice, therefore, sunk from the elevated tone of maternal authority into a whimpering, apologetic sort of strain, and she proceeded to say: "It is no that I have ony ill thoughts of the Border riders, for Tibb Tacket there has often heard me say that I thought spear and bridle as natural to a Border man as a pen to a priest, or a feather-fan to a lady; and—have you not heard me say it, Tibb?"

Tibb showed something less than her expected alacrity in attesting her mistress's deep respect for the freebooters of the southland hills; but, thus conjured, did at length reply: "Hout ay, mistress, I'se warrant I have heard you say something like that."

"Mother!" said Halbert, in a firm and commanding tone of voice, "what or whom is it that you fear under my father's roof? I well hope that it harbours not a guest in whose presence you are afraid to say your pleasure to me or my brother? I am sorry I have been detained so late, being ignorant of the fair company which I should encounter on my return. I pray you, let this excuse suffice; and what satisfies you will, I trust, be nothing less than acceptable to your guests."

An answer calculated so justly betwixt the submission due to his parent, and the natural feeling of dignity in one who was by birth master of the mansion, excited universal satisfaction. And as Elspeth herself confessed to Tibb on the same evening: "She did not think it had been in the callant. Till that night, he took pets and passions if he was spoke to, and lap through the house like a four-year-auld at the least word of advice that was minted at him, but now he spoke as grave and as douce as the lord abbot himself. She kendna," she said, "what might be the upshot of it, but it was like he was a wonderfu' callant even now."

The party then separated, the young men retiring to their

apartments, the elder to their household cares. While Christie went to see his horse properly accommodated, Edward betook himself to his book, and Halbert, who was as ingenious
in employing his hands as he had hitherto appeared imperfect
in mental exertion, applied himself to constructing a place of
concealment in the floor of his apartment by raising a plank,
beneath which he resolved to deposit that copy of the Holy
Scriptures which had been so strangely regained from the possession of men and spirits.

In the mean while, Sir Piercie Shafton sate still as a stone,
in the chair in which he had deposited himself, his hands
folded on his breast, his legs stretched straight out before him
and resting upon the heels, his eyes cast up to the ceiling as
if he had meant to count every mesh of every cobweb with
which the arched roof was canopied, wearing at the same time
a face of as solemn and imperturbable gravity as if his existence had depended on the accuracy of his calculation.

He could scarce be roused from his listless state of contemplative absorption so as to take some supper, a meal at which
the younger females appeared not. Sir Piercie stared around
twice or thrice as if he missed something; but he asked not
for them, and only evinced his sense of a proper audience
being wanting by his abstraction and absence of mind, seldom
speaking until he was twice addressed, and then replying,
without trope or figure, in that plain English which nobody
could speak better when he had a mind.

Christie, finding himself in undisturbed possession of the
conversation, indulged all who chose to listen with details of
his own wild and inglorious warfare, while Dame Elspeth's
curch bristled with horror, and Tibb Tacket, rejoiced to find
herself once more in the company of a jack-man, listened to
his tales, like Desdemona to Othello's, with undisguised delight. Meantime, the two young Glendinnings were each
wrapped up in his own reflections, and only interrupted in
them by the signal to move bedward.

CHAPTER XV.

He strikes no coin 'tis true, but coins new phrases,
And vends them forth as knaves vend gilded counters,
Which wise men scorn, and fools accept in payment.

Old Play.

IN the morning Christie of the Clinthill was nowhere to be seen. As this worthy personage did seldom pique himself on sounding a trumpet before his movements, no one was surprised at his moonlight departure, though some alarm was excited lest he had not made it empty-handed. So, in the language of the national ballad,

Some ran to cupboard, and some to kist,
But nought was gone that could be mist.

All was in order, the key of the stable left above the door, and that of the iron grate in the inside of the lock. In short, the retreat had been made with scrupulous attention to the security of the garrison, and so far Christie left them nothing to complain of.

The safety of the premises was ascertained by Halbert, who, instead of catching up a gun or a cross-bow, and sallying out for the day as had been his frequent custom, now, with a gravity beyond his years, took a survey of all around the tower, and then returned to the spence, or public apartment, in which, at the early hour of seven, the morning meal was prepared.

There he found the Euphuist in the same elegant posture of abstruse calculation which he had exhibited on the preceding evening, his arms folded in the same angle, his eyes turned up to the same cobwebs, and his heels resting on the ground as before. Tired of this affectation of indolent importance, and not much flattered with his guest's persevering in it to the last, Halbert resolved at once to break the ice, being determined to know what circumstances had brought to the Tower of Glendinning [Glendearg] a guest at once so supercilious and so silent.

"Sir knight," he said with some firmness, "I have twice given you good morning, to which the absence of your mind hath, I presume, prevented you from yielding attention, or from making return. This exchange of courtesy is at your pleasure to give or withhold; but, as what I have farther to say concerns your comfort and your motions in an especial manner, I will entreat you to give me some signs of attention, that I may be sure I am not wasting my words on a monumental image."

At this unexpected address, Sir Piercie Shafton opened his eyes, and afforded the speaker a broad stare; but, as Halbert returned the glance without either confusion or dismay, the knight thought proper to change his posture, draw in his legs, raise his eyes, fix them on young Glendinning, and assume the appearance of one who listens to what is said to him. Nay, to make his purpose more evident, he gave voice to his resolution in these words: "Speak! we do hear."

"Sir knight," said the youth, "it is the custom of this halidome, or patrimony, of St. Mary's to trouble with inquiries no guests who receive our hospitality, providing they tarry in our house only for a single revolution of the sun. We know that both criminals and debtors come hither for sanctuary, and we scorn to extort from the pilgrim, whom chance may make our guest, an avowal of the cause of his pilgrimage and penance. But when one so high above our rank as yourself, sir knight, and especially one to whom the possession of such pre-eminence is not indifferent, shows his determination to be our guest for a longer time, it is our usage to inquire of him whence he comes, and what is the cause of his journey."

The English knight gaped twice or thrice before he answered, and then replied in a bantering tone: "Truly, good villagio, your question hath in it somewhat of embarrassment, for you ask me of things concerning which I am not as yet altogether determined what answer I may find it convenient to make. Let it suffice thee, kind juvenal, that thou hast the lord abbot's authority for treating me to the best of that power of thine, which, indeed, may not always so well suffice for my accommodation as either of us would desire."

"I must have a more precise answer than this, sir knight," said the young Glendinning.

"Friend," said the knight, "be not outrageous. It may suit your northern manners thus to press harshly upon the secrets of thy betters; but believe me that, even as the lute, struck by an unskilful hand, doth produce discords, so——"

At this moment the door of the apartment opened, and Mary Avenel presented herself. "But who can talk of discords," said the knight, assuming his complimentary vein and humour, "when the soul of harmony descends upon us in the presence of surpassing beauty? For even as foxes, wolves, and other animals void of sense and reason do fly from the presence of the resplendent sun of heaven when he arises in his glory, so do strife, wrath, and all ireful passions retreat, and, as it were, scud away, from the face which now beams upon us, with power to compose our angry passions, illuminate our errors and difficulties, soothe our wounded minds, and lull to rest our disorderly apprehensions; for as the heat and warmth of the eye of day is to the material and physical world, so is the eye which I now bow down before to that of the intellectual microcosm."

He concluded with a profound bow; and Mary Avenel, gazing from one to the other, and plainly seeing that something was amiss, could only say: "For Heaven's sake, what is the meaning of this?"

The newly-acquired tact and intelligence of her foster-brother was as yet insufficient to enable him to give an answer. He was quite uncertain how he ought to deal with a guest who, preserving a singularly high tone of assumed superiority and importance, seemed nevertheless so little serious in what he said that it was quite impossible to discern with accuracy whether he was in jest or earnest.

Forming, however, the internal resolution to bring Sir Piercie Shafton to a reckoning at a more fit place and season, he resolved to prosecute the matter no farther at present; and the entrance of his mother with the damsel of the mill, and the return of the honest miller from the stack-yard, where he had been numbering and calculating the probable amount of the season's grist, rendered further discussion impossible for the moment.

In the course of the calculation, it could not but strike the man of meal and grindstones that, after the church's dues were paid, and after all which he himself could by any means deduct from the crop, still the residue which must revert to Dame Glendinning could not be less than considerable. I wot not if this led the honest miller to nourish any plans similar to those adopted by Elspeth; but it is certain that he accepted with grateful alacrity an invitation which the dame gave to his daughter to remain a week or two as her guest at Glendearg.

The principal persons being thus in high good-humour with each other, all business gave place to the hilarity of the morning repast; and so much did Sir Piercie appear gratified by the attention which was paid to every word that he uttered by the nut-brown Mysie, that, notwithstanding his high birth and distinguished quality, he bestowed on her some of the more ordinary and second-rate tropes of his elocution.

Mary Avenel, when relieved from the awkwardness of feeling the full weight of his conversation addressed to herself, enjoyed it much more; and the good knight, encouraged by those conciliating marks of approbation from the sex for whose sake he cultivated his oratorical talents, made speedy intimation of his purpose to be more communicative than he had shown himself in his conversation with Halbert Glendinning, and gave them to understand that it was in consequence of some pressing danger that he was at present their involuntary guest.

The conclusion of the breakfast was a signal for the separation of the company. The miller went to prepare for his departure; his daughter to arrange matters for her unexpected stay; Edward was summoned to consultation by Martin concerning some agricultural matter, in which Halbert could not be brought to interest himself; the dame left the room upon her household concerns; and Mary was in the act of following her, when she suddenly recollected that, if she did so, the strange knight and Halbert must be left alone together, at the risk of another quarrel.

The maiden no sooner observed this circumstance than she instantly returned from the door of the apartment, and, seating herself in a small stone window-seat, resolved to maintain that curb which she was sensible her presence imposed on Halbert Glendinning, of whose quick temper she had some apprehensions.

The stranger marked her motions, and, either interpreting them as inviting his society, or obedient to those laws of gallantry which permitted him not to leave a lady in silence and solitude, he instantly placed himself near to her side, and opened the conversation as follows:

"Credit me, fair lady," he said, addressing Mary Avenel, "it much rejoiceth me, being, as I am, a banished man from the delights of mine own country, that I shall find here, in this obscure and silvan cottage of the north, a fair form and a candid soul, with whom I may explain my mutual sentiments. And let me pray you in particular, lovely lady, that, according to the universal custom now predominant in our court, the garden of superior wits, you will exchange with me some epithet whereby you may mark my devotion to your service. Be henceforward named, for example, my Protection, and let me be your Affability." [1]

"Our northern and country manners, sir knight, do not permit us to exchange epithets with those to whom we are strangers," replied Mary Avenel.

"Nay, but see now," said the knight, "how you are startled! even as the unbroken steed, which swerves aside from the shaking of a handkerchief, though he must in time encounter the waving of a pennon. This courtly exchange of epithets of honour is no more than the compliments which pass between valour and beauty, wherever they meet, and under whatever circumstances. Elizabeth of England herself calls Philip Sidney her Courage, and he in return calls that princess his Inspiration. Wherefore, my fair Protection, for by such epithet it shall be mine to denominate you——"

[1] See Usage of Epithets. Note 12.

"Not without the young lady's consent, sir," interrupted Halbert. "Most truly do I hope your courtly and quaint breeding will not so far prevail over the more ordinary rules of civil behaviour."

"Fair tenant of an indifferent copyhold," replied the knight, with the same coolness and civility of mien, but in a tone somewhat more lofty than he used to the young lady, "we do not, in the southern parts, much intermingle discourse, save with those with whom we may stand on some footing of equality; and I must, in all discretion, remind you that the necessity which makes us inhabitants of the same cabin doth not place us otherwise on a level with each other."

"By St. Mary," replied young Glendinning, "it is my thought that it does; for plain men hold that he who asks the shelter is indebted to him who gives it; and so far, therefore, is our rank equalised while this roof covers us both."

"Thou art altogether deceived," answered Sir Piercie; "and that thou mayst fully adapt thyself to our relative condition, know that I account not myself thy guest, but that of thy master, the Lord Abbot of St. Mary's, who, for reasons best known to himself and me, chooseth to administer his hospitality to me through the means of thee, his servant and vassal, who art, therefore, in good truth, as passive an instrument of my accommodation as this ill-made and rugged joint-stool on which I sit, or as the wooden trencher from which I eat my coarse commons. Wherefore," he added, turning to Mary, "fairest mistress, or rather, as I said before, most lovely Protection——"

Mary Avenel was about to reply to him, when the stern, fierce, and resentful expression of voice and countenance with which Halbert exclaimed, "Not from the King of Scotland, did he live, would I brook such terms!" induced her to throw herself between him and the stranger, exclaiming: "For God's sake, Halbert, beware what you do!"

"Fear not, fairest Protection," replied Sir Piercie, with the utmost serenity, "that I can be provoked by this rustical and mistaught juvenal to do aught misbecoming your presence or mine own dignity; for as soon shall the gunner's linstock give fire unto the icicle, as the spark of passion inflame my blood, tempered as it is to serenity by the respect due to the presence of my gracious Protection."

"You may well call her your protection, sir knight," said Halbert; "by St. Andrew, it is the only sensible word I have heard you speak! But we may meet where her protection shall no longer afford you shelter."

"Fairest Protection," continued the courtier, not even honouring with a look, far less with a direct reply, the threat of the incensed Halbert, "doubt not that thy faithful Affability will be more commoved by the speech of this rudesby than the bright and serene moon is perturbed by the baying of the cottage cur, proud of the height of his own dunghill, which, in his conceit, lifteth him nearer unto the majestic luminary."

To what lengths so unsavoury a simile might have driven Halbert's indignation is left uncertain; for at that moment Edward rushed into the apartment with the intelligence that two most important officers of the convent, the kitchener and refectioner, were just arrived with a sumpter mule, loaded with provisions, announcing that the lord abbot, the subprior, and the sacristan were on their way thither. A circumstance so very extraordinary had never been recorded in the annals of St. Mary's, or in the traditions of Glendearg, though there was a faint legendary report that a certain abbot had dined there in old days, after having been bewildered in a hunting expedition amongst the wilds which lie to the northward. But that the present lord abbot should have taken a voluntary journey to so wild and dreary a spot, the very Kamtschatka of the halidome, was a thing never dreamt of; and the news excited the greatest surprise in all the members of the family, saving Halbert alone.

This fiery youth was too full of the insult he had received to think of anything as unconnected with it. "I am glad of it," he exclaimed—"I am glad the abbot comes hither. I will know of him by what right this stranger is sent hither to domineer over us under our father's roof, as if we were slaves and not freemen. I will tell the proud priest to his beard——"

"Alas! alas! my brother," said Edward, "think what these words may cost thee!"

"And what will, or what can, they cost me," said Halbert, "that I should sacrifice my human feelings and my justifiable resentment to the fear of what the abbot can do?"

"Our mother—our mother!" exclaimed Edward; "think, if she is deprived of her home, expelled from her property, how can you amend what your rashness may ruin?"

"It is too true, by Heaven!" said Halbert, striking his forehead. Then, stamping his foot against the floor to express the full energy of the passion to which he dared no longer give vent, he turned round and left the apartment.

Mary Avenel looked at the stranger knight, while she was endeavouring to frame a request that he would not report the intemperate violence of her foster-brother, to the prejudice of his family in the mind of the abbot. But Sir Piercie, the very pink of courtesy, conjectured her meaning from her embarrassment, and waited not to be entreated.

"Credit me, fairest Protection," said he, "your Affability is less than capable of seeing or hearing, far less of reciting or reiterating, aught of an unseemly nature which may have chanced while I enjoyed the Elysium of your presence. The winds of idle passion may indeed rudely agitate the bosom of the rude; but the heart of the courtier is polished to resist them. As the frozen lake receives not the influence of the breeze, even so——"

The voice of Dame Glendinning, in shrill summons, here demanded Mary Avenel's attendance, who instantly obeyed, not a little glad to escape from the compliments and similes of this courtlike gallant. Nor was it apparently less a relief on his part; for no sooner was she past the threshold of the room than he exchanged the look of formal and elaborate politeness which had accompanied each word he had uttered hitherto for an expression of the utmost lassitude and *ennui;* and after indulging in one or two portentous yawns, broke forth into a soliloquy.

"What the foul fiend sent this wench hither? As if it were not sufficient plague to be harboured in a hovel that would hardly serve for a dog's kennel in England, baited by a rude peasant-boy, and dependent on the faith of a mercenary ruffian, but I cannot even have time to muse over my own mishap, but must come aloft, frisk, fidget, and make speeches to please this pale hectic phantom, because she has gentle blood in her veins! By mine honour, setting prejudice aside, the mill-wench is the more attractive of the two. But *patienza*, Piercie Shafton; thou most not lose thy well-earned claim to be accounted a devout servant of the fair sex, a witty-brained, prompt, and accomplished courtier. Rather thank Heaven, Piercie Shafton, which hath sent thee a subject, wherein, without derogating from thy rank—since the honours of the Avenel family are beyond dispute—thou mayst find a whetstone for thy witty compliments, a strop whereon to sharpen thine acute ingine, a butt whereat to shoot the arrows of thy gallantry. For even as a Bilboa blade, the more it is rubbed the brighter and the sharper will it prove, so—— But what need I waste my stock of similitudes in holding converse with myself? Yonder comes the monkish retinue, like some half-score of crows winging their way slowly up the valley. I hope, a'gad, they have not forgotten my trunk-mails of apparel amid the ample provision they have made for their own belly-timber. Mercy, a'gad, I were finely holped up if the vesture has miscarried among the thievish Borderers!"

Stung by this reflection, he ran hastily downstairs, and caused his horse to be saddled, that he might, as soon as possible, ascertain this important point, by meeting the lord abbot and his retinue as they came up the glen. He had not ridden a mile before he met them advancing with the slowness and decorum which became persons of their dignity and profession. The knight failed not to greet the lord abbot with all the formal compliments with which men of rank at that period exchanged courtesies. He had the good fortune to find that his mails were numbered among the train of baggage which attended upon the party; and, satisfied in that particular, he turned his horse's head and accompanied the abbot to the Tower of Glendearg.

Great, in the mean while, had been the turmoil of the good

Dame Elspeth and her coadjutors to prepare for the fitting reception of the father lord abbot and his retinue. The monks had indeed taken care not to trust too much to the state of her pantry; but she was not the less anxious to make such additions as might enable her to claim the thanks of her feudal lord and spiritual father. Meeting Halbert, as, with his blood on fire, he returned from his altercation with her guest, she commanded him instantly to go forth to the hill, and not to return without venison; reminding him that he was apt enough to go thither for his own pleasure, and must now do so for the credit of the house.

The miller, who was now hastening his journey homewards, promised to send up some salmon by his own servant. Dame Elspeth, who by this time thought she had guests enough, had begun to repent of her invitation to poor Mysie, and was just considering by what means, short of giving offence, she could send off the Maid of the Mill behind her father, and adjourn all her own aerial architecture till some future opportunity, when this unexpected generosity on the part of the sire rendered any present attempt to return his daughter on his hands too highly ungracious to be further thought on. So the miller departed alone on his homeward journey.

Dame Elspeth's sense of hospitality proved in this instance its own reward; for Mysie had dwelt too near the convent to be altogether ignorant of the noble art of cookery, which her father patronised to the extent of consuming on festival days such dainties as his daughter could prepare in emulation of the luxuries of the abbot's kitchen. Laying aside, therefore, her holiday kirtle, and adopting a dress more suitable to the occasion, the good-humoured maiden bared her snowy arms above the elbows; and, as Elspeth acknowledged, in the language of the time and country, took "entire and aefauld part with her" in the labours of the day; showing unparalleled talent, and indefatigable industry, in the preparation of *mortreux, blanc-manger,* and Heaven knows what delicacies besides, which Dame Glendinning, unassisted by her skill, dared not even have dreamt of presenting.

Leaving this able substitute in the kitchen, and regretting

that Mary Avenel was so brought up that she could entrust nothing to her care, unless it might be seeing the great chamber strewed with rushes, and ornamented with such flowers and branches as the season afforded, Dame Elspeth hastily donned her best attire, and with a beating heart presented herself at the door of her little tower, to make her obeisance to the lord abbot as he crossed her humble threshold. Edward stood by his mother, and felt the same palpitation, which his philosophy was at a loss to account for. He was yet to learn how long it is ere our reason is enabled to triumph over the force of external circumstances, and how much our feelings are affected by novelty, and blunted by use and habit.

On the present occasion, he witnessed with wonder and awe the approach of some half-score of riders, sober men upon sober palfreys, muffled in their long black garments, and only relieved by their white scapularies, showing more like a funeral procession than aught else, and not quickening their pace beyond that which permitted easy conversation and easy digestion. The sobriety of the scene was indeed somewhat enlivened by the presence of Sir Piercie Shafton, who, to show that his skill in the manege was not inferior to his other accomplishments, kept alternately pressing and checking his gay courser, forcing him to piaffe, to caracole, to passage, and to do all the other feats of the school, to the great annoyance of the lord abbot, the wonted sobriety of whose palfrey became at length discomposed by the vivacity of its companion, while the dignitary kept crying out in bodily alarm, "I do pray you, sir—sir knight—good now, Sir Piercie—— Be quiet, Benedict, there is a good steed—soh, poor fellow!" and uttering all the other precatory and soothing exclamations by which a timid horseman usually bespeaks the favour of a frisky companion, or of his own unquiet nag, and concluding the bead-roll with a sincere *Deo gratias* so soon as he alighted in the courtyard of the Tower of Glendearg.

The inhabitants unanimously knelt down to kiss the hand of the lord abbot, a ceremony which even the monks were often condemned to. Good Abbot Boniface was too much fluttered by the incidents of the latter part of his journey to go through this ceremony with much solemnity, or indeed with much patience. He kept wiping his brow with a snow-white handkerchief with one hand, while another was abandoned to the homage of his vassals; and then signing the cross with his outstretched arm, and exclaiming, "Bless ye—bless ye, my children!" he hastened into the house, and murmured not a little at the darkness and steepness of the rugged winding stair, whereby he at length scaled the spence destined for his entertainment, and, overcome with fatigue, threw himself, I do not say into an easy chair, but into the easiest the apartment afforded.

CHAPTER XVI.

> A courtier extraordinary, who by diet
> Of meats and drinks, his temperate exercise,
> Choice music, frequent bath, his horary shifts
> Of shirts and waistcoats, means to immortalise
> Mortality itself, and makes the essence
> Of his whole happiness the trim of court.
>
> *Magnetic Lady.*

WHEN the lord abbot had suddenly and superciliously vanished from the eyes of his expectant vassals, the sub-prior made amends for the negligence of his principal by the kind and affectionate greeting which he gave to all the members of the family, but especially to Dame Elspeth, her foster-daughter, and her son Edward. "Where," he even condescended to inquire, "is that naughty Nimrod, Halbert? He hath not yet, I trust, turned, like his great prototype, his hunting-spear against man?"

"Oh no, an it please your reverence," said Dame Glendinning; "Halbert is up the glen to get some venison, or surely he would not have been absent when such a day of honour dawned upon me and mine."

"Oh, to get savoury meat, such as our soul loveth," muttered the sub-prior; "it has been at times an acceptable gift. I bid you good morrow, my good dame, as I must attend upon his lordship the father abbot."

"And oh, reverend sir," said the good widow, detaining him, "if it might be your pleasure to take part with us if there is anything wrong; and if there is anything wanted, to say that it is just coming, or to make some excuses your learning best knows how. Every bit of vassail and silver work have we been spoiled of since Pinkie Cleuch, when I lost poor Simon Glendinning, that was the warst of a'."

"Never mind—never fear," said the sub-prior, gently extricating his garment from the anxious grasp of Dame Elspeth, "the refectioner has with him the abbot's plate and drinking-cups; and I pray you to believe that whatever is short in your entertainment will be deemed amply made up in your good-will."

So saying, he escaped from her and went into the spence, where such preparations as haste permitted were making for the noon collation of the abbot and the English knight. Here he found the lord abbot, for whom a cushion, composed of all the plaids in the house, had been unable to render Simon's huge elbow-chair a soft or comfortable place of rest.

"*Benedicite!*" said Abbot Boniface, "now marry fie upon these hard benches with all my heart; they are as uneasy as the *scabella* of our novices. St. Jude be with us, sir knight, how have you contrived to pass over the night in this dungeon? An your bed was no softer than your seat, you might as well have slept on the stone couch of St. Pacomius. After trotting a full ten miles, a man needs a softer seat than has fallen to my hard lot."

With sympathising faces, the sacristan and the refectioner ran to raise the lord abbot, and to adjust his seat to his mind, which was at length accomplished in some sort, although he continued alternately to bewail his fatigue and to exult in the conscious sense of having discharged an arduous duty. "You errant cavaliers," said he, addressing the knight, "may now perceive that others have their travail and their toils to undergo as well as your honoured faculty. And this I will say for myself and the soldiers of St. Mary, among whom I may be termed captain, that it is not our wont to flinch from the heat of the service, or to withdraw from the good fight.

14

No, by St. Mary!—no sooner did I learn that you were here, and dared not for certain reasons come to the monastery, where with as good will, and with more convenience, we might have given you a better reception, than, striking the table with my hammer, I called a brother. 'Timothy,' said I, 'let them saddle Benedict—let them saddle my black palfrey, and bid the sub-prior and some half-score of attendants be in readiness to-morrow after matins; we would ride to Glendearg.' Brother Timothy stared, thinking, I imagine, that his ears had scarce done him justice; but I repeated my commands, and said: 'Let the kitchener and refectioner go before to aid the poor vassals to whom the place belongs in making a suitable collation.' So that you will consider, good Sir Piercie, our mutual incommodities, and forgive whatever you may find amiss."

"By my faith," said Sir Piercie Shafton, "there is nothing to forgive. If you spiritual warriors have to submit to the grievous incommodities which your lordship narrates, it would ill become me, a sinful and secular man, to complain of a bed as hard as a board, of broth which relished as if made of burnt wool, of flesh which, in its sable and singed shape, seemed to put me on a level with Richard Cœur-de-Lion, when he ate up the head of a Moor carbonadoed, and of other viands savouring rather of the rusticity of this northern region."

"By the good saints, sir," said the abbot, somewhat touched in point of his character for hospitality, of which he was in truth a most faithful and zealous professor, "it grieves me to the heart that you have found our vassals no better provided for your reception. Yet I crave leave to observe that, if Sir Piercie Shafton's affairs had permitted him to honour with his company our poor house of St. Mary's, he might have had less to complain of in respect of easements."

"To give your lordship the reasons," said Sir Piercie Shafton, "why I could not at this present time approach your dwelling, or avail myself of its well-known and undoubted hospitality, craves either some delay or (looking around him) a limited audience."

The lord abbot immediately issued his mandate to the refectioner: "Hie thee to the kitchen, Brother Hilarius, and there make inquiry of our brother the kitchener within what time he opines that our collation may be prepared, since sin and sorrow it were, considering the hardships of this noble and gallant knight, no whit mentioning or weighing those we ourselves have endured, if we were now either to advance or retard the hour of refection beyond the time when the viands are fit to be set before us."

Brother Hilarius parted with an eager alertness to execute the will of his superior, and returned with the assurance that punctually at one after noon would the collation be ready.

"Before that time," said the accurate refectioner, "the wafers, flams, and pastry-meat will scarce have had the just degree of fire which learned pottingers prescribe as fittest for the body; and if it should be past one o'clock, were it but ten minutes, our brother the kitchener opines that the haunch of venison would suffer, in spite of the skill of the little turn-broche whom he has recommended to your holiness by his praises."

"How!" said the abbot, "a haunch of venison! From whence comes that dainty? I remember not thou didst intimate its presence in thy hamper of vivers."

"So please your holiness and lordship," said the refectioner, "he is a son of the woman of the house who hath shot it and sent it in—killed but now; yet, as the animal heat hath not left the body, the kitchener undertakes it shall eat as tender as a young chicken; and this youth hath a special gift in shooting deer, and never misses the heart or the brain; so that the blood is not driven through the flesh, as happens too often with us. It is a hart of grease; your holiness has seldom seen such a haunch."

"Silence, Brother Hilarius," said the abbot, wiping his mouth; "it is not beseeming our order to talk of food so earnestly, especially as we must oft have our animal powers exhausted by fasting, and be accessible, as being ever mere mortals, to those signs of longing (he again wiped his mouth) which arise on the mention of victuals to an hungry man.

Minute down, however, the name of that youth; it is fitting merit should be rewarded, and he shall hereafter be a *frater ad succurrendum* in the kitchen and buttery."

"Alas! reverend father and my good lord," replied the refectioner, "I did inquire after the youth, and I learn he is one who prefers the casque to the cowl, and the sword of the flesh to the weapons of the spirit."

"And if it be so," said the abbot, "see that thou retain him as a deputy-keeper and man-at-arms, and not as a lay brother of the monastery; for old Tallboy, our forester, waxes dim-eyed, and hath twice spoiled a noble buck by hitting him unwarily on the haunch. Ah! 'tis a foul fault, the abusing by evil-killing, evil-dressing, evil appetite, or otherwise, the good creatures indulged to us for our use. Wherefore, secure us the service of this youth, Brother Hilarius, in the way that may best suit him. And now, Sir Piercie Shafton, since the fates have assigned us a space of wellnigh an hour ere we dare hope to enjoy more than the vapour or savour of our repast, may I pray you, of your courtesy, to tell me the cause of this visit; and, above all, to inform us why you will not approach our more pleasant and better furnished *hospitium?*"

"Reverend father and my very good lord," said Sir Piercie Shafton, "it is well known to your wisdom that there are stone walls which have ears, and that secrecy is to be looked to in matters which concern a man's head."

The abbot signed to his attendants, excepting the sub-prior, to leave the room, and then said: "Your valour, Sir Piercie, may freely unburden yourself before our faithful friend and counsellor Father Eustace, the benefits of whose advice we may too soon lose, inasmuch as his merits will speedily recommend him to an higher station, in which, we trust, he may find the blessing of a friend and adviser as valuable as himself, since I may say of him, as our claustral rhyme goeth, [1]

> Dixit Abbas ad prioris,
> Tu es homo boni moris
> Quia semper sanioris
> Mihi das concilia.

---

[1] The rest of this doggerel rhyme may be found in Fosbrooke's learned work on *British Monarchism*.

Indeed," he added, "the office of sub-prior is altogether be-neath our dear brother; nor can we elevate him unto that of prior, which, for certain reasons, is at present kept vacant amongst us. Howbeit, Father Eustace is fully possessed of my confidence, and worthy of yours, and well may it be said of him, *Intravit in secretis nostris.*"

Sir Piercie Shafton bowed to the reverend brethren, and, heaving a sigh, as if he would have burst his steel cuirass, he thus commenced his speech:

"Certes, reverend sirs, I may well heave such a suspiration, who have, as it were, exchanged heaven for purgatory, leaving the lightsome sphere of the royal court of England for a remote nook in this inaccessible desert; quitting the tiltyard, where I was ever ready among my compeers to splinter a lance, either for the love of honour or for the honour of love, in order to couch my knightly spear against base and pilfering besognios and marauders; exchanging the lighted halls, where-in I used nimbly to pace the swift coranto, or to move with a loftier grace in the stately galliard, for this rugged and decayed dungeon of rusty-coloured stone; quitting the gay theatre for the solitary chimney-nook of a Scottish dog-house; bartering the sounds of the soul-ravishing lute and the love-awakening viol-de-gamba for the discordant squeak of a northern bagpipe; above all, exchanging the smiles of those beauties who form a galaxy around the throne of England for the cold courtesy of an untaught damsel and the bewildered stare of a miller's maiden. More might I say, of the exchange of the conversa-tion of gallant knights and gay courtiers of mine own order and capacity, whose conceits are bright and vivid as the light-ning, for that of monks and churchmen—but it were discour-teous to urge that topic."

The abbot listened to this list of complaints with great round eyes, which evinced no exact intelligence of the orator's mean-ing; and when the knight paused to take breath, he looked with a doubtful and inquiring eye at the sub-prior, not well knowing in what tone he should reply to an exordium so extra-ordinary. The sub-prior accordingly stepped in to the relief of his principal.

" We deeply sympathise with you, sir knight, in the several mortifications and hardships to which fate has subjected you, particularly in that which has thrown you into the society of those who, as they were conscious they deserved not such an honour, so neither did they at all desire it. But all this goes little way to expound the cause of this train of disasters, or, in plainer words, the reason which has compelled you into a situation having so few charms for you."

"Gentle and reverend sir," replied the knight, "forgive an unhappy person who, in giving a history of his miseries, dilateth upon them extremely, even as he who, having fallen from a precipice, looketh upward to measure the height from which he hath been precipitated."

"Yea, but," said Father Eustace, "methinks it were wiser in him to tell those who come to lift him up which of his bones have been broken."

"You, reverend sir," said the knight, "have, in the encounter of our wits, made a fair attaint; whereas I may be in some sort said to have broken my staff across.[1] Pardon me, grave sir, that I speak the language of the tiltyard, which is doubtless strange to your reverend ears. Ah! brave resort of the noble, the fair, and the gay! Ah! throne of love, and citadel of honour! Ah! celestial beauties, by whose bright eyes it is graced! Never more shall Piercie Shafton advance, as the centre of your radiant glances, couch his lance, and spur his horse at the sound of the spirit-stirring trumpets, nobly called the voice of war; never more shall he baffle his adversary's encounter boldly, break his spear dexterously, and, ambling around the lovely circle, receive the rewards with which beauty honours chivalry!"

Here he paused, wrung his hands, looked upwards, and seemed lost in contemplation of his own fallen fortunes.

"Mad—very mad," whispered the abbot to the sub-prior; "I would we were fairly rid of him; for, of a truth, I expect he will proceed from raving to mischief. Were it not better to call up the rest of the brethren?"

But the sub-prior knew better than his superior how to dis-

[1] See Attaint. Note 13.

tinguish the jargon of affectation from the ravings of insanity, and although the extremity of the knight's passion seemed altogether fantastic, yet he was not ignorant to what extravagancies the fashion of the day can conduct its votaries.

Allowing, therefore two minutes' space to permit the knight's enthusiastic feelings to exhaust themselves, he again gravely reminded him that the lord abbot had taken a journey, unwonted to his age and habits, solely to learn in what he could serve Sir Piercie Shafton; that it was altogether impossible he could do so without his receiving distinct information of the situation in which he had now sought refuge in Scotland. "The day wore on," he observed, looking at the window; "and if the abbot should be obliged to return to the monastery without obtaining the necessary intelligence, the regret might be mutual, but the inconvenience was like to be all on Sir Piercie's own side."

The hint was not thrown away.

"O goddess of courtesy!" said the knight, "can I have so far forgotten thy behests as to make this good prelate's ease and time a sacrifice to my vain complaints! Know, then, most worthy, and not less worshipful, that I, your poor visitor and guest, am by birth nearly bound to the Piercie of Northumberland whose fame is so widely blown through all parts of the world where English worth hath been known. Now, this present Earl of Northumberland, of whom I propose to give you the brief history——"

"It is altogether unnecessary," said the abbot; "we know him to be a good and true nobleman, and a sworn upholder of our Catholic faith, in the spite of the heretical woman who now sits upon the throne of England. And it is specially as his kinsman, and as knowing that ye partake with him in such devout and faithful belief and adherence to our holy Mother Church, that we say to you, Sir Piercie Shafton, that ye be heartily welcome to us, and that, an we wist how, we would labour to do you good service in your extremity."

"For such kind offer I rest your most humble debtor," said Sir Piercie; "nor need I at this moment say more than that my right honourable cousin of Northumberland, having devised with me and some others, the choice and picked spirits of the age, how and by what means the worship of God, according to the Catholic Church, might be again introduced into this distracted kingdom of England—even as one deviseth, by the assistance of his friend, to catch and to bridle a runaway steed—it pleased him so deeply to entrust me in those communications that my personal safety becomes, as it were, entwined or complicated therewith. Natheless, as we have had sudden reason to believe, this Princess Elizabeth, who maintaineth around her a sort of counsellors skilful in tracking whatever schemes may be pursued for bringing her title into challenge, or for erecting again the discipline of the Catholic Church, has obtained certain knowledge of the trains which we had laid before we could give fire unto them. Wherefore, my right honourable cousin of Northumberland, thinking it best belike that one man should take both blame and shame for the whole, did lay the burden of all this trafficking upon my back; which load I am the rather content to bear, in that he hath always shown himself my kind and honourable kinsman, as well as that my estate, I wot not how, hath of late been somewhat insufficient to maintain the expense of those braveries wherewith it is incumbent on us, who are chosen and selected spirits, to distinguish ourselves from the vulgar."

"So that possibly," said the sub-prior, "your private affairs rendered a foreign journey less incommodious to you than it might have been to the noble earl, your right worthy cousin?"

"You are right, reverend sir," answered the courtier; "*rem acu*—you have touched the point with a needle. My cost and expenses had been indeed somewhat lavish at the late triumphs and tourneys, and the flat-capp'd citizens had shown themselves unwilling to furnish my pocket for new gallantries for the honour of the nation, as well as for mine own peculiar glory; and, to speak truth, it was in some part the hope of seeing these matters amended that led me to desire a new world in England."

"So that the miscarriage of your public enterprise, with the derangement of your own private affairs," said the sub-prior, "have induced you to seek Scotland as a place of refuge?"

"*Rem acu*, once again," said Sir Piercie; "and not without good cause, since my neck, if I remained, might have been brought within the circumstances of an halter; and so speedy was my journey northward, that I had but time to exchange my peach-coloured doublet of Genoa velvet, thickly laid over with goldsmith's work, for this cuirass, which was made by Bonamico of Milan, and travelled northward with all speed, judging that I might do well to visit my right honourable cousin of Northumberland at one of his numerous castles. But as I posted towards Alnwick, even with the speed of a star which, darting from its native sphere, shoots wildly downwards, I was met at Northallerton by one Henry Vaughan, a servant of my right honourable kinsman, who showed me that as then I might not with safety come to his presence, seeing that, in obedience to orders from his court, he was obliged to issue out letters for my incarceration."

"This," said the abbot, "seems but hard measure on the part of your honourable kinsman."

"It might be so judged, my lord," replied Sir Piercie; "nevertheless, I will stand to the death for the honour of my right honourable cousin of Northumberland. Also, Henry Vaughan gave me, from my said cousin, a good horse, and a purse of gold, with two Border prickers, as they are called, for my guides, who conducted me, by such roads and bye-paths as have never been seen since the days of Sir Lancelot and Sir Tristrem, into this kingdom of Scotland, and to the house of a certain baron, or one who holds the style of such, called Julian Avenel, with whom I found such reception as the place and party could afford."

"And that," said the abbot, "must have been right wretched; for, to judge from the appetite which Julian showeth when abroad, he hath not, I judge, over-abundant provision at home."

"You are right, sir—your reverence is in the right," continued Sir Piercie: "we had but lenten fare, and, what was worse, a score to clear at the departure; for though this Julian Avenel called us to no reckoning, yet he did so extravagantly admire the fashion of my poniard—the *poignet* being of silver exquisitely hatched, and indeed the weapon being altogether a piece of exceeding rare device and beauty—that in faith I could not for very shame's sake but pray his acceptance of it; words which he gave me not the trouble of repeating twice, before he had stuck it into his greasy buff-belt, where, credit me, reverend sir, it showed more like a butcher's knife than a gentleman's dagger."

"So goodly a gift might at least have purchased you a few days' hospitality," said Father Eustace.

"Reverend sir," said Sir Piercie, "had I abidden with him, I should have been complimented out of every remnant of my wardrobe—acutally flayed, by the hospitable gods I swear it! Sir, he secured my spare doublet, and had a pluck at my galligaskins; I was enforced to beat a retreat before I was altogether unrigged. That Border knave, his serving-man, had a pluck at me too, and usurped a scarlet cassock and steel cuirass belonging to the page of my body, whom I was fain to leave behind me. In good time I received a letter from my right honourable cousin, showing me that he had written to you in my behalf, and sent to your charge two mails filled with wearing apparel—namely, my rich crimson silk doublet, slashed out and lined with cloth of gold, and which I wore at the last revels, with baldric and trimmings to correspond; also two pair black silk slops, with hanging garters of carnation silk; also the flesh-coloured silken doublet, with the trimmings of fur, in which I danced the salvage man at the Gray's Inn mummery; also——"

"Sir knight," said the sub-prior, "I pray you to spare the further inventory of your wardrobe. The monks of St. Mary's are no freebooting barons, and whatever part of your vestments arrived at our house have been this day faithfully brought hither, with the mails which contained them. I may presume from what has been said, as we have indeed been given to understand by the Earl of Northumberland, that your desire is to remain for the present as unknown and as unnoticed as may be consistent with your high worth and distinction?"

"Alas, reverend father!" replied the courtier, "a blade when it is in the scabbard cannot give lustre, a diamond when it is in the casket cannot give light, and worth, when it is compelled by circumstances to obscure itself, cannot draw observation: my retreat can only attract the admiration of those few to whom circumstances permit its displaying itself."

"I conceive now, my venerable father and lord," said the sub-prior, "that your wisdom will assign such a course of conduct to this noble knight as may be alike consistent with his safety and with the weal of the community. For you wot well that perilous strides have been made in these audacious days to the destruction of all ecclesiastical foundations, and that our holy community has been repeatedly menaced. Hitherto they have found no flaw in our raiment; but a party, friendly as well to the Queen of England as to the heretical doctrines of the schismatical church, or even to worse and wilder forms of heresy, prevails now at the court of our sovereign, who dare not yield to her suffering clergy the protection she would gladly extend to them."

"My lord and reverend sir," said the knight, "I will gladly relieve ye of my presence, while ye canvass this matter at your freedom; and to speak truly, I am desirous to see in what case the chamberlain of my noble kinsman hath found my wardrobe, and how he hath packed the same, and whether it has suffered from the journey. There are four suits of as pure and elegant device as ever the fancy of a fair lady doated upon, every one having a treble and appropriate change of ribbons, trimmings, and fringes, which, in case of need, may, as it were, renew each of them, and multiply the four into twelve. There is also my sad-coloured riding-suit, and three cut-work shirts with falling bands; I pray you, pardon me, I must needs see how matters stand with them without farther dallying."

Thus speaking, he left the room; and the sub-prior, looking after him significantly, added: "Where the treasure is will the heart be also."

"St. Mary preserve our wits!" said the abbot, stunned with the knight's abundance of words; "were man's brains ever so stuffed with silk and broadcloth, cut-work, and I wot not what besides! And what could move the Earl of Northumberland to assume for his bosom counsellor, in matters of depth and danger, such a feather-brained coxcomb as this!"

"Had he been other than what he is, venerable father," said the sub-prior, "he had been less fitted for the part of scapegoat, to which his right honourable cousin had probably destined him from the commencement, in case of their plot failing. I know something of this Piercie Shafton. The legitimacy of his mother's descent from the Piercie family, the point on which he is most jealous, hath been called in question. If hare-brained courage and an outrageous spirit of gallantry can make good his pretensions to the high lineage he claims, these qualities have never been denied him. For the rest, he is one of the ruffling gallants of the time, like Rowland Yorke, Stukely,[1] and others, who wear out their fortunes and endanger their lives in idle braveries, in order that they may be esteemed the only choice gallants of the time; and afterwards endeavour to repair their estate by engaging in the desperate plots and conspiracies which wiser heads have devised. To use one of his own conceited similitudes, such courageous fools resemble hawks, which the wiser conspirator keeps hooded and blindfolded on his wrist until the quarry is on the wing, and who are then flown at them."

"St. Mary," said the abbot, "he were an evil guest to introduce into our quiet household. Our young monks make bustle enough, and more than is beseeming God's servants, about their outward attire already: this knight were enough to turn their brains, from the *vestiarius* down to the very scullion boy."

"A worse evil might follow," said the sub-prior. "In these bad days, the patrimony of the church is bought and sold, forfeited and distrained, as if it were the unhallowed soil appertaining to a secular baron. Think what penalty awaits us, were we convicted of harbouring a rebel to her whom they call the Queen of England! There would neither be wanting Scottish parasites to beg the lands of the foundation, nor an army from England to burn and harry the halidome. The men of Scotland were once Scotsmen, firm and united in their

[1] See Rowland Yorke and Stukely. Note 14.

love of their country, and throwing every other consideration aside when the frontier was menaced; now they are—what shall I call them?—the one part French, the other part English, considering their dear native country merely as a prize-fighting stage, upon which foreigners are welcome to decide their quarrels."

"*Benedicite!*" replied the abbot, "they are indeed slippery and evil times."

"And therefore," said Father Eustace, "we must walk warily: we must not, for example, bring this man—this Sir Piercie Shafton, to our house of St. Mary's."

"But how then shall we dispose of him?" replied the abbot. "Bethink thee that he is a sufferer for Holy Church's sake; that his patron, the Earl of Northumberland, hath been our friend, and that, lying so near us, he may work us weal or woe according as we deal with his kinsman."

"And, accordingly," said the sub-prior, "for these reasons, as well as for discharge of the great duty of Christian charity, I would protect and relieve this man. Let him not go back to Julian Avenel; that unconscientious baron would not stick to plunder the exiled stranger. Let him remain here: the spot is secluded, and if the accommodation be beneath his quality, discovery will become the less likely. We will make such means for his convenience as we can devise."

"Will he be persuaded, thinkest thou?" said the abbot; "I will leave my own travelling-bed for his repose, and send up a suitable easy-chair."

"With such easements," said the sub-prior, "he must not complain; and then, if threatened by any sudden danger, he can soon come down to the sanctuary, where we will harbour him in secret until means can be devised of dismissing him in safety."

"Were we not better," said the abbot, "send him on to the court, and get rid of him at once?"

"Ay, but at the expense of our friends: this butterfly may fold his wings, and lie under cover in the cold air of Glendearg; but were he at Holyrood, he would, did his life depend on it, expand his spangled drapery in the eyes of the queen and court. Rather than fail of distinction, he would sue for love to our gracious sovereign: the eyes of all men would be upon him in the course of three short days, and the international peace of the two ends of the island endangered for a creature who, like a silly moth, cannot abstain from fluttering round a light."

"Thou hast prevailed with me, Father Eustace," said the abbot, "and it will go hard but I improve on thy plan. I will send up in secret not only household stuff, but wine and wassell-bread. There is a young swankie here who shoots venison well. I will give him directions to see that the knight lacks none."

"Whatever accommodation he can have, which infers not a risk of discovery," said the sub-prior, "it is our duty to afford him."

"Nay," said the abbot, "we will do more, and will instantly despatch a servant express to the keeper of our revestiary to send us such things as he may want, even this night. See it done, good father."

"I will," answered Father Eustace; "but I hear the gull clamorous for some one to truss his points.[1] He will be fortunate if he lights on any one here who can do him the office of groom of the chamber."

"I would he would appear," said the abbot "for here comes the refectioner with the collation. By my faith, the ride hath given me a sharp appetite!"

[1] See Note 15.

CHAPTER XVII.

I'll seek for other aid. Spirits, they say,
Flit round invisible, as thick as motes
Dance in the sunbeam. If that spell
Or necromancer's sigil can compel them,
They shall hold counsel with me.

JAMES DUFF.

THE reader's attention must be recalled to Halbert Glendin-ning, who had left the Tower of Glendearg immediately after his quarrel with its new guest, Sir Piercie Shafton. As he walked with a rapid pace up the glen, Old Martin followed him, beseeching him to be less hasty.

"Halbert," said the old man, "you will never live to have white hair, if you take fire thus at every spark of provocation."

"And why should I wish it, old man," said Halbert, "if I am to be the butt that every fool may aim a shaft of scorn against? What avails it, old man, that you yourself move, sleep, and wake, eat thy niggard meal, and repose on thy hard pallet? Why art thou so well pleased that the morning should call thee up to daily toil, and the evening again lay thee down a wearied-out wretch? Were it not better sleep and wake no more, than to undergo this dull exchange of labour for insensibility, and of insensibility for labour?"

"God help me," answered Martin, "there may be truth in what thou sayest; but walk slower, for my old limbs cannot keep pace with your young legs—walk slower, and I will tell you why age, though unlovely, is yet endurable."

"Speak on then," said Halbert, slackening his pace; "but remember we must seek venison to refresh the fatigues of these holy men, who will this morning have achieved a journey of ten miles; and if we reach not the Brocksburn head, we are scarce like to see an antler."

"Then know, my good Halbert," said Martin, "whom I love as my own son, that I am satisfied to live till death calls me, because my Maker wills it. Ay, and although I spend what men call a hard life, pinched with cold in winter and burnt with heat in summer, though I feed hard and sleep hard, and am held mean and despised, yet I bethink me, that were I of no use on the face of this fair creation, God would withdraw me from it."

"Thou poor old man," said Halbert, "and can such a vain conceit as this of thy fancied use reconcile thee to a world where thou playest so poor a part?"

"My part was nearly as poor," said Martin, "my person nearly as much despised, the day that I saved my mistress and her child from perishing in the wilderness."

"Right, Martin," answered Halbert; "there, indeed, thou didst what might be a sufficient apology for a whole life of insignificance."

"And do you account it for nothing, Halbert, that I should have the power of giving you a lesson of patience and submission to the destinies of Providence? Methinks there is use for the grey hairs on the old scalp, were it but to instruct the green head by precept and by example."

Halbert held down his face and remained silent for a minute or two, and then resumed his discourse: "Martin, seest thou aught changed in me of late?"

"Surely," said Martin. "I have always known you hasty, wild, and inconsiderate, rude, and prompt to speak at the volley and without reflection; but now, methinks, your bearing, without losing its natural fire, has something in it of force and dignity which it had not before. It seems as if you had fallen asleep a carle and awakened a gentleman."

"Thou canst judge, then, of noble bearing?" said Halbert.

"Surely," answered Martin, "in some sort I can; for I have travelled through court, and camp, and city with my master, Walter Avenel, although he could do nothing for me in the long run but give me room for two score of sheep on the hill; and surely even now, while I speak with you, I feel sensible that my language is more refined than it is my wont to use, and that, though I know not the reason, the rude northern dialect, so familiar to my tongue, has given place to a more town-bred speech."

"And this change in thyself and me thou canst by no means account for?" said young Glendinning.

"Change!" replied Martin, "by Our Lady, it is not so much a change which I feel as a recalling and renewing sentiments and expressions which I had some thirty years since, ere Tibb and I set up our humble household. It is singular that your society should have this sort of influence over me, Halbert, and that I should never have experienced it ere now."

"Thinkest thou," said Halbert, "thou seest in me aught that can raise me from this base, low, despised state into one where I may rank with those proud men who now despise my clownish poverty?"

Martin paused an instant, and then answered: "Doubtless you may, Halbert; as broken a ship has come to land. Heard ye never of Hughie Dun, who left this halidome some thirty-five years gone by? A deliverly fellow was Hughie—could read and write like a priest, and could wield brand and buckler with the best of the riders. I mind him; the like of him was never seen in the halidome of St. Mary's, and so was seen of the preferment that God sent him."

"And what was that?" said Halbert, his eyes sparkling with eagerness.

"Nothing less," answered Martin, "than body-servant to the Archbishop of St. Andrews!"

Halbert's countenance fell. "A servant—and to a priest! Was this all that knowledge and activity could raise him to?"

Martin, in his turn, looked with wistful surprise in the face of his young friend. "And to what could fortune lead him farther?" answered he. "The son of a kirk-feuar is not the stuff that lords and knights are made of. Courage and school-craft cannot change churl's blood into gentle blood, I trow. I have heard, forbye, that Hughie Dun left a good five hundred punds of Scots money to his only daughter, and that she married the bailie of Pittenweem."

At this moment, and while Halbert was embarrassed with devising a suitable answer, a deer bounded across their path. In an instant the cross-bow was at the youth's shoulder, the

15

bolt whistled, and the deer, after giving one bound upright, dropt dead on the green sward.

"There lies the venison our dame wanted," said Martin; "who would have thought of an out-lying stag being so low down the glen at this season? And it is a hart of grease too, in full season, and three inches of fat on the brisket. Now this is all your luck, Halbert, that follows you, go where you like. Were you to put in for it, I would warrant you were made one of the abbot's yeomen prickers, and ride about in a purple doublet as bold as the best."

"Tush, man," answered Halbert, "I will serve the Queen or no one. Take thou care to have down the venison to the tower, since they expect it. I will on to the moss. I have two or three bird-bolts at my girdle, and it may be I shall find wild-fowl."

He hastened his pace, and was soon out of sight. Martin paused for a moment, and looked after him. "There goes the making of a right gallant stripling, an ambition have not the spoiling of him. Serve the Queen! said he. By my faith, and she hath worse servants, from all that I e'er heard of him. And wherefore should he not keep a high head? They that ettle to the top of the ladder will at least get up some rounds. They that mint at a gown of gold will always get a sleeve of it. But come, sir (addressing the stag), you shall go to Glendearg on my two legs somewhat more slowly than you were frisking it even now on your own four nimble shanks. Nay, by my faith, if you be so heavy, I will content me with the best of you, and that's the haunch and the nombles, and e'en heave up the rest on the old oak-tree yonder, and come back for it with one of the yauds."

While Martin returned to Glendearg with the venison, Halbert prosecuted his walk, breathing more easily since he was free of his companion. "The domestic of a proud and lazy priest—body-squire to the Archbishop of St. Andrews," he repeated to himself; "and this, with the privilege of allying his blood with the bailie of Pittenweem, is thought a preferment worth a brave man's struggling for; nay more, a preferment which, if allowed, should crown the hopes, past, present, and to come, of the son of a kirk-vassal! By Heaven, but that I find in me reluctance to practise their acts of nocturnal rapine, I would rather take the jack and lance, and join with the Border riders. Something I will do. Here, degraded and dishonoured, I will not live the scorn of each whiffling stranger from the South, because, forsooth, he wears tinkling spurs on a tawny boot. This thing—this phantom, be it what it will, I will see it once more. Since I spoke with her, and touched her hand, thoughts and feelings have dawned on me of which my former life had not even dreamed; but shall I, who feel my father's glen too narrow for my expanding spirit, brook to be bearded in it by this vain gewgaw of a courtier, and in the sight too of Mary Avenel? I will not stoop to it, by Heaven!"

As he spoke thus, he arrived in the sequestered glen of Corrie-nan-Shian, as it verged upon the hour of noon. A few moments he remained looking upon the fountain, and doubting in his own mind with what countenance the White Lady might receive him. She had not indeed expressly forbidden his again evoking her; but yet there was something like such a prohibition implied in the farewell, which recommended him to wait for another guide.

Halbert Glendinning did not long, however, allow himself to pause. Hardihood was the natural characteristic of his mind; and under the expansion and modification which his feelings had lately undergone it had been augmented rather than diminished. He drew his sword, undid the buskin from his foot, bowed three times with deliberation towards the fountain, and as often towards the tree, and repeated the same rhyme as formerly:

> "Thrice to the holly brake,
>   Thrice to the well;
> I bid thee awake,
>   White Maid of Avenel!
>
> Noon gleams on the lake,
>   Noon glows on the fell;
> Wake thee, O wake,
>   White Maid of Avenel!"

His eye was on the holly bush as he spoke the last line; and

it was not without an involuntary shuddering that he saw the
air betwixt his eye and that object become more dim, and con-
dense, as it were, into the faint appearance of a form, through
which, however, so thin and transparent was the first appearance of the phantom, he could discern the outline of the bush,
as through a veil of fine crape.   But gradually it darkened
into a more substantial appearance, and the White Lady stood
before him with displeasure on her brow.   She spoke, and her
speech was still song, or rather measured chant; but, as if now
more familiar, it flowed occasionally in modulated blank-verse,
and at other times in the lyrical measure which she had used
at their former meeting.

> " This is the day when the fairy kind
>   Sit weeping alone for their hopeless lot,
>   And the wood-maiden sighs to the sighing wind,
>   And the mermaiden weeps in her crystal grot:
>   For this is a day that a deed was wrought
>   In which we have neither part nor share,
>   For the children of clay was salvation bought,
>   But not for the forms of sea or air !
>   And ever the mortal is most forlorn,
>   Who meeteth our race on the Friday morn."

" Spirit," said Halbert Glendinning, boldly, " it is bootless
to threaten one who holds his life at no rate.   Thine anger
can but slay; nor do I think thy power extendeth, or thy will
stretcheth, so far.   The terrors which your race produce upon
others are vain against me.   My heart is hardened against fear,
as by a sense of despair.   If I am, as thy words infer, of a
race more peculiarly the care of Heaven than thine, it is mine
to call, it must be thine to answer.   I am the nobler being."

As he spoke, the figure looked upon him with a fierce and
ireful countenance, which, without losing the similitude of
that which it usually exhibited, had a wilder and more exag-
gerated cast of features.   The eyes seemed to contract and
become more fiery, and slight convulsions passed over the
face, as if it was about to be transformed into something hideous.   The whole appearance resembled those faces which the
imagination summons up when it is disturbed by laudanum,
but which do not remain under the visionary's command, and,

beautiful in their first appearance, become wild and grotesque ere we can arrest them.

But when Halbert had concluded his bold speech, the White Lady stood before him with the same pale, fixed, and melancholy aspect which she usually bore. He had expected the agitation which she exhibited would conclude in some frightful metamorphosis. Folding her arms on her bosom, the phantom replied:

> " Daring youth! for thee it is well,
> Here calling me in haunted dell,
> That thy heart has not quail'd,
> Nor thy courage fail'd,
> And that thou couldst brook
> The angry look
> Of her of Avenel.
> Did one limb shiver,
> Or an eyelid quiver,
> Thou wert lost for ever.
> Though I am form'd from the ether blue,
> And my blood is of the unfallen dew,
> And thou art framed of mud and dust,
> 'Tis thine to speak, reply I must."

" I demand of thee, then," said the youth, " by what charm it is that I am thus altered in mind and in wishes; that I think no longer of deer or dog, of bow or bolt; that my soul spurns the bounds of this obscure glen; that my blood boils at an insult from one by whose stirrup I would some days since have run for a whole summer's morn, contented and honoured by the notice of a single word? Why do I now seek to mate me with princes, and knights, and nobles? Am I the same who but yesterday, as it were, slumbered in contented obscurity, but who am to-day awakened to glory and ambition? Speak—tell me, if thou canst, the meaning of this change! Am I spell-bound, or have I till now been under the influence of a spell, that I feel as another being, yet am conscious of remaining the same? Speak and tell me, is it to thy influence that the change is owing?"

The White Lady replied:

> " A mightier wizard far than I
> Wields o'er the universe his power;
> Him owns the eagle in the sky,
> The turtle in the bower.

> Changeful in shape, yet mightiest still,
> He wields the heart of man at will,
> From ill to good, from good to ill,
> 　　In cot and castle-tower.''

"Speak not thus darkly," said the youth, colouring so deeply that face, neck, and hands were in a sanguine glow; "make me sensible of thy purpose."

The spirit answered:

> "Ask thy heart, whose secret cell
> Is fill'd with Mary Avenel!
> Ask thy pride, why scornful look
> In Mary's view it will not brook?
> Ask it, why thou seek'st to rise
> Among the mighty and the wise,
> Why thou spurn'st thy lowly lot,
> Why thy pastimes are forgot,
> Why thou wouldst in bloody strife
> Mend thy luck or lose thy life?
> Ask thy heart, and it shall tell,
> Sighing from its secret cell,
> 'Tis for Mary Avenel.''

"Tell me, then," said Halbert, his cheek still deeply crimsoned, "thou who hast said to me that which I dared not to say myself, by what means shall I urge my passion—by what means make it known?"

The White Lady replied:

> "Do not ask me;
> On doubts like these thou canst not task me.
> We only see the passing show
> Of human passions' ebb and flow;
> And view the pageant's idle glance
> As mortals eye the northern dance,
> When thousand streamers, flashing bright,
> Career it o'er the brow of night,
> And gazers mark their changeful gleams,
> But feel no influence from their beams."

"Yet thine own fate," replied Halbert, "unless men greatly err, is linked with that of mortals?"

The phantom answered:

> "By ties mysterious link'd, our fated race
> Holds strange connection with the sons of men.
> The star that rose upon the house of Avenel,
> When Norman Ulric first assumed the name,

> That star, when culminating in its orbit,
> Shot from its sphere a drop of diamond dew,
> And this bright font received it; and a Spirit
> Rose from the fountain, and her date of life
> Hath co-existence with the house of Avenel,
> And with the star that rules it."

"Speak yet more plainly," answered young Glendinning; "of this I can understand nothing. Say what hath forged thy weirded link of destiny with the house of Avenel? Say, especially, what fate now overhangs that house?"

The White Lady replied:

> "Look on my girdle—on this thread of gold,
> 'Tis fine as web of lightest gossamer,
> And, but there is a spell on't, would not bind,
> Light as they are, the folds of my thin robe.
> But when 'twas donn'd, it was a massive chain,
> Such as might bind the champion of the Jews,
> Even when his locks were longest; it hath dwindled
> Hath minish'd in its substance and its strength,
> As sunk the greatness of the house of Avenel.
> When this frail thread gives way, I to the elements
> Resign the principles of life they lent me.
> Ask me no more of this! the stars forbid it."

"Then canst thou read the stars," answered the youth, "and mayst tell me the fate of my passion, if thou canst not aid it?"

The White Lady again replied:

> "Dim burns the once bright star of Avenel,
> Dim as the beacon when the morn is nigh,
> And the o'er-wearied warder leaves the light-house;
> There is an influence sorrowful and fearful,
> That dogs its downward course. Disastrous passion,
> Fierce hate and rivalry, are in the aspect
> That lowers upon its fortunes."

"And rivalry!" repeated Glendinning. "It is then as I feared! But shall that English silkworm presume to beard me in my father's house, and in the presence of Mary Avenel? Give me to meet him, spirit—give me to do away the vain distinction of rank on which he refuses me the combat. Place us on equal terms, and gleam the stars with what aspect they will, the sword of my father shall control their influences."

She answered as promptly as before:

> "Complain not of me, child of clay,
> If to thy harm I yield the way.
> We, who soar thy sphere above,
> Know not aught of hate or love;
> As will or wisdom rules thy mood,
> My gifts to evil turn, or good."

"Give me to redeem my honour," said Halbert Glendinning—"give me to retort on my proud rival the insults he has thrown on me, and let the rest fare as it will. If I cannot revenge my wrong, I shall sleep quiet, and know nought of my disgrace."

The phantom failed not to reply:

> "When Piercie Shafton boasteth high,
> Let this token meet his eye.
> The sun is westering from the dell,
> Thy wish is granted, fare thee well!"

As the White Lady spoke or chanted these last words, she undid from her locks a silver bodkin around which they were twisted, and gave it to Halbert Glendinning; then shaking her dishevelled hair till it fell like a veil around her, the outlines of her form gradually became as diffuse as her flowing tresses, her countenance grew pale as the moon in her first quarter, her features became indistinguishable, and she melted into the air.

Habit inures us to wonders; but the youth did not find himself alone by the fountain without experiencing, though in a much less degree, the revulsion of spirits which he had felt upon the phantom's former disappearance. A doubt strongly pressed upon his mind, whether it were safe to avail himself of the gifts of a spirit which did not even pretend to belong to the class of angels, and might, for aught he knew, have a much worse lineage than that which she was pleased to avow. "I will speak of it," he said, "to Edward, who is clerkly learned, and will tell me what I should do. And yet, no—Edward is scrupulous and wary. I will prove the effect of her gift on Sir Piercie Shafton if he again braves me, and by the issue I will be myself a sufficient judge whether there is danger in resorting to her counsel. Home, then—home, and we shall soon learn whether that home shall longer hold me; for not again will I brook insult, with my father's sword by my side and Mary for the spectator of my disgrace."

CHAPTER XVIII.

I give thee eighteenpence a day,
    And my bow shalt thou bear,
And over all the north country,
    I make thee the chief rydere.
And I thirteenpence a day, quoth the queen,
    By God and by my faye;
Come fetch thy payment when thou wilt,
    No man shall say thee nay.

William of Cloudesley.

THE manners of the age did not permit the inhabitants of Glendearg to partake of the collation which was placed in the spence of that ancient tower before the lord abbot and his attendants and Sir Piercie Shafton. Dame Glendinning was excluded both by inferiority of rank and by sex; for (though it was a rule often neglected) the superior of St. Mary's was debarred from taking his meals in female society. To Mary Avenel the latter, and to Edward Glendinning the former, incapacity attached; but it pleased his lordship to require their presence in the apartment, and to say sundry kind words to them upon the ready and hospitable reception which they had afforded him.

The smoking haunch now stood upon the table; a napkin, white as snow, was, with due reverence, tucked under the chin of the abbot by the refectioner; and nought was wanting to commence the repast, save the presence of Sir Piercie Shafton, who at length appeared, glittering like the sun, in a carnation-velvet doublet, slashed and puffed out with cloth of silver, his hat of the newest block, surrounded by a hatband of goldsmith's work, while around his neck he wore a collar of gold, set with rubies and topazes so rich that it vindicated his anxiety for the safety of his baggage from being founded upon his love of mere finery. This gorgeous collar or chain, resembling those worn by the knights of the highest orders of chivalry, fell down on his breast, and terminated in a medallion.

"We waited for Sir Piercie Shafton," said the abbot, hastily assuming his place in the great chair which the kitchener advanced to the table with ready hand.

"I pray your pardon, reverend father and my good lord," replied that pink of courtesy; "I did but wait to cast my riding slough, and to transmew myself into some civil form meeter for this worshipful company."

"I cannot but praise your gallantry, sir knight," said the abbot, "and your prudence also, for choosing the fitting time to appear thus adorned. Certes, had that goodly chain been visible in some part of your late progress, there was risk that the lawful owner might have parted company therewith."

"This chain, said your reverence?" answered Sir Piercie. "Surely it is but a toy, a trifle, a slight thing, which shows but poorly with this doublet; marry, when I wear that of the murrey-coloured, double-piled Genoa velvet, puffed out with ciprus, the gems, being relieved and set off by the darker and more grave ground of the stuff, show like stars giving a lustre through dark clouds."

"I nothing doubt it," said the abbot; "but I pray you to sit down at the board."

But Sir Piercie had now got into his element, and was not easily interrupted. "I own," he continued, "that, slight as the toy is, it might perchance have had some captivation for Julian—— Sancta Maria!" said he, interrupting himself; "what was I about to say, and my fair and beauteous Protection, or shall I rather term her my Discretion, here in presence! Indiscreet had it been in your Affability, O most lovely Discretion, to suffer a stray word to have broke out of the pen-fold of his mouth, that might overleap the fence of civility, and trespass on the manor of decorum."

"Marry!" said the abbot, somewhat impatiently, "the greatest discretion that I can see in the matter is to eat our victuals being hot. Father Eustace, say the *Benedicite*, and cut up the haunch."

The sub-prior readily obeyed the first part of the abbot's injunction, but paused upon the second. "It is Friday, most reverend," he said in Latin, desirous that the hint should escape, if possible, the ears of the stranger.

"We are travellers," said the abbot, in reply, "and *viatoribus licitum est*. You know the canon: a traveller must eat what food his hard fate sets before him. I grant you all a dispensation to eat flesh this day, conditionally that you, brethren, say the *confiteor* at curfew time, that the knight give alms to his ability, and that all and each of you fast from flesh on such day within the next month that shall seem most convenient; wherefore fall to and eat your food with cheerful countenances; and you, father refectioner, *da mixtus*."

While the abbot was thus stating the conditions on which his indulgence was granted, he had already half-finished a slice of the noble haunch, and now washed it down with a flagon of Rhenish, modestly tempered with water.

"Well is it said," he observed, as he required from the refectioner another slice, "that virtue is its own reward; for though this is but humble fare, and hastily prepared, and eaten in a poor chamber, I do not remember me of having had such an appetite since I was a simple brother in the Abbey of Dundrennan, and was wont to labour in the garden from morning until nones, when our abbot struck the *cymbalum*. Then would I enter keen with hunger, parched with thirst—*da mihi vinum, quæso, et merum sit*—and partake with appetite of whatever was set before us, according to our rule; feast or fast-day, *caritas* or *pœnitentia*, was the same to me. I had no stomach complaints then, which now crave both the aid of wine and choice cookery to render my food acceptable to my palate, and easy of digestion."

"It may be, holy father," said the sub-prior, "an occasional ride to the extremity of St. Mary's patrimony may have the same happy effect on your health as the air of the garden at Dundrennan."

"Perchance, with our patroness's blessing, such progresses

may advantage us," said the abbot; "having an especial eye that our venison is carefully killed by some woodman that is master of his craft."

"If the lord abbot will permit me," said the kitchener, "I think the best way to assure his lordship on that important point would be to retain as a yeoman pricker, or deputy-ranger, the eldest son of this good woman, Dame Glendinning, who is here to wait upon us. I should know by mine office what belongs to killing of game, and I can safely pronounce that never saw I, or any other *coquinarius,* a bolt so justly shot. It has cloven the very heart of the buck."

"What speak you to us of one good shot, father?" said Sir Piercie; "I would advise you that such no more maketh a shooter than doth one swallow make a summer. I have seen this springald of whom you speak, and if his hand can send forth his shafts as boldly as his tongue doth utter presumptuous speeches, I will own him as good an archer as Robin Hood."

"Marry," said the abbot, "and it is fitting we know the truth of this matter from the dame herself; for ill-advised were we to give way to any rashness in this matter, whereby the bounties which Heaven and our patroness provide might be unskilfully mangled, and rendered unfit for worthy men's use. Stand forth, therefore, Dame Glendinning, and tell to us, as thy liege lord and spiritual superior, using plainness and truth, without either fear or favour, as being a matter wherein we are deeply interested, doth this son of thine use his bow as well as the father kitchener avers to us?"

"So please your noble fatherhood," answered Dame Glendinning, with a deep courtesy, "I should know somewhat of archery to my cost, seeing my husband—God assoilzie him!—was slain in the field of Pinkie with an arrow-shot, while he was fighting under the Kirk's banner, as became a liege vassal of the halidome. He was a valiant man, please your reverence, and an honest; and saving that he loved a bit of venison, and shifted for his living at a time, as Border men will sometimes do, I wot not of sin that he did. And yet, though I have paid for mass after mass, to the matter of a forty shilling, besides a quarter of wheat and four firlots of rye, I can have no assurance yet that he has been delivered from purgatory."

"Dame," said the lord abbot, "this shall be looked into heedfully; and since thy husband fell, as thou sayest, in the Kirk's quarrel, and under her banner, rely upon it that we will have him out of purgatory forthwith—that is, always provided he be there. But it is not of thy husband whom we now devise to speak, but of thy son; not of a shot Scotsman, but of a shot deer. Wherefore I say answer me to the point, is thy son a practised archer, ay or no?"

"Alack! my reverend lord," replied the widow, "and my croft would be better tilled if I could answer your reverence that he is not. Practised archer! Marry, holy sir, I would he would practise something else—cross-bow and long-bow, hand-gun and hackbut, falconet and saker, he can shoot with them all. And if it would please this right honourable gentleman, our guest, to hold out his hat at the distance of a hundred yards, our Halbert shall send shaft, bolt, or bullet through it—so that right honourable gentleman swerve not, but hold out steady—and I will forfeit a quarter of barley if he touch but a knot of his ribands. I have seen our Old Martin do as much, and so has our right reverend the sub-prior, if he be pleased to remember it."

"I am not like to forget it, dame," said Father Eustace; "for I knew not which most to admire, the composure of the young marksman or the steadiness of the old mark. Yet I presume not to advise Sir Piercie Shafton to subject his valuable beaver, and yet more valuable person, to such a risk, unless it should be his own special pleasure."

"Be assured it is not," said Sir Piercie Shafton, something hastily—"be well assured, holy father, that it is not. I dispute not the lad's qualities, for which your reverence vouches. But bows are but wood, strings are but flax, or the silkworm's excrement at best, archers are but men: fingers may slip, eyes may dazzle, the blindest may hit the butt, the best marker may shoot a bow's length beside. Therefore will we try no perilous experiments."

"Be that as you will, Sir Piercie," said the abbot; "meantime, we will name this youth bow-bearer in the forest granted to us by good King David, that the chase might recreate our wearied spirits, the flesh of the deer improve our poor commons, and the hides cover the books of our library; thus tending at once to the sustenance of body and soul."

"Kneel down, woman—kneel down," said the refectioner and the kitchener with one voice to Dame Glendinning, "and kiss his lordship's hand for the grace which he has granted to thy son."

They then, as if they had been chanting the service and the responses, set off in a sort of duetto, enumerating the advantages of the situation.

"A green gown and a pair of leathern galligaskins every Pentecost," said the kitchener.

"Four marks by the year at Candlemas," answered the refectioner.

"An hogshead of ale at Martlemas, of the double strike, and single ale at pleasure, as he shall agree with the cellarer——"

"Who is a reasonable man," said the abbot, "and will encourage an active servant of the convent."

"A mess of broth and a dole of mutton or beef at the kitchener's on each high holiday," resumed the kitchener.

"The gang of two cows and a palfrey on Our Lady's meadow," answered his brother-officer.

"An ox-hide to make buskins of yearly, because of the brambles," echoed the kitchener.

"And various other perquisites, *quæ nunc præscribere longum*," said the abbot, summing, with his own lordly voice, the advantages attached to the office of conventual bow-bearer.

Dame Glendinning was all this while on her knees, her head mechanically turning from the one church-officer to the other, which, as they stood one on each side of her, had much the appearance of a figure moved by clock-work, and so soon as they were silent, most devoutly did she kiss the munificent hand of the abbot. Conscious, however, of Halbert's intractability in some points, she could not help qualifying her grateful and reiterated thanks for the abbot's bountiful proffer with a hope that Halbert would see his wisdom, and accept of it.

"How," said the abbot, bending his brows, "accept of it! Woman, is thy son in his right wits?"

Elspeth, stunned by the tone in which this question was asked, was altogether unable to reply to it. Indeed, any answer she might have made could hardly have been heard, as it pleased the two office-bearers of the abbot's table again to recommence their alternate dialogue.

"Refuse!" said the kitchener.

"Refuse!" answered the refectioner, echoing the other's word in a tone of still louder astonishment.

"Refuse four marks by the year!" said the one.

"Ale and beer—broth and mutton—cow's grass and palfrey's!" shouted the kitchener.

"Gown and galligaskins!" responded the refectioner.

"A moment's patience, my brethren," answered the subprior, "and let us not be thus astonished before cause is afforded of our amazement. This good dame best knoweth the temper and spirit of her son; this much I can say, that it lieth not towards letters or learning, of which I have in vain endeavoured to instil into him some tincture. Nevertheless, he is a youth of no common spirit, but much like those, in my judgment, whom God raises up among a people when He meaneth that their deliverance shall be wrought out with strength of hand and valour of heart. Such men we have seen marked by a waywardness, and even an obstinacy, of character which hath appeared intractability and stupidity to those among whom they walked and were conversant, until the very opportunity hath arrived in which it was the will of Providence that they should be the fitting instrument of great things."

"Now, in good time hast thou spoken, Father Eustace," said the abbot; "and we will see this swankie before we decide upon the means of employing him. How say you, Sir Piercie Shafton, is it not the court fashion to suit the man to the office, and not the office to the man?"

"So please your reverence and lordship," answered the Northumbrian knight, "I do partly, that is, in some sort, subscribe to what your wisdom hath delivered. Nevertheless, under reverence of the sub-prior, we do not look for gallant leaders and national deliverers in the hovels of the mean common people. Credit me, that if there be some flashes of martial spirit about this young person, which I am not called upon to dispute, though I have seldom seen that presumption and arrogance were made good upon the upshot by deed and action; yet still these will prove insufficient to distinguish him, save in his own limited and lowly sphere, even as the glowworm, which makes a goodly show among the grass of the field, would be of little avail if deposited in a beacon-grate."

"Now, in good time," said the sub-prior, "and here comes the young huntsman to speak for himself"; for, being placed opposite to the window, he could observe Halbert as he ascended the little mound on which the tower was situated.

"Summon him to our presence," said the lord abbot; and with an obedient start the two attendant monks went off with emulous alertness. Dame Glendinning sprung away at the same moment, partly to gain an instant to recommend obedience to her son, partly to prevail with him to change his apparel before coming in presence of the abbot. But the kitchener and refectioner, both speaking at once, had already seized each an arm, and were leading Halbert in triumph into the apartment, so that she could only ejaculate: "His will be done; but an he had but had on him his Sunday's hose!"

Limited and humble as this desire was, the fates did not grant it; for Halbert Glendinning was hurried into the presence of the lord abbot and his party without a word of explanation, and without a moment's time being allowed to assume his holiday hose, which, in the language of the time, implied both breeches and stockings.

Yet, though thus suddenly presented amid the centre of all eyes, there was something in Halbert's appearance which commanded a certain degree of respect from the company into which he was so unceremoniously intruded, and the greater part of whom were disposed to consider him with hauteur, if not with absolute contempt. But his appearance and reception we must devote to another chapter.

CHAPTER XIX.

Now choose thee, gallant, betwixt wealth and honour;
There lies the pelf, in sum to bear thee through
The dance of youth and he turmoil of manhood,
Yet leave enough for age's chimney-corner;
But an thou grasp to it, farewell ambition,
Farewell each hope of bettering thy condition,
And raising thy low rank above the churls
That till the earth for bread.

Old Play.

IT is necessary to dwell for some brief space on the appearance and demeanour of young Glendinning, ere we proceed to describe his interview with the abbot of St. Mary's, at this momentous crisis of his life.

Halbert was now about nineteen years old, tall and active rather than strong, yet of that hardy conformation of limb and sinew which promises great strength when the growth shall be complete and the system confirmed. He was perfectly well made, and, like most men who have that advantage, possessed a grace and natural ease of manner and carriage which prevented his height from being the distinguished part of his external appearance. It was not until you had compared his stature with that of those amongst or near to whom he stood that you became sensible that the young Glendinning was upwards of six feet high. In the combination of unusual height with perfect symmetry, ease, and grace of carriage, the young heir of Glendearg, notwithstanding his rustic birth and education, had greatly the advantage even of Sir Piercie Shafton himself, whose stature was lower, and his limbs, though there was no particular point to object to, were on the whole less exactly proportioned. On the other hand, Sir Piercie's very handsome countenance afforded him as decided an advantage over the Scotsman as regularity of features and brilliance of complexion could give over traits which were rather strongly marked than beautiful, and upon whose complexion the "skyey influences," to which he was constantly exposed, had blended the red and white into the purely nutbrown hue, which coloured alike cheeks, neck, and forehead,

16

and blushed only in a darker glow upon the former. Halbert's eyes supplied a marked and distinguished part of his physiognomy. They were large and of a hazel [1] colour, and sparkled in moments of animation with such uncommon brilliancy that it seemed as if they actually emitted light. Nature had closely curled the locks of dark-brown hair, which relieved and set off the features, such as we have described them, displaying a bold and animated disposition, much more than might have been expected from his situation, or from his previous manners, which hitherto had seemed bashful, homely, and awkward.

Halbert's dress was certainly not of that description which sets off to the best advantage a presence of itself prepossessing. His jerkin and hose were of coarse rustic cloth, and his cap of the same. A belt round his waist served at once to sustain the broadsword which we have already mentioned, and to hold five or six arrows and bird-bolts, which were stuck into it on the right side, along with a large knife hilted with buck-horn, or, as it was then called, a dudgeon-dagger. To complete his dress, we must notice his loose buskins of deer's-hide, formed so as to draw up on the leg as high as the knee, or at pleasure to be thrust down lower than the calves. These were generally used at the period by such as either had their principal occupation or their chief pleasure in silvan sports, as they served to protect the legs against the rough and tangled thickets into which the pursuit of game frequently led them. And these trifling particulars complete his external appearance.

It is not so easy to do justice to the manner in which young Glendinning's soul spoke through his eyes, when ushered so suddenly into the company of those whom his earliest education had taught him to treat with awe and reverence. The degree of embarrassment which his demeanour evinced had nothing in it either meanly servile or utterly disconcerted. It was no more than became a generous and ingenuous youth of a bold spirit, but totally inexperienced, who should for the first time be called upon to think and act for himself in such society, and under such disadvantageous circumstances.

[1] [See p. 71 above.]

There was not in his carriage a grain either of forwardness or of timidity which a friend could have wished away.

He kneeled and kissed the abbot's hand, then rose, and, retiring two paces, bowed respectfully to the circle around, smiling gently as he received an encouraging nod from the sub-prior, to whom alone he was personally known, and blushing as he encountered the anxious look of Mary Avenel, who beheld with painful interest the sort of ordeal to which her foster-brother was about to be subjected. Recovering from the transient flurry of spirits into which the encounter of her glance had thrown him, he stood composedly awaiting till the abbot should express his pleasure.

The ingenuous expression of countenance, noble form, and graceful attitude of the young man failed not to prepossess in his favour the churchmen in whose presence he stood. The abbot looked round and exchanged a gracious and approving glance with his counsellor, Father Eustace, although probably the appointment of a ranger, or bow-bearer, was one in which he might have been disposed to proceed without the sub-prior's advice, were it but to show his own free agency. But the good mien of the young man now in nomination was such that he rather hastened to exchange congratulation on meeting with so proper a subject of promotion than to indulge any other feeling. Father Eustace enjoyed the pleasure which a well-constituted mind derives from seeing a benefit light on a deserving object; for, as he had not seen Halbert since circumstances had made so material a change in his manner and feelings, he scarce doubted that the proffered appointment would, notwithstanding his mother's uncertainty, suit the disposition of a youth who had appeared devoted to woodland sports, and a foe alike to sedentary or settled occupation of any kind. The refectioner and kitchener were so well pleased with Halbert's prepossessing appearance that they seemed to think that the salary, emoluments, and perquisites, the dole, the grazing, the gown, and the galligaskins could scarce be better bestowed than on the active and graceful figure before them.

Sir Piercie Shafton, whether from being more deeply engaged in his own cogitations or that the subject was unworthy of his notice, did not seem to partake of the general feeling of approbation excited by the young man's presence. He sate with his eyes half-shut, and his arms folded, appearing to be wrapped in contemplations of a nature deeper than those arising out of the scene before him. But, notwithstanding his seeming abstraction and absence of mind, there was a flutter of vanity in Sir Piercie's very handsome countenance, an occasional change of posture from one striking attitude (or what he conceived to be such) to another, and an occasional stolen glance at the female part of the company, to spy how far he succeeded in riveting their attention, which gave a marked advantage, in comparison, to the less regular and more harsh features of Halbert Glendinning, with their composed, manly, and deliberate expression of mental fortitude.

Of the females belonging to the family of Glendearg, the miller's daughter alone had her mind sufficiently at leisure to admire, from time to time, the graceful attitudes of Sir Piercie Shafton; for both Mary Avenel and Dame Glendinning were waiting in anxiety and apprehension the answer which Halbert was to return to the abbot's proposal, and fearfully anticipating the consequences of his probable refusal. The conduct of his brother Edward, for a lad constitutionally shy, respectful, and even timid, was at once affectionate and noble. This younger son of Dame Elspeth had stood unnoticed in a corner, after the abbot, at the request of the sub-prior, had honoured him with some passing notice, and asked him a few commonplace questions about his progress in Donatus, and in the *Promptuarium Parvulorum*, without waiting for the answers. From his corner he now glided round to his brother's side, and keeping a little behind him, slid his right hand into the huntsman's left, and by a gentle pressure, which Halbert instantly and ardently returned, expressed at once his interest in his situation and his resolution to share his fate.

The group was thus arranged when, after the pause of two or three minutes, which he employed in slowly sipping his cup of wine, in order that he might enter on his proposal with

due and deliberate dignity, the abbot at length expressed himself thus:

"My son, we, your lawful superior, and the abbot, under
God's favour, of the community of St. Mary's, have heard of
your manifold good gifts—a-hem—especially touching wood-
craft, and the huntsman-like fashion in which you strike your
game, truly and as a yeoman should, not abusing Heaven's
good benefits by spoiling the flesh, as is too often seen in
careless rangers—a-hem." He made here a pause, but observing that Glendinning only replied to his compliment by
a bow, he proceeded: "My son, we commend your modesty;
nevertheless, we will that thou shouldst speak freely to us
touching that which we have premeditated for thine advancement, meaning to confer on thee the office of bow-bearer and
ranger, as well over the chases and forests wherein our house
hath privilege by the gifts of pious kings and nobles, whose
souls now enjoy the fruits of their bounties to the church, as
to those which belong to us in exclusive right of property and
perpetuity. Thy knee, my son, that we may, with our own
hand, and without loss of time, induct thee into office."

"Kneel down," said the kitchener on the one side; and
"Kneel down," said the refectioner on the other.

But Halbert Glendinning remained standing.

"Were it to show gratitude and good-will for your reverend
lordship's noble offer, I could not," he said, "kneel low enough,
or remain long enough kneeling. But I may not kneel to take
investiture of your noble gift, my lord abbot, being a man determined to seek my fortune otherwise."

"How is that, sir?" said the abbot, knitting his brows;
"do I hear you speak aright? and do you, a born vassal of
the halidome, at the moment when I am destining to you such
a noble expression of my good-will, propose exchanging my
service for that of any other?"

"My lord," said Halbert Glendinning, "it grieves me to
think you hold me capable of undervaluing your gracious
offer, or of exchanging your service for another. But your
noble proffer doth but hasten the execution of a determination
which I have long since formed."

"Ay, my son," said the abbot, "is i. indeed so? right early have you learned to form resolutions without consulting those on whom you naturally depend. But what may it be, this sagacious resolution, if I may so far pray you?"

"To yield up to my brother and mother," answered Halbert, "mine interest in the fief of Glendearg, lately possessed by my father, Simon Glendinning; and having prayed your lordship to be the same kind and generous master to them that your predecessors, the venerable abbots of St. Mary's, have been to my fathers in time past—for myself, I am determined to seek my fortune where I may best find it."

Dame Glendinning here ventured, emboldened by maternal anxiety, to break silence with an exclamation of "O my son!" Edward, clinging to his brother's side, half-spoke, half-whispered a similar ejaculation of "Brother! brother!"

The sub-prior took up the matter in a tone of grave reprehension, which, as he conceived, the interest he had always taken in the family of Glendearg required at his hand.

"Wilful young man," he said, "what folly can urge thee to push back the hand that is stretched out to aid thee? What visionary aim hast thou before thee, that can compensate for the decent and sufficient independence which thou art now rejecting with scorn?"

"Four marks by the year, duly and truly," said the kitchener.

"Cow's grass, doublet, and galligaskins," responded the refectioner.

"Peace, my brethren," said the sub-prior; "and may it please your lordship, venerable father, upon my petition, to allow this headstrong youth a day for consideration, and it shall be my part so to indoctrinate him as to convince him what is due on this occasion to your lordship, and to his family, and to himself."

"Your kindness, reverend father," said the youth, "craves my dearest thanks; it is the continuance of a long train of benevolence towards me, for which I give you my gratitude, for I have nothing else to offer. It is my mishap, not your fault, that your intentions have been frustrated. But my

present resolution is fixed and unalterable. I cannot accept
the generous offer of the lord abbot; my fate calls me elsewhere, to scenes where I shall end it or mend it."

"By Our Lady," said the abbot, "I think the youth be mad
indeed; or that you, Sir Piercie, judged of him most truly,
when you prophesied that he would prove unfit for the promotion we designed him. It may be you knew something of
this wayward humour before?"

"By the mass, not I," answered Sir Piercie Shafton, with
his usual indifference. "I but judged of him by his birth
and breeding; for seldom doth a good hawk come out of a
kite's egg."

"Thou art thyself a kite, and kestrel to boot," replied Halbert Glendinning, without a moment's hesitation.

"This in our presence, and to a man of worship!" said the
abbot, the blood rushing to his face.

"Yes, my lord," answered the youth; "even in your presence I return to this gay man's face the causeless dishonour
which he has flung on my name. My brave father, who fell
in the cause of his country, demands that justice at the hands
of his son!"

"Unmannered boy!" said the abbot.

"Nay, my good lord," said the knight, "praying pardon for
the coarse interruption, let me entreat you not to be wroth
with this rustical. Credit me, the north wind shall as soon
puff one of your rocks from its basis, as aught which I hold
so slight and inconsiderate as the churlish speech of an untaught churl shall move the spleen of Piercie Shafton."

"Proud as you are, sir knight," said Halbert, "in your
imagined superiority, be not too confident that you cannot be
moved."

"Faith, by nothing that thou canst urge," said Sir Piercie.

"Knowest thou then this token?" said young Glendinning,
offering to him the silver bodkin which he had received from
the White Lady.

Never was such an instant change, from the most contemptuous serenity to the most furious state of passion, as that
which Sir Piercie Shafton exhibited. It was the difference

between a cannon lying quiet in its embrasure and the same
gun when touched by the linstock. He started up, every
limb quivering with rage, and his features so inflamed and
agitated by passion that he more resembled a demoniac than
a man under the regulation of reason. He clenched both his
fists, and, thrusting them forward, offered them furiously at
the face of Glendinning, who was even himself startled at the
frantic state of excitement which his action had occasioned.
The next moment he withdrew them, struck his open palm
against his own forehead, and rushed out of the room in a
state of indescribable agitation. The whole matter had been
so sudden that no person present had time to interfere.

When Sir Piercie Shafton had left the apartment, there was
a moment's pause of astonishment, and then a general demand
that Halbert Glendinning should instantly explain by what
means he had produced such a violent change in the deport-
ment of the English cavalier.

"I did nought to him," answered Halbert Glendinning, "but
what you all saw. Am I to answer for his fantastic freaks of
humour?"

"Boy," said the abbot, in his most authoritative manner,
"these subterfuges shall not avail thee. This is not a man
to be driven from his temperament without some sufficient
cause. That cause was given by thee, and must have been
known to thee. I command thee, as thou wilt save thyself
from worse measure, to explain to me by what means thou
hast moved our friend thus. We choose not that our vassals
shall drive our guests mad in our very presence, and we remain ignorant of the means whereby that purpose is effected."

"So may it please your reverence, I did but show him this
token," said Halbert Glendinning, delivering it at the same
time to the abbot, who looked at it with much attention, and
then, shaking his head, gravely delivered it to the sub-prior,
without speaking a word.

Father Eustace looked at the mysterious token with some
attention; and then addressing Halbert in a stern and severe
voice, said: "Young man, if thou wouldst not have us suspect
thee of some strange double-dealing in this matter, let us in-

stantly know whence thou hadst this token, and how it possesses an influence on Sir Piercie Shafton?"

It would have been extremely difficult for Halbert, thus
hard pressed, to have either evaded or answered so puzzling
a question. To have avowed the truth might, in those times,
have occasioned his being burnt at a stake, although in ours
his confession would have only gained for him the credit of
a liar beyond all rational credibility. He was fortunately relieved by the return of Sir Piercie Shafton himself, whose ear
caught, as he entered, the sound of the sub-prior's question.

Without waiting until Halbert Glendinning replied, he came
forward, whispering to him as he passed: "Be secret; thou
shalt have the satisfaction thou hast dared to seek for."

When he returned to his place, there were still marks of
discomposure on his brow; but, becoming apparently collected
and calm, he looked around him, and apologised for the inde-
corum of which he had been guilty, which he ascribed to sudden and severe indisposition. All were silent, and looked on
each other with some surprise.

The lord abbot gave orders for all to retire from the apartment, save himself, Sir Piercie Shafton, and the sub-prior.
"And have an eye," he added, "on that bold youth, that he
escape not; for if he hath practised by charm, or otherwise,
on the health of our worshipful guest, I swear by the alb and
mitre which I wear that his punishment shall be most exemplary."

"My lord and venerable father," said Halbert, bowing respectfully, "fear not but that I will abide my doom. I think
you will best learn from the worshipful knight himself what
is the cause of his distemperature, and how slight my share
in it has been."

"Be assured," said the knight, without looking up, however, while he spoke, "I will satisfy the lord abbot."

With these words the company retired, and with them
young Glendinning.

When the abbot, the sub-prior, and the English knight
were left alone, Father Eustace, contrary to his custom, could
not help speaking the first. "Expound unto us, noble sir,"

he said, "by what mysterious means the production of this simple toy could so far move your spirit, and overcome your patience, after you had shown yourself proof to all the provo-cation offered by this self-sufficient and singular youth."

The knight took the silver bodkin from the good father's hand, looked at it with great composure, and having examined it all over, returned it to the sub-prior, saying at the same time: "In truth, venerable father, I cannot but marvel that the wisdom implied alike in your silver hairs and in your eminent rank should, like a babbling hound—excuse the similitude—open thus loudly on a false scent. I were, indeed, more slight to be moved than the leaves of the aspen-tree, which wag at the least breath of heaven, could I be touched by such a trifle as this, which in no way concerns me more than if the same quantity of silver were stricken into so many groats. Truth is, that from my youth upward I have been subjected to such a malady as you saw me visited with even now—a cruel and searching pain, which goeth through nerve and bone, even as a good brand in the hands of a brave soldier sheers through limb and sinew; but it passes away speedily, as you yourselves may judge."

"Still," said the sub-prior, "this will not account for the youth offering to you this piece of silver, as a token by which you were to understand something, and, as we must needs conjecture, something disagreeable."

"Your reverence is to conjecture what you will," said Sir Piercie; "but I cannot pretend to lay your judgment on the right scent when I see it at fault. I hope I am not liable to be called upon to account for the foolish actions of a malapert boy?"

"Assuredly," said the sub-prior, "we shall prosecute no inquiry which is disagreeable to our guest. Nevertheless," said he, looking to his superior, "this chance may, in some sort, alter the plan your lordship had formed for your worshipful guest's residence for a brief term in this tower, as a place alike of secrecy and of security; both of which, in the terms which we now stand on with England, are circumstances to be desired."

"In truth," said the abbot, "and the doubt is well thought on, were it as well removed; for I scarce know in the hali-dome so fitting a place of refuge, yet see I not how to recommend it to our worshipful guest, considering the unrestrained petulance of this headstrong youth."

"Tush! reverend sirs, what would you make of me?" said Sir Piercie Shafton. "I protest, by mine honour, I would abide in this house were I to choose. What! I take no exceptions at the youth for showing a flash of spirit, though the spark may light on mine own head. I honour the lad for it. I protest I will abide here, and he shall aid me in striking down a deer. I must needs be friends with him, an he be such a shot; and we will speedily send down to my lord abbot a buck of the first head, killed so artificially as shall satisfy even the reverend kitchener."

This was said with such apparent ease and good-humour that the abbot made no farther observation on what had passed, but proceeded to acquaint his guest with the details of furniture, hangings, provisions, and so forth which he proposed to send up to the Tower of Glendearg for his accommodation. This discourse, seasoned with a cup or two of wine, served to prolong the time until the reverend abbot ordered his cavalcade to prepare for their return to the monastery.

"As we have," he said, "in the course of this our toilsome journey, lost our meridian, indulgence shall be given to those of our attendants who shall, from very weariness, be unable to attend the duty at prime, and this by way of misericord [1] or *indulgentia*."

Having benevolently intimated a boon to his faithful followers which he probably judged would be far from unacceptable, the good abbot, seeing all ready for his journey, bestowed his blessing on the assembled household; gave his hand to be kissed by Dame Glendinning, himself kissed the cheek of Mary Avenel, and even of the miller's maiden, when they approached to render him the same homage; commanded Halbert to rule his temper, and to be aiding and obedient in all things to the English knight; admonished Edward to be *discipulus impiger*

[1] See **Note** 16.

atque strenuus; then took a courteous farewell of Sir Piercie Shafton, advising him to lie close, for fear of the English Borderers, who might be employed to kidnap him; and having discharged these various offices of courtesy, moved forth to the courtyard, followed by the whole establishment. Here, with a heavy sigh approaching to a groan, the venerable father heaved himself upon his palfrey, whose dark purple housings swept the ground; and, greatly comforted that the discretion of the animal's pace would be no longer disturbed by the gambadoes of Sir Piercie and his prancing war-horse, he set forth at a sober and steady trot upon his return to the monastery.

When the sub-prior had mounted to accompany his principal, his eye sought out Halbert, who, partly hidden by a projection of the outward wall of the court, stood apart from, and gazing upon, the departing cavalcade and the group which assembled around them. Unsatisfied with the explanation he had received concerning the mysterious transaction of the silver bodkin, yet interesting himself in the youth, of whose character he had formed a favourable idea, the worthy monk resolved to take an early opportunity of investigating that matter. In the mean while, he looked upon Halbert with a serious and warning aspect, and held up his finger to him as he signed farewell. He then joined the rest of the churchmen, and followed his superior down the valley.

CHAPTER XX.

I hope you'll give me cause to think you noble,
And do me right with your sword, sir, as becomes
One gentleman of honour to another;
All this is fair, sir—let us make no days on't,
I'll lead your way.

Love's Pilgrimage.

THE look and sign of warning which the sub-prior gave to Halbert Glendinning as they parted went to his heart; for, although he had profited much less than Edward by the good man's instructions, he had a sincere reverence for his person; and even the short time he had for deliberation tended to show him he was embarked in a perilous adventure. The nature of the provocation which he had given to Sir Piercie Shafton he could not even conjecture; but he saw that it was of a mortal quality, and he was now to abide the consequences.

That he might not force these consequences forward by any premature renewal of their quarrel, he resolved to walk apart for an hour, and consider on what terms he was to meet this haughty foreigner. The time seemed propitious for his doing so without having the appearance of wilfully shunning the stranger, as all the members of the little household were dispersing, either to perform such tasks as had been interrupted by the arrival of the dignitaries, or to put in order what had been deranged by their visit.

Leaving the tower, therefore, and descending, unobserved, as he thought, the knoll on which it stood, Halbert gained the little piece of level ground which extended betwixt the descent of the hill and the first sweep made by the brook after washing the foot of the eminence on which the tower was situated, where a few straggling birch and oak trees served to secure him from observation. But scarcely had he reached the spot when he was surprised to feel a smart tap upon the shoulder, and, turning around, he perceived he had been closely followed by Sir Piercie Shafton.

When, whether from our state of animal spirits, want of confidence in the justice of our cause, or any other motive, our own courage happens to be in a wavering condition, nothing tends so much altogether to disconcert us as a great appearance of promptitude on the part of our antagonist. Halbert Glendinning, both morally and constitutionally intrepid, was nevertheless somewhat troubled at seeing the stranger, whose resentment he had provoked, appear at once before him, and with an aspect which boded hostility. But, though his heart might beat somewhat thicker, he was too high-spirited to exhibit any external signs of emotion. " What is your pleasure, Sir Piercie?" he said to the English knight, enduring without apparent discomposure all the terrors which his antagonist had summoned into his aspect.

"What is my pleasure?" answered Sir Piercie; "a goodly question, after the part you have acted towards me. Young men, I know not what infatuation has led thee to place thyself in direct and insolent opposition to one who is a guest of thy liege lord the abbot, and who, even from the courtesy due to thy mother's roof, had a right to remain there without meeting insult. Neither do I ask, or care, by what means thou hast become possessed of the fatal secret by which thou hast dared to offer me open shame. But I must now tell thee that the possession of it hath cost thee thy life."

"Not, I trust, if my hand and sword can defend it." replied Halbert, boldly.

"True," said the Englishman; "I mean not to deprive thee of thy fair chance of self-defence. I am only sorry to think that, young and country-bred as thou art, it can but little avail thee. But thou must be well aware that in this quarrel I shall use no terms of quarter."

"Rely on it, proud man," answered the youth, "that I shall ask none; and although thou speakest as if I lay already at thy feet, trust me that, as I am determined never to ask thy mercy, so I am not fearful of needing it."

"Thou wilt, then," said the knight, "do nothing to avert the certain fate which thou hast provoked with such wantonness?"

"And how were that to be purchased?" replied Halbert Glendinning, more with the wish of obtaining some farther insight into the terms on which he stood with this stranger than to make him the submission which he might require.

"Explain to me instantly," said Sir Piercie, "without equivocation or delay, by what means thou wert enabled to wound my honour so deeply; and shouldst thou point out to me by so doing an enemy more worthy of my resentment, I will permit thine own obscure insignificance to draw a veil over thine insolence."

"This is too high a flight," said Glendinning, fiercely, "for thine own presumption to soar without being checked. Thou hast come to my father's house, as well as I can guess, a fugitive and an exile, and thy first greeting to its inhabitants has been that of contempt and injury. By what means I have been able to retort that contempt, let thine own conscience tell thee. Enough for me that I stand on the privilege of a free Scotchman, and will brook no insult unreturned and no injury unrequited."

"It is well, then," said Sir Piercie Shafton; "we will dispute this matter to-morrow morning with our swords. Let the time be daybreak, and do thou assign the place. We will go forth as if to strike a deer."

"Content," replied Halbert Glendinning; "I will guide thee to a spot where an hundred men might fight and fall without any chance of interruption."

"It is well," answered Sir Piercie Shafton. "Here then we part. Many will say that, in thus indulging the right of a gentleman to the son of a clod-breaking peasant, I derogate from my sphere, even as the blessed sun would derogate should he condescend to compare and match his golden beams with the twinkle of a pale, blinking, expiring, gross-fed taper. But no consideration of rank shall prevent my avenging the insult thou hast offered me. We bear a smooth face, observe me, sir villagio, before the worshipful inmates of yonder cabin, and to-morrow we try conclusions with our swords." So saying, he turned away towards the tower.

It may not be unworthy of notice, that in the last speech only had Sir Piercie used some of those flowers of rhetoric which characterised the usual style of his conversation. Apparently, a sense of wounded honour, and the deep desire of vindicating his injured feelings, had proved too strong for the fantastic affectation of his acquired habits. Indeed, such is usually the influence of energy of mind, when called forth and exerted, that Sir Piercie Shafton had never appeared in the eyes of his youthful antagonist half so much deserving of esteem and respect as in this brief dialogue, by which they exchanged mutual defiance. As he followed him slowly to the tower, he could not help thinking to himself that, had the English knight always displayed this superior tone of bearing and feeling, he would not probably have felt so earnestly disposed to take offence at his hand. Mortal offence, however, had been exchanged, and the matter was to be put to mortal arbitrement.

The family met at the evening meal, when Sir Piercie Shafton extended the benignity of his countenance and the graces of his conversation far more generally over the party than he had hitherto condescended to do. The greater part of his attention was, of course, still engrossed by his divine and inimitable Discretion, as he chose to term Mary Avenel; but, nevertheless, there were interjectional flourishes to the Maid of the Mill, under the title of Comely Damsel, and to the dame, under that of Worthy Matron. Nay, lest he should fail to excite their admiration by the graces of his rhetoric, he generously, and without solicitation, added those of his voice; and after regretting bitterly the absence of his viol-de-gamba, he regaled them with a song, "which," said he, "the inimitable Astrophel, whom mortals call Philip Sidney, composed in the nonage of his muse, to show the world what they are to expect from his riper years, and which will one day see the light in that not-to-be-paralleled perfection of human wit which he has addressed to his sister, the matchless Parthenope, whom men call Countess of Pembroke; a work," he continued, "whereof his friendship hath permitted me, though unworthy, to be an occasional partaker, and whereof I may well say that the deep afflictive tale which awakeneth our sorrows is so relieved with brilliant similitudes, dulcet descriptions, pleasant poems, and engaging interludes that they seem as the stars of the firmament beautifying the dusky robe of night. And though I wot well how much the lovely and quaint language will suffer by my widowed voice—widowed in that it is no longer matched by my beloved viol-de-gamba—I will essay to give you a taste of the ravishing sweetness of the poesy of the un-to-be-imitated Astrophel."

So saying, he sung without mercy or remorse about five hundred verses, of which the two first and the four last may suffice for a specimen:

> " What tongue can her perfections tell,
> On whose each part all pens may dwell?
>
> .   .   .   .
>
> Of whose high praise and praiseful bliss,
> Goodness the pen, Heaven paper is;
> The ink immortal fame doth send,
> As I began so I must end."

As Sir Piercie Shafton always sung with his eyes half-shut, it was not until, agreeably to the promise of his poetry, he had fairly made an end that, looking round, he discovered that the greater part of his audience had, in the mean while, yielded to the charms of repose. Mary Avenel, indeed, from a natural sense of politeness, had contrived to keep awake through all the prolixities of the divine Astrophel; but Mysie was transported in dreams back to the dusty atmosphere of her father's mill; Edward himself, who had given his attention for some time, had at length fallen fast asleep; and the good dame's nose, could its tones have been put under regulation, might have supplied the bass of the lamented viol-de-gamba. Halbert, however, who had no temptation to give way to the charms of slumber, remained awake, with his eyes fixed on the songster; not that he was better entertained with the words, or more ravished with the execution, than the rest of the company, but rather because he admired, or perhaps envied, the composure which could thus spend the evening in interminable madrigals, when the next morning was to be devoted to deadly combat. Yet it struck his natural acuteness of observation that the eye of the gallant cavalier did now and then, furtively as it were, seek a glance of his countenance, as if to discover how he was taking the exhibition of his antagonist's composure and serenity of mind.

"He shall read nothing in my countenance," thought Halbert, proudly, "that can make him think my indifference less than his own."

And taking from the shelf a bag full of miscellaneous matters collected for the purpose, he began with great industry to dress hooks, and had finished half a dozen of flies (we are enabled, for the benefit of those who admire the antiquities of the gentle art of angling, to state that they were brown

17

hackles) by the time that Sir Piercie had arrived at the conclu·
sion of his long-winded strophes of the divine Astrophel.   So
that he also testified a magnanimous contempt of that which
to-morrow should bring forth.

As it now waxed late, the family of Glendearg separated for
the evening; Sir Piercie first saying to the dame that "Her
son Albert——"

"Halbert," said Elspeth, with emphasis—"Halbert; after
his goodsire, Halbert Brydone."

"Well, then, I have prayed your son, Halbert, that we may
strive to-morrow, with the sun's earliness, to wake a stag from
his lair, that I may see whether he be as prompt at that sport
as fame bespeaks him."

"Alas! sir," answered Dame Elspeth, "he is but too prompt,
an you talk of promptitude, at anything that has steel at one
end of it and mischief at the other.   But he is at your honourable disposal, and I trust you will teach him how obedience
is due to our venerable father and lord, the abbot, and prevail
with him to take the bow-bearer's place in fee; for, as the two
worthy monks said, it will be a great help to a widow woman."

"Trust me, good dame," replied Sir Piercie, "it is my purpose so to indoctrinate him touching his conduct and bearing
towards his betters that he shall not lightly depart from the
reverence due to them.   We meet, then, beneath the birch-
trees in the plain," he said, looking to Halbert, "so soon as
the eye of day hath opened its lids."   Halbert answered with
a sign of acquiescence, and the knight proceeded: "And now,
having wished to my fairest Discretion those pleasant dreams
which wave their pinions around the couch of sleeping beauty,
and to this comely damsel the bounties of Morpheus, and to all
others the common good-night, I will crave you leave to depart
to my place of rest, though I may say with the poet:

> Ah rest!—no rest but change of place and posture;
> Ah sleep!—no sleep but worn-out Nature's swooning:
> Ah bed!—no bed but cushion fill'd with stones:
> Rest, sleep, nor bed await not on an exile."

With a delicate obeisance he left the room, evading Dame
Glendinning, who hastened to assure him he would find his

accommodations for repose much more agreeable than they had been the night before, there having been store of warm coverlets and a soft feather-bed sent up from the abbey. But the good knight probably thought that the grace and effect of his exit would be diminished if he were recalled from his heroics to discuss such sublunary and domestic topics, and therefore hastened away without waiting to hear her out.

"A pleasant gentleman," said Dame Glendinning; "but I will warrant him an humorous. And sings a sweet song, though it is somewhat of the longest. Well, I make mine avow he is goodly company. I wonder when he will go away."

Having thus expressed her respect for her guest, not without intimation that she was heartily tired of his company, the good dame gave the signal for the family to disperse, and laid her injunctions on Halbert to attend Sir Piercie Shafton at daybreak, as he required.

When stretched on his pallet by his brother's side, Halbert had no small cause to envy the sound sleep which instantly settled on the eyes of Edward, but refused him any share of its influence. He saw now too well what the Spirit had darkly indicated, that, in granting the boon which he had asked so unadvisedly, she had contributed more to his harm than his good. He was now sensible, too late, of the various dangers and inconveniences with which his dearest friends were threatened, alike by his discomfiture or his success in the approaching duel. If he fell, he might say personally, "Good-night all." But it was not the less certain that he should leave a dreadful legacy of distress and embarrassment to his mother and family—an anticipation which by no means tended to render the front of death, in itself a grisly object, more agreeable to his imagination. The vengeance of the abbot, his conscience told him, was sure to descend on his mother and brother, or could only be averted by the generosity of the victor. And Mary Avenel—he should have shown himself, if he succumbed in the present combat, as inefficient in protecting her as he had been unnecessarily active in bringing disaster on her, and on the house in which she had been protected from infancy.

And to this view of the case were to be added all those embittered and anxious feelings with which the bravest men, even in a better or less doubtful quarrel, regard the issue of a dubious conflict, the first time when it has been their fate to engage in an affair of that nature.

But, however disconsolate the prospect seemed in the event of his being conquered, Halbert could expect from victory little more than the safety of his own life and the gratification of his wounded pride. To his friends—to his mother and brother—especially to Mary Avenel—the consequences of his triumph would be more certain destruction than the contingency of his defeat and death. If the English knight survived, he might in courtesy extend his protection to them; but if he fell, nothing was likely to screen them from the vindictive measures which the abbot and convent would surely adopt against the violation of the peace of the halidome, and the slaughter of a protected guest by one of their own vassals, within whose house they had lodged him for shelter. These thoughts, in which neither view of the case augured aught short of ruin to his family, and that ruin entirely brought on by his own rashness, were thorns in Halbert Glendinning's pillow, that deprived his soul of peace and his eyes of slumber.

There appeared no middle course, saving one which was marked by degradation, and which, even if he stooped to it, was by no means free of danger. He might indeed confess to the English knight the strange circumstances which led to his presenting him with that token which the White Lady (in her displeasure, as it now seemed) had given him, that he might offer it to Sir Piercie Shafton. But to this avowal his pride could not stoop, and reason, who is wonderfully ready to be of counsel with pride on such occasions, offered many arguments to show it would be useless as well as mean so far to degrade himself. "If I tell a tale so wonderful," thought he, "shall I not either be stigmatised as a liar or punished as a wizard? Were Sir Piercie Shafton generous, noble, and benevolent, as the champions of whom we near in romance, I might indeed gain his ear, and, without demeaning myself, escape from the situation in which I am placed. But as he is, or at least seems to be, self-conceited, arrogant, vain, and presumptuous, I should but humble myself in vain; and I will not humble myself!" he said, starting out of bed, grasping to his broadsword, and brandishing it in the light of the moon, which streamed through the deep niche that served them as a window; when, to his extreme surprise and terror, an airy form stood in the moonlight, but intercepted not the reflection on the floor. Dimly as it was expressed, the sound of the voice soon made him sensible he saw the White Lady.

At no time had her presence seemed so terrific to him; for when he had invoked her, it was with the expectation of the apparition, and the determination to abide the issue. But now she had come uncalled, and her presence impressed him with a sense of approaching misfortune, and with the hideous apprehension that he had associated himself with a demon, over whose motions he had no control, and of whose powers and quality he had no certain knowledge. He remained, therefore, in mere terror, gazing on the apparition, which chanted or recited in cadence the following lines:

> " He whose heart for vengeance sued,
> Must not shrink from shedding blood;
> The knot that thou hast tied with word,
> Thou must loose by edge of sword."

"Avaunt thee, false Spirit!" said Halbert Glendinning; "I have bought thy advice too dearly already. Begone, in the name of God!"

The Spirit laughed; and the cold, unnatural sound of her laughter had something in it more fearful than the usual melancholy tones of her voice. She then replied:

> " You have summon'd me once—you have summon'd me twice,
> And without e'er a summons I come to you thrice;
> Unask'd for, unsued for, you came to my glen;
> Unsued and unask'd, I am with you again."

Halbert Glendinning gave way for a moment to terror, and called on his brother; "Edward! waken—waken, for Our Lady's sake!"

Edward awaked accordingly, and asked what he wanted.

"Look out," said Halbert—"look up! seest thou no one in the room?"

"No, upon my good word," said Edward, looking out.

"What! seest thou nothing in the moonshine upon the floor there?"

"No, nothing," answered Edward, "save thyself, resting on thy naked sword. I tell thee, Halbert, thou shouldst trust more to thy spiritual arms, and less to those of steel and iron. For this many a night hast thou started and moaned, and cried out of fighting, and of spectres, and of goblins: thy sleep hath not refreshed thee, thy waking hath been a dream. Credit me, dear Halbert, say the *pater* and *credo*, resign thyself to the protection of God, and thou wilt sleep sound and wake in comfort."

"It may be," said Halbert, slowly, and having his eye still bent on the female form which to him seemed distinctly visible—"it may be. But tell me, dear Edward, seest thou no one on the chamber floor but me?"

"No one," answered Edward, raising himself on his elbow; "dear brother, lay aside thy weapon, say thy prayers, and lay thee down to rest."

While he thus spoke, the Spirit smiled at Halbert as if in scorn; her wan cheek faded in the wan moonlight even before the smile had passed away, and Halbert himself no longer beheld the vision to which he had so anxiously solicited his brother's attention. "May God preserve my wits!" he said, as, laying aside his weapon, he again threw himself on his bed.

"Amen! my dearest brother," answered Edward; "but we must not provoke that Heaven in our wantonness which we invoke in our misery. Be not angry with me, my dear brother: I know not why you have totally of late estranged yourself from me. It is true, I am neither so athletic in body nor so alert in courage as you have been from your infancy; yet, till lately, you have not absolutely cast off my society. Believe me, I have wept in secret, though I forbore to intrude myself on your privacy. The time has been when you held me not so cheap; and when, if I could not follow the game so closely, or mark it so truly, as you, I could fill up our intervals of pastime with pleasant tales of the olden times, which I had read or heard, and which excited even your attention as we sate and ate our provision by some pleasant spring; but now, I have, though I know not why, lost thy regard and affection. Nay, toss not thy arms about thee thus wildly," said the younger brother; "from thy strange dreams, I fear some touch of fever hath affected thy blood; let me draw closer around thee thy mantle."

"Forbear," said Halbert; "your care is needless—your complaints are without reason—your fears on my account are in vain."

"Nay, but hear me, brother," said Edward. "Your speech in sleep, and now even your waking dreams, are of beings which belong not to this world, or to our race. Our good Father Eustace says that, howbeit we may not do well to receive all idle tales of goblins and spectres, yet there is warrant from Holy Scripture to believe that the fiends haunt waste and solitary places; and that those who frequent such wildernesses alone are the prey, or the sport, of these wandering demons. And therefore I pray thee, brother, let me go with you when you go next up the glen, where, as you well know, there be places of evil reputation. Thou carest not for my escort; but, Halbert, such dangers are more safely encountered by the wise in judgment than by the bold in bosom; and though I have small cause to boast of my own wisdom, yet I have that which ariseth from the written knowledge of elder times."

There was a moment during this discourse when Halbert had wellnigh come to the resolution of disburdening his own breast by entrusting Edward with all that weighed upon it. But when his brother reminded him that this was the morning of a high holiday, and that, setting aside all other business or pleasure, he ought to go to the monastery and shrive himself before Father Eustace, who would that day occupy the confessional, pride stepped in and confirmed his wavering resolution. "I will not avow," he thought, "a tale so extraordinary, that I may be considered as an impostor or something worse: I will not fly from this Englishman, whose arm and sword may be no better than my own. My fathers have faced his betters, were he as much distinguished in battle as he is by his quaint discourse."

Pride, which has been said to save man, and woman too, from falling, has yet a stronger influence on the mind when it embraces the cause of passion, and seldom fails to render it victorious over conscience and reason. Halbert once determined, though not to the better course, at length slept soundly, and was only awakened by the dawn of day.

CHAPTER XXI.

Indifferent, but indifferent—pshaw, he doth it not
Like one who is his craft's master—ne'ertheless
I have seen a clown confer a bloody coxcomb
On one who was a master of defence.

Old Play.

WITH the first grey peep of dawn, Halbert Glendinning arose and hastened to dress himself, girded on his weapon, and took a cross-bow in his hand, as if his usual sport had been his sole object. He groped his way down the dark and winding staircase, and undid with as little noise as possible the fastenings of the inner door, and of the exterior iron grate. At length he stood free in the courtyard, and looking up to the tower, saw a signal made with a handkerchief from the window. Nothing doubting that it was his antagonist, he paused expecting him. But it was Mary Avenel, who glided like a spirit from under the low and rugged portal.

Halbert was much surprised, and felt, he knew not why, like one caught in the act of a meditated trespass. The presence of Mary Avenel had till that moment never given him pain. She spoke, too, in a tone where sorrow seemed to mingle with reproach, while she asked him with emphasis: "What he was about to do?"

He showed his cross-bow and was about to express the pretext he had meditated, when Mary interrupted him.

"Not so, Halbert; that evasion were unworthy of one whose

word has hitherto been truth. You meditate not the destruction of the deer: your hand and your heart are aimed at other game—you seek to do battle with this stranger."

"And wherefore should I quarrel with our guest?" answered Halbert, blushing deeply.

"There are, indeed, many reasons why you should not," replied the maiden, "nor is there one of avail wherefore you should; yet, nevertheless, such a quarrel you are now searching after."

"Why should you suppose so, Mary?" said Halbert, endeavouring to hide his conscious purpose; "he is my mother's guest; he is protected by the abbot and the community, who are our masters; he is of high degree also; and wherefore should you think that I can, or dare, resent a hasty word, which he has perchance thrown out against me more from the wantonness of his wit than the purpose of his heart?"

"Alas!" answered the maiden, "the very asking that question puts your resolution beyond a doubt. Since your childhood you were ever daring, seeking danger rather than avoiding it, delighting in whatever had the air of adventure and of courage; and it is not from fear that you will now blench from your purpose. O let it then be from pity!—from pity, Halbert, to your aged mother, whom your death or victory will alike deprive of the comfort and stay of her age."

"She has my brother Edward," said Halbert, turning suddenly from her.

"She has indeed," said Mary Avenel, "the calm, the noble-minded, the considerate Edward, who has thy courage, Halbert, without thy fiery rashness, thy generous spirit, with more of reason to guide it. He would not have heard his mother, would not have heard his adopted sister, beseech him in vain not to ruin himself, and tear up their future hopes of happiness and protection."

Halbert's heart swelled as he replied to this reproach: "Well—what avails it speaking? You have him that is better than me, wiser, more considerate, braver for aught that I know: you are provided with a protector, and need care no more for me."

Again he turned to depart, but Mary Avenel laid her hand on his arm so gently that he scarce felt her hold, yet felt that it was impossible for him to strike it off. There he stood, one foot advanced to leave the courtyard, but so little determined on departure that he resembled a traveller arrested by the spell of a magician, and unable either to quit the attitude of motion or to proceed on his course.

Mary Avenel availed herself of his state of suspense. "Hear me," she said—"hear me, Halbert! I am an orphan, and even Heaven hears the orphan. I have been the companion of your infancy, and if *you* will not hear me for an instant, from whom may Mary Avenel claim so poor a boon?"

"I hear you," said Halbert Glendinning, "but be brief, dear Mary; you mistake the nature of my business; it is but a morning of summer sport which we propose."

"Say not thus," said the maiden, interrupting him—"say not thus to me; others thou mayst deceive, but me thou canst not. There has been that in me from the earliest youth which fraud flies from, and which imposture cannot deceive. For what fate has given me such a power I know not; but, bred an ignorant maiden in this sequestered valley, mine eyes can too often see what man would most willingly hide. I can judge of the dark purpose, though it is hid under the smiling brow, and a glance of the eye says more to me than oaths and protestations do to others."

"Then," said Halbert, "if thou canst so read the human heart, say, dear Mary, what dost thou see in mine? tell me that—say that what thou seest—what thou readest in this bosom, does not offend thee—say but *that*, and thou shalt be the guide of my actions, and mould me now and henceforward to honour or to dishonour at thy own free will!"

Mary Avenel became first red and then deadly pale as Halbert Glendinning spoke. But when, turning round at the close of his address, he took her hand, she gently withdrew it, and replied: "I cannot read the heart, Halbert, and I would not of my will know aught of yours, save what beseems us both; I only can judge of signs, words, and actions of little outward import more truly than those around me, as my eyes, thou knowest, have seen objects not presented to those of others."

"Let them gaze then on one whom they shall never see more," said Halbert, once more turning from her, and rushing out of the courtyard without again looking back.

Mary Avenel gave a faint scream, and clasped both her hands firmly on her forehead and eyes. She had been a minute in this attitude when she was thus greeted by a voice from behind: "Generously done, my most clement Discretion, to hide those brilliant eyes from the far inferior beams which even now begin to gild the eastern horizon. Certes, peril there were that Phœbus, outshone in splendour, might in very shamefacedness turn back his car, and rather leave the world in darkness than incur the disgrace of such an encounter. Credit me, lovely Discretion——"

But as Sir Piercie Shafton (the reader will readily set down these flowers of eloquence to the proper owner) attempted to take Mary Avenel's hand, in order to proceed in his speech, she shook him abruptly off, and regarding him with an eye which evinced terror and agitation, rushed past him into the tower.

The knight stood looking after her with a countenance in which contempt was strongly mingled with mortification. "By my knighthood!" he ejaculated, "I have thrown away upon this rude rustic Phidele a speech which the proudest beauty at the court of Felicia—so let me call the Elysium from which I am banished—might have termed the very matins of Cupid. Hard and inexorable was the fate that sent thee thither, Piercie Shafton, to waste thy wit upon country wenches and thy valour upon hobnailed clowns! But that insult—that affront—had it been offered to me by the lowest plebeian, he must have died for it by my hand, in respect the enormity of the offence doth countervail the inequality of him by whom it was given. I trust I shall find this clownish roisterer not less willing to deal in blows than in taunts."

While he held this conversation with himself, Sir Piercie Shafton was hastening to the little tuft of birch-trees which had been assigned as the place of meeting. He greeted his antagonist with a courtly salutation, followed by this commentary: "I pray you to observe that I doff my hat to you, though so much my inferior in rank, without derogation on my part, inasmuch as my having so far honoured you in receiving and admitting your defiance doth, in the judgment of the best martialists, in some sort, and for the time, raise you to a level with me—an honour which you may and ought to account cheaply purchased even with the loss of your life, if such should chance to be the issue of this duello."

"For which condescension," said Halbert, "I have to thank the token which I presented to you."

The knight changed colour, and grinded his teeth with rage. "Draw your weapon!" said he to Glendinning.

"Not in this spot," answered the youth; "we should be liable to interruption. Follow me, and I will bring you to a place where we shall encounter no such risk."

He proceeded to walk up the glen, resolving that their place of combat should be in the entrance of the Corrie-nan-Shian; both because the spot, lying under the reputation of being haunted, was very little frequented, and also because he regarded it as a place which to him might be termed fated, and which he therefore resolved should witness his death or victory.

They walked up the glen for some time in silence, like honourable enemies who did not wish to contend with words, and who had nothing friendly to exchange with each other. Silence, however, was always an irksome state with Sir Piercie, and, moreover, his anger was usually a hasty and short-lived passion. As, therefore, he went forth, in his own idea, in all love and honour towards his antagonist, he saw not any cause for submitting longer to the painful restraint of positive silence. He began by complimenting Halbert on the alert activity with which he surmounted the obstacles and impediments of the way.

"Trust me," said he, "worthy rustic, we have not a lighter or a firmer step in our courtlike revels, and if duly set forth by a silk hose, and trained unto that stately exercise, your leg would make an indifferent good show in a pavin or a galliard. And I doubt nothing," he added, "that you have availed yourself of some opportunity to improve yourself in the art of fence, which is more akin than dancing to our present purpose?"

"I know nothing more of fencing," said Halbert, "than hath been taught me by an old shepherd of ours called Martin, and at whiles a lesson from Christie of the Clinthill; for the rest, I must trust to good sword, strong arm, and sound heart."

"Marry and I am glad of it, young Audacity—I will call you my Audacity, and you may call me your Condescension, while we are on these terms of unnatural equality—I am glad of your ignorance with all my heart. For we martialists proportion the punishments which we inflict upon our opposites to the length and hazard of the efforts wherewith they oppose themselves to us. And I see not why you, being but a tyro, may not be held sufficiently punished for your outrecuidance and orgillous presumption by the loss of an ear, an eye, or even of a finger, accompanied by some flesh-wound of depth and severity, suited to your error; whereas, had you been able to stand more effectually on your defence, I see not how less than your life could have atoned sufficiently for your presumption."

"Now, by God and Our Lady," said Halbert, unable any longer to restrain himself, "thou art thyself over-presumptuous, who speakest thus daringly of the issue of a combat which is not yet even begun. Are you a god, that you already dispose of my life and limbs? or are you a judge in the justice chair, telling, at your ease and without risk, how the head and quarters of a condemned criminal are to be disposed of?"

"Not so, O thou whom I have well permitted to call thyself my Audacity! I, thy Condescension, am neither a god to judge the issue of the combat before it is fought, nor a judge to dispose at my ease and in safety of the limbs and head of a condemned criminal; but I am an indifferent good master of fence, being the first pupil of the first master of the first school of fence that our royal England affords, the said master being no other than the truly noble and all-unutterably-skilful Vincentio Saviola, from whom I learned the firm step, quick eye, and nimble hand—of which qualities thou, O my most rustical Audacity, art full like to reap the fruits, so soon as we shall find a piece of ground fitting for such experiments."

They had now reached the gorge of the ravine where Halbert had at first intended to stop; but when he observed the narrowness of the level ground, he began to consider that it was only by superior agility that he could expect to make up his deficiency in the science, as it was called, of defence. He found no spot which afforded sufficient room to traverse/ for this purpose, until he gained the well-known fountain, by whose margin, and in front of the huge rock from which it sprung, was an amphitheatre of level turf, of small space indeed, compared with the great height of the cliffs with which it was surrounded on every point save that from which the rivulet issued forth, yet large enough for their present purpose.

When they had reached this spot of ground, fitted well by its gloom and sequestered situation to be a scene of mortal strife, both were surprised to observe that a grave was dug close by the foot of the rock with great neatness and regularity, the green turf being laid down upon the one side, and the earth thrown out in a heap upon the other. A mattock and shovel lay by the verge of the grave.

Sir Piercie Shafton bent his eye with unusual seriousness upon Halbert Glendinning, as he asked him sternly: "Does this bode treason, young man? And have you purpose to set upon me here as in an *emboscata* or place of vantage?"

"Not on my part, by Heaven!" answered the youth. "I told no one of our purpose, nor would I for the throne of Scotland take odds against a single arm."

"I believe thou wouldst not, mine Audacity," said the knight, resuming the affected manner which was become a second nature to him; "nevertheless, this fosse is curiously well shaped, and might be the masterpiece of nature's last bed-maker—I would say the sexton. Wherefore, let us be thankful to chance, or some unknown friend, who hath thus provided for one of us the decencies of sepulture, and let us proceed to determine which shall have the advantage of enjoying this place of undisturbed slumber."

So saying, he stripped off his doublet and cloak, which he folded up with great care and deposited upon a large stone, while Halbert Glendinning, not without some emotion, followed his example. Their vicinity to the favourite haunt of the White Lady led him to form conjectures concerning the incident of the grave. "It must have been her work!" he thought: "the Spirit foresaw and has provided for the fatal event of the combat. I must return from this place a homicide, or I must remain here for ever!"

The bridge seemed now broken down behind him, and the chance of coming off honourably without killing or being killed (the hope of which issue has cheered the sinking heart of many a duellist) seemed now to be altogether removed. Yet the very desperation of his situation gave him, on an instant's reflection, both firmness and courage, and presented to him one sole alternative—conquest, namely, or death.

"As we are here," said Sir Piercie Shafton, "unaccompanied by any patrons or seconds, it were well you should pass your hands over my side, as I shall over yours; not that I suspect you to use any quaint device of privy armour, but in order to comply with the ancient and laudable custom practised on all such occasions."

While, complying with his antagonist's humour, Halbert Glendinning went through this ceremony, Sir Piercie Shafton did not fail to solicit his attention to the quality and fineness of his wrought and embroidered shirt. "In this very shirt," said he, "O mine Audacity—I say in this very garment, in which I am now to combat a Scottish rustic like thyself, it was my envied lot to lead the winning party at that wondrous match at ballon made betwixt the divine Astrophel—our matchless Sidney—and the right honourable my very good lord of Oxford. All the beauties of Felicia—by which name I distinguish our beloved England—stood in the gallery, waving their kerchiefs at each turn of the game, and cheering the winners by their plaudits. After which noble sport we were refreshed by a suitable banquet, whereat it pleased the noble Urania—being the unmatched Countess of Pembroke—to accommodate me with her own fan for the cooling my somewhat too much inflamed visage, to requite with courtesy I said, casting my features into a smiling yet melancholy fashion "O divinest Urania! receive again that too fatal gift, which not like the Zephyr cooleth, but like the hot breath of the Sirocco heateth yet more that which is already inflamed." Whereupon, looking upon me somewhat scornfully, yet not so but what the experienced courtier might perceive a certain cast of approbative affection——"

Here the knight was interrupted by Halbert, who had waited with courteous patience for some little time, till he found that, far from drawing to a close, Sir Piercie seemed rather inclined to wax prolix in his reminiscences.

"Sir knight," said the youth, "if this matter be not very much to the purpose, we will, if you object not, proceed to that which we have in hand. You should have abidden in England had you desired to waste time in words, for here we spend it in blows."

"I crave your pardon, most rusticated Audacity," answered Sir Piercie; "truly I become oblivious of everything beside when the recollections of the divine court of Felicia press upon my weakened memory, even as a saint is dazzled when he bethinks him of the beatific vision. Ah, felicitous Feliciana! delicate nurse of the fair, chosen abode of the wise, the birthplace and cradle of nobility, the temple of courtesy, the fane of sprightly chivalry! Ah, heavenly court, or rather courtly heaven! cheered with dances, lulled asleep with harmony, wakened with sprightly sports and tourneys, decored with silks and tissues, glittering with diamonds and jewels, standing on end with double-piled velvets, satins, and satinettas!"

"The token, sir knight—the token!" exclaimed Halbert Glendinning, who, impatient of Sir Piercie's interminable oratory, reminded him of the ground of their quarrel, as the best way to compel him to the purpose of their meeting.

And he judged right; for Sir Piercie Shafton no sooner

heard him speak than he exclaimed: "Thy death-hour has struck: betake thee to thy sword. *Via!*"

Both swords were unsheathed, and the combatants commenced their engagement. Halbert became immediately aware that, as he had expected, he was far inferior to his adversary in the use of his weapon. Sir Piercie Shafton had taken no more than his own share of real merit when he termed himself an absolutely good fencer; and Glendinning soon found that he should have great difficulty in escaping with life and honour from such a master of the sword. The English knight was master of all the mystery of the *stoccata, imbrocata, punto reverso, incartata*, and so forth, which the Italian masters of defence had lately introduced into general practice. But Glendinning, on his part, was no novice in the principles of the art, according to the old Scottish fashion, and possessed the first of all qualities, a steady and collected mind. At first, being desirous to try the skill, and become acquainted with the play, of his enemy, he stood on his defence, keeping his foot, hand, eye, and body in perfect unison, and holding his sword short, and with the point towards his antagonist's face, so that Sir Piercie, in order to assail him, was obliged to make actual passes, and could not avail himself of his skill in making feints; while, on the other hand, Halbert was prompt to parry these attacks, either by shifting his ground or with the sword. The consequence was that, after two or three sharp attempts on the part of Sir Piercie, which were evaded or disconcerted by the address of his opponent, he began to assume the defensive in his turn, fearful of giving some advantage by being repeatedly the assailant. But Halbert was too cautious to press on a swordsman whose dexterity had already more than once placed him within a hair's-breadth of death, which he had only escaped by uncommon watchfulness and agility.

When each had made a feint or two, there was a pause in the conflict, both as if by one assent dropping their sword's point, and looking on each other for a moment without speaking. At length Halbert Glendinning, who felt perhaps more uneasy on account of his family than he had done before he

18

had displayed his own courage and proved the strength o_ his antagonist, could not help saying: "Is the subject of our quarrel, sir knight, so mortal that one of our two bodies must needs fill up that grave? or may we with honour, having proved ourselves against each other, sheathe our swords and depart friends?"

"Valiant and most rustical Audacity," said the Southron knight, "to no man on earth could you have put a question on the code of honour who was more capable of rendering you a reason. Let us pause for the space of one venue, until I give you my opinion on this dependence; for certain it is that brave men should not run upon their fate like brute and furious wild beasts, but should slay each other deliberately, decently, and with reason. Therefore, if we coolly examine the state of our dependence, we may the better apprehend whether the sisters three have doomed one of us to expiate the same with his blood. Dost thou understand me?"

"I have heard Father Eustace," said Halbert, after a moment's recollection, "speak of the three furies, with their thread and their shears."

"Enough—enough," interrupted Sir Piercie Shafton, crimsoning with a new fit of rage, "the thread of thy life is spun!"

And with these words he attacked with the utmost ferocity the Scottish youth, who had but just time to throw himself into a posture of defence. But the rash fury of the assailant, as frequently happens, disappointed its own purpose; for, as he made a desperate thrust, Halbert Glendinning avoided it, and, ere the knight could recover his weapon, requited him (to use his own language) with a resolute *stoccata*, which passed through his body, and Sir Piercie Shafton fell to the ground.

CHAPTER XXII.

Yes, life hath left him : every busy thought,
Each fiery passion, every strong affection,
All sense of outward ill and inward sorrow,
Are fled at once from the pale trunk before me ;
And I have given that which spoke and moved,
Thought, acted, suffer'd as a living man,
To be a ghastly form of bloody clay,
Soon the foul food for reptiles.

Old Play.

I BELIEVE few successful duellists, if the word successful can be applied to a superiority so fatal, have beheld their dead antagonist stretched on the earth at their feet without wishing they could redeem with their own blood that which it has been their fate to spill. Least of all could such indifference be the lot of so young a man as Halbert Glendinning, who, unused to the sight of human blood, was not only struck with sorrow, but with terror, when he beheld Sir Piercie Shafton lie stretched on the greensward before him, vomiting gore as if impelled by the strokes of a pump. He threw his bloody sword on the ground, and hastened to kneel down and support him, vainly striving, at the same time, to stanch his wound, which seemed rather to bleed inwardly than externally.

The unfortunate knight spoke at intervals, when the syncope would permit him, and his words, so far as intelligible, partook of his affected and conceited, yet not ungenerous, character.

"Most rustical youth," he said, "thy fortune hath prevailed over knightly skill, and Audacity hath overcome Condescension, even as the kite hath sometimes hawked at and struck down the falcon-gentle. Fly and save thyself! Take my purse; it is in the nether pocket of my carnation-coloured hose, and is worth a clown's acceptance. See that my mails, with my vestments, be sent to the Monastery of St. Mary's (here his voice grew weak, and his mind and recollection seemed to waver). I bestow the cut velvet jerkin, with close breeches conforming, for—oh!—the good of my soul."

"Be of good comfort, sir," said Halbert, half-distracted with his agony of pity and remorse. "I trust you shall yet do well. O for a leech!"

"Were there twenty physicians, O most generous Audacity —and that were a grave spectacle—I might not survive: my life is ebbing fast. Commend me to the rustical nymph whom I called my Discretion. O Claridiana! true empress of this bleeding heart, which now bleedeth in sad earnest! Place me on the ground at my length, most rustical victor, born to quench the pride of the burning light of the most felicitous court of Feliciana. O saints and angels—knights and ladies— masques and theatres—quaint devices—chain-work and broidery—love, honour, and beauty——!"

While muttering these last words, which slid from him, as it were unawares, while doubtless he was recalling to mind the glories of the English court, the gallant Sir Piercie Shafton stretched out his limbs, groaned deeply, shut his eyes, and became motionless.

The victor tore his hair for very sorrow, as he looked on the pale countenance of his victim. Life, he thought, had not utterly fled, but without better aid than his own he saw not how it could be preserved.

"Why," he exclaimed, in vain penitence—"why did I provoke him to an issue so fatal! Would to God I had submitted to the worst insult man could receive from man, rather than be the bloody instrument of this bloody deed; and doubly cursed be this evil-boding spot, which, haunted as I knew it to be by a witch or a devil, I yet chose for the place of combat! In any other place save this there had been help to be gotten by speed of foot or by uplifting of voice; but here there is no one to be found by search, no one to hear my shouts, save the evil spirit who has counselled this mischief. It is not her hour—I will essay the spell howsoever; and if she can give me aid, she *shall* do it, or know of what a madman is capable even against those of another world!"

He spurned his bloody shoe from his foot, and repeated the spell with which the reader is well acquainted; but there was nether voice, apparition, nor signal of answer. The youth, in the impatience of his despair, and with the rash hardihood which formed the basis of his character, shouted aloud: "Witch—sorceress—fiend! art thou deaf to my cries for help, and so ready to appear and answer those of vengeance? Arise and speak to me, or I will choke up thy fountain, tear down thy holly-bush, and leave thy haunt as waste and bare as thy fatal assistance has made me waste of comfort and bare of counsel!" This furious and raving invocation was suddenly interrupted by a distant sound, resembling a halloo, from the gorge of the ravine. "Now may St. Mary be praised," said the youth, hastily fastening his sandal, "I hear the voice of some living man, who may give me counsel and help in this fearful extremity!"

Having donned his sandal, Halbert Glendinning, hallooing at intervals, in answer to the sound which he had heard, ran with the speed of a hunted buck down the rugged defile, as if paradise had been before him, hell and all her furies behind, and his eternal happiness or misery had depended upon the speed which he exerted. In a space incredibly short for any one but a Scottish mountaineer having his nerves strung by the deepest and most passionate interest, the youth reached the entrance of the ravine, through which the rill that flows down Corrie-nan-Shian discharges itself, and unites with the brook that waters the little valley of Glendearg.

Here he paused, and looked around him upwards and downwards through the glen, without perceiving a human form. His heart sank within him. But the windings of the glen intercepted his prospect, and the person whose voice he had heard might, therefore, be at no great distance, though not obvious to his sight. The branches of an oak-tree, which shot straight out from the face of a tall cliff, proffered to his bold spirit, steady head, and active limbs the means of ascending it as a place of outlook, although the enterprise was what most men would have shrunk from. But by one bound from the earth the active youth caught hold of the lower branch, and swung himself up into the tree, and in a minute more gained the top of the cliff, from which he could easily descry a human figure descending the valley. It was not that of a shepherd or of a hunter, and scarcely any others use to traverse this deserted solitude, especially coming from the north, since the reader may remember that the brook took its rise from an extensive and dangerous morass which lay in that direction.

But Halbert Glendinning did not pause to consider who the traveller might be, or what might be the purpose of his journey. To know that he saw a human being, and might receive, in the extremity of his distress, the countenance and advice of a fellow-creature, was enough for him at the moment. He threw himself from the pinnacle of the cliff once more into the arms of the projecting oak-tree, whose boughs waved in middle air, anchored by the roots in a huge rift or chasm of the rock. Catching at the branch which was nearest to him, he dropped himself from that height upon the ground; and such was the athletic springiness of his youthful sinews, that he pitched there as lightly, and with as little injury, as the falcon stooping from her wheel.

To resume his race at full speed up the glen was the work of an instant; and as he turned angle after angle of the indented banks of the valley without meeting that which he sought, he became half afraid that the form which he had seen at such a distance had already melted into thin air, and was either a deception of his own imagination or of the elementary spirits by which the valley was supposed to be haunted.

But, to his inexpressible joy, as he turned round the base of a huge and distinguished crag, he saw, straight before and very near to him, a person whose dress, as he viewed it hastily, resembled that of a pilgrim.

He was a man in advanced life, and wearing a long beard, having on his head a large slouched hat, without either band or brooch. His dress was a tunic of black serge, which, like those commonly called hussar cloaks, had an upper part, which covered the arms and fell down on the lower; a small scrip and bottle, which hung at his back, with a stout staff in his hand, completed his equipage. His step was feeble, like that of one exhausted by a toilsome journey.

"Save ye, good father!" said the youth. "God and Our Lady have sent you to my assistance."

"And in what, my son, can so frail a creature as I am be of service to you?" said the old man, not a little surprised at being thus accosted by so handsome a youth, his features discomposed by anxiety, his face flushed with exertion, his hands and much of his dress stained with blood.

"A man bleeds to death in the valley here, hard by. Come with me—come with me! You are aged—you have experience—you have at least your senses—and mine have wellnigh left me."

"A man, and bleeding to death—and here in this desolate spot?" said the stranger.

"Stay not to question it, father," said the youth, "but come instantly to his rescue. Follow me—follow me, without an instant's delay."

"Nay, but, my son," said the old man, "we do not lightly follow the guides who present themselves thus suddenly in the bosom of a howling wilderness. Ere I follow thee, thou must expound to me thy name, thy purpose, and the cause."

"There is no time to expound anything," said Halbert; "I tell thee a man's life is at stake, and thou must come to aid him, or I will carry thee thither by force!"

"Nay, thou shalt not need," said the traveller; "if it indeed be as thou sayest, I will follow thee of free will, the rather that I am not wholly unskilled in leechcraft, and have in my scrip that which may do thy friend a service. Yet walk more slowly, I pray thee, for I am already wellnigh forespent with travel."

With the indignant impatience of the fiery steed when compelled by his rider to keep pace with some slow drudge upon the highway, Halbert accompanied the wayfarer, burning with anxiety, which he endeavoured to subdue, that he might not alarm his companion, who was obviously afraid to trust him. When they reached the place where they were to turn off the wider glen into the Corrie, the traveller made a doubtful pause, as if unwilling to leave the broader path. "Young man," he said, "if thou meanest aught but good to these grey

hairs, thou wilt gain little by thy cruelty: I have no earthly
treasure to tempt either robber or murderer."

"And I," said the youth, "am neither; and yet—God of
Heaven!—I *may* be a murderer, unless your aid comes in time
to this wounded wretch!"

"Is it even so?" said the traveller; "and do human passions disturb the breast of nature even in her deepest solitude? Yet why should I marvel that where darkness abides
the works of darkness should abound? By its fruits is the
tree known. Lead on, unhappy youth—I follow thee!"

And with better will to the journey than he had evinced
hitherto, the stranger exerted himself to the uttermost, and
seemed to forget his own fatigue in his efforts to keep pace
with his impatient guide.

What was the surprise of Halbert Glendinning when, upon
arriving at the fatal spot, he saw no appearance of the body
of Sir Piercie Shafton! The traces of the fray were otherwise sufficiently visible. The knight's cloak had indeed vanished as well as the body, but his doublet remained where he
had laid it down, and the turf on which he had been stretched
was stained with blood in many a dark crimson spot.

As he gazed round him in terror and astonishment, Halbert's eyes fell upon the place of sepulture which had so lately
appeared to gape for a victim. It was no longer open, and it
seemed that earth had received the expected tenant; for the
usual narrow hillock was piled over what had lately been an
open grave, and the green sod was adjusted over all with the
accuracy of an experienced sexton. Halbert stood aghast.
The idea rushed on his mind irresistibly that the earth-heap
before him inclosed what had lately been a living, moving,
and sentient fellow-creature, whom, on little provocation, his
fell act had reduced to a clod of the valley, as senseless and
as cold as the turf under which he rested. The hand that
scooped the grave had completed its work; and whose hand
could it be save that of the mysterious being of doubtful quality whom his rashness had invoked, and whom he had suffered
to intermingle in his destinies?

As he stood with clasped hands and uplifted eyes, bitterly

ruing his rashness, he was roused by the voice of the stranger, whose suspicions of his guide had again been awakened by finding the scene so different from what Halbert had led him to expect. "Young man," he said, "hast thou baited thy tongue with falsehood, to cut perhaps only a few days from the life of one whom nature will soon call home, without guilt on thy part to hasten his journey?"

"By the blessed Heaven!—by our dear Lady!" ejaculated Halbert——

"Swear not at all!" said the stranger, interrupting him, "neither by Heaven, for it is God's throne, nor by earth, for it is His footstool; nor by the creatures whom He hath made, for they are but earth and clay as we are. Let thy yea be yea, and thy nay nay. Tell me in a word, why and for what purpose thou hast feigned a tale to lead a bewildered traveller yet farther astray?"

"As I am a Christian man," said Glendinning, "I left him here bleeding to death; and now I nowhere spy him, and much I doubt that the tomb that thou seest has closed on his mortal remains!"

"And who is he for whose fate thou art so anxious?" said the stranger; "or how is it possible that this wounded man could have been either removed from, or interred in, a place so solitary?"

"His name," said Halbert, after a moment's pause, "is Piercie Shafton; there, on that very spot, I left him bleeding; and what power has conveyed him hence, I know no more than thou dost."

"Piercie Shafton?" said the stranger—"Sir Piercie Shafton of Wilverton, a kinsman, as it is said, of the great Piercie of Northumberland? If thou hast slain him, to return to the territories of the proud abbot is to give thy neck to the gallows. He is well known—that Piercie Shafton—the meddling tool of wiser plotters—a hare-brained trafficker in treason—a champion of the Pope, employed as a forlorn hope by those more politic heads, who have more will to work mischief than valour to encounter danger. Come with me, youth, and save thyself from the evil consequences of this deed. Guide me to the Castle of Avenel, and thy reward shall be protection and safety."

Again Halbert paused, and summoned his mind to a hasty council. The vengeance with which the abbot was likely to visit the slaughter of Shafton, his friend, and in some measure his guest, was likely to be severe; yet, in the various contingencies which he had considered previous to their duel, he had unaccountably omitted to reflect what was to be his line of conduct in case of Sir Piercie falling by his hand. If he returned to Glendearg, he was sure to draw on his whole family, including Mary Avenel, the resentment of the abbot and community, whereas it was possible that flight might make him be regarded as the sole author of the deed, and might avert the indignation of the monks from the rest of the inhabitants of his paternal tower. Halbert recollected also the favour expressed for the household, and especially for Edward, by the sub-prior; and he conceived that he could, by communicating his own guilt to that worthy ecclesiastic, when at a distance from Glendearg, secure his powerful interposition in favour of his family. These thoughts rapidly passed through his mind, and he determined on flight. The stranger's company and his promised protection came in aid of that resolution; but he was unable to reconcile the invitation which the old man gave him to accompany him for safety to the Castle of Avenel with the connexions of Julian, the present usurper of that inheritance. "Good father," he said, "I fear that you mistake the man with whom you wish me to harbour. Avenel guided Piercie Shafton into Scotland, and his henchman, Christie of the Clinthill, brought the Southron hither."

"Of that," said the old man, "I am well aware. Yet if thou wilt trust to me, as I have shown no reluctance to confide in thee, thou shalt find with Julian Avenel welcome, or at least safety."

"Father," replied Halbert, "though I can ill reconcile what thou sayest with what Julian Avenel hath done, yet caring little about the safety of a creature so lost as myself, and as thy words seem those of truth and honesty, and finally, as thou didst render thyself frankly up to my conduct, I will return the confidence thou hast shown, and accompany thee to the Castle of Avenel by a road which thou thyself couldst never have discovered." He led the way, and the old man followed for some time in silence.

CHAPTER XXIII.

'Tis when the wound is stiffening with the cold
The warrior first feels pain ; 'tis when the heat
And fiery fever of his soul is pass'd,
The sinner feels remorse.

Old Play.

THE feelings of compunction with which Halbert Glendinning was visited upon this painful occasion were deeper than belonged to an age and country in which human life was held so cheap. They fell far short certainly of those which might have afflicted a mind regulated by better religious precepts, and more strictly trained under social laws; but still they were deep and severely felt, and divided in Halbert's heart even the regret with which he parted from Mary Avenel and the tower of his fathers.

The old traveller walked silently by his side for some time, and then addressed him. "My son, it has been said that sorrow must speak or die. Why art thou so much cast down? Tell me thy unhappy tale, and it may be that my grey head may devise counsel and aid for your young life."

"Alas!" said Halbert Glendinning, "can you wonder why I am cast down? I am at this instant a fugitive from my father's house, from my mother and from my friends, and I bear on my head the blood of a man who injured me but in idle words, which I have thus bloodily requited. My heart now tells me I have done evil: it were harder than these rocks if it could bear unmoved the thought that I have sent this man to a long account, unhouseled and unshrieved!"

"Pause there, my son," said the traveller. "That thou hast defaced God's image in thy neighbour's person, that thou hast sent dust to dust in idle wrath or idler pride, is indeed a sin of the deepest dye; that thou hast cut short the space which Heaven might have allowed him for repentance makes it yet more deadly; but for all this there is balm in Gilead."

"I understand you not, father," said Halbert, struck by the solemn tone which was assumed by his companion.

The old man proceeded. "Thou hast slain thine enemy— it was a cruel deed; thou hast cut him off perchance in his sins—it is a fearful aggravation. Do yet by my counsel, and in lieu of him whom thou hast perchance consigned to the kingdom of Satan, let thine efforts wrest another subject from the reign of the Evil One."

"I understand you, father," said Halbert; "thou wouldst have me atone for my rashness by doing service to the soul of my adversary. But how may this be? I have no money to purchase masses, and gladly would I go barefoot to the Holy Land to free his spirit from purgatory, only that——"

"My son," said the old man, interrupting him, "the sinner for whose redemption I entreat you to labour is not the dead but the living. It is not for the soul of thine enemy I would exhort thee to pray, that has already had its final doom from a Judge as merciful as He is just; nor, wert thou to coin that rock into ducats, and obtain a mass for each one, would it avail the departed spirit. Where the tree hath fallen it must lie. But the sapling, which hath in it yet the vigour and juice of life, may be bended to the point to which it ought to incline."

"Art thou a priest, father?" said the young man, "or by what commission dost thou talk of such high matters?"

"By that of my Almighty Master," said the traveller, "under whose banner I am an enlisted soldier."

Halbert's acquaintance with religious matters was no deeper than could be derived from the Archbishop of St. Andrews' Catechism, and the pamphlet called the *Twa-pennie Faith*, both which were industriously circulated and recommended by the monks of St. Mary's. Yet, however indifferent and superficial a theologian, he began to suspect that he was now in company with one of the gospellers, or heretics, before whose influence the ancient system of religion now tottered to the very foundation. Bred up, as may well be presumed, in a holy horror against these formidable sectaries, the youth's first feelings were those of a loyal and devoted church vassal. "Old man," he said, "wert thou able to make good with thy hand the words that thy tongue hath spoken against our Holy Mother Church, we should have tried upon this moor which of our creeds hath the better champion."

"Nay," said the stranger, "if thou art a true soldier of Rome, thou wilt not pause from thy purpose because thou hast the odds of years and of strength on thy side. Hearken to me, my son. I have showed thee how to make thy peace with Heaven, and thou hast rejected my proffer. I will now show thee how thou shalt make thy reconciliation with the powers of this world. Take this grey head from the frail body which supports it, and carry it to the chair of proud Abbot Boniface; and when thou tellest him thou hast slain Piercie Shafton, and his ire rises at the deed, lay the head of Henry Warden at his foot, and thou shalt have praise instead of censure."

Halbert Glendinning stepped back in surprise. "What! are you that Henry Warden so famous among the heretics that even Knox's name is scarce more frequently in their mouths? Art thou he, and darest thou to approach the halidome of St. Mary's?"

"I am Henry Warden of a surety," said the old man, "far unworthy to be named in the same breath with Knox, but yet willing to venture on whatever dangers my Master's service may call me to."

"Hearken to me, then," said Halbert; "to slay thee I have no heart; to make thee prisoner were equally to bring thy blood on my head; to leave thee in this wild without a guide were little better. I will conduct thee, as I promised, in safety to the Castle of Avenel; but breathe not, while we are on the journey, a word against the doctrines of the holy church of which I am an unworthy, but, though an ignorant, a zealous member. When thou art there arrived, beware of thyself: there is a high price upon thy head, and Julian Avenel loves the glance of gold bonnet-pieces."

"Yet thou sayest not," answered the Protestant preacher, for such he was, "that for lucre he would sell the blood of his guest?"

"Not if thou comest an invited stranger, relying on his faith," said the youth: "evil as Julian may be, he dare not break the rites of hospitality; for, loose as we on these marches may be in all other ties, these are respected amongst us even to idolatry, and his nearest relations would think it incumbent on them to spill his blood themselves, to efface the disgrace such treason would bring upon their name and lineage. But if thou goest self-invited, and without assurance of safety, I promise thee thy risk is great."

"I am in God's hand," answered the preacher; "it is on His errand that I traverse these wilds amidst dangers of every kind; while I am useful for my Master's service, they shall not prevail against me, and when, like the barren fig-tree, I can no longer produce fruit, what imports it when or by whom the axe is laid to the root?"

"Your courage and devotion," said Glendinning, "are worthy of a better cause."

"That," said Warden, "cannot be: mine is the very best."

They continued their journey in silence, Halbert Glendinning tracing with the utmost accuracy the mazes of the dangerous and intricate morasses and hills which divided the halidome from the barony of Avenel. From time to time he was obliged to stop in order to assist his companion to cross the black intervals of quaking bog, called in the Scottish dialect "hags," by which the firmer parts of the morass were intersected.

"Courage, old man," said Halbert, as he saw his companion almost exhausted with fatigue, "we shall soon be upon hard ground. And yet, soft as this moss is, I have seen the merry falconers go through it as light as deer when the quarry was upon the flight."

"True, my son," answered Warden, "for so I will still call you, though you term me no longer father; and even so doth headlong youth pursue its pleasures, without regard to the mire and the peril of the paths through which they are hurried."

"I have already told thee," answered Halbert Glendinning, sternly, "that I will hear nothing from thee that savours of doctrine."

"Nay, but, my son, answered Warden, "thy spiritual father himself would surely not dispute the truth of what I have now spoken for your edification?"

Glendinning stoutly replied: "I know not how that may be; but I wot well it is the fashion of your brotherhood to bait your hook with fair discourse, and to hold yourselves up as angels of light, that you may the better extend the kingdom of darkness."

"May God," replied the preacher, "pardon those who have thus reported of His servants! I will not offend thee, my son, by being instant out of season. Thou speakest but as thou art taught; yet sure I trust that so goodly a youth will be still rescued, like a brand from the burning."

While he thus spoke, the verge of the morass was attained, and their path lay on the declivity. Greensward it was, and, viewed from a distance, chequered with its narrow and verdant line the dark-brown heath which it traversed, though the distinction was not so easily traced when they were walking on it.[1] The old man pursued his journey with comparative ease; and, unwilling again to awaken the jealous zeal of his young companion for the Roman faith, he discoursed on other matters. The tone of his conversation was still grave, moral, and instructive. He had travelled much, and knew both the language and manners of other countries, concerning which Halbert Glendinnng, already anticipating the possibility of being obliged to quit Scotland for the deed he had done, was naturally and anxiously desirous of information. By degrees he was more attracted by the charms of the stranger's conversation than repelled by the dread of his dangerous character as a heretic, and Halbert had called him father more than once ere the turrets of Avenel Castle came in view.

The situation of this ancient fortress was remarkable. It

---

[1] This species of path, visible when looked at from a distance, but not to be seen when you are upon it, is called on the Border by the significant name of a "blind road."

occupied a small rocky islet in a mountain lake, or tarn, as such a piece of water is called in Westmoreland. The lake might be about a mile in circumference, surrounded by hills of considerable height, which, except where old trees and brushwood occupied the ravines that divided them from each other, were bare and heathy. The surprise of the spectator was chiefly excited by finding a piece of water situated in that high and mountainous region, and the landscape around had features which might rather be termed wild than either romantic or sublime; yet the scene was not without its charms. Under the burning sun of summer, the clear azure of the deep unruffled lake refreshed the eye, and impressed the mind with a pleasing feeling of deep solitude. In winter, when the snow lay on the mountains around, these dazzling masses appeared to ascend far beyond their wonted and natural height, while the lake, which stretched beneath, and filled their bosom with all its frozen waves, lay like the surface of a darkened and broken mirror around the black and rocky islet, and the walls of the grey castle with which it was crowned.

As the castle occupied, either with its principal buildings or with its flanking and outward walls, every projecting point of rock, which served as its site, it seemed as completely surrounded by water as the nest of a wild swan, save where a narrow causeway extended betwixt the islet and the shore. But the fortress was larger in appearance than in reality; and of the buildings which it actually contained, many had become ruinous and uninhabitable. In the times of the grandeur of the Avenel family, these had been occupied by a considerable garrison of followers and retainers, but they were now in a great measure deserted; and Julian Avenel would probably have fixed his habitation in a residence better suited to his diminished fortunes, had it not been for the great security which the situation of the old castle afforded to a man of his precarious and perilous mode of life. Indeed, in this respect the spot could scarce have been more happily chosen, for it could be rendered almost completely inaccessible at the pleasure of the inhabitant. The distance betwixt the nearest shore and the islet was not indeed above an hundred yards; but then the causeway which connected them was extremely narrow, and completely divided by two cuts, one in the midway between the islet and shore, and another close under the outward gate of the castle. These formed a formidable, and almost insurmountable, interruption to any hostile approach. Each was defended by a drawbridge, one of which, being that nearest to the castle, was regularly raised at all times during the day, and both were lifted at night.[1]

The situation of Julian Avenel, engaged in a variety of feuds, and a party to almost every dark and mysterious transaction which was on foot in that wild and military frontier, required all these precautions for his security. His own ambiguous and doubtful course of policy had increased these dangers; for as he made professions to both parties in the state, and occasionally united more actively with either the one or the other, as chanced best to serve his immediate purpose, he could not be said to have either firm allies and protectors or determined enemies. His life was a life of expedients and of peril; and while, in pursuit of his interest, he made all the doubles which he thought necessary to attain his object, he often overran his prey, and missed that which he might have gained by observing a straighter course.

CHAPTER XXIV.

I'll walk on tiptoe; arm my eye with caution,
My heart with courage, and my hand with weapon,
Like him who ventures on a lion's den.

Old Play.

WHEN, issuing from the gorge of a pass which terminated upon the lake, the travellers came in sight of the ancient castle of Avenel, the old man paused, and, resting upon his pilgrim staff, looked with earnest attention upon the scene before him. The castle was, as we have said, in many places ruinous, as was evident, even at this distance, by the broken, rugged, and irregular outline of the walls and of the towers.

[1] See Castle of Avenel. Note 17.

In others it seemed more entire, and a pillar of dark smoke, which ascended from the chimneys of the donjon, and spread its long dusky pennon through the clear ether, indicated that it was inhabited. But no cornfields or inclosed pasture-grounds on the side of the lake showed that provident attention to comfort and subsistence which usually appeared near the houses of the greater, and even of the lesser, barons. There were no cottages with their patches of infield, and their crofts and gardens, surrounded by rows of massive sycamores; no church with its simple tower in the valley; no herds of sheep among the hills; no cattle on the lower ground; nothing which intimated the occasional prosecution of the arts of peace and of industry. It was plain that the inhabitants, whether few or numerous, must be considered as the garrison of the castle, living within its defended precincts, and subsisting by means which were other than peaceful.

Probably it was with this conviction that the old man, gazing on the castle, muttered to himself, " *Lapis offensionis et petra scandali!* " and then, turning to Halbert Glendinning, he added: " We may say of yonder fort as King James did of another fastness in this province, that he who built it was a thief in his heart." [1]

" But it was not so," answered Glendinning; " yonder castle was built by the old lords of Avenel, men as much beloved in peace as they were respected in war. They were the bulwark of the frontiers against foreigners, and the protectors of the natives from domestic oppression. The present usurper of their inheritance no more resembles them than the night-prowling owl resembles a falcon because she builds on the same rock."

" This Julian Avenel, then, holds no high place in the love and regard of his neighbours?" said Warden.

" So little," answered Halbert, " that, besides the jack-men and riders with whom he has associated himself, and of whom he has many at his disposal, I know of few who voluntarily

---

[1] It was of Lochwood, the hereditary fortress of the Johnstones of Annandale, a strong castle situated in the centre of a quaking bog, that James VI. made this remark.

associate with him. He has been more than once outlawed both by England and Scotland, his lands declared forfeited, and his head set at a price. But in these unquiet times a man so daring as Julian Avenel has ever found some friends willing to protect him against the penalties of the law, on condition of his secret services."

"You describe a dangerous man," replied Warden.

"You may have experience of that," replied the youth, "if you deal not the more warily; though it may be that he also has forsaken the communion of the church, and gone astray in the path of heresy."

"What your blindness terms the path of heresy," answered the Reformer, "is indeed the straight and narrow way, wherein he who walks turns not aside, whether for worldly wealth or for worldly passions. Would to God this man were moved by no other and no worse spirit than that which prompts my poor endeavours to extend the kingdom of Heaven! This Baron of Avenel is personally unknown to me, is not of our congregation or of our counsel; yet I bear to him charges touching my safety from those whom he must fear if he does not respect them, and upon that assurance I will venture upon his hold. I am now sufficiently refreshed by these few minutes of repose."

"Take, then, this advice for your safety," said Halbert, "and believe that it is founded upon the usage of this country and its inhabitants. If you can better shift for yourself, go not to the Castle of Avenel; if you do risk going thither, obtain from him, if possible, his safe-conduct, and beware that he swears it by the Black Rood. And lastly, observe whether he eats with you at the board, or pledges you in the cup; for if he gives you not these signs of welcome, his thoughts are evil towards you."

"Alas!" said the preacher, "I have no better earthly refuge for the present than these frowning towers, but I go thither trusting to aid which is not of this earth. But thou, good youth, needest thou trust thyself in this dangerous den?"

"I," answered Halbert, "am in no danger. I am well known to Christie of the Clinthill, the henchman of this

Julian Avenel; and, what is a yet better protection, I have nothing either to provoke malice or to tempt plunder."

The tramp of a steed, which clattered along the shingly banks of the loch, was now heard behind them; and, when they looked back, a rider was visible, his steel cap and the point of his long lance glancing in the setting sun, as he rode rapidly towards them.

Halbert Glendinning soon recognised Christie of the Clint-hill, and made his companion aware that the henchman of Julian Avenel was approaching.

" Ha, youngling!" said Christie to Halbert, as he came up to them, " thou hast made good my word at last, and come to take service with my noble master, hast thou not? Thou shalt find me a good friend and a true; and ere St. Barnaby come round again, thou shalt know every pass betwixt Millburn Plain and Netherby, as if thou hadst been born with a jack on thy back and a lance in thy hand. What old carle hast thou with thee? He is not of the brotherhood of St. Mary's; at least he has not the buist of these black cattle."

" He is a wayfaring man," said Halbert, " who has concerns with Julian of Avenel. For myself, I intend to go to Edin-burgh to see the court and the Queen, and when I return hither we will talk of your proffer. Meantime, as thou hast often in-vited me to the castle, I crave hospitality there to-night for myself and my companion."

" For thyself, and welcome, young comrade," replied Christie; " but we harbour no pilgrims, nor aught that looks like a pilgrim."

" So please you," said Warden, " I have letters of commen-dation to thy master from a sure friend, whom he will right willingly oblige in higher matters than in affording me a brief protection. And I am no pilgrim, but renounce the same, with all its superstitious observances."

He offered his letters to the horseman, who shook his head.

" These," he said, " are matters for my master, and it will be well if he can read them himself; for me, sword and lance are my book and psalter, and have been since I was twelve years old. But I will guide you to the castle, and the Baron of Avenel will himself judge of your errand."

By this time the party had reached the causeway, along which Christie advanced at a trot, intimating his presence to the warders within the castle by a shrill and peculiar whistle. At this signal the farther drawbridge was lowered. The horseman passed it, and disappeared under the gloomy portal which was beyond it.

Glendinning and his companion, advancing more leisurely along the rugged causeway, stood at length under the same gateway, over which frowned in dark red freestone the ancient armorial bearings of the house of Avenel, which represented a female figure shrouded and muffled, which occupied the whole field.[1] The cause of their assuming so singular a device was uncertain, but the figure was generally supposed to represent the mysterious being called the White Lady of Avenel. The sight of this mouldering shield awakened in the mind of Halbert the strange circumstances which had connected his fate with that of Mary Avenel, and with the doings of the spiritual being who was attached to her house, and whom he saw here represented in stone, as he had before seen her effigy upon the seal ring of Walter Avenel, which, with other trinkets formerly mentioned, had been saved from pillage and brought to Glendearg, when Mary's mother was driven from her habitation.

"You sigh, my son," said the old man, observing the impression made on his youthful companion's countenance, but mistaking the cause; "if you fear to enter, we may yet return."

"That can you not," said Christie of the Clinthill, who emerged at that instant from the side door under the archway. "Look yonder, and choose whether you will return skimming the water like a wild duck, or winging the air like a plover."

They looked, and saw that the drawbridge which they had just crossed was again raised, and now interposed its planks betwixt the setting sun and the portal of the castle, deepening

[1] There is an ancient English family, I believe, which bears, or did bear, a ghost or spirit passant sable in a field argent. This seems to have been a device of a punning or "canting" herald.

the gloom of the arch under which they stood. Christie laughed, and bid them follow him, saying, by way of encouragement, in Halbert's ear: "Answer boldly and readily to whatever the Baron asks you. Never stop to pick your words, and above all show no fear of him: the devil is not so black as he is painted."

As he spoke thus, he introduced them into the large stone hall, at the upper end of which blazed a huge fire of wood. The long oaken table, which, as usual, occupied the midst of the apartment, was covered with rude preparations for the evening meal of the Baron and his chief domestics, five or six of whom, strong, athletic, savage-looking men, paced up and down the lower end of the hall, which rang to the jarring clang of their long swords that clashed as they moved, and to the heavy tramp of their high-heeled jack-boots. Iron jacks, or coats of buff, formed the principal part of their dress, and steel bonnets, or large slouched hats with Spanish plumes drooping backwards, were their head attire.

The Baron of Avenel was one of those tall, muscular, martial figures which are the favourite subjects of Salvator Rosa. He wore a cloak which had been once gaily trimmed, but which, by long wear and frequent exposure to the weather, was now faded in its colours. Thrown negligently about his tall person, it partly hid and partly showed a short doublet of buff, under which was in some places visible that light shirt of mail which was called a "secret," because worn instead of more ostensible armour, to protect against private assassination. A leathern belt sustained a large and heavy sword on one side, and on the other that gay poniard which had once called Sir Piercie Shafton master, of which the hatchments and gildings were already much defaced, either by rough usage or neglect.

Notwithstanding the rudeness of his apparel, Julian Avenel's manner and countenance had far more elevation than those of the attendants who surrounded him. He might be fifty or upwards, for his dark hair was mingled with grey, but age had neither tamed the fire of his eye nor the enterprise of his disposition. His countenance had been handsome, for beauty was an attribute of the family; but the lines were roughened by fatigue and exposure to the weather, and rendered coarse by the habitual indulgence of violent passions.

He seemed in deep and moody reflection, and was pacing at a distance from his dependants along the upper end of the hall, sometimes stopping from time to time to caress and feed a goshawk, which sat upon his wrist, with its jesses (*i.e.* the leathern straps fixed to its legs) wrapt around his hand. The bird, which seemed not insensible to its master's attention, answered his caresses by ruffling forward its feathers and pecking playfully at his finger. At such intervals the Baron smiled, but instantly resumed the darksome air of sullen meditation. He did not even deign to look upon an object which few could have passed and repassed so often without bestowing on it a transient glance.

This was a woman of exceeding beauty, rather gaily than richly attired, who sat on a low seat close by the huge hall chimney. The gold chains round her neck and arms; the gay gown of green which swept the floor; the silver-embroidered girdle, with its bunch of keys, depending in housewifely pride by a silver chain; the yellow silken *couvre-chef* (Scotticé, curch) which was disposed around her head, and partly concealed her dark profusion of hair; above all, the circumstances so delicately touched in the old ballad, that "the girdle was too short," the "gown of green all too strait," for the wearer's present shape, would have intimated the Baron's lady. But then the lowly seat; the expression of deep melancholy, which was changed into a timid smile whenever she saw the least chance of catching the eye of Julian Avenel; the subdued look of grief, and the starting tear for which that constrained smile was again exchanged when she saw herself entirely disregarded —these were not the attributes of a wife, or [rather] they were those of a dejected and afflicted female who had yielded her love on less than legitimate terms.

Julian Avenel, as we have said, continued to pace the hall without paying any of that mute attention which is rendered to almost every female either by affection or courtesy. He

seemed totally unconscious of her presence, or of that of his
attendants, and was only roused from his own dark reflections
by the notice he paid to the falcon, to which, however, the
lady seemed to attend, as if studying to find either an opportunity of speaking to the Baron, or of findigg something enig-
matical in the expressions which he used to the bird. All this
the strangers had time enough to remark; for no sooner had
they entered the apartment than their usher, Christie of the
Clinthill, after exchanging a significant glance with the menials or troopers at the lower end of the apartment, signed to
Halbert Glendinning and to his companion to stand still near
the door, while he himself, advancing nearer the table, placed
himself in such a situation as to catch the Baron's observation
when he should be disposed to look around, but without presuming to intrude himself on his master's notice. Indeed,
the look of this man, naturally bold, hardy, and audacious,
seemed totally changed when he was in presence of his lord,
and resembled the dejected and cowering manner of a quar-
relsome dog when rebuked by his owner, or when he finds himself obliged to deprecate the violence of a superior adversary
of his own species.

In spite of the novelty of his own situation, and every painful feeling connected with it, Halbert felt his curiosity interested in the female who sate by the chimney unnoticed and
unreguarded. He marked with what keen and trembling solicitude she watched the broken words of Julian, and how her
glance stole towards him, ready to be averted upon the slightest chance of his perceiving himself to be watched.

Meantime, he went on with his dalliance with his feathered
favourite, now giving, now withholding, the morsel with which
he was about to feed the bird, and so exciting its appetite and
gratifying it by turns. "What! more yet? Thou foul kite,
thou wouldst never have done: give thee part thou wilt have
all. Ay, prune thy feathers, and prink thyself gay—much
thou wilt make of it now; dost think I know thee not? dost
think I see not that all that ruffling and pluming of wing and
feathers is not for thy master, but to try what thou canst
make of him, thou greedy gled? Well—there—take it then,

and rejoice thyself; little boon goes far with thee, and with all thy sex—and so it should."

He ceased to look on the bird, and again traversed the apartment. Then taking another small piece of raw meat from the trencher, on which it was placed ready cut for his use, he began once again to tempt and tease the bird, by offering and withdrawing it, until he awakened its wild and bold disposition. "What! struggling, fluttering, aiming at me with beak and single?[1] So la! so la! wouldst mount? wouldst fly? the jesses are round thy clutches, fool: thou canst neither stir nor soar, but by my will. Beware thou come to reclaim, wench, else I will wring thy head off one of these days. Well, have it then, and welfare thou with it. So ho, Jenkin!" One of the attendants stepped forward. "Take the foul gled hence to the mew—or, stay, leave her, but look well to her casting and to her bathing; we will see her fly to-morrow. How now, Christie, so soon returned?"

Christie advanced to his master, and gave an account of himself and his journey, in the way in which a police-officer holds communication with his magistrate, that is, as much by signs as by words.

"Noble sir," said that worthy satellite, "the Laird of ——," he named no place, but pointed with his finger in a southwestern direction, "may not ride with you the day he purposed, because the Lord Warden has threatened that he will——"

Here another blank, intelligibly enough made up by the speaker touching his own neck with his left forefinger, and leaning his head a little to one side.

"Cowardly caitiff!" said Julian. "By Heaven! the whole world turns sheer naught—it is not worth a brave man's living in; ye may ride a day and night, and never see a feather wave or hear a horse prance; the spirit of our fathers is dead amongst us—the very brutes are degenerated—the cattle we bring home at our life's risk are mere carrion—our hawks are riflers—our hounds are turnspits and trindle-tails—our men are women—and our women are——"

---

[1] In the *kindly* language of hawking, as Lady Juliana Berners terms it, hawks' talons are called singles.

He looked at the female for the first time, and stopped short
in the midst of what he was about to say, though there was
something so contemptuous in the glance that the blank might
have been thus filled up: "Our women are such as she is."

He said it not, however, and, as if desirous of attracting his
attention at all risks, and in whatever manner, she rose and
came forward to him, but with a timorousness ill-disguised
by affected gaiety. "Our women, Julian—what would you
say of the women?"

"Nothing," answered Julian Avenel, "at least nothing but
that they are kind-hearted wenches like thyself, Kate." The
female coloured deeply, and returned to her seat. "And what
strangers hast thou brought with thee, Christie, that stand
yonder like two stone statues?" said the Baron.

"The taller," answered Christie, "is, so please you, a young
fellow called Halbert Glendinning, the eldest son of the old
widow at Glendearg."

"What brings him here?" said the Baron. "Hath he any
message from Mary Avenel?"

"Not as I think," said Christie; "the youth is roving the
country: he was always a wild slip, for I have known him
since he was the height of my sword."

"What qualities hath he?" said the Baron.

"All manner of qualities," answered his follower: "he can
strike a buck, track a deer, fly a hawk, halloo to a hound; he
shoots in the long and cross-bow to a hair's-breadth, wields a
lance or sword like myself nearly, backs a horse manfully and
fairly; I wot not what more a man need to do to make him a
gallant companion."

"And who," said the Baron, "is the old miser[1] who stands
beside him?"

"Some cast of a priest as I fancy; he says he is charged
with letters to you."

"Bid them come forward," said the Baron; and no sooner
had they approached him more nearly, than, struck by the
fine form and strength displayed by Halbert Glendinning, he

---

[1] Used in the sense in which it often occurs in Spenser, and which is
indeed its literal import, "wretched old man."

addressed him thus: "I am told, young swankie, that you are roaming the world to seek your fortune; if you will serve Julian Avenel, you may find it without going farther."

"So please you," answered Glendinning, "something has chanced to me that makes it better I should leave this land, and I am bound for Edinburgh."

"What! thou hast stricken some of the king's deer, I warrant; or lightened the meadows of St. Mary's of some of their beeves; or thou hast taken a moonlight leap over the Border?"

"No, sir," said Halbert, "my case is entirely different."

"Then I warrant thee," said the Baron, "thou hast stabbed some brother churl in a fray about a wench; thou art a likely lad to wrangle in such a cause."

Ineffably disgusted at his tone and manner, Halbert Glendinning remained silent, while the thought darted across his mind, what would Julian Avenel have said, had he known the quarrel, of which he spoke so lightly, had arisen on account of his own brother's daughter! "But be thy cause of flight what it will," said Julian, in continuation, "dost thou think the law or its emissaries can follow thee into this island, or arrest thee under the standard of Avenel? Look at the depth of the lake, the strength of the walls, the length of the causeway; look at my men, and think if they are likely to see a comrade injured, or if I, their master, am a man to desert a faithful follower, in good or evil. I tell thee, it shall be an eternal day of truce betwixt thee and justice, as they call it, from the instant thou hast put my colours into thy cap: thou shalt ride by the warden's nose as thou wouldst pass an old market-woman, and ne'er a cur which follows him shall dare to bay at thee!"

"I thank you for your offers, noble sir," replied Halbert, "but I must answer in brief, that I cannot profit by them; my fortunes lead me elsewhere."

"Thou art a self-willed fool for thy pains," said Julian, turning from him; and signing Christie to approach, he whispered in his ear: "There is promise in that young fellow's looks, Christie, and we want men of limbs and sinews so compacted; those thou hast brought to me of late are the mere refuse of mankind, wretches scarce worth the arrow that ends them: this youngster is limbed like St. George. Ply him with wine and wassail; let the wenches weave their meshes about him like spiders—thou understandest?" Christie gave a sagacious nod of intelligence, and fell back to a respectful distance from his master. "And thou, old man," said the Baron, turning to the elder traveller, "hast thou been roaming the world after fortune too? it seems not she has fallen into thy way."

"So please you," replied Warden, "I were perhaps more to be pitied than I am now had I indeed met with that fortune which, like others, I have sought in my greener days."

"Nay, understand me, friend," said the Baron; "if thou art satisfied with thy buckram gown and long staff, I also am well content thou shouldst be as poor and contemptible as is good for the health of thy body and soul. All I care to know of thee is, the cause which hath brought thee to my castle, where few crows of thy kind care to settle. Thou art, I warrant thee, some ejected monk of a suppressed convent, paying in his old days the price of the luxurious idleness in which he spent his youth. Ay, or it may be some pilgrim with a budget of lies from St. James of Compostella or Our Lady of Loretto; or thou mayest be some pardoner with his budget of relics from Rome, forgiving sins at a penny a dozen, and one to the tale. Ay, I guess why I find thee in this boy's company, and doubtless thou wouldst have such a strapping lad as he to carry thy wallet, and relieve thy lazy shoulders; but, by the mass, I will cross thy cunning. I make my vow to sun and moon, I will not see a proper lad so misleard as to run the country with an old knave, like Simmie and his brother. Away with thee!" he added, rising in wrath, and speaking so fast as to give no opportunity of answer, being probably determined to terrify the elder guest into an abrupt flight— "away with thee, with thy clouted coat, scrip, and scallop-shell, or, by the name of Avenel, I will have them loose the hounds on thee!"

Warden waited with the greatest patience until Julian Avenel, astonished that the threats and violence of his language made no impression on him, paused in a sort of wonder, and said in a less imperious tone: "Why the fiend dost thou not answer me?"

"When you have done speaking," said Warden, in the same composed manner, "it will be full time to reply."

"Say on, man, in the devil's name; but take heed—beg not here—were it but for the rinds of cheese, the refuse of the rats, or a morsel that my dogs would turn from—neither a grain of meal, nor the nineteenth part of a grey groat, will I give to any feigned limmar of thy coat."

"It may be," answered Warden, "that you would have less quarrel with my coat if you knew what it covers. I am neither friar nor mendicant, and would be right glad to hear thy testimony against these foul deceivers of God's church, and usurpers of His rights over the Christian flock, were it given in Christian charity."

"And who or what art thou, then," said Avenel, "that thou comest to this Borderland, and art neither monk, nor soldier, nor broken man?"

"I am an humble teacher [preacher] of the Holy Word," answered Warden. "This letter from a most noble person will speak why I am here at this present time."

He delivered the letter to the Baron, who regarded the seal with some surprise, and then looked on the letter itself, which seemed to excite still more. He then fixed his eyes on the stranger, and said, in a menacing tone: "I think thou darest not betray me or deceive me?"

"I am not the man to attempt either," was the concise reply.

Julian Avenel carried the letter to the window, where he perused, or at least attempted to peruse, it more than once, often looking from the paper and gazing on the stranger who had delivered it, as if he meant to read the purport of the missive in the face of the messenger. Julian at length called to the female: "Catherine, bestir thee, and fetch me presently that letter which I bade thee keep ready at hand in thy casket, having no sure lockfast place of my own."

Catherine went with the readiness of one willing to be employed; and as she walked, the situation which requires a

wider gown and a longer girdle, and in which woman claims
from man a double portion of the most anxious care, was still
more visible than before. She soon returned with the paper,
and was rewarded with a cold, "I thank thee, wench; thou
art a careful secretary."

This second paper he also perused and reperused more than
once, and still, as he read it, bent from time to time a wary
and observant eye upon Henry Warden. This examination
and re-examination, though both the man and the place were
dangerous, the preacher endured with the most composed and
steady countenance, seeming, under the eagle, or rather the vul-
ture, eye of the Baron, as unmoved as under the gaze of an ordinary and peaceful peasant. At length Julian Avenel folded
both papers, and having put them into the pocket of his cloak,
cleared his brow, and, coming forward, addressed his female
companion. "Catherine," said he, "I have done this good
man injustice, when I mistook him for one of the drones of
Rome. He is a preacher, Catherine—a preacher of the—the
new doctrine of the Lords of the Congregation."

"The doctrine of the blessed Scriptures," said the preacher,
"purified from the devices of men."

"Sayest thou?" said Julian Avenel. "Well, thou mayest
call it what thou lists; but to me it is recommended because
it flings off all those sottish dreams about saints and angels
and devils, and unhorses the lazy monks that have ridden us
so long, and spur-galled us so hard. No more masses and
corpse-gifts; no more tithes and offerings to make men poor;
no more prayers or psalms to make men cowards; no more
christenings and penances, and confessions and marriages."

"So please you," said Henry Warden, "it is against the
corruptions, not against the fundamental doctrines, of the
church, which we desire to renovate, and not to abolish."

"Prithee, peace, man," said the Baron; "we of the laity
care not what you set up, so you pull merrily down what
stands in our way. Specially it suits well with us of the
southland fells; for it is our profession to turn the world upside down, and we live ever the blythest life when the downer
side is uppermost."

Warden would have replied; but the Baron allowed him not time, striking the table with the hilt of his dagger, and crying out: "Ha! you loitering knaves, bring our supper meal quickly. See you not this holy man is exhausted for lack of food? Heard ye ever of priest or preacher that devoured not his five meals a day?"

The attendants bustled to and fro, and speedily brought in several large smoking platters, filled with huge pieces of beef, boiled and roasted, but without any variety whatsoever, without vegetables, and almost without bread, though there was at the upper end a few oat-cakes in a basket.

Julian Avenel made a sort of apology to Warden. "You have been commended to our care, sir preacher, since that is your style, by a person whom we highly honour."

"I am assured," said Warden, "that the most noble Lord——"

"Prithee, peace, man," said Avenel; "what need of naming names, so we understand each other? I meant but to speak in reference to your safety and comfort, of which he desires us to be chary. Now, for your safety, look at my walls and water. But touching your comfort, we have no corn of our own, and the meal-girnels of the south are less easily transported than their beeves, seeing they have no legs to walk upon. But what though? a stoup of wine thou shalt have, and of the best; thou shalt sit betwixt Catherine and me at the board-end. And, Christie, do thou look to the young springald, and call to the cellarer for a flagon of the best."

The Baron took his wonted place at the upper end of the board; his Catherine sate down, and courteously pointed to a seat betwixt them for their reverend guest. But, notwithstanding the influence both of hunger and fatigue, Henry Warden retained his standing posture.

CHAPTER XXV.

When lovely woman stoops to folly,
And finds too late that men betray——

JULIAN AVENEL saw with surprise the demeanour of the reverend stranger. "Beshrew me," he said, "these new-fashioned religioners have fast-days, I warrant me; the old ones used to confer these blessings chiefly on the laity."

"We acknowledge no such rule," said the preacher. "We hold that our faith consists not in using or abstaining from special meats on special days; and in fasting we rend our hearts, and not our garments."

"The better—the better for yourselves, and the worse for Tom Tailor," said the Baron; "but come, sit down, or, if thou needs must e'en give us a cast of thine office, mutter thy charm."

"Sir Baron," said the preacher, "I am in a strange land, where neither mine office nor my doctrine are known, and where, it would seem, both are greatly misunderstood. It is my duty so to bear me that in my person, however unworthy, my Master's dignity may be respected, and that sin may take no confidence from relaxation of the bonds of discipline."

"Ho la! halt there," said the Baron; "thou wert sent hither for thy safety, but not, I think, to preach to or control me. What is it thou wouldst have, sir preacher? Remember thou speakest to one somewhat short of patience, who loves a short health and a long draught."

"In a word, then," said Henry Warden, "that lady——"

"How!" said the Baron, starting—"what of her? What hast thou to say of that dame?"

"Is she thy house-dame?" said the preacher, after a moment's pause, in which he seemed to seek for the best mode of expressing what he had to say—"is she, in brief, thy wife?"

The unfortunate young woman pressed both her hands on her face, as if to hide it, but the deep blush which crimsoned her brow and neck showed that her cheeks were also glowing;

and the bursting tears, which found their way betwixt her slender fingers, bore witness to her sorrow, as well as to her shame.

"Now, by my father's ashes!" said the Baron, rising and spurning from him his footstool with such violence that it hit the wall on the opposite side of the apartment; then instantly constraining himself, he muttered: "What need to run myself into trouble for a fool's word?" Then resuming his seat, he answered coldly and scornfully: "No, sir priest or sir preacher, Catherine is not my wife—Cease thy whimpering, thou foolish wench!—She is not my wife, but she is handfasted with me, and that makes her as honest a woman."

"Handfasted!" repeated Warden.

"Knowest thou not that rite, holy man?" said Avenel, in the same tone of derision; "then I will tell thee. We Border men are more wary than your inland clowns of Fife and Lothian: no jump in the dark for us, no clenching the fetters around our wrists till we know how they will wear with us: we take our wives, like our horses, upon trial. When we are handfasted, as we term it, we are man and wife for a year and day; that space gone by, each may choose another mate, or, at their pleasure, may call the priest to marry them for life; and this we call handfasting." [1]

"Then," said the preacher, "I tell thee, noble Baron, in brotherly love to thy soul, it is a custom licentious, gross, and corrupted, and, if persisted in, dangerous, yea damnable. It binds thee to the frailer being while she is the object of desire; it relieves thee when she is most the subject of pity; it gives all to brutal sense, and nothing to generous and gentle affection. I say to thee, that he who can meditate the breach of such an engagement, abandoning the deluded woman and the helpless offspring, is worse than the birds of prey; for of them the males remain with their mates until the nestlings can take wing. Above all, I say it is contrary to the pure Christian doctrine, which assigns woman to man as the partner of his labour, the soother of his evil, his helpmate in peril, his friend in affliction; not as the toy of his looser hours,

1 See Note 18.

or as a flower which, once cropped, he may throw aside at pleasure."

"Now, by the saints, a most virtuous homily!" said the Baron; "quaintly conceived and curiously pronounced, and to a well-chosen congregation. Hark ye, sir gospeller! trow ye to have a fool in hand? Know I not that your sect rose by bluff Harry Tudor, merely because ye aided him to change *his* Kate; and wherefore should I not use the same Christian liberty with *mine?* Tush, man! bless the good food, and meddle not with what concerns thee not; thou hast no gull in Julian Avenel."

"He hath gulled and cheated himself," said the preacher, "should he even incline to do that poor sharer of his domestic cares the imperfect justice that remains to him. Can he now raise her to the rank of a pure and uncontaminated matron? Can he deprive his child of the misery of owing birth to a mother who has erred. He can indeed give them both the rank, the state of married wife and of lawful son; but, in public opinion, their names will be smirched and sullied with a stain which his tardy efforts cannot entirely efface. Yet render it to them, Baron of Avenel—render to them this late and imperfect justice. Bid me bind you together for ever, and celebrate the day of your bridal, not with feasting or wassail, but with sorrow for past sin, and the resolution to commence a better life. Happy then will the chance have been that has drawn me to this castle, though I come driven by calamity, and unknowing where my course is bound, like a leaf travelling on the north wind."

The plain, and even coarse, features of the zealous speaker were warmed at once and ennobled by the dignity of his enthusiasm; and the wild Baron, lawless as he was, and accustomed to spurn at the control whether of religious or moral law, felt, for the first time perhaps in his life, that he was under subjection to a mind superior to his own. He sat mute and suspended in his deliberations, hesitating betwixt anger and shame, yet borne down by the weight of the just rebuke thus boldly fulminated against him.

The unfortunate young woman, conceiving hopes from her

tyrant's silence and apparent indecision, forgot both her fear and shame in her timid expectation that Avenel would relent; and fixing upon him her anxious and beseeching eyes, gradually drew near and nearer to his seat, till at length, laying a trembling hand on his cloak, she ventured to utter: "O noble Julian, listen to the good man!"

The speech and the motion were ill-timed, and wrought on that proud and wayward spirit the reverse of her wishes.

The fierce Baron started up in fury, exclaiming: "What! thou foolish callet, art thou confederate with this strolling vagabond, whom thou hast seen beard me in mine own hall! Hence with thee, and think that I am proof both to male and female hypocrisy!"

The poor girl started back, astounded at his voice of thunder and looks of fury, and, turning pale as death, endeavoured to obey his orders, and tottered towards the door. Her limbs failed in the attempt, and she fell on the stone floor in a manner which her situation might have rendered fatal. The blood gushed from her face. Halbert Glendinning brooked not a sight so brutal, but, uttering a deep imprecation, started from his seat, and laid his hand on his sword, under the strong impulse of passing it through the body of the cruel and hardhearted ruffian. But Christie of the Clinthill, guessing his intention, threw his arms around him, and prevented him from stirring to execute his purpose.

The impulse to such a dangerous act of violence was indeed but momentary, as it instantly appeared that Avenel himself, shocked at the effects of his violence, was lifting up and endeavouring to soothe in his own way the terrified Catherine.

" Peace," he said—" prithee, peace, thou silly minion; why, Kate, though I listen not to this tramping preacher, I said not what might happen an thou dost bear me a stout boy. There —there—dry thy tears—call thy women. So ho! where be these queans? Christie — Rowley — Hutcheon — drag them hither by the hair of the head!"

A half-dozen of startled, wild-looking females rushed into the room, and bore out her who might be either termed their mistress or their companion. She showed little sign of life, except by groaning faintly and keeping her hand on her side.

No sooner had this luckless female been conveyed from the apartment than the Baron, advancing to the table, filled and drank a deep goblet of wine; then putting an obvious restraint on his passions, turned to the preacher, who stood horror-struck at the scene he had witnessed, and said: "You have borne too hard on us, sir preacher; but coming with the commendations which you have brought me, I doubt not but your meaning was good. But we are a wilder folk than you inland men of Fife and Lothian. Be advised, therefore, by me. Spur not an unbroken horse; put not your ploughshare too deep into new land. Preach to us spiritual liberty, and we will hearken to you; but we will give no way to spiritual bondage. Sit, therefore, down, and pledge me in old sack, and we will talk over other matters."

"It is *from* spiritual bondage," said the preacher, in the same tone of admonitory reproof, "that I came to deliver you —it is from a bondage more fearful than that of the heaviest earthly gyves: it is from your own evil passions."

"Sit down," said Avenel, fiercely—"sit down while the play is good, else by my father's crest and my mother's honour——!"

"Now," whispered Christie of the Clinthill to Halbert, "if he refuse to sit down, I would not give a grey groat for his head."

"Lord Baron," said Warden, "thou hast placed me in ex-tremity. But if the question be, whether I am to hide the light which I am commanded to show forth or to lose the light of this world, my choice is made. I say to thee, like the Holy Baptist to Herod, it is not lawful for thee to have this woman; and I say it, though bonds and death be the consequence, counting my life as nothing in comparison of the ministry to which I am called."

Julian Avenel, enraged at the firmness of this reply, flung from his right hand the cup in which he was about to drink to his guest, and from the other cast off the hawk, which flew wildly through the apartment. His first motion was to lay

hand upon his dagger. But, changing his resolution, he exclaimed: "To the dungeon with this insolent stroller! I will
hear no man speak a word for him. Look to the falcon,
Christie, thou fool; an she escape, I will despatch you after
her every man. Away with that hypocritical dreamer; drag
him hence if he resist!"

He was obeyed in both points. Christie of the Clinthill
arrested the hawk's flight by putting his foot on her jesses,
and so holding her fast, while Henry Warden was led off,
without having shown the slightest symptom of terror, by
two of the Baron's satellites. Julian Avenel walked the
apartment for a short space in sullen silence, and despatch-
ing one of his attendants with a whispered message, which
probably related to the health of the unfortunate Catherine, he said aloud, "These rash and meddling priests! By
Heaven! they make us worse than we should be without
them."[1]

The answer which he presently received seemed somewhat
to pacify his angry mood, and he took his place at the board,
commanding his retinue to do the like. All sat down in silence, and began the repast.

During the meal, Christie in vain attempted to engage his
youthful companion in carousal, or, at least, in conversation.
Halbert Glendinning pleaded fatigue, and expressed himself
unwilling to take any liquor stronger than the heather ale,
which was at that time frequently used at meals. Thus every
effort at joviality died away, until the Baron, striking his hand
against the table, as if impatient of the long unbroken silence,
cried out aloud: "What, ho! my masters, are ye Border riders, and sit as mute over your meal as a mess of monks and
friars? Some one sing, if no one list to speak. Meat eaten
without either mirth or music is ill of digestion. Louis," he
added, speaking to one of the youngest of his followers, "thou
art ready enough to sing when no one bids thee."

The young man looked first at his master, then up to the
arched roof of the hall, then drank off the horn of ale, or
wine, which stood beside him, and with a rough yet not un-

melodious voice sung the following ditty to the ancient air of
" Blue Bonnets over the Border":

> March, march, Ettrick and Teviotdale,
>   Why the deil dinna ye march forward in order?
> March, march, Eskdale and Liddesdale,
>   All the Blue Bonnets are bound for the Border.
>   Many a banner spread,
>   Flutters above your head,
>   Many a crest that is famous in story;
>   Mount and make ready then,
>   Sons of the mountain glen,
>   Fight for the Queen and the old Scottish glory!
>
> Come from the hills where the hirsels are grazing,
>   Come from the glen of the buck and the roe ;
> Come to the crag where the beacon is blazing,
>   Come with the buckler, the lance, and the bow.
>   Trumpets are sounding,
>   War-steeds are bounding,
>   Stand to your arms then, and march in good order;
>   England shall many a day
>   Tell of the bloody fray,
>   When the Blue Bonnets came over the Border ! "

The song, rude as it was, had in it that warlike character
which at any other time would have roused Halbert's spirit;
but at present the charm of minstrelsy had no effect upon
him. He made it his request to Christie to suffer him to retire to rest, a request with which that worthy person, seeing
no chance of making a favourable impression on his intended
proselyte in his present humour, was at length pleased to
comply.   But no Sergeant Kite who ever practised the profession of recruiting was more attentive that his object should
not escape him than was Christie of the Clinthill.   He indeed
conducted Halbert Glendinning to a small apartment overlook-
ing the lake, which was accommodated with a truckle-bed.
But before quitting him Christie took special care to give a
look to the bars which crossed the outside of the window, and
when he left the apartment he failed not to give the key a
double turn—circumstances which convinced young Glendinning that there was no intention of suffering him to depart
from the Castle of Avenel at his own time and pleasure.   He
judged it, however, most prudent to let these alarming symptoms pass without observation.

No sooner did he find himself in undisturbed solitude than he ran rapidly over the events of the day in his recollection, and to his surprise found that his own precarious fate, and even the death of Piercie Shafton, made less impression on him than the singularly bold and determined conduct of his companion, Henry Warden. Providence, which suits its instruments to the end they are to achieve, had awakened in the cause of Reformation in Scotland a body of preachers of more energy than refinement, bold in spirit, and strong in faith, contenmers of whatever stood betwixt them and their principal object, and seeking the advancement of the great cause in which they laboured by the roughest road, provided it were the shortest. The soft breeze may wave the willow, but it requires the voice of the tempest to agitate the boughs of the oak; and, accordingly, to milder hearers, and in a less rude age, their manners would have been ill adapted, but they were singularly successful in their mission to the rude people to whom it was addressed.

Owing to these reasons, Halbert Glendinning, who had resisted and repelled the arguments of the preacher, was forcibly struck by the firmness of his demeanour in the dispute with Julian Avenel. It might be discourteous, and most certainly it was incautious, to choose such a place and such an audience, for upbraiding with his transgressions a baron whom both manners and situation placed in full possession of independent power. But the conduct of the preacher was uncompromising, firm, manly, and obviously grounded upon the deepest conviction which duty and principle could afford; and Glendinning, who had viewed the conduct of Avenel with the deepest abhorrence, was proportionally interested in the brave old man, who had ventured life rather than withhold the censure due to guilt. This pitch of virtue seemed to him to be in religion what was demanded by chivalry of her votaries in war— an absolute surrender of all selfish feelings, and a combination of every energy proper to the human mind to discharge the task which duty demanded.

Halbert was at the period when youth is most open to generous emotions, and knows best how to appreciate them in others, and he felt, although he hardly knew why, that, whether Catholic or heretic, the safety of this man deeply interested him. Curiosity mingled with the feeling, and led him to wonder what the nature of those doctrines could be which stole their votary so completely from himself, and devoted him to chains or to death as their sworn champion. He had indeed been told of saints and martyrs of former days who had braved for their religious faith the extremity of death and torture. But their spirit of enthusiastic devotion had long slept in the ease and indolent habits of their successors, and their adventures, like those of knights-errant, were rather read for amusement than for edification. A new impulse had been necessary to rekindle the energies of religious zeal, and that impulse was now operating in favour of a purer religion, with one of whose steadiest votaries the youth had now met for the first time.

The sense that he himself was a prisoner, under the power of this savage chieftain, by no means diminished Halbert's interest in the fate of his fellow-sufferer, while he determined at the same time so far to emulate his fortitude that neither threats nor suffering should compel him to enter into the service of such a master. The possibility of escape next occurred to him, and, though with little hope of effecting it in that way, Glendinning proceeded to examine more particularly the window of the apartment. This apartment was situated in the first story of the castle, and was not so far from the rock on which it was founded but that an active and bold man might with little assistance descend to a shelf of the rock which was immediately below the window, and from thence either leap or drop himself down into the lake which lay below his eye, clear and blue in the placid light of a full summer's moon. "Were I once placed on that ledge," thought Glendinning, "Julian Avenel and Christie had seen the last of me." The size of the window favoured such an attempt, but the stanchions or iron bars seemed to form an insurmountable obstacle.

While Halbert Glendinning gazed from the window with that eagerness of hope which was prompted by the energy of his character and his determination not to yield to circumstances, his ear caught some sounds from below, and listening with more attention, he could distinguish the voice of the preacher engaged in his solitary devotions. To open a correspondence with him became immediately his object, and failing to do so by less marked sounds, he at length ventured to speak, and was answered from beneath, "Is it thou, my son?" The voice of the prisoner now sounded more distinctly than when it was first heard, for Warden had approached the small aperture which, serving his prison for a window, opened just betwixt the wall and the rock, and admitted a scanty portion of light through a wall of immense thickness. This *soupirail* being placed exactly under Halbert's window, the contiguity permitted the prisoners to converse in a low tone, when Halbert declared his intention to escape, and the possibility he saw of achieving his purpose, but for the iron stanchions of the window. "Prove thy strength, my son, in the name of God!" said the preacher. Halbert obeyed him more in despair than hope, but to his great astonishment, and somewhat to his terror, the bar parted asunder near the bottom, and the longer part being easily bent outwards and not secured with lead in the upper socket, dropt out into Halbert's hand. He immediately whispered, but as energetically as a whisper could be expressed, "By Heaven, the bar has given way in my hand!"

"Thank Heaven, my son, instead of swearing by it," answered Warden from his dungeon.

With little effort Halbert Glendinning forced himself through the opening thus wonderfully effected, and using his leathern sword-belt as a rope to assist him, let himself safely drop on the shelf of rock upon which the preacher's window opened. But through this no passage could be effected, being scarce larger than a loophole for musketry, and apparently constructed for that purpose.

"Are there no means by which I can assist your escape, my father?" said Halbert.

"There are none, my son," answered the preacher; "but if thou wilt ensure my safety, that may be in thy power."

"I will labour earnestly for it," said the youth.

"Take then a letter which I will presently write, for I have the means of light and writing materials in my scrip. Hasten towards Edinburgh, and on the way thou wilt meet a body of horse marching southwards. Give this to their leader, and acquaint him of the state in which thou hast left me. It may hap that thy doing so will advantage thyself."

In a minute or two the light of a taper gleamed through the shot-hole, and very shortly after the preacher, with the assistance of his staff, pushed a billet to Glendinning through the window.

"God bless thee, my son," said the old man, "and complete the marvellous work which He hath begun!"

"Amen!" answered Halbert, with solemnity, and proceeded on his enterprise.

He hesitated a moment whether he should attempt to descend to the edge of the water; but the steepness of the rock, notwithstanding the clearness of the night, rendered the enterprise too dangerous. He clasped his hands above his head, and boldly sprung from the precipice, shooting himself forward into the air as far as he could for fear of sunken rocks, and alighted on the lake, head foremost, with such force as sunk him for a minute below the surface. But, strong, long-breathed, and accustomed to such exercise, Halbert, even though encumbered with his sword, dived and rose like a sea-fowl, and swam across the lake in the northern direction. When he landed and looked back on the castle, he could observe that the alarm had been given, for lights glanced from window to window, and he heard the drawbridge lowered, and the tread of horses' feet upon the causeway. But, little alarmed for the consequence of a pursuit during the darkness, he wrung the water from his dress, and, plunging into the moors, directed his course to the northeast by the assistance of the polar star.

CHAPTER XXVI.

Why, what an intricate impeach is this !
I think you all have drank of Circe's cup.
If here you housed him, here he would have been;
If he were mad, he would not plead so coldly.
Comedy of Errors.

THE course of our story, leaving for the present Halbert Glendininng to the guidance of his courage and his fortune, returns to the Tower of Glendearg, where matters in the mean while fell out with which it is most fitting that the reader should be acquainted.

The meal was prepared at noontide with all the care which Elspeth and Tibb, assisted by the various accommodations which had been supplied from the monastery, could bestow on it. Their dialogue ran on as usual in the intervals of their labour, partly as between mistress and servant, partly as maintained by gossips of nearly equal quality.

"Look to the minced meat, Tibb," said Elspeth; "and turn the broach even, thou good-for-nothing Simmie: thy wits are harrying birds' nests, child. Weel, Tibb, this is a fasheous job—this Sir Piercie lying leaguer with us up here, and wha kens for how lang?"

"A fasheous job, indeed," answered her faithful attendant, "and little good did the name ever bring to fair Scotland. Ye may have your hands fuller of them than they are yet. Mony a sair heart have the Piercies given to Scots wife and bairns with their pricking on the Borders. There was Hotspur, and many more of that bloody kindred, have sate in our skirts since Malcolm's time, as Martin says!"

"Martin should keep a weel-scrapit tongue in his head," said Elspeth, "and not slander the kin of anybody that quarters at Glendearg; forbye, that Sir Piercie Shafton is much respected with the holy fathers of the community, and they will make up to us ony fasherie that we may have with him, either by good word or good deed, I'se warrant them. He is a considerate lord, the lord abbot."

"And weel he likes a saft seat to his hinder end," said Tibb; "I have seen a belted baron sit on a bare bench, and find nae fault. But an ye are pleased, mistress, I am pleased."

"Now, in good time, here comes Mysie of the Mill. And whare hae ye been, lass, for a's gane wrang without you?" said Elspeth.

"I just gaed a blink up the burn," said Mysie, "for the young lady has been down on her bed, and is no just that weel. So I gaed a gliff up the burn."

"To see the young lads come hame frae the sport, I will warrant you," said Elspeth. "Ay, ay, Tibb, that's the way the young folk guide us, Tibbie; leave us to do the wark, and out to the play themsells."

"Ne'er a bit of that, mistress," said the Maid of the Mill, stripping her round pretty arms, and looking actively and good-humouredly about her for some duty that she could discharge; "but just—I thought ye might like to ken if they were coming back, just to get the dinner forward."

"And saw you aught of them, then?" demanded Elspeth.

"Not the least tokening," said Mysie, "though I got to the head of a knowe, and though the English knight's beautiful white feather could have been seen over all the bushes in the shaw."

"The knight's white feather!" said Dame Glendinning; "ye are a sillie hempie—my Halbert's high head will be seen farther than his feather, let it be as white as it like, I trow."

Mysie made no answer, but began to knead dough for wastel-cake with all despatch, observing that Sir Piercie had partaken of that dainty, and commended it, upon the preceding day. And presently, in order to place on the fire the girdle or iron plate on which these cakes were to be baked, she displaced a stew-pan in which some of Tibb's delicacies were submitted to the action of the kitchen fire. Tibb muttered betwixt her teeth: "And it is the broth for my sick bairn that maun make room for the dainty Southron's wastel-bread! It was a blythe time in Wight Wallace's day, or good King Robert's, when the pock-puddings gat naething here but hard straiks and bloody crowns. But we will see how it will a' end."

Elspeth did not think it proper to notice these discontented expressions of Tibbie, but they sunk into her mind; for she was apt to consider her as a sort of authority in matters of war and policy, with which her former experience as bower-woman at Avenel Castle made her better acquainted than were the peaceful inhabitants of the halidome. She only spoke, however, to express her surprise that the hunters did not return.

"An they come not back the sooner," said Tibb, "they will fare the waur, for the meat will be roasted to a cinder; and there is poor Simmie that can turn the spit nae langer: the bairn is melting like an icicle in warm water. Gang awa', bairn, and take a mouthful of the caller air, and I will turn the broach till ye come back."

"Rin up to the bartizan at the tower head, callant," said Dame Glendinning, "the air will be callerer there than ony gate else, and bring us word if our Halbert and the gentleman are coming down the glen."

The boy lingered long enough to allow his substitute, Tibb Tacket, heartily to tire of her own generosity and of his cricket-stool by the side of a huge fire. He at length returned with the news that he had seen nobody.

The matter was not remarkable so far as Halbert Glendinning was concerned, for, patient alike of want and of fatigue, it was no uncommon circumstance for him to remain in the wilds till curfew time. But nobody had given Sir Pierce Shafton credit for being so keen a sportsman, and the idea of an Englishman preferring the chase to his dinner was altogether inconsistent with their preconceptions of the national character. Amidst wondering and conjecturing, the usual dinner hour passed long away; and the inmates of the tower, taking a hasty meal themselves, adjourned their more solemn preparations until the hunters' return at night, since it seemed now certain that their sport had either carried them to a greater distance, or engaged them for a longer time, than had been expected.

About four hours after noon, arrived, not the expected sportsmen, but an unlooked-for visitant, the sub-prior from the monastery. The scene of the preceding day had dwelt on the mind of Father Eustace, who was of that keen and penetrating cast of character which loves not to leave unascertained whatever of mysterious is subjected to its inquiry. His kindness was interested in the family of Glendearg, which he had now known for a long time; and besides, the community was interested in the preservation of the peace betwixt Sir Piercie Shafton and his youthful host, since whatever might draw public attention on the former could not fail to be prejudicial to the monastery, which was already threatened by the hand of power. He found the family assembled all but Mary Avenel, and was informed that Halbert Glendinning had accompanied the stranger on a day's sport. So far was well. They had not returned; but when did youth and sport conceive themselves bound by set hours? and the circumstance excited no alarm in his mind.

While he was conversing with Edward Glendinning touching his progress in the studies he had pointed out to him, they were startled by a shriek from Mary Avenel's apartment, which drew the whole family hither in headlong haste. They found her in a swoon in the arms of Old Martin, who was bitterly accusing himself of having killed her: so indeed it seemed, for her pale features and closed eyes argued rather a dead corpse than a living person. The whole family were instantly in tumult. Snatching her from Martin's arms with the eagerness of affectionate terror, Edward bore her to the casement, that she might receive the influence of the open air; the sub-prior, who, like many of his profession, had some knowledge of medicine, hastened to prescribe the readiest remedies which occurred to him; and the terrified females contended with, and impeded each other, in their rival efforts to be useful.

"It has been ane of her weary ghaists," said Dame Glendinning.

"It's just a trembling on her spirits, as her blessed mother used to have," said Tibb.

"It's some ill news has come ower her," said the miller's

maiden; while burnt feathers, cold water, and all the usual means of restoring suspended animation, were employed alternately, and with little effect.

At length a new assistant, who had joined the group unobserved, tendered his aid in the following terms: "How is this, my most fair Discretion? What cause hath moved the ruby current of life to rush back to the citadel of the heart, leaving pale those features in which it should have delighted to meander for ever! Let me approach her," he said, "with this sovereign essence, distilled by the fair hands of the divine Urania, and powerful to recall fugitive life, even if it were trembling on the verge of departure."

Thus speaking, Sir Piercie Shafton knelt down, and most gracefully presented to the nostrils of Mary Avenel a silver pouncet-box, exquisitely chased, containing a sponge dipt in the essence which he recommended so highly. Yes, gentle reader, it was Sir Piercie Shafton himself who thus unexpectedly proffered his good offices!—his cheeks, indeed, very pale, and some part of his dress stained with blood, but not otherwise appearing different from what he was on the preceding evening. But no sooner had Mary Avenel opened her eyes and fixed them on the figure of the officious courtier, than she screamed faintly, and exclaimed: "Secure the murderer!"

Those present stood aghast with astonishment, and none more so than the Euphuist, who found himself so suddenly and so strangely accused by the patient whom he was endeavouring to succour, and who repelled his attempts to yield her assistance with all the energy of abhorrence.

"Take him away!" she exclaimed—"take away the murderer!"

"Now, by my knighthood," answered Sir Piercie, "your lovely faculties either of mind or body are, O my most fair Discretion, obnubilated by some strange hallucination! For either your eyes do not discern that it is Piercie Shafton, your most devoted Affability, who stands before you, or else, your eyes discerning truly, your mind has most erroneously concluded that he has been guilty of some delict or violence to which his hand is a stranger. No murder, O most scornful Discretion, hath been this day done, saving but that which your angry glances are now performing on your most devoted captive."

He was here interrupted by the sub-prior, who had, in the mean time, been speaking with Martin apart, and had received from him an account of the circumstances which, suddenly communicated to Mary Avenel, had thrown her into this state. "Sir knight," said the sub-prior, in a very solemn tone, yet with some hesitation, "circumstances have been communicated to us of a nature so extraordinary that, reluctant as I am to exercise such authority over a guest of our venerable community, I am constrained to request from you an explanation of them. You left this tower early in the morning, accompanied by a youth, Halbert Glendinning, the eldest son of this good dame, and you return hither without him. Where, and at what hour, did you part company from him?"

The English knight paused for a moment, and then replied: "I marvel that your reverence employs so grave a tone to enforce so light a question. I parted with the villagio whom you call Halbert Glendinning some hour or twain after sunrise."

"And at what place, I pray you?" said the monk.

"In a deep ravine, where a fountain rises at the base of a huge rock, an earth-born Titan, which heaveth up its grey head, even as——"

"Spare us further description," said the sub-prior; "we know the spot. But that youth hath not since been heard of, and it will fall on you to account for him."

"My bairn!—my bairn!" exclaimed Dame Glendinning. "Yes, holy father, make the villain account for my bairn!"

"I swear, good woman, by bread and by water, which are the props of our life——"

"Swear by wine and wastel-bread, for these are the props of *thy* life, thou greedy Southron!" said Dame Glendinning; "a base belly-god, to come here to eat the best, and practise on our lives that give it to him!"

"I tell thee, woman," said Sir Piercie Shafton, "I did but go with thy son to the hunting."

"A black hunting it has been to him, poor bairn," replied Tibb; "and sae I said it wad prove since I first saw the false Southron snout of thee. Little good comes of a Piercie's hunting, from Chevy Chase till now."

"Be silent, woman," said the sub-prior, "and rail not upon the English knight; we do not yet know of anything beyond suspicion."

"We will have his heart's blood!" said Dame Glendinning; and, seconded by the faithful Tibbie, she made such a sudden onslaught on the unlucky Euphuist as must have terminated in something serious, had not the monk, aided by Mysie Happer, interposed to protect him from their fury. Edward had left the apartment the instant the disturbance broke out, and now entered sword in hand, followed by Martin and Jasper, the one having a hunting-spear in his hand, the other a cross-bow.

"Keep the door," he said to his two attendants; "shoot him or stab him without mercy should he attempt to break forth; if he offers an escape, by Heaven he shall die!"

"How now, Edward," said the sub-prior; "how is this that you so far forget yourself? meditating violence to a guest, and in my presence, who represent your liege lord?"

Edward stepped forward with his drawn sword in his hand. "Pardon me, reverend father," he said, "but in this matter the voice of nature speaks louder and stronger than yours. I turn my sword's point against this proud man, and I demand of him the blood of my brother—the blood of my father's son—of the heir of our name! If he denies to give me a true account of him, he shall not deny me vengeance."

Embarrassed as he was, Sir Piercie Shafton showed no personal fear. "Put up thy sword," he said, "young man; not in the same day does Piercie Shafton contend with two peasants."

"Hear him! he confesses the deed, holy father," said Edward.

"Be patient, my son," said the sub-prior, endeavouring to soothe the feelings which he could not otherwise control—"be patient, thou wilt attain the ends of justice better through my

means than thine own violence. And you, women, be silent.
Tibb, remove your mistress and Mary Avenel."

While Tibb, with the assistance of the other females of the
household, bore the poor mother and Mary Avenel into separate apartments, and while Edward, still keeping his sword in
his hand, hastily traversed the room, as if to prevent the possibility of Sir Piercie Shafton's escape, the sub-prior insisted
upon knowing from the perplexed knight the particulars which
he knew respecting Halbert Glendinning. His situation became extremely embarrassing, for what he might with safety
have told of the issue of their combat was so revolting to his
pride that he could not bring himself to enter into the detail;
and of Halbert's actual fate he knew, as the reader is well
aware, absolutely nothing.

The father in the mean while pressed him with remon-
strances, and prayed him to observe, he would greatly prejudice himself by declining to give a full account of the
transactions of the day. "You cannot deny," he said, "that
yesterday you seemed to take the most violent offence at this
unfortunate youth; and that you suppressed your resentment
so suddenly as to impress us all with surprise. Last night
you proposed to him this day's hunting party, and you set
out together by break of day. You parted, you said, at the
fountain near the rock, about an hour or twain after sunrise,
and it appears that before you parted you had been at strife
together."

"I said not so," replied the knight. "Here is a coil indeed
about the absence of a rustical bondsman, who, I dare say,
hath gone off—if he be gone—to join the next rascally band of
freebooters! Ye ask me, a knight of the Piercie's lineage, to
account for such an insignificant fugitive, and I answer, let
me know the price of his head, and I will pay it to your convent treasurer."

"You admit, then, that you have slain my brother?" said
Edward, interfering once more; "I will presently show you
at what price we Scots rate the lives of our friends!"

"Peace, Edward—peace, I entreat—I command thee!" said
the sub-prior. "And you, sir knight, think better of us than

to suppose you may spend Scottish blood, and reckon for it as for wine spilt in a drunken revel. This youth was no bonds-man; thou well knowest that, in thine own land, thou hadst not dared to lift thy sword against the meanest subject of England but her laws would have called thee to answer for the deed. Do not hope it will be otherwise here, for you will but deceive yourself."

"You drive me beyond my patience," said the Euphuist, "even as the over-driven ox is urged into madness! What can I tell you of a young fellow whom I have not seen since the second hour after sunrise?"

"But can you explain in what circumstances you parted with him?" said the monk.

"What *are* the circumstances, in the devil's name, which you desire should be explained? for although I protest against this constraint as alike unworthy and inhospitable, yet would I willingly end this fray, provided that by words it may be ended," said the knight.

"If these end it not," said Edward, "blows shall, and that full speedily."

"Peace, impatient boy!" said the sub-prior; "and do you, Sir Piercie Shafton, acquaint me why the ground is bloody by the verge of the fountain in Corrie-nan-Shian, where, as you say yourself, you parted from Halbert Glendinning."

Resolute not to avow his defeat if possibly he could avoid it, the knight answered, in a haughty tone, that he supposed it was no unusual thing to find the turf bloody where hunters had slain a deer.

"And did you bury your game as well as kill it?" inquired the monk. "We must know from you who is the tenant of that grave—that newly-made grave, beside the very fountain whose margin is so deeply crimsoned with blood. Thou seest thou canst not evade me; therefore be ingenuous, and tell us the fate of this unhappy youth, whose body is doubtless lying under that bloody turf."

"If it be," said Sir Piercie, "they must have buried him alive; for I swear to thee, reverend father, that this rustic juvenal parted from me in perfect health. Let the grave be

searched, and if his body be found, then deal with me as
ye list."

"It is not my sphere to determine thy fate, sir knight, but
that of the lord abbot and the right reverend chapter.   It is
but my duty to collect such information as may best possess
their wisdom with the matters which have chanced."

"Might I presume so far, reverend father," said the knight,
"I should wish to know the author and evidence of all these
suspicions, so unfoundedly urged against me?"

"It is soon told," said the sub-prior; "nor do I wish to
disguise it, if it can avail you in your defence.   This maiden,
Mary Avenel, apprehending that you nourished malice against
her foster-brother under a friendly brow, did advisedly send
up the old man, Martin Tacket, to follow your footsteps, and
to prevent mischief.   But it seems that your evil passions had
outrun precaution; for when he came to the spot, guided by
your footsteps upon the dew, he found but the bloody turf and
the new-covered grave; and after long and vain search through
the wilds after Halbert and yourself, he brought back the
sorrowful news to her who had sent him."

"Saw he not my doublet, I pray you?" said Sir Piercie;
"for when I came to myself I found that I was wrapped in
my cloak, but without my under garment, as your reverence
may observe."

So saying, he opened his cloak, forgetting, with his charac-
teristical inconsistency, that he showed his shirt stained with
blood.

"How! cruel man," said the monk, when he observed this
confirmation of his suspicions; "wilt thou deny the guilt, even
while thou bearest on thy person the blood thou hast shed?
Wilt thou longer deny that thy rash hand has robbed a mother
of a son, our community of a vassal, the Queen of Scotland of
a liege subject?   And what canst thou expect, but that, at the
least, we deliver thee up to England, as undeserving our further protection?"

"By the saints!" said the knight, now driven to extremity,
"if this blood be the witness against me, it is but rebel blood,
since this morning at sunrise it flowed within my own veins."

"How were that possible, Sir Piercie Shafton," said the monk, "since I see no wound from whence it can have flowed?"

"That," said the knight, "is the most mysterious part of the transaction. See here!"

So saying, he undid his shirt collar, and, opening his bosom, showed the spot through which Halbert's sword had passed, but already cicatrised, and bearing the appearance of a wound lately healed.

"This exhausts my patience, sir knight," said the subprior, "and is adding insult to violence and injury. Do you hold me for a child or an idiot, that you pretend to make me believe that the fresh blood with which your shirt is stained flowed from a wound which has been healed for weeks or months? Unhappy mocker, thinkest thou thus to blind us? Too well do we know that it is the blood of your victim, wrestling with you in the desparate and mortal struggle, which has thus dyed your apparel."

The knight, after a moment's recollection, said in reply: "I will be open with you, my father; bid these men stand out of ear-shot, and I will tell you all I know of this mysterious business; and muse not, good father, though it may pass thy wit to expound it, for I avouch to you it is too dark for mine own."

The monk commmanded Edward and the two men to withdraw, assuring the former that his conference with the prisoner should be brief, and giving him permission to keep watch at the door of the apartment; without which allowance he might, perhaps, have had some difficulty in procuring his absence. Edward had no sooner left the chamber than he despatched messengers to one or two families of the halidome, with whose sons his brother and he sometimes associated, to tell them that Halbert Glendinning had been murdered by an Englishman, and to require them to repair to the Tower of Glendearg without delay. The duty of revenge in such cases was held so sacred that he had no reason to doubt they would instantly come with such assistance as would ensure the detention of the prisoner. He then locked the doors of the tower, both inner and outer, and also the gate of the courtyard. Having taken these precautions, he made a hasty visit to the females of the family, exhausting himself in efforts to console them, and in protestations that he would have vengeance for his murdered brother.

———————◆———————

CHAPTER XXVII.

Now, by Our Lady, sheriff, 'tis hard reckoning,
That I, with every odds of birth and barony,
Should be detain'd here for the casual death
Of a wild forester, whose utmost having
Is but the brazen buckle of the belt
In which he sticks his hedge-knife.
Old Play.

WHILE Edward was making preparations for securing and punishing the supposed murderer of his brother, with an intense thirst for vengeance which had not hitherto shown itself as part of his character, Sir Piercie Shafton made such communications as it pleased him to the sub-prior, who listened with great attention, though the knight's narrative was none of the clearest, especially as his self-conceit led him to conceal or abridge the details which were necessary to render it intelligible.

"You are to know," he said, "reverend father, that this rustical juvenal having chosen to offer me, in the presence of your venerable superior, yourself, and other excellent and worthy persons, besides the damsel Mary Avenel, whom I term my Discretion in all honour and kindness, a gross insult, rendered yet more intolerable by the time and place, my just resentment did so gain the mastery over my discretion, that I resolved to allow him the privileges of an equal, and to indulge him with the combat."

"But, sir knight," said the sub-prior, "you still leave two matters very obscure. First, why the token he presented to you gave you so much offence, as I with others witnessed; and then again, how the youth, whom you then met for the first, or at least the second, time, knew so much of your history as enabled him so greatly to move you."

The knight coloured very deeply.

"For your first query," he said, "most reverend father, we will, if you please, pretermit it as nothing essential to the matter in hand; and for the second, I protest to you that I know as little of his means of knowledge as you do, and that I am wellnigh persuaded he deals with Sathanas, of which more anon. Well, sir—in the evening, I failed not to veil my purpose with a pleasant brow, as is the custom amongst us martialists, who never display the bloody colours of defiance in our countenance until our hand is armed to fight under them. I amused the fair Discretion with some canzonettes and other toys, which could not but be ravishing to her inexperienced ears. I arose in the morning, met my antagonist, who, to say truth, for an inexperienced villagio, comported himself as stoutly as I could have desired. So, coming to the encounter, reverend sir, I did try his mettle with some half a dozen of downright passes, with any one of which I could have been through his body, only that I was loth to take so fatal an advantage, but rather, mixing mercy with my just indignation, studied to inflict upon him some flesh-wound of no very fatal quality. But, sir, in the midst of my clemency, he, being instigated, I think, by the devil, did follow up his first offence with some insult of the same nature. Whereupon, being eager to punish him, I made an estramazone, and my foot slipping at the same time—not from any fault of fence on my part or any advantage of skill on his, but the devil having, as I said, taken up the matter in hand, and the grass being slippery—ere I recovered my position I encountered his sword, which he had advanced, with my undefended person, so that, as I think, I was in some sort run through the body. My juvenal, being beyond measure appalled at his own unexpected and unmerited success in this strange encounter, takes the flight and leaves me there, and I fall into a dead swoon for the lack of the blood I had lost so foolishly; and when I awake as from a sound sleep, I find myself lying, an it like you, wrapt up in my cloak at the foot of one of the birch-trees which stand together in a clump near to this place. I feel my limbs, and experience little pain, but much weakness; I put my hand to the wound—it was whole and skinned over as you now see it; I rise and come hither; and in these words you have my whole day's story."

"I can only reply to so strange a tale," answered the monk, "that it is scarce possible that Sir Piercie Shafton can expect me to credit it. Here is a quarrel, the cause of which you conceal; a wound received in the morning, of which there is no recent appearance at sunset; a grave filled up, in which no body is deposited; the vanquished found alive and well; the victor departed no man knows whither. These things, sir knight, hang not so well together that I should receive them as gospel."

"Reverend father," answered Sir Piercie Shafton, "I pray you in the first place to observe, that if I offer peaceful and civil justification of that which I have already averred to be true, I do so only in devout deference to your dress and to your order, protesting, that to any other opposite, saving a man of religion, a lady, or my liege prince, I would not deign to support that which I had once attested, otherwise than with the point of my good sword. And so much being premised, I have to add, that I can but gage my honour as a gentleman, and my faith as a Catholic Christian, that the things which I have described to you have happened to me as I have described them, and not otherwise."

"It is a deep assertion, sir knight," answered the sub-prior; "yet, bethink you, it is only an assertion, and that no reason can be alleged why things should be believed which are so contrary to reason. Let me pray you to say whether the grave which has been seen at your place of combat was open or closed when your encounter took place?"

"Reverend father," said the knight, "I will veil from you nothing, but show you each secret of my bosom; even as the pure fountain revealeth the smallest pebble which graces the sand at the bottom of its crystal mirror, and as——"

"Speak in plain terms, for the love of Heaven!" said the monk; "these holiday phrases belong not to solemn affairs. Was the grave open when the conflict began?"

"It was," answered the knight, "I acknowledge it; even as he that acknowledgeth——"

"Nay, I pray you, fair son, forbear these similitudes, and observe me. On yesterday at even no grave was found in that place, for Old Martin chanced, contrary to his wont, to go thither in quest of a strayed sheep. At break of day, by your own confession, a grave was opened in that spot, and there a combat was fought; only one of the combatants appears, and he is covered with blood, and to all appearance woundless." Here the knight made a gesture of impatience. "Nay, fair son, hear me but one moment—the grave is closed and covered by the sod; what can we believe, but that it conceals the bloody corpse of the fallen duellist?"

"By Heaven, it cannot!" said the knight, "unless the juvenal hath slain himself, and buried himself, in order to place me in the predicament of his murderer."

"The grave shall doubtless be explored, and that by tomorrow's dawn," said the monk; "I will see it done with mine own eyes."

"But," said the prisoner, "I protest against all evidence which may arise from its contents, and do insist beforehand that whatever may be found in that grave shall not prejudicate me in my defence. I have been so haunted by diabolical deceptions in this matter, that what do I know but that the devil may assume the form of this rustical juvenal, in order to procure me farther vexation? I protest to you, holy father, it is my very thought that there is witchcraft in all that hath befallen me. Since I entered into this northern land, in which men say that sorceries do abound, I, who am held in awe and regard even by the prime gallants in the court of Feliciana, have been here bearded and taunted by a clod-treading clown. I, whom Vincentio Saviola termed his nimblest and most agile disciple, was, to speak briefly, foiled by a cow-boy, who knew no more of fence than is used at every country wake. I am run, as it seemed to me, through the body, with a very sufficient *stoccata*, and faint on the spot; and yet, when I recover, I find myself without either wem or wound, and lacking nothing of my apparel, saving my murrey-coloured doublet, slashed with satin, which I will pray may be inquired after, lest the devil, who transported me, should have dropped it in his passage among some of the trees or bushes—it being a choice and most fanciful piece of raiment, which I wore for the first time at the Queen's pageant in Southwark."

"Sir knight," said the monk, "you do again go astray from this matter. I inquire of you respecting that which concerns the life of another man, and, it may be, touches your own also, and you answer me with the tale of an old doublet!"

"Old!" exclaimed the knight; "now, by the gods and saints, if there be a gallant at the British court more fancifully considerate and more considerately fanciful, more quaintly curious and more curiously quaint, in frequent changes of all rich articles of vesture, becoming one who may be accounted point-device a courtier, I will give you leave to term me a slave and a liar."

The monk thought, but did not say, that he had already acquired right to doubt the veracity of the Euphuist, considering the marvellous tale which he had told. Yet his own strange adventure, and that of Father Philip, rushed on his mind, and forbade his coming to any conclusion. He contented himself, therefore, with observing, that these were certainly strange incidents, and requested to know if Sir Piercie Shafton had any other reason for suspecting himself to be in a manner so particularly selected for the sport of sorcery and witchcraft.

"Sir sub-prior," said the Euphuist, "the most extraordinary circumstance remains behind, which alone, had I neither been bearded in dispute nor foiled in combat, nor wounded and cured in the space of a few hours, would nevertheless of itself, and without any other corroborative, have compelled me to believe myself the subject of some malevolent fascination. Reverend sir, it is not to your ears that men should tell tales of love and gallantry, nor is Sir Piercie Shafton one who, to any ears whatsoever, is wont to boast of his fair acceptance with the choice and prime beauties of the court; insomuch that a lady, none of the least resplendent constellations which revolve in that hemisphere of honour, pleasure, and beauty, but whose name I here pretermit, was wont to call me her Taciturnity. Nevertheless, truth must be spoken;

and I cannot but allow, as the general report of the court, allowed in camps, and echoed back by city and country, that in the alacrity of the accost, the tender delicacy of the regard, the facetiousness of the address, the adopting and pursuing of the fancy, the solemn close and the graceful fall-off, Piercie Shafton was accounted the only gallant of the time, and so well accepted amongst the choicer beauties of the age that no silk-hosed reveller of the presence-chamber, or plumed jouster of the tilt-yard, approached him by a bow's-length in the ladies' regard, being the mark at which every well-born and generous juvenal aimeth his shaft. Nevertheless, reverend sir, having found in this rude place something which by blood and birth might be termed a lady, and being desirous to keep my gallant humour in exercise, as well as to show my sworn devotion to the sex in general, I did shoot off some arrows of compliment at this Mary Avenel, terming her my Discretion, with other quaint and well-imagined courtesies, rather bestowed out of my bounty than warranted by her merit, or perchance like unto the boyish fowler, who, rather than not exercise his bird-piece, will shoot at crows or magpies for lack of better game——"

"Mary Avenel is much obliged by your notice," answered the monk; "but to what does all this detail of past and present gallantry conduct us?"

"Marry, to this conclusion," answered the knight; "that either this my Discretion or I myself am little less than bewitched; for, instead of receiving my accost with a gratified bow, answering my regard with a suppressed smile, accompanying my falling off or departure with a slight sigh—honours with which I protest to you the noblest dancers and proudest beauties in Feliciana have graced my poor services— she hath paid me as little and as cold regard as if I had been some hob-nailed clown of these bleak mountains! Nay, this very day, while I was in the act of kneeling at her feet to render her the succours of this pungent quintessence of purest spirit distilled by the fairest hands of the court of Feliciana, she pushed me from her with looks which savoured of repugnance, and, as I think, thrust at me with her foot as if to spurn me from her presence. These things, reverend father, are strange, portentous, unnatural, and befall not in the current of mortal affairs, but are symptomatic of sorcery and fascination. So that, having given to your reverence a perfect, simple, and plain account of all that I know concerning this matter, I leave it to your wisdom to solve what may be found soluble in the same, it being my purpose to-morrow, with the peep of dawn, to set forward towards Edinburgh."

"I grieve to be an interruption to your designs, sir knight," said the monk, "but that purpose of thine may hardly be fulfilled."

"How, reverend father!" said the knight, with an air of the utmost surprise; "if what you say respects my departure, understand that it *must* be, for I have so resolved it."

"Sir knight," reiterated the sub-prior, "I must once more repeat, this *cannot* be, until the abbot's pleasure be known in the matter."

"Reverend sir," said the knight, drawing himself up with great dignity, "I desire my hearty and thankful commendations to the abbot; but in this matter I have nothing to do with his reverend pleasure, designing only to consult my own."

"Pardon me," said the sub-prior; "the lord abbot hath in this matter a voice potential."

Sir Piercie Shafton's colour began to rise. "I marvel," he said, "to hear your reverence talk thus. What! will you, for the imagined death of a rude, low-born frampler and wrangler, venture to impinge upon the liberty of the kinsman of the house of Piercie?"

"Sir knight," returned the sub-prior, civilly, "your high lineage and your kindling anger will avail you nothing in this matter. You shall not come here to seek a shelter, and then spill our blood as if it were water."

"I tell you," said the knight, "once more, as I have told you already, that there was no blood spilled but mine own!"

"That remains to be proved," replied the sub-prior; "we of the community of St. Mary's of Kennaquhair use not to take fairy tales in exchange for the lives of our liege vassals."

"We of the house of Piercie," answered Shafton, "brook

neither threats nor restraint. I say I will travel to-morrow,
happen what may!"

"And I," answered the sub-prior, in the same tone of determination, "say that I will break your journey, come what
may!"

"Who shall gainsay me?" said the knight, "if I make my
way by force?"

"You will judge wisely to think ere you make such an attempt," answered the monk, with composure; "there are men
enough in the halidome to vindicate its rights over those who
dare to infringe them."

"My cousin of Northumberland will know how to revenge
this usage to a beloved kinsman so near to his blood," said
the Englishman.

"The lord abbot will know how to protect the rights of his
territory, both with the temporal and spiritual sword," said
the monk. "Besides, consider, were we to send you to your
kinsman at Alnwick or Warkworth to-morrow, he dare do
nothing but transmit you in fetters to the Queen of England.
Bethink, sir knight, that you stand on slippery ground, and
will act most wisely in reconciling yourself to be a prisoner
in this place until the abbot shall decide the matter. There
are armed men enow to countervail all your efforts at escape.
Let patience and resignation, therefore, arm you to a necessary submission."

So saying, he clapped his hands and called aloud. Edward
entered, accompanied by two young men who had already
joined him and were well armed.

"Edward," said the sub-prior, "you will supply the English
knight here in this spence with suitable food and accommodation for the night, treating him with as much kindness as if
nothing had happened between you. But you will place a
sufficient guard, and look carefully that he make not his escape.
Should he attempt to break forth, resist him to the death;
but in no other case harm a hair of his head, as you shall be
answerable."

Edward Glendinning replied: "That I may obey your commands, reverend sir, I will not again offer myself to this per-

son's presence; for shame it were to me to break the peace of
the halidome, but not less shame to leave my brother's death
unavenged."

As he spoke, his lips grew livid, the blood forsook his
cheek, and he was about to leave the apartment, when the
sub-prior recalled him, and said in a solemn tone: "Edward,
I have known you from infancy. I have done what lay
within my reach to be of use to you. I say nothing of what
you owe to me as the representative of your spiritual superior. I say nothing of the duty from the vassal to the sub-
prior. But Father Eustace expects from the pupil whom he
has nurtured—he expects from Edward Glendinning, that he
will not, by any deed of sudden violence, however justified
in his own mind by the provocation, break through the respect due to public justice, or that which he has an especial
right to claim from him."

"Fear nothing, my reverend father, for so in an hundred
senses may I well term you," said the young man; "fear not,
I would say, that I will in anything diminish the respect I
owe to the venerable community by whom we have so long
been protected, far less that I will do aught which can be
personally less than respectful to you. But the blood of my
brother must not cry for vengeance in vain: your reverence
knows our Border creed."

" 'Vengeance is mine, saith the Lord, and I will requite it,' "
answered the monk. "The heathenish custom of deadly feud
which prevails in this land, through which each man seeks
vengeance at his own hand when the death of a friend or
kinsman has chanced, hath already deluged our vales with the
blood of Scottish men, spilled by the hands of countrymen and
kindred. It were endless to count up the fatal results. On
the Eastern Border, the Homes are at feud with the Swintons
and Cockburns; in our Middle Marches, the Scotts and Kerrs
have spilled as much brave blood in domestic feud as might
have fought a pitched field in England, could they have but
forgiven and forgotten a casual rencounter that placed their
names in opposition to each other. On the west frontier, the
Johnstones are at war with the Maxwells, the Jardines with

the Bells, drawing with them the flower of the country, which should place their breasts as a bulwark against England, into private and bloody warfare, of which it is the only end to waste and impair the forces of the country, already divided in itself. Do not, my dear son Edward, permit this bloody prejudice to master your mind. I cannot ask you to think of the crime supposed as if the blood spilled had been less dear to you. Alas! I know that is impossible. But I do require you, in proportion to your interest in the supposed sufferer—for as yet the whole is matter of supposition—to bear on your mind the evidence on which the guilt of the accused person must be tried. He hath spoken with me, and I confess his tale is so extraordinary that I should have, without a moment's hesitation, rejected it as incredible, but that an affair which chanced to myself in this very glen—— More of that another time. Suffice it for the present to say that, from what I have myself experienced, I deem it possible—that, extraordinary as Sir Piercie Shafton's story may seem, I hold it not utterly impossible."

"Father," said Edward Glendinning, when he saw that his preceptor paused, unwilling farther to explain upon what grounds he was inclined to give a certain degree of credit to Sir Piercie Shafton's story, while he admitted it as improbable—"father to me you have been in every sense. You know that my hand grasped more readily to the book than to the sword; and that I lacked utterly the ready and bold spirit which distinguished——" Here his voice faltered, and he paused for a moment, and then went on with resolution and rapidity—"I would say, that I was unequal to Halbert in promptitude of heart and of hand; but Halbert is gone, and I stand his representative, and that of my father—his successor in all his rights (while he said this his eyes shot fire), and bound to assert and maintain them as he would have done; therefore I am a changed man, increased in courage as in my rights and pretensions. And, reverend father, respectfully, but plainly and firmly, do I say, his blood, if it has been shed by this man, shall be atoned. Halbert shall not sleep neglected in his lonely grave, as if with him the spirit of my father had ceased for ever. His blood flows in my veins, and while his has been poured forth unrequited, mine will permit me no rest. My poverty and meanness of rank shall not avail the lordly murderer. My calm nature and peaceful studies shall not be his protection. Even the obligations, holy father, which I acknowlege to you, shall not be his protection. I wait with patience the judgment of the abbot and chapter for the slaughter of one of their most anciently descended vassals. If they do right to my brother's memory, it is well. But mark me, father, if they shall fail in rendering me that justice, I bear a heart and a hand which, though I love not such extremities, are capable of remedying such an error. He who takes up my brother's succession must avenge his death."

The monk perceived with surprise that Edward, with his extreme diffidence, humility, and obedient assiduity, for such were his general characteristics, had still boiling in his veins the wild principles of those from whom he was descended, and by whom he was surrounded. His eyes sparkled, his frame was agitated, and the extremity of his desire of vengeance seemed to give a vehemence to his manner resembling the restlessness of joy.

"May God help us," said Father Eustace, "for, frail wretches as we are, we cannot help ourselves under sudden and strong temptation. Edward, I will rely on your word that you do nothing rashly."

"That will I not," said Edward—"that, my better than father, I surely will not. But the blood of my brother—the tears of my mother—and—and—and of Mary Avenel, shall not be shed in vain. I will not deceive you, father: if this Piercie Shafton hath slain my brother, he dies, if the whole blood of the whole house of Piercie were in his veins."

There was a deep and solemn determination in the utterance of Edward Glendinning, expressive of a rooted resolution. The sub-prior sighed deeply, and for the moment yielded to circumstances, and urged the acquiescence of his pupil no farther. He commanded lights to be placed in the lower chamber, which for a time he paced in silence.

A thousand ideas, and even differing principles, debated with each other in his bosom. He greatly doubted the English knight's account of the duel, and of what had followed it. Yet the extraordinary and supernatural circumstances which had befallen the sacristan and himself in that very glen prevented him from being absolutely incredulous on the score of the wonderful wound and recovery of Sir Piercie Shafton, and prevented him from at once condemning as impossible that which was altogether improbable. Then he was at a loss how to control the fraternal affections of Edward, with respect to whom he felt something like the keeper of a wild animal, a lion's whelp or tiger's cub, which he has held under his command from infancy, but which, when grown to maturity, on some sudden provocation displays his fangs and talons, erects his crest, resumes his savage nature, and bids defiance at once to his keeper and to all mankind.

How to restrain and mitigate an ire which the universal example of the times rendered deadly and inveterate, was sufficient cause of anxiety to Father Eustace. But he had also to consider the situation of his community, dishonoured and degraded by submitting to suffer the slaughter of a vassal to pass unavenged—a circumstance which of itself might in those difficult times have afforded pretext for a revolt among their wavering adherents, or, on the other hand, exposed the community to imminent danger, should they proceed against a subject of England of high degree, connected with the house of Northumberland and other northern families of high rank, who, as they possessed the means, could not be supposed to lack inclination to wreak upon the patrimony of St. Mary of Kennaquhair any violence which might be offered to their kinsman.

In either case, the sub-prior well knew that, the ostensible cause of feud, insurrection, or incursion being once afforded, the case would not be ruled either by reason or by evidence, and he groaned in spirit when, upon counting up the chances which arose in this ambiguous dilemma, he found he had only a choice of difficulties. He was a monk, but he felt also, as a man, indignant at the supposed slaughter of young Glendinning by one skilful in all the practice of arms, in which the vassal of the monastery was most likely to be deficient; and to aid the resentment which he felt for the loss of a youth whom he had known from infancy, came in full force the sense of dishonour arising to his community from passing over so gross an insult unavenged. Then the light in which it might be viewed by those who at present presided in the stormy court of Scotland, attached as they were to the Reformation, and allied by common faith and common interest with Queen Elizabeth, was a formidable subject of apprehension. The sub-prior well knew how they lusted after the revenues of the church (to express it in the ordinary phrase of the religious of the time), and how readily they would grasp at such a pretext for encroaching on those of St. Mary's as would be afforded by the suffering to pass unpunished the death of a native Scottishman by a Catholic Englishman, a rebel to Queen Elizabeth.

On the other hand, to deliver up to England, or, which was nearly the same thing, to the Scottish administration, an English knight leagued with the Piercie by kindred and political intrigue, a faithful follower of the Catholic Church, who had fled to the halidome for protection, was, in the estimation of the sub-prior, an act most unworthy in itself, and meriting the malediction of Heaven, besides being, moreover, fraught with great temporal risk. If the government of Scotland was now almost entirely in the hands of the Protestant party, the Queen was still a Catholic, and there was no knowing when, amid the sudden changes which agitated that tumultuous country, she might find herself at the head of her own affairs, and able to protect those of her own faith. Then if the court of England and its Queen were zealously Protestant, the northern counties, whose friendship or enmity were of most consequence in the first instance to the community of St. Mary's, contained many Catholics, the heads of whom were able, and must be supposed willing, to avenge any injury suffered by Sir Piercie Shafton.

On either side, the sub-prior, thinking, according to his sense of duty, most anxiously for the safety and welfare of his monastery, saw the greatest risk of damage, blame, inroad, and confiscation. The only course on which he could determine was to stand by the helm like a resolute pilot, watch every contingence, do his best to weather each reef and shoal, and commit the rest to Heaven and his patroness.

As he left the apartment, the knight called after him, beseeching he would order his trunk-mails to be sent in to his apartment, understanding he was to be guarded there for the night, as he wished to make some alteration in his apparel.[1]

"Ay, ay," said the monk, muttering as he went up the winding stair, "carry him his trumpery with all despatch. Alas! that man, with so many noble objects of pursuit, will amuse himself like a jackanape with a laced jerkin and a cap and bells! I must now to the melancholy work of consoling that which is wellnigh inconsolable, a mother weeping for her first-born."

Advancing, after a gentle knock, into the apartment of the women, he found that Mary Avenel had retired to bed extremely indisposed, and that Dame Glendinning and Tibb were indulging their sorrows by the side of a decaying fire, and by the light of a small iron lamp, or cruize, as it was termed. Poor Elspeth's apron was thrown over her head, and bitterly did she sob and weep for "her beautiful, her brave—the very image of her dear Simon Glendinning, the stay of her widowhood and the support of her old age."

The faithful Tibb echoed her complaints, and, more violently clamorous, made deep promises of revenge on Sir Piercie Shafton, "if there were a man left in the south that could draw a whinger, or a woman that could thraw a rape." The presence of the sub-prior imposed silence on these clamours. He sate down by the unfortunate mother, and essayed, by such topics as his religion and reason suggested, to interrupt the current of Dame Glendinning's feelings; but the attempt was in vain. She listened, indeed, with some little interest, while he pledged his word and his influence with the abbot that the family which had lost their eldest-born by means of a guest received at his command should experience particular

[1] See Foppery of the Sixteenth Century. Note 20.

protection at the hands of the community; and that the fief
which belonged to Simon Glendinning should, with extended
bounds and added privileges, be conferred on Edward; but
it was only for a very brief space that the mother's sobs were
apparently softer and her grief more mild.   She soon blamed
herself for casting a moment's thought upon world's gear
while poor Halbert was lying stretched in his bloody shirt.
The sub-prior was not more fortunate when he promised that
Halbert's body "should be removed to hallowed ground, and
his soul secured by the prayers of the church in his behalf."
Grief would have its natural course, and the voice of the com-
forter was wasted in vain.

CHAPTER XXVIII.

He is at liberty, I have ventured for him!
.   .   .   .   . if the law
Find and condemn me for't, some living wenches,
Some honest-hearted maids will sing my dirge,
And tell to memory my death was noble,
Dying almost a martyr.
                                   The Two Noble Kinsmen.

THE sub-prior of St. Mary's, in taking his departure from
the spence in which Sir Piercie Shafton was confined, and in
which some preparations were made for his passing the night,
as the room which might be most conveniently guarded, left
more than one perplexed person behind him.   There was connected with this chamber, and opening into it, a small "out-
shot," or projecting part of the building, occupied by a little
sleeping apartment, which upon ordinary occasions was that
of Mary Avenel, and which, in the unusual number of guests
who had come to the tower on the former evening, had also
accommodated Mysie Happer, the miller's daughter; for anciently, as well as in the present day, a Scottish house was
always rather too narrow and limited for the extent of the
owner's hospitality, and some shift and contrivance was necessary, upon any unusual occasion, to ensure the accommodation of all the guests.

The fatal news of Halbert Glendinning's death had thrown all former arrangements into confusion. Mary Avenel, whose case required immediate attention, had been transported into the apartment hitherto occupied by Halbert and his brother, as the latter proposed to watch all night in order to prevent the escape of the prisoner. Poor Mysie had been altogether overlooked, and had naturally enough betaken herself to the little apartment which she had hitherto occupied, ignorant that the spence, through which lay the only access to it, was to be the sleeping-chamber of Sir Piercie Shafton. The measures taken for securing him there had been so sudden that she was not aware of it, until she found that the other females had been removed from the spence by the sub-prior's direction, and having once missed the opportunity of retreating along with them, bashfulness, and the high respect which she was taught to bear to the monks, prevented her venturing forth alone, and intruding herself on the presence of Father Eustace, while in secret conference with the Southron. There appeared no remedy but to wait till their interview was over; and, as the door was thin, and did not shut very closely, she could hear every word which passed betwixt them.

It thus happened, that without any intended intrusion on her part, she became privy to the whole conversation of the sub-prior and the English knight, and could also observe from the window of her little retreat that more than one of the young men summoned by Edward arrived successively at the tower. These circumstances led her to entertain most serious apprehension that the life of Sir Piercie Shafton was in great and instant peril.

Woman is naturally compassionate, and not less willingly so when youth and fair features are on the side of him who claims her sympathy. The handsome presence, elaborate dress and address of Sir Piercie Shafton, which had failed to make any favourable impression on the grave and lofty character of Mary Avenel, had completely dazzled and bewildered the poor Maid of the Mill. The knight had perceived this result, and flattered by seeing that his merit was not universally underrated, he had bestowed on Mysie a good deal more of his courtesy than in his opinion her rank warranted. It was not cast away, but received with a devout sense of his condescension, and with gratitude for his personal notice, which, joined to her fears for his safety and the natural tenderness of her disposition, began to make wild work in her heart.

"To be sure it was very wrong in him to slay Halbert Glendinning," it was thus she argued the case with herself, "but then he was a gentleman born, and a soldier, and so gentle and courteous withal that she was sure the quarrel had been all of young Glendinning's own seeking; for it was well known that both these lads were so taken up with that Mary Avenel that they never looked at another lass in the halidome, more than if they were of a different degree. And then Halbert's dress was as clownish as his manners were haughty; and this poor young gentleman, who was habited like any prince, banished from his own land, was first drawn into a quarrel by a rude brangler, and then persecuted and like to be put to death by his kin and allies."

Mysie wept bitterly at the thought, and then her heart rising against such cruelty and oppression to a defenceless stranger, who dressed with so much skill, and spoke with so much grace, she began to consider whether she could not render him some assistance in his extremity.

Her mind was now entirely altered from its original purpose. At first her only anxiety had been to find the means of escaping from the interior apartment, without being noticed by any one; but now she began to think that Heaven had placed her there for the safety and protection of the persecuted stranger. She was of a simple and affectionate, but at the same time an alert and enterprising, character, possessing more than female strength of body, and more than female courage, though with feelings as capable of being bewildered with gallantry of dress and language as a fine gentleman of any generation would have desired to exercise his talents upon. "I will save him," she thought, "that is the first thing to be resolved; and then I wonder what he will say to the poor miller's maiden, that has done for him what all the dainty dames in London or Holyrood would have been afraid to venture upon."

Prudence began to pull her sleeve as she indulged speculations so hazardous, and hinted to her that the warmer Sir Piercie Shafton's gratitude might prove, it was the more likely to be fraught with danger to his benefactress. Alas! poor Prudence, thou mayst say with our moral teacher:

I preach for ever, but I preach in vain.

The miller's maiden, while you pour your warning into her unwilling bosom, has glanced her eye on the small mirror by which she has placed her little lamp, and it returns to her a countenance and eyes, pretty and sparkling at all times, but ennobled at present with the energy of expression proper to those who have dared to form, and stand prepared to execute, deeds of generous audacity.

"Will these features—will these eyes, joined to the benefit I am about to confer upon Sir Piercie Shafton, do nothing towards removing the distance of rank between us?"

Such was the question which female vanity asked of fancy; and though even fancy dared not answer in a ready affirmative, a middle conclusion was adopted. "Let me first succour the gallant youth, and trust to fortune for the rest."

Banishing, therefore, from her mind everything that was personal to herself, the rash but generous girl turned her whole thoughts to the means of executing this enterprise.

The difficulties which interposed were of no ordinary nature. The vengeance of the men of that country, in cases of deadly feud, that is, in cases of a quarrel excited by the slaughter of any of their relations, was one of their most marked characteristics; and Edward, however gentle in other respects, was so fond of his brother that there could be no doubt that he would be as signal in his revenge as the customs of the country authorised. There were to be passed the inner door of the apartment, the two gates of the tower itself, and the gate of the courtyard, ere the prisoner was at liberty; and then a guide and means of flight were to be provided, otherwise ultimate escape was impossible. But where the will of woman is strongly bent on the accomplishment of such a purpose, her wit is seldom baffled by difficulties, however embarrassing.

The sub-prior had not long left the apartment ere Mysie had devised a scheme for Sir Piercie Shafton's freedom, daring indeed, but likely to be successful, if dexterously conducted. It was necessary, however, that she should remain where she was till so late an hour that all in the tower should have betaken themselves to repose, excepting those whose duty made them watchers. The interval she employed in observing the movements of the person in whose service she was thus boldly a volunteer.

She could hear Sir Piercie Shafton pace the floor to and fro, in reflection doubtless on his own untoward fate and precarious situation. By and by she heard him making a rustling among his trunks, which, agreeably to the order of the sub-prior, had been placed in the apartment to which he was confined, and which he was probably amusing more melancholy thoughts by examining and arranging. Then she could hear him resume his walk through the room, and, as if his spirits had been somewhat relieved and elevated by the survey of his wardrobe, she could distinguish that at one turn he half-recited a sonnet, at another half-whistled a galliard, and at the third hummed a saraband. At length she could understand that he extended himself on the temporary couch which had been allotted to him, after muttering his prayers hastily, and in a short time she concluded he must be fast asleep.

She employed the moments which intervened in considering her enterprise under every different aspect; and, dangerous as it was, the steady view which she took of the various perils accompanying her purpose furnished her with plausible devices for obviating them. Love and generous compassion, which give singly such powerful impulse to the female heart, were in this case united, and championed her to the last extremity of hazard.

It was an hour past midnight. All in the tower slept soundly but those who had undertaken to guard the English prisoner; or if sorrow and suffering drove sleep from the bed of Dame Glendinning and her foster-daughter, they were too much wrapt in their own griefs to attend to external sounds. The means of striking light were at hand in the small apartment, and thus the miller's maiden was enabled to light and trim a small lamp. With a trembling step and throbbing heart, she undid the door which separated her from the apartment in which the Southron knight was confined, and almost flinched from her fixed purpose when she found herself in the same room with the sleeping prisoner. She scarcely trusted herself to look upon him, as he lay wrapped in his cloak, and fast asleep upon the pallet bed, but turned her eyes away while she gently pulled his mantle with no more force than was just equal to awaken him. He moved not until she had twitched his cloak a second and a third time, and then at length looking up, was about to make an exclamation in the suddenness of his surprise.

Mysie's bashfulness was conquered by her fear. She placed her fingers in her lips, in token that he must observe the most strict silence, and then pointed to the door to intimate that it was watched.

Sir Piercie Shafton now collected himself, and sat upright on his couch. He gazed with surprise on the graceful figure of the young woman who stood before him; her well-formed person, her flowing hair, and the outline of her features showed dimly, and yet to advantage, by the partial and feeble light which she held in her hand. The romantic imagination of the gallant would soon have coined some compliment proper for the occasion, but Mysie left him not time.

"I come," she said, "to save your life, which is else in great peril; if you answer me, speak as low as you can, for they have sentinelled your door with armed men."

"Comeliest of millers' daughters," answered Sir Piercie, who by this time was sitting upright in his couch, "dread nothing for my safety. Credit me that, as in very truth I have not spilled the red puddle, which these villagios call the blood, of their most uncivil relation, so I am under no apprehension whatever for the issue of this restraint, seeing that it cannot but be harmless to me. Natheless, to thee, O most molendinar beauty, I return the thanks which thy courtesy may justly claim."

"Nay, but, sir knight," answered the maiden, in a whisper as low as is was tremulous, "I deserve no thanks, unless you will act by my counsel. Edward Glendinning hath sent for Dan of the Howlethirst and young Adie of Aikenshaw, and they are come with three men more, and with bow, and jack, and spear, and I heard them say to each other and to Edward, as they alighted in the court, that they would have amends for the death of their kinsman, if the monk's cowl should smoke for it. And the vassals are so wilful now that the abbot himself dare not control them, for fear they turn heretics, and refuse to pay their feu-duties."

"In faith," said Sir Piercie Shafton, "it may be a shrewd temptation, and perchance the monks may rid themselves of trouble and cumber by handing me over the march to Sir John Foster or Lord Hunsdon, the English wardens, and so make peace with their vassals and with England at once. Fairest Molinara, I will for once walk by thy rede, and if thou dost contrive to extricate me from this vile kennel, I will so celebrate thy wit and beauty that the Baker's Nymph of Raphael d'Urbino shall seem but a gipsy in comparison of my Molinara."

"I pray you, then, be silent," said the miller's daughter; "for if your speech betrays that you are awake, my scheme fails utterly, and it is Heaven's mercy and Our Lady's that we are not already overheard and discovered."

"I am silent," replied the Southron, "even as the starless night; but yet, if this contrivance of thine should endanger thy safety, fair and no less kind than fair damsel, it were utterly unworthy of me to accept it at thy hand."

"Do not think of me," said Mysie, hastily; "I am safe—I will take thought for myself, if I once saw you out of this dangerous dwelling; if you would provide yourself with any part of your apparel or goods, lose no time."

The knight, *did*, however, lose some time ere he could settle in his own mind what to take and what to abandon of his wardrobe, each article of which seemed endeared to him by recol-

lection of the feasts and revels at which it had been exhibited.
For some little while Mysie left him to make his selections at
leisure, for she herself had also some preparations to make for
flight. But when, returning from the chamber into which she
had retired, with a small bundle in her hand, she found him
still indecisive, she insisted in plain terms that he should
either make up his baggage for the enterprise or give it up
entirely. Thus urged, the disconsolate knight hastily made up
a few clothes into a bundle, regarded his trunk-mails with a
mute expression of parting sorrow, and intimated his readiness to wait upon his kind guide.

She led the way to the door of the apartment, having first
carefully extinguished her lamp, and motioning to the knight
to stand close behind her, tapped once or twice at the door.
She was at length answered by Edward Glendinning, who demanded to know who knocked within, and what was desired.

"Speak low," said Mysie Happer, "or you will awaken the
English knight. It is I, Mysie Happer, who knock; I wish
to get out; you have locked me up, and I was obliged to wait
till the Southron slept."

"Locked you up!" replied Edward, in surprise.

"Yes," answered the miller's daughter, "you have locked
me up into this room: I was in Mary Avenel's sleeping apartment."

"And can you not remain there till morning," replied Edward, "since it has so chanced?"

"What!" said the miller's daughter, in a tone of offended
delicacy, "*I* remain here a moment longer than I can get out
without discovery! I would not, for all the halidome of St.
Mary's, remain a minute longer in the neighbourhood of a
man's apartment than I can help it. For whom or for what
do you hold me? I promise you, my father's daughter has
been better brought up than to put in peril her good name."

"Come forth, then, and get to thy chamber in silence," said
Edward.

So saying, he undid the bolt. The staircase without was
in utter darkness, as Mysie had before ascertained. So soon
as she stept out, she took hold of Edward as if to support

herself, thus interposing her person betwixt him and Sir Piercie Shafton, by whom she was closely followed. Thus screened from observation, the Englishman slipped past on tiptoe, unshod and in silence, while the damsel complained to Edward that she wanted a light.

"I cannot get you a light," said he, "for I cannot leave this post; but there is a fire below."

"I will sit below till morning," said the Maid of the Mill and, tripping downstairs, heard Edward bolt and bar the door of the now tenantless apartment with vain caution.

At the foot of the stair which she descended, she found the object of her care waiting her farther directions. She recommended to him the most absolute silence, which, for once in his life, he seemed not unwilling to observe, conducted him with as much caution as if he were walking on cracked ice to a dark recess used for depositing wood, and instructed him to ensconce himself behind the fagots. She herself lighted her lamp once more at the kitchen fire, and took her distaff and spindle, that she might not seem to be unemployed in case any one came into the apartment. From time to time, however, she stole towards the window on tiptoe to catch the first glance of the dawn, for the farther prosecution of her adventurous project. At length she saw, to her great joy, the first peep of the morning brighten upon the grey clouds of the east, and, clasping her hands together, thanked Our Lady for the sight, and implored protection during the remainder of her enterprise. Ere she had finished her prayer, she started at feeling a man's arm across her shoulder, while a rough voice spoke in her ear: "What! menseful Mysie of the Mill so soon at her prayers? Now, benison on the bonny eyes that open so early! I'll have a kiss for good-morrow's sake."

Dan of the Howlethirst, for he was the gallant who paid Mysie this compliment, suited the action with the word, and the action, as is usual in such cases of rustic gallantry, was rewarded with a cuff, which Dan received as a fine gentleman receives a tap with a fan, but which, delivered by the energetic arm of the miller's maiden, would have certainly astonished a less robust gallant.

"How now, sir coxcomb!" said she, "and must you be away from your guard over the English knight to plague quiet folk with your horse-tricks!"

"Truly you are mistaken, pretty Mysie," said the clown, "for I have not yet relieved Edward at his post; and were it not a shame to let him stay any longer, by my faith, I could find it in my heart not to quit you these two hours."

"Oh, you have hours and hours enough to see any one," said Mysie; "but you must think of the distress of the household even now, and get Edward to sleep for a while, for he has kept watch this whole night."

"I will have another kiss first," answered Dan of the Howlethirst.

But Mysie was now on her guard, and, conscious of the vicinity of the wood-hole, offered such strenuous resistance that the swain cursed the nymph's bad humour with very unpastoral phrase and emphasis, and ran upstairs to relieve the guard of his comrade. Stealing to the door, she heard the new sentinel hold a brief conversation with Edward, after which the latter withdrew, and the former entered upon the duties of his watch.

Mysie suffered him to walk there a little while undisturbed, until the dawning became more general, by which time she supposed he might have digested her coyness, and then presenting herself before the watchful sentinel, demanded of him "the keys of the outer tower, and of the courtyard gate."

"And for what purpose?" answered the warder.

"To milk the cows, and drive them out to their pasture," said Mysie; "you would not have the poor beasts kept in the byre a' morning, and the family in such distress that there isna ane fit to do a turn but the byre-woman and myself?"

"And where is the byre-woman?" said Dan.

"Sitting with me in the kitchen, in case these distressed folk want anything."

"There are the keys then, Mysie Dorts," said the sentinel.

"Many thanks, Dan Ne'er-do-Weel," answered the Maid of the Mill, and escaped downstairs in a moment.

To hasten to the wood-hole, and there to robe the English

knight in a short gown and petticoat, which she had provided
for the purpose, was the work of another moment.   She then
undid the gates of the tower, and made towards the byre or
cow-house, which stood in one corner of the courtyard.   Sir
Piercie Shafton remonstrated against the delay which this
would occasion.

"Fair and generous Molinara," he said, "had we not better
undo the outward gate, and make the best of our way hence,
even like a pair of sea-mews who make towards shelter of the
rocks as the storm waxes high?"

"We must drive out the cows first," said Mysie, "for a sin
it were to spoil the poor widow's cattle, both for her sake and
the poor beasts' own; and I have no mind any one shall leave
the tower in a hurry to follow us.   Besides, you must have
your horse, for you will need a fleet one ere all be done."

So saying, she locked and double-locked both the inward
and outward door of the tower, proceeded to the cow-house,
turned out the cattle, and, giving the knight his own horse to
lead, drove them before her out at the courtyard gate, intend-
ing to return for her own palfrey.   But the noise attending the
first operation caught the wakeful attention of Edward, who,
starting to the bartizan, called to know what the matter was.

Mysie answered with great readiness, that "She was driving out the cows, for that they would be spoiled for want of
looking to."

"I thank thee, kind maiden," said Edward; "and yet," he
added, after a moment's pause, "what damsel is that thou
hast with thee?"

Mysie was about to answer, when Sir Piercie Shafton, who
apparently did not desire that the great work of his liberation
should be executed without the interposition of his own inge-
nuity, exclaimed from beneath: "I am she, O most bucolical
juvenal, under whose charge are placed the milky mothers of
the herd."

"Hell and darkness!" exclaimed Edward, in a transport of
fury and astonishment, "it is Piercie Shafton.   What! treason! treason! — ho! — Dan — Jasper — Martin — the villain
escapes!"

"To horse! to horse!" cried Mysie, and in an instant mounted behind the knight, who was already in the saddle.

Edward caught up a cross-bow and let fly a bolt, which whistled so near Mysie's ear that she called to her companion: "Spur—spur, sir knight! the next will not miss us. Had it been Halbert instead of Edward who bent that bow, we had been dead."

The knight pressed his horse, which dashed past the cows, and down the knoll on which the tower was situated. Then taking the road down the valley, the gallant animal, reckless of its double burden, soon conveyed them out of hearing of the tumult and alarm with which their departure filled the Tower of Glendearg.

Thus it strangely happened that two men were flying in different directions at the same time, each accused of being the other's murderer.

CHAPTER XXIX.

> Sure he cannot
> Be so unmanly as to leave me here;
> If he do, maids will not so easily
> Trust men again.
> *The Two Noble Kinsmen.*

THE knight continued to keep the good horse at a pace as quick as the road permitted, until they had cleared the valley of Glendearg, and entered upon the broad dale of the Tweed, which now rolled before them in crystal beauty, displaying on its opposite bank the huge grey Monastery of St. Mary's, whose towers and pinnacles were scarce yet touched by the newly-risen sun, so deeply the edifice lies shrouded under the mountains which rise to the southward.

Turning to the left, the knight continued his road down the northern bank of the river, until they arrived nearly opposite to the wear, or dam-dike, where Father Philip concluded his extraordinary aquatic excursion.

Sir Piercie Shafton, whose brain seldom admitted more than

one idea at a time, had hitherto pushed forward without very distinctly considering where he was going. But the sight of the monastery so near to him reminded him that he was still on dangerous ground, and that he must necessarily provide for his safety by choosing some settled plan of escape. The situation of his guide and deliverer also occurred to him, for he was far from being either selfish or ungrateful. He listened, and discovered that the miller's daughter was sobbing and weeping bitterly as she rested her head on his shoulder.

"What ails thee," he said, "my generous Molinara? is there aught that Piercie Shafton can do which may show his gratitude to his deliverer?" Mysie pointed with her finger across the river, but ventured not to turn her eyes in that direction. "Nay, but speak plain, most generous damsel," said the knight, who, for once, was puzzled as much as his own elegance of speech was wont to puzzle others, "for I swear to you that I comprehend nought by the extension of thy fair digit."

"Yonder is my father's house," said Mysie, in a voice interrupted by the increased burst of her sorrow.

"And I was carrying thee discourteously to a distance from thy habitation?" said Shafton, imagining he had found out the source of her grief. "Woe worth the hour that Piercie Shafton, in attention to his own safety, neglected the accommodation of any female, far less of his most beneficent liberatrice! Dismount, then, O lovely Molinara, unless thou wouldst rather that I should transport thee on horseback to the house of thy molendinary father, which, if thou sayest the word, I am prompt to do, defying all dangers which may arise to me personally, whether by monk or miller."

Mysie suppressed her sobs, and with considerable difficulty muttered her desire to alight, and take her fortune by herself. Sir Piercie Shafton, too devoted a squire of dames to consider the most lowly as exempted from a respectful attention, independent of the claims which the miller's maiden possessed over him, dismounted instantly from his horse, and received in his arms the poor girl, who still wept bitterly, and, when placed on the ground, seemed scarce able to support herself, or at least still clung, though, as it appeared, unconsciously, to the support he had afforded. He carried her to a weeping birch-tree, which grew on the greensward bank around which the road winded, and, placing her on the ground beneath it, exhorted her to compose herself. A strong touch of natural feeling struggled with, and half overcame, his acquired affectation, while he said: "Credit me, most generous damsel, the service you have done to Piercie Shafton he would have deemed too dearly bought had he foreseen it was to cost you these tears and singults. Show me the cause of your grief, and if I can do aught to remove it, believe that the rights you have acquired over me will make your commands sacred as those of an empress. Speak then, fair Molinara; and command him whom fortune hath rendered at once your debtor and your champion. What are your orders?"

"Only that you will fly and save yourself," said Mysie, mustering up her utmost efforts to utter these few words.

"Yet," said the knight, "let me not leave you without some token of remembrance." Mysie would have said there needed none, and most truly would she have spoken, could she have spoken for weeping. "Piercie Shafton is poor," he continued, "but let this chain testify he is not ungrateful to his deliverer."

He took from his neck the rich chain and medallion we have formerly mentioned, and put it into the powerless hand of the poor maiden, who neither received nor rejected it, but, occupied with more intense feelings, seemed scarce aware of what he was doing.

"We shall meet again," said Sir Piercie Shafton, "at least I trust so; meanwhile, weep no more, fair Molinara, an thou lovest me."

The phrase of conjuration was but used as an ordinary commonplace expression of the time, but bore a deeper sense to poor Mysie's ear. She dried her tears; and when the knight, in all kind and chivalrous courtesy, stooped to embrace her at their parting, she rose humbly up to receive the proffered honour in a posture of more deference, and meekly and gratefully accepted the offered salute. Sir Piercie Shafton mounted his horse, and began to ride off; but curiosity, or perhaps a stronger feeling, soon induced him to look back, when he beheld the miller's daughter standing still motionless on the spot where they had parted, her eyes turned after him, and the unheeded chain hanging from her hand.

It was at this moment that a glimpse of the real state of Mysie's affections, and of the motive from which she had acted in the whole matter, glanced on Sir Piercie Shafton's mind. The gallants of that age, disinterested, aspiring, and lofty-minded even in their coxcombry, were strangers to those degrading and mischievous pursuits which are usually termed low amours. They did not " chase the humble maidens of the plain," or degrade their own rank to deprive rural innocence of peace and virtue. It followed of course that, as conquests in this class were no part of their ambition, they were in most cases totally overlooked and unsuspected, left unimproved, as a modern would call it, where, as on the present occasion, they were casually made. The companion of Astrophel, and flower of the tiltyard of Feliciana, had no more idea that his graces and good parts could attach the love of Mysie Happer than a first-rate beauty in the boxes dreams of the fatal wound which her charms may inflict on some attorney's romantic apprentice in the pit. I suppose, in any ordinary case, the pride of rank and distinction would have pronounced on the humble admirer the doom which Beau Fielding denounced against the whole female world, " Let them look and die"; but the obligations under which he lay to the enamoured maiden, miller's daughter as she was, precluded the possibility of Sir Piercie's treating the matter *en cavalier*, and, much embarrassed, yet a little flattered at the same time, he rode back to try what could be done for the damsel's relief.

The innate modesty of poor Mysie could not prevent her showing too obvious signs of joy at Sir Piercie Shafton's return. She was betrayed by the sparkle of the rekindling eye, and a caress which, however timidly bestowed, she could not help giving to the neck of the horse which brought back the beloved rider.

" What farther can I do for you, kind Molinara?" said Sir Piercie Shafton, himself hesitating and blushing; for, to the grace of Queen Bess's age be it spoken, her courtiers wore more iron on their breasts than brass on their foreheads, and even amid their vanities preserved still the decaying spirit of chivalry, which inspired of yore the very gentle knight of Chaucer,

> Who in his port was modest as a maid.

Mysie blushed deeply, with her eyes fixed on the ground, and Sir Piercie proceeded in the same tone of embarrassed kindness. "Are you afraid to return home alone, my kind Molinara? would you that I should accompany you?"

"Alas!" said Mysie, looking up, and her cheek changing from scarlet to pale, "I have no home left!"

"How! no home?" said Shafton. "Says my generous Molinara she hath no home, when yonder stands the house of her father, and but a crystal stream between?"

"Alas!" answered the miller's maiden, "I have no longer either home or father. He is a devoted servant to the abbey; I have offended the abbot, and if I return home my father will kill me."

"He dare not injure thee, by Heaven!" said Sir Piercie. "I swear to thee, by my honour and knighthood, that the forces of my cousin of Northumberland shall lay the monastery so flat that a horse shall not stumble as he rides over it, if they should dare to injure a hair of your head! Therefore be hopeful and content, kind Mysinda, and know you have obliged one who can and will avenge the slightest wrong offered to you."

He sprung from his horse as he spoke, and in the animation of his argument grasped the willing hand of Mysie, or Mysinda, as he had now christened her. He gazed too upon full black eyes, fixed upon his own with an expression which, however subdued by maidenly shame, it was impossible to mistake, on cheeks where something like hope began to restore the natural colour, and on two lips which, like double rosebuds, were kept a little apart by expectation, and showed within a line of teeth as white as pearl. All this was dangerous to look upon, and Sir Piercie Shafton, after repeating with less and less force his request that the fair Mysinda would allow him to carry her to her father's, ended by asking the fair Mysinda to go along with him. "At least," he added, "until I shall be able to conduct you to a place of safety."

Mysie Happer made no answer; but, blushing scarlet betwixt joy and shame, mutely expressed her willingness to accompany the Southron knight, by knitting her bundle closer and preparing to resume her seat *en croupe*. "And what is your pleasure that I should do with this?" she said, holding up the chain as if she had been for the first time aware that it was in her hand.

"Keep it, fairest Mysinda, for my sake," said the knight.

"Not so, sir," answered Mysie, gravely; "the maidens of my country take no such gifts from their superiors, and I need no token to remind me of this morning."

Most earnestly and courteously did the knight urge her acceptance of the proposed guerdon; but on this point Mysie was resolute, feeling, perhaps, that to accept of anything bearing the appearance of reward would be to place the service she had rendered him on a mercenary footing. In short, she would only agree to conceal the chain, lest it might prove the means of detecting the owner, until Sir Piercie should be placed in perfect safety.

They mounted and resumed their journey, of which Mysie, as bold and sharp-witted in some points as she was simple and susceptible in others, now took in some degree the direction, having only inquired its general destination, and learned that Sir Piercie Shafton desired to go to Edinburgh, where he hoped to find friends and protection. Possessed of this information, Mysie availed herself of her local knowledge to get as soon as possible out of the bounds of the halidome, and into those of a temporal baron, supposed to be addicted to the Reformed doctrines, and upon whose limits, at least, she thought their pursuers would not attempt to hazard any violence. She was not indeed very apprehensive of a pursuit, reckoning with some confidence that the inhabitants of the Tower of Glendearg would find it a matter of difficulty to surmount the obstacles arising from their own bolts and bars, with which she had carefully secured them before setting forth on the retreat.

They journeyed on, therefore, in tolerable security, and Sir Piercie Shafton found leisure to amuse the time in high-flown speeches and long anecdotes of the court of Feliciana, to which Mysie bent an ear not a whit less attentive that she did not understand one word out of three which was uttered by her fellow-traveller. She listened, however, and admired upon trust, as many a wise man has been contented to treat the conversation of a handsome but silly mistress. As for Sir Piercie, he was in his element; and well assured of the interest and full approbation of his auditor, he went on spouting Euphuism of more than usual obscurity, and at more than usual length. Thus passed the morning, and noon brought them within sight of a winding stream, on the side of which arose an ancient baronial castle, surrounded by some large trees. At a small distance from the gate of the mansion extended, as in those days was usual, a straggling hamlet, having a church in the centre.

"There are two hostelries in this Kirktown," said Mysie, "but the worst is best for our purpose; for it stands apart from the other houses, and I ken the man weel, for he has dealt with my father for malt."

This *causa scientiæ*, to use a lawyer's phrase, was ill chosen for Mysie's purpose; for Sir Piercie Shafton had, by dint of his own loquacity, been talking himself all this while into a high esteem for his fellow-traveller, and, pleased with the gracious reception which she afforded to his powers of conversation, had wellnigh forgotten that she was not herself one of those high-born beauties of whom he was recounting so many stories, when this unlucky speech at once placed the most disadvantageous circumstances attending her lineage under his immediate recollection. He said nothing, however. What indeed could he say? Nothing was so natural as that a miller's daughter should be acquainted with publicans who dealt with her father for malt, and all that was to be wondered at was the concurrence of events which had rendered such a female the companion and guide of Sir Piercie Shafton of

Wilverton, kinsman of the great Earl of Northumberland, whom princes and sovereigns themselves termed cousin, because of the Piercie blood.[1] He felt the disgrace of strolling through the country with a miller's maiden on the crupper behind him, and was even ungrateful enough to feel some emotions of shame when he halted his horse at the door of the little inn.

But the alert intelligence of Mysie Happer spared him further sense of derogation, by instantly springing from the horse, and cramming the ears of mine host, who came out with his mouth agape to receive a guest of the knight's appearance, with an imagined tale, in which circumstance on circumstance were huddled so fast as to astonish Sir Piercie Shafton, whose own invention was none of the most brilliant. She explained to the publican that this was a great English knight travelling from the monastery to the court of Scotland, after having paid his vows to St. Mary, and that she had been directed to conduct him so far on the road; and that Ball, her palfrey, had fallen by the way, because he had been overwrought with carrying home the last melder of meal to the portioner of Langhope; and that she had turned in Ball to graze in the Tasker's Park, near Cripplecross, for he had stood as still as Lot's wife with very weariness; and that the knight had courteously insisted she should ride behind him; and that she had brought him to her kenn'd friend's hostelry rather than to proud Peter Peddie's, who got his malt at the Mellerstain mills; and that he must get the best that the house afforded, and that he must get it ready in a moment of time, and that she was ready to help in the kitchen.

All this ran glibly off the tongue without pause on the part of Mysie Happer, or doubt on that of the landlord. The guest's horse was conducted to the stable, and he himself installed in the cleanest corner and best seat which the place afforded. Mysie, ever active and officious, was at once engaged in preparing food, in spreading the table, and in mak-

---

[1] Froissart tells us somewhere (the readers of romances are indifferent to accurate reference) that the King of France called one of the Piercies cousin, because of the blood of Northumberland.

ing all the better arrangements which her experience could suggest for the honour and comfort of her companion. He would fain have resisted this; for while it was impossible not to be gratified with the eager and alert kindness which was so active in his service, he felt an indefinable pain in seeing Mysinda engaged in these menial services, and discharging them, moreover, as one to whom they were but too familiar. Yet this jarring feeling was mixed with, and perhaps balanced by, the extreme grace with which the neat-handed maiden executed these tasks, however mean in themselves, and gave to the wretched corner of a miserable inn of the period the air of a bower, in which an enamoured fairy, or at least a shepherdess of Arcadia, was displaying, with unavailing solicitude, her designs on the heart of some knight, destined by fortune to higher thoughts and a more splendid union.

The lightness and grace with which Mysie covered the little round table with a snow-white cloth, and arranged upon it the hastily-roasted capon, with its accompanying stoup of Bourdeaux, were but plebeian graces in themselves; but yet there were very flattering ideas excited by each glance. She was so very well made, agile at once and graceful, with her hand and arm as white as snow, and her face in which a smile contended with a blush, and her eyes which looked ever at Shafton when he looked elsewhere, and were dropped at once when they encountered his, that she was irresistible! In fine, the affectionate delicacy of her whole demeanour, joined to the promptitude and boldness she had so lately evinced, tended to ennoble the services she had rendered, as if some

> Sweet engaging Grace
> Put on some clothes to come abroad,
> And took a waiter's place.

But, on the other hand, came the damning reflection that these duties were not taught her by love, to serve the beloved only, but arose from the ordinary and natural habits of a miller's daughter, accustomed, doubtless, to render the same service to every wealthier churl who frequented her father's mill. This stopped the mouth of vanity, and of the love which vanity had been hatching, as effectually as a peck of literal flour would have done.

Amidst this variety of emotions, Sir Piercie Shafton forgot not to ask the object of them to sit down and partake the good cheer which she had been so anxious to provide and to place in order. He expected that this invitation would have been bashfully, perhaps, but certainly most thankfully, accepted; but he was partly flattered and partly piqued by the mixture of deference and resolution with which Mysie declined his invitation. Immediately after, she vanished from the apartment, leaving the Euphuist to consider whether he was most gratified or displeased by her disappearance.

In fact, this was a point on which he would have found it difficult to make up his mind, had there been any necessity for it. As there was none, he drank a few cups of claret, and sang (to himself) a strophe or two of the canzonettes of the divine Astrophel. But in spite both of wine and of Sir Philip Sidney, the connexion in which he now stood, and that which he was in future to hold, with the lovely Molinara, or Mysinda, as he had been pleased to denominate Mysie Happer, recurred to his mind. The fashion of the times, as we have already noticed, fortunately coincided with his own natural generosity of disposition, which indeed amounted almost to extravagance, in prohibiting, as a deadly sin, alike against gallantry, chivalry, and morality, his rewarding the good offices he had received from this poor maiden by abusing any of the advantages which her confidence in his honour had afforded. To do Sir Piercie justice, it was an idea which never entered into his head; and he would probably have dealt the most scientific *imbrocata, stoccata,* or *punto reverso,* which the school of Vincent Saviola had taught him, to any man who had dared to suggest to him such selfish and ungrateful meanness. On the other hand, he was a man, and foresaw various circumstances which might render their journey together in this intimate fashion a scandal and a snare. Moreover, he was a coxcomb and a courtier, and felt there was something ridiculous in travelling the land with a miller's daughter behind his saddle, giving rise to suspicions not very creditable to either, and to ludicrous constructions, so far as he himself was concerned.

"I would," he said half-aloud, "that, if such might be done without harm or discredit to the too-ambitious, yet too-well-distinguishing Molinara, she and I were fairly severed, and bound on our different courses; even as we see the goodly vessel bound for the distant seas hoist sails and bear away into the deep, while the humble flyboat carries to shore those friends who, with wounded hearts and watery eyes, have committed to their higher destinies the more daring adventurers by whom the fair frigate is manned."

He had scarce uttered the wish when it was gratified; for the host entered to say that his worshipful knighthood's horse was ready to be brought forth as he had desired; and on his inquiry for "the—the—damsel—that is—the young woman——"

"Mysie Happer," said the landlord, "has returned to her father's; but she bade me say, you could not miss the road for Edinburgh, in respect it was neither far way nor foul gate."

It is seldom we are exactly blessed with the precise fulfilment of our wishes at the moment when we utter them; perhaps because Heaven wisely withholds what, if granted, would be often received with ingratitude. So at least it chanced in the present instance; for, when mine host said that Mysie was returned homeward, the knight was tempted to reply with an ejaculation of surprise and vexation, and a hasty demand whither and when she had departed. The first emotions his prudence suppressed, the second found utterance.

"Where is she gane?" said the host, gazing on him, and repeating his question. "She is gane hame to her father's, it is like; and she gaed just when she gave orders about your worship's horse, and saw it weel fed—she might have trusted me, but millers and millers' kin think a'body as thief-like as themselves—an' she's three miles on the gate by this time."

"Is she gone, then?" muttered Sir Piercie, making two or three hasty strides through the narrow apartment—"is she gone? Well, then, let her go. She could have had but disgrace by abiding by me, and I little credit by her society.

That I should have thought there was such difficulty in shaking her off! I warrant she is by this time laughing with some clown she has encountered; and my rich chain will prove a good dowry. And ought it not to prove so? and has she not deserved it, were it ten times more valuable? Piercie Shafton! Piercie Shafton! dost thou grudge thy deliverer the guerdon she hath so dearly won? The selfish air of this northern land hath infected thee, Piercie Shafton, and blighted the blossoms of thy generosity, even as it is said to shrivel the flowers of the mulberry. Yet I thought," he added, after a moment's pause, "that she would not so easily and voluntarily have parted from me. But it skills not thinking of it. Cast my reckoning, mine host, and let your groom lead forth my nag."

The good host seemed also to have some mental point to discuss, for he answered not instantly, debating perhaps whether his conscience would bear a double charge for the same guests. Apparently his conscience replied in the negative, though not without hesitation, for he at length replied: "It's daffing to lee; it winna deny that the lawing is clean paid. Ne'ertheless, if your worshipful knighthood pleases to give aught for increase of trouble——"

"How!" said the knight; "the reckoning paid! and by whom, I pray you?"

"E'en by Mysie Happer, if truth maun be spoken, as I said before," answered the honest landlord, with as many compunctious visitings for telling the verity as another might have felt for making a lie in the circumstances; "and out of the monies supplied for your honour's journey by the abbot, as she tauld to me. And laith were I to surcharge any gentleman that darkens my doors." He added, in the confidence of honesty which his frank avowal entitled him to entertain: "Ne'ertheless, as I said before, if it pleases your knighthood of free good-will to consider extraordinary trouble——"

The knight cut short his argument by throwing the landlord a rose-noble, which probably doubled the value of a Scottish reckoning, though it would have defrayed but a half one at the Three Cranes or [in] the Vintry. The bounty so much delighted mine host that he ran to fill the stirrup-cup (for which no charge was ever made) from a butt yet charier than that which he had pierced for the former stoup. The knight paced slowly to horse, partook of his courtesy, and thanked him with the stiff condescension of the court of Elizabeth; then mounted and followed the northern path, which was pointed out as the nearest to Edinburgh, and which, though very unlike a modern highway, bore yet so distinct a resemblance to a public and frequented road as not to be easily mistaken.

"I shall not need her guidance it seems," said he to himself, as he rode slowly onward; "and I suppose that was one reason of her abrupt departure, so different from what one might have expected. Well, I am well rid of her. Do we not pray to be liberated from temptation? Yet that she should have erred so much in estimation of her own situation and mine as to think of defraying the reckoning! I would I saw her once more, but to explain to her the solecism of which her inexperience hath rendered her guilty. And I fear," he added, as he emerged from some straggling trees, and looked out upon a wild moorish country, composed of a succession of swelling lumpish hills—"I fear I shall soon want the aid of this Ariadne, who might afford me a clue through the recesses of yonder mountainous labyrinth."

As the knight thus communed with himself, his attention was caught by the sound of a horse's footsteps; and a lad, mounted on a little grey Scottish nag, about fourteen hands high, coming along a path which led from behind the trees, joined him on the highroad, if it could be termed such.

The dress of the lad was completely in village fashion, yet neat and handsome in appearance. He had a jerkin of grey cloth slashed and trimmed, with black hose of the same, with deer-skin rullions or sandals, and handsome silver spurs. A cloak of a dark mulberry colour was closely drawn round the upper part of his person, and the cape in part muffled his face, which was also obscured by his bonnet of black velvet cloth, and its little plume of feathers.

Sir Piercie Shafton, fond of society, desirous also to have a guide, and, moreover, prepossessed in favour of so handsome a youth, failed not to ask him whence he came, and whither he was going. The youth looked another way, as he answered, that he was going to Edinburgh, "to seek service in some nobleman's family."

"I fear me you have run away from your last master," said Sir Piercie, "since you dare not look me in the face while you answer my question."

"Indeed, sir, I have not," answered the lad, bashfully, while, as if with reluctance, he turned round his face, and instantly withdrew it. It was a glance, but the discovery was complete. There was no mistaking the dark full eye, the cheek in which much embarrassment could not altogether disguise an expression of comic humour, and the whole figure at once betrayed, under her metamorphosis, the Maid of the Mill. The recognition was joyful, and Sir Piercie Shafton was too much pleased to have regained his companion to remember the various good reasons which had consoled him for losing her.

To his questions respecting her dress, she answered that she had obtained it in the Kirktown from a friend; it was the holiday suit of a son of hers, who had taken the field with his liege lord, the baron of the land. She had borrowed the suit under pretence she meant to play in some mumming or rural masquerade. She had left, she said, her own apparel in exchange, which was better worth ten crowns than this was worth four.

"And the nag, my ingenious Molinara," said Sir Piercie— "whence comes the nag?"

"I borrowed him from our host at the Gled's Nest," she replied; and added, half-stifling a laugh, "he has sent to get, instead of it, our Ball, which I left in the Tasker's Park at Cripplecross. He will be lucky if he find it there."

"But then the poor man will lose his horse, most argute Mysinda," said Sir Piercie Shafton, whose English notions of property were a little startled at a mode of acquisition more congenial to the ideas of a miller's daughter, and he a Border miller to boot, than with those of an English person of quality.

"And if he does lose his horse," said Mysie, laughing, "surely he is not the first man on the marches who has had such a mischance? But he will be no loser, for I warrant he will stop the value out of monies which he has owed my father this many a day."

"But then your father will be the loser," objected yet again the pertinacious uprightness of Sir Piercie Shafton.

"What signifies it now to talk of my father?" said the damsel, pettishly; then instantly changing to a tone of deep feeling, she added: "My father has this day lost that which will make him hold light the loss of all the gear he has left."

Struck with the accents of remorseful sorrow in which his companion uttered these few words, the English knight felt himself bound both in honour and conscience to expostulate with her as strongly as he could on the risk of the step which she had now taken, and on the propriety of her returning to her father's house. The matter of his discourse, though adorned with many unnecessary flourishes, was honourable both to his head and heart.

The Maid of the Mill listened to his flowing periods with her head sunk on her bosom as she rode, like one in deep thought or deeper sorrow. When he had finished, she raised up her countenance, looked full on the knight, and replied with great firmness: "If you are weary of my company, Sir Piercie Shafton, you have but to say so, and the miller's daughter will be no farther cumber to you. And do not think I will be a burden to you, if we travel together to Edinburgh: I have wit enough and pride enough to be a willing burden to no man. But if you reject not my company at present, and fear not it will be burdensome to you hereafter, speak no more to me of returning back. All that you can say to me I have said to myself; and that I am now here is a sign that I have said it to no purpose. Let this subject, therefore, be for ever ended betwixt us. I have already, in some small fashion, been useful to you, and the time may come I may be more so; for this is not your land of England, where men say justice is done with little fear or favour to great and to small; but it is a land where men do by the strong hand, and defend by the

ready wit, and I know better than you the perils you are exposed to."

Sir Piercie Shafton was somewhat mortified to find that the
damsel conceived her presence useful to him as a protectress
as well as guide, and said something of seeking protection
from nought save his own arm and his good sword. Mysie
answered very quietly, that she nothing doubted his bravery;
but it was that very quality of bravery which was most likely
to involve him in danger. Sir Piercie Shafton, whose head
never kept very long in any continued train of thinking, acquiesced without much reply, resolving in his own mind that
the maiden only used this apology to disguise her real motive
of affection to his person. The romance of the situation flattered his vanity and elevated his imagination, as placing him
in the situation of one of those romantic heroes of whom he
had read the histories, where similar transformations made a
distinguished figure.

He took many a sidelong glance at his page, whose habits
of country sport and country exercise had rendered her quite
adequate to sustain the character she had assumed. She
managed the little nag with dexterity, and even with grace;
nor did anything appear which could have betrayed her disguise, except when a bashful consciousness of her companion's
eyes being fixed on her gave her an appearance of temporary
embarrassment, which greatly added to her beauty.

The couple rode forward as in the morning, pleased with
themselves and with each other, until they arrived at the village where they were to repose for the night, and where all
the inhabitants of the little inn, both male and female, joined
in extolling the good grace and handsome countenance of the
English knight, and the uncommon beauty of his youthful attendant.

It was here that Mysie Happer first made Sir Piercie Shafton sensible of the reserved manner in which she proposed to
live with him. She announced him as her master, and, waiting upon him with the reverent demeanour of an actual domestic, permitted not the least approach to familiarity, not even
such as the knight might with the utmost innocence have ven-

tured upon. For example, Sir Piercie, who, as we know, was a great connoisseur in dress, was detailing to her the advantageous change which he proposed to make in her attire as soon as they should reach Edinburgh, by arraying her in his own colours of pink and carnation. Mysie Happer listened with great complacency to the unction with which he dilated upon welts, laces, slashes, and trimmings, until, carried away by the enthusiasm with which he was asserting the superiority of the falling band over the Spanish ruff, he approached his hand, in the way of illustration, towards the collar of his page's doublet. She instantly stepped back, and gravely reminded him that she was alone, and under his protection.

"You cannot but remember the cause which has brought me here," she continued; "make the least approach to any familiarity which you would not offer to a princess surrounded by her court, and you have seen the last of the miller's daughter. She will vanish as the chaff disappears from the shieling-hill, when the west wind blows."

"I do protest, fair Molinara," said Sir Piercie Shafton— but the fair Molinara had disappeared before his protest could be uttered. "A most singular wench," said he to himself; "and by this hand as discreet as she is fair-featured. Certes, shame it were to offer her scathe or dishonour! She makes similes, too, though somewhat savouring of her condition. Had she but read *Euphues*, and forgotten that accursed mill and shieling-hill, it is my thought that her converse would be broidered with as many and as choice pearls of compliment as that of the most rhetorical lady in the court of Feliciana. I trust she means to return to bear me company!"

But that was no part of Mysie's prudential scheme. It was then drawing to dusk, and he saw her not again until the next morning, when the horses were brought to the door, that they might prosecute their journey.

But our story here necessarily leaves the English knight and his page, to return to the Tower of Glendearg.

CHAPTER XXX.

You call it an ill angel—it may be so;
But sure I am, among the ranks which fell,
'Tis the first fiend e'er counsell'd man to rise,
And win the bliss the sprite himself had forfeited.
Old Play.

WE must resume our narrative at the period when Mary
Avenel was conveyed to the apartment which had been formerly occupied by the two Glendinnings, and when her faithful attendant, Tibbie, had exhausted herself in useless attempts
to compose and to comfort her.   Father Eustace also dealt forth
with well-meant kindness those apothegms and dogmata of consolation which friendship almost always offers to grief, though
they are uniformly offered in vain.   She was at length left to
indulge in the desolation of her own sorrowful feelings.   She
felt as those who, loving for the first time, have lost what
they loved, before time and repeated calamity have taught
them that every loss is to a certain extent reparable or endurable.

Such grief may be conceived better than it can be described,
as is well known to those who have experienced it.   But Mary
Avenel had been taught by the peculiarity of her situation to
regard herself as the child of destiny; and the melancholy and
reflecting turn of her disposition gave to her sorrows a depth
and breadth peculiar to her character.   The grave—and it was
a bloody grave—had closed, as she believed, over the youth to
whom she was secretly, but most warmly, attached; the force
and ardour of Halbert's character bearing a singular correspondence to the energy of which her own was capable.   Her
sorrow did not exhaust itself in sighs or in tears, but, when
the first shock had passed away, concentrated itself with deep
and steady meditation to collect and calculate, like a bankrupt
debtor, the full amount of her loss.   It seemed as if all that
connected her with earth had vanished with this broken tie.
She had never dared to anticipate the probability of an ultimate union with Halbert, yet now his supposed fall seemed
that of the only tree which was to shelter her from the storm.

She respected the more gentle character and more peaceful attainments of the younger Glendinning; but it had not escaped her (what never indeed escaped woman in such circumstances) that he was disposed to place himself in competition with what she, the daughter of a proud and warlike race, deemed the more manly qualities of his elder brother; and there is no time when a woman does so little justice to the character of a surviving lover as when comparing him with the preferred rival of whom she has been recently deprived.

The motherly but coarse kindness of Dame Glendinning, and the doting fondness of her old domestic, seemed now the only kind feeling of which she formed the object; and she could not but reflect how little these were to be compared with the devoted attachment of a high-souled youth, whom the least glance of her eye could command, as the high-mettled steed is governed by the bridle of the rider. It was when plunged among these desolating reflections that Mary Avenel felt the void of mind arising from the narrow and bigoted ignorance in which Rome then educated the children of her church. Their whole religion was a ritual, and their prayers were the formal iteration of unknown words, which, in the hour of affliction, could yield but little consolation to those who from habit resorted to them. Unused to the practice of mental devotion, and of personal approach to the Divine Presence by prayer, she could not help exclaiming in her distress: "There is no aid for me on earth, and I know not how to ask it from Heaven!"

As she spoke thus in an agony of sorrow, she cast her eyes into the apartment, and saw the mysterious Spirit which waited upon the fortunes of her house standing in the moonlight in the midst of the room. The same form, as the reader knows, had more than once offered itself to her sight; and either her native boldness of mind, or some peculiarity attached to her from her birth, made her now look upon it without shrinking. But the White Lady of Avenel was now more distinctly visible, and more closely present, than she had ever before seemed to be, and Mary was appalled by her presence. She would, however, have spoken; but there ran a tradition,

that though others who had seen the White Lady had asked
questions and received answers, yet those of the house of Avenel who had ventured to speak to her had never long survived
the colloquy. The figure, besides, as, sitting up in her bed,
Mary Avenel gazed on it intently, seemed by its gestures to
caution her to keep silence, and at the same time to bespeak
attention.

The White Lady then seemed to press one of the planks of
the floor with her foot, while, in her usual low, melancholy,
and musical chant, she repeated the following verses:

> " Maiden, whose sorrows wail the living dead,
>   Whose eyes shall commune with the dead alive,
> Maiden, attend ! Beneath my foot lies hid
>   The Word, the Law, the Path, which thou dost strive
> To find, and canst not find. Could spirits shed
>   Tears for their lot, it were my lot to weep,
> Showing the road which I shall never tread,
>   Though my foot points it. Sleep, eternal sleep,
> Dark, long, and cold forgetfulness my lot !
>   But do not thou at human ills repine,
> Secure there lies full guerdon in this spot
>   For all the woes that wait frail Adam's line:
> Stoop then and make it yours—I may not make it mine ! "

The phantom stooped towards the floor as she concluded, as
if with the intention of laying her hand on the board on which
she stood. But, ere she had completed that gesture, her form
became indistinct, was presently only like the shade of a
fleecy cloud which passed betwixt earth and the moon, and
was soon altogether invisible.

A strong impression of fear, the first which she had experienced in her life to any agitating extent, seized upon the mind
of Mary Avenel, and for a minute she felt a disposition to faint.
She repelled it, however, mustered her courage, and addressed
herself to saints and angels, as her church recommended.
Broken slumbers at length stole on her exhausted mind and
frame, and she slept until the dawn was about to arise, when
she was awakened by the cry of " Treason! treason! follow—
follow!" which arose in the tower, when it was found that
Piercie Shafton had made his escape.

Apprehensive of some new misfortune, Mary Avenel hastily

arranged the dress which she had not laid aside, and, venturing to quit her chamber, learned from Tibb, who, with her grey hairs dishevelled like those of a sibyl, was flying from room to room, that "The bloody Southron villain had made his escape, and that Halbert Glendinning, poor bairn, would sleep unrevenged and unquiet in his bloody grave." In the lower apartments the young men were roaring like thunder, and venting in oaths and exclamations against the fugitives the rage which they experienced in finding themselves locked up within the tower, and debarred from their vindictive pursuit by the wily precautions of Mysie Happer. The authoritative voice of the sub-prior commanding silence was next heard; upon which Mary Avenel, whose tone of feeling did not lead her to enter into counsel or society with the rest of the party, again retired to her solitary chamber.

The rest of the family held counsel in the spence, Edward almost beside himself with rage, and the sub-prior in no small degree offended at the effrontery of Mysie Happer in attempting such a scheme, as well as at the mingled boldness and dexterity with which it had been executed. But neither surprise nor anger availed aught. The windows, well secured with iron bars for keeping assailants out, proved now as effectual for detaining the inhabitants within. The battlements were open, indeed; but, without ladder or ropes to act as a substitute for wings, there was no possibility of descending from them. They easily succeeded in alarming the inhabitants of the cottages beyond the precincts of the court; but the men had been called in to strengthen the guard for the night, and only women and children remained, who could contribute nothing in the emergency, except their useless exclamations of surprise; and there were no neighbours for miles around. Dame Elspeth, however, though drowned in tears, was not so unmindful of external affairs but that she could find voice enough to tell the women and children without to "leave their skirling, and look after the cows that she couldna get minded, what wi' the awfu' distraction of her mind, what wi' that fause slut having locked them up in their ain tower as fast as if they had been in the Jeddart tolbooth."

Meanwhile, the men, finding other modes of exit impossible, unanimously concluded to force the doors with such tools as the house afforded for the purpose. These were not very proper for the occasion, and the strength of the doors was great. The interior one, formed of oak, occupied them for three mortal hours, and there was little prospect of the iron door being forced in double the time.

While they were engaged in this ungrateful toil, Mary Avenel had with much less labour acquired exact knowledge of what the Spirit had intimated in her mystic rhyme. On examining the spot which the phantom had indicated by her gestures, it was not difficult to discover that a board had been loosened, which might be raised at pleasure. On removing this piece of plank, Mary Avenel was astonished to find the Black Book, well remembered by her as her mother's favourite study, of which she immediately took possession, with as much joy as her present situation rendered her capable of feeling.

Ignorant in a great measure of its contents, Mary Avenel had been taught from her infancy to hold this volume in sacred veneration. It is probable that the deceased lady of Walter Avenel only postponed initiating her daughter into the mysteries of the Divine Word until she should be better able to comprehend both the lessons which it taught and the risk at which, in those times, they were studied. Death interposed, and removed her before the times became favourable to the Reformers, and before her daughter was so far advanced in age as to be fit to receive religious instruction of this deep import. But the affectionate mother had made preparations for the earthly work which she had most at heart. There were slips of paper inserted in the volume, in which, by an appeal to, and a comparison of, various passages in Holy Writ, the errors and human inventions with which the Church of Rome had defaced the simple edifice of Christianity, as erected by its Divine architect, were pointed out. These controversial topics were treated with a spirit of calmness and Christian charity which might have been an example to the theologians of the period; but they were clearly, fairly, and plainly argued, and supported by the necessary proofs and references. Other papers there were which had no reference whatever to polemics, but were the simple effusions of a devout mind communing with itself. Among these was one frequently used, as it seemed from the state of the manuscript, on which the mother of Mary had transcribed and placed together those affecting texts to which the heart has recourse in affliction, and which assure us at once of the sympathy and protection afforded to the children of the promise. In Mary Avenel's state of mind, these attracted her above all the other lessons which, coming from a hand so dear, had reached her at a time so critical, and in a manner so touching. She read the affecting promise, "I will never leave thee nor forsake thee," and the consoling exhortation, "Call upon me in the day of trouble, and I will deliver thee." She read them, and her heart acquiesced in the conclusion, Surely this is the Word of God!

There are those to whom a sense of religion has come in storm and tempest; there are those whom it has summoned amid scenes of revelry and idle vanity; there are those, too, who have heard its "still small voice" amid rural leisure and placid contentment. But perhaps the knowledge which causeth not to err is most frequently impressed upon the mind during seasons of affliction; and tears are the softened showers which cause the seed of Heaven to spring and take root in the human breast. At least it was thus with Mary Avenel. She was insensible to the discordant noise which rang below, the clang of bars and the jarring symphony of the levers which they used to force them, the measured shouts of the labouring inmates as they combined their strength for each heave, and gave time with their voices to the exertion of their arms, and their deeply-muttered vows of revenge on the fugitives who had bequeathed them at their departure a task so toilsome and difficult. Not all this din, combined in hideous concert, and expressive of aught but peace, love, and forgiveness, could divert Mary Avenel from the new course of study on which she had so singularly entered. "The serenity of Heaven," she said, "is above me; the sounds which are around are but those of earth and earthly passion."

Meanwhile, the noon was passed, and little impression was made on the iron grate, when they who laboured at it received a sudden reinforcement by the unexpected arrival of Christie of the Clinthill. He came at the head of a small party, consisting of four horsemen, who bore in their caps the sprig of holly which was the badge of Avenel.

"What, ho! my masters," he said, "I bring you a prisoner."

"You had better have brought us liberty," said Dan of the Howlethirst.

Christie looked at the state of affairs with great surprise. "An I were to be hanged for it," he said, "as I may for as little a matter, I could not forbear laughing at seeing men peeping through their own bars like so many rats in a rat-trap, and he with the beard behind, like the oldest rat in the cellar!"

"Hush, thou unmannered knave," said Edward, "it is the sub-prior; and this is neither time, place, nor company for your ruffian jests."

"What, ho! is my young master malapert?" said Christie; "why, man, were he my own carnal father, instead of being father to half the world, I would have my laugh out. And now it is over, I must assist you, I reckon, for you are setting very greenly about this gear; put the pinch nearer the staple, man, and hand me an iron crow through the grate, for that's the fowl to fly away with a wicket on its shoulders. I have broke into as many grates as you have teeth in your young head; ay, and broke out of them, too, as the captain of the Castle of Lochmaben knows full well."

Christie did not boast more skill than he really possessed; for, applying their combined strength, under the direction of that experienced engineer, bolt and staple gave way before them, and in less than half an hour the grate, which had so long repelled their force, stood open before them.

"And now," said Edward, "to horse, my mates, and pursue the villain Shafton!"

"Halt there," said Christie of the Clinthill; "pursue your guest, my master's friend and my own! There go two words to that bargain. What the foul fiend would you pursue him for?"

"Let me pass," said Edward, vehemently, "I will be staid by no man; the villain has murdered my brother."

"What says he?" said Christie, turning to the others; "murdered? who is murdered, and by whom?"

"The Englishman, Sir Piercie Shafton," said Dan of the Howlethirst, "has murdered young Halbert Glendinning yesterday morning, and we have all risen to the fray."

"It is a bedlam business, I think," said Christie. "First I find you all locked up in your own tower, and next I am come to prevent you revenging a murder that was never committed!"

"I tell you," said Edward, "that my brother was slain and buried yesterday morning by this false Englishman."

"And I tell you," answered Christie, "that I saw him alive and well last night. I would I knew his trick of getting out of the grave; most men find it more hard to break through a green sod than a grated door."

Everybody now paused, and looked on Christie in astonishment, until the sub-prior, who had hitherto avoided communication with him, came up, and required earnestly to know whether he meant really to maintain that Halbert Glendinning lived.

"Father," he said, with more respect than he usually showed to any one save his master, "I confess I may sometimes jest with those of your coat, but not with you; because, as you may partly recollect, I owe you a life. It is certain as the sun is in heaven that Halbert Glendinning supped at the house of my master the Baron of Avenel last night, and that he came thither in company with an old man, of whom more anon."

"And where is he now?"

"The devil only can answer that question," replied Christie, "for the devil has possessed the whole family, I think. He took fright, the foolish lad, at something or other which our Baron did in his moody humour, and so he jumped into the lake and swam ashore like a wild duck. Robin of Redcastle spoiled a good gelding in chasing him this morning."

"And why did he chase the youth?" said the sub-prior; "what harm had he done?"

"None that I know of," said Christie; "but such was the Baron's order, being in his mood, and all the world having gone mad, as I have said before."

"Whither away so fast, Edward?" said the monk.

"To Corrie-nan-Shian, father," answered the youth. "Martin and Dan, take pickaxe and mattock, and follow me if you be men!"

"Right," said the monk, "and fail not to give us instant notice what you find."

"If you find aught there like Halbert Glendinning," said Christie, hallooing after Edward, "I will be bound to eat him unsalted. 'Tis a sight to see now how that fellow takes the bent! It is in the time of action men see what lads are made of. Halbert was aye skipping up and down like a roe, and his brother used to sit in the chimney-nook, with his book and sic-like trash. But the lad was like a loaded hackbut, which will stand in the corner as quiet as an old crutch until ye draw the trigger, and then there is nothing but flash and smoke. But here comes my prisoner; and, setting other matters aside, I must pray a word with you, sir sub-prior, respecting him. I came on before to treat about him, but I was interrupted with this fasherie."

As he spoke, two more of Avenel's troopers rode into the courtyard, leading betwixt them a horse, on which, with his hands bound to his side, sate the Reformed preacher, Henry Warden.

CHAPTER XXXI.

> At school I knew him—a sharp-witted youth,
> Grave, thoughtful, and reserved among his mates,
> Turning the hours of sport and food to labour,
> Starving his body to inform his mind.
> *Old Play.*

THE sub-prior, at the Borderer's request, had not failed to return to the tower, into which he was followed by Christie of the Clinthill, who, shutting the door of the apartment, drew near, and began his discourse with great confidence and familiarity.

"My master," he said, "sends me with his commendations to you, sir sub-prior, above all the community of St. Mary's, and more specially than even to the abbot himself; for, though he be termed, 'my lord,' and so forth, all the world knows that you are the tongue of the trump."

"If you have aught to say to me concerning the community," said the sub-prior, "it were well you proceeded in it without further delay. Time presses, and the fate of young Glendinning dwells on my mind."

"I will be caution for him, body for body," said Christie. "I do protest to you, as sure as I am a living man, so surely is he one."

"Should I not tell his unhappy mother the joyful tidings?" said Father Eustace; "and yet better wait till they return from searching the grave. Well, sir jack-man, your message to me from your master?"

"My lord and master," said Chrisie, "hath good reason to believe that, from the information of certain back-friends, whom he will reward at more leisure, your reverend community hath been led to deem him ill attached to Holy Church, allied with heretics and those who favour heresy, and a hungerer after the spoils of your abbey."

"Be brief, good henchman," said the sub-prior, "for the devil is ever most to be feared when he preacheth."

"Briefly then—my master desires your friendship; and to excuse himself from the maligners' calumnies, he sends to your abbot that Henry Warden whose sermons have turned the world upside down, to be dealt with as Holy Church directs, and as the abbot's pleasure may determine."

The sub-prior's eyes sparkled at the intelligence; for it had been accounted a matter of great importance that this man should be arrested, possessed, as he was known to be, of so much zeal and popularity that scarcely the preaching of Knox himself had been more awakening to the people, and more formidable to the Church of Rome.

In fact, that ancient system, which so well accommodated its doctrines to the wants and wishes of a barbarous age, had, since the art of printing and the gradual diffusion of knowl-

edge, lain floating like some huge leviathan, into which ten
thousand reforming fishers were darting their harpoons. The
Roman Church of Scotland, in particular, was at her last gasp,
actually bowing blood and water, yet still with unremitted,
though animal, exertions maintaining the conflict with the assailants, who on every side were plunging their weapons into
her bulky body. In many large towns the monasteries had
been suppressed by the fury of the populace; in other places,
their possessions had been usurped by the power of the Reformed nobles; but still the hierarchy made a part of the
common law of the realm, and might claim both its property
and its privileges wherever it had the means of asserting them.
The community of St. Mary's of Kennaquhair was considered
as being particularly in this situation. They had retained,
undiminished, their territorial power and influence; and the
great barons in the neighbourhood, partly from their attachment to the party in the state who still upheld the old system
of religion, partly because each grudged the share of the prey
which the others must necessarily claim, had as yet abstained
from despoiling the halidome. The community was also understood to be protected by the powerful Earls of Northumberland and Westmoreland, whose zealous attachment to the
Catholic faith caused at a later period the great rebellion of
the tenth of Elizabeth.

Thus happily placed, it was supposed by the friends of the
decaying cause of the Roman Catholic faith that some determined example of courage and resolution, exercised where the
franchises of the church were yet entire, and her jurisdiction
undisputed, might awe the progress of the new opinions into
activity; and, protected by the laws which still existed and
by the favour of the sovereign, might be the means of securing the territory which Rome yet preserved in Scotland, and
perhaps of recovering that which she had lost.

The matter had been considered more than once by the
northern Catholics of Scotland, and they had held communication with those of the south. Father Eustace, devoted by
his public and private vows, had caught the flame, and had
eagerly advised that they should execute the doom of heresy

on the first Reformed preacher, or, according to his sense, on the first heretic of eminence, who should venture within the precincts of the halidome. A heart naturally kind and noble was, in this instance, as it has been in many more, deceived by its own generosity. Father Eustace would have been a bad administrator of the inquisitorial power of Spain, where that power was omnipotent, and where judgment was exercised without danger to those who inflicted it. In such a situation his rigour might have relented in favour of the criminal, whom it was at his pleasure to crush or to place at freedom. But in Scotland during this crisis the case was entirely different. The question was, whether one of the spirituality dared, at the hazard of his own life, to step forward to assert and exercise the rights of the church. Was there any one who would venture to wield the thunder in her cause, or must it remain like that in the hand of a painted Jupiter, the object of derision instead of terror? The crisis was calculated to awake the soul of Eustace; for it comprised the question, whether he dared, at all hazards to himself, to execute with stoical severity a measure which, according to the general opinion, was to be advantageous to the church, and, according to ancient law, and to his firm belief, was not only justifiable, but meritorious.

While such resolutions were agitated amongst the Catholics, chance placed a victim within their grasp. Henry Warden had, with the animation proper to the enthusiastic Reformers of the age, transgressed, in the vehemence of his zeal, the bounds of the discretional liberty allowed to his sect so far that it was thought the Queen's personal dignity was concerned in bringing him to justice. He fled from Edinburgh, with recommendations, however, from Lord James Stuart, afterwards the celebrated Earl of Murray, to some of the Border chieftains of inferior rank, who were privately conjured to procure him safe passage into England. One of the principal persons to whom such recommendation was addressed was Julian Avenel; for as yet, and for a considerable time afterwards, the correspondence and interest of Lord James lay rather with the subordinate leaders than with the chiefs of great power and men of distinguished influence upon the Border. Julian Avenel had intrigued without scruple with both parties; yet, bad as he was, he certainly would not have practised aught against the guest whom Lord James had recommended to his hospitality, had it not been for what he termed the preacher's officious intermeddling in his family affairs. But when he had determined to make Warden rue the lecture he had read him, and the scene of public scandal which he had caused in his hall, Julian resolved, with the constitutional shrewdness of his disposition, to combine his vengeance with his interest. And therefore, instead of doing violence on the person of Henry Warden within his own castle, he determined to deliver him up to the community of St. Mary's, and at once make them the instruments of his own revenge and found a claim of personal recompense, either in money or in a grant of abbey lands at a low quit-rent, which last began now to be the established form in which the temporal nobles plundered the spirituality.

The sub-prior, therefore, of St. Mary's unexpectedly saw the steadfast, active, and inflexible enemy of the church delivered into his hand, and felt himself called upon to make good his promises to the friends of the Catholic faith, by quenching heresy in the blood of one of its most zealous professors.

To the honour more of Father Eustace's heart than of his consistency, the communication that Henry Warden was placed within his power struck him with more sorrow than triumph; but his next feelings were those of exultation. "It is sad," he said to himself, "to cause human suffering, it is awful to cause human blood to be spilled; but the judge to whom the sword of St. Paul, as well as the keys of St. Peter, are confided must not flinch from his task. Our weapon returns into our own bosom if not wielded with a steady and unrelenting hand against the irreconcilable enemies of the Holy Church. *Pereat iste!* It is the doom he has incurred, and were all the heretics in Scotland armed and at his back, they should not prevent its being pronounced, and, if possible, enforced. Bring the heretic before me," he said, issuing his commands aloud and in a tone of authority.

Henry Warden was led in, his hands still bound, but his feet at liberty.

"Clear the apartment," said the sub-prior, "of all but the necessary guard on the prisoner."

All retired excepting Christie of the Clinthill, who, having dismissed the inferior troopers whom he commanded, unsheathed his sword, and placed himself beside the door, as if taking upon him the character of sentinel.

The judge and the accused met face to face, and in that of both was enthroned the noble confidence of rectitude. The monk was about, at the utmost risk to himself and his community, to exercise what in his ignorance he conceived to be his duty. The preacher, actuated by a better-informed, yet not a more ardent, zeal, was prompt to submit to execution for God's sake, and to seal, were it necessary, his mission with his blood. Placed at such a distance of time as better enables us to appreciate the tendency of the principles on which they severally acted, we cannot doubt to which the palm ought to be awarded. But the zeal of Father Eustace was as free from passion and personal views as if it had been exerted in a better cause.

They approached each other, armed each and prepared for intellectual conflict, and each intently regarding his opponent, as if either hoped to spy out some defect, some chasm in the armour of his antagonist. As they gazed on each other, old recollections began to awake in either bosom, at the sight of features long unseen and much altered, but not forgotten. The brow of the sub-prior dismissed by degrees its frown of command, the look of calm yet stern defiance gradually vanished from that of Warden, and both lost for an instant that of gloomy solemnity. They had been ancient and intimate friends in youth at a foreign university, but had been long separated from each other; and the change of name, which the preacher had adopted from motives of safety, and the monk from the common custom of the convent, had prevented the possibility of their hitherto recognising each other in the opposite parts which they had been playing in the great polemical and political drama. But now the sub-prior exclaimed, "Henry Wellwood!" and the preacher replied, "William Allan!" and, stirred by the old familiar names and never-to-be-forgotten recollections of college studies and college intimacy, their hands were for a moment locked in each other.

"Remove his bonds," said the sub-prior, and assisted Christie in performing that office with his own hands, although the prisoner scarcely would consent to be unbound, repeating with emphasis that he rejoiced in the cause for which he suffered shame. When his hands were at liberty, however, he showed his sense of the kindness by again exchanging a grasp and a look of affection with the sub-prior.

The salute was frank and generous on either side, yet it was but the friendly recognition and greeting which is wont to take place betwixt adverse champions, who do nothing in hate, but all in honour. As each felt the pressure of the situation in which they stood, he quitted the grasp of the other's hand, and they fell back, confronting each other with looks more calm and sorrowful than expressive of any other passion.

The sub-prior was the first to speak. "And is this, then, the end of that restless activity of mind, that bold and indefatigable love of truth, that urged investigation to its utmost limits, and seemed to take Heaven itself by storm: is this the termination of Wellwood's career? And having known and loved him during the best years of our youth, do we meet in our old age as judge and criminal?"

"Not as judge and criminal," said Henry Warden, for to avoid confusion we describe him by his later and best-known name—"not as judge and criminal do we meet, but as a misguided oppressor and his ready and devoted victim. I too may ask, are these the harvest of the rich hopes excited by the classical learning, acute logical powers, and varied knowledge of William Allan, that he should sink to be the solitary drone of a cell, graced only above the swarm with the high commission of executing Roman malice on all who oppose Roman imposture?"

"Not to thee," answered the sub-prior, "be assured—not unto thee, nor unto mortal man, will I render an account of the power with which the church may have invested me. It was granted but as a deposit for her welfare; for her welfare it shall at every risk be exercised, without fear and without favour."

"I expected no less from your misguided zeal," answered the preacher; "and in me have you met one on whom you may fearlessly exercise your authority, secure that his mind at least will defy your influence, as the snows of that Mont Blanc which we saw together shrink not under the heat of the hottest summer sun."

"I do believe thee," said the sub-prior—"I do believe that thine is indeed metal unmalleable by force. Let it yield then to persuasion. Let us debate these matters of faith as we once were wont to conduct our scholastic disputes, when hours, nay days, glided past in the mutual exercise of our intellectual powers. It may be thou mayst yet hear the voice of the shepherd, and return to the universal fold."

"No, Allan," replied the prisoner, "this is no vain question, devised by dreaming scholiasts, on which they may whet their intellectual faculties until the very metal be wasted away. The errors which I combat are like those fiends which are only cast out by fasting and prayer. Alas! not many wise, not many learned are chosen; the cottage and the hamlet shall in our days bear witness against the schools and their disciples. Thy very wisdom, which is foolishness, hath made thee, as the Greeks of old, hold as foolishness that which is the only true wisdom."

"This," said the sub-prior, sternly, "is the mere cant of ignorant enthusiasm, which appealeth from learning and from authority, from the sure guidance of that lamp which God hath afforded us in the councils and in the fathers of the church, to a rash, self-willed, and arbitrary interpretation of the Scriptures, wrested according to the private opinion of each speculating heretic."

"I disdain to reply to the charge," replied Warden. "The question at issue between your church and mine is, whether we will be judged by the Holy Scriptures, or by the devices and decisions of men not less subject to error than ourselves, and who have defaced our holy religion with vain devices, reared up idols of stone and wood, in form of those who, when they lived, were but sinful creatures, to share the worship due only to the Creator; established a toll-house betwixt Heaven and Hell, that profitable purgatory of which the Pope keeps the keys, like an iniquitous judge commutes punishment for bribes, and——"

"Silence, blasphemer," said the sub-prior, sternly, "or I will have thy blatant obloquy stopped with a gag!"

"Ay," replied Warden, "such is the freedom of the Christian conference to which Rome's priests so kindly invite us! —the gag—the rack—the axe—is the *ratio ultima Romœ*. But know thou, mine ancient friend, that the character of thy former companion is not so changed by age but that he still dares to endure for the cause of truth all that thy proud hierarchy shall dare to inflict."

"Of that," said the monk, "I nothing doubt. Thou wert ever a lion to turn against the spear of the hunter, not a stag to be dismayed at the sound of his bugle." He walked through the room in silence. "Wellwood," he said at length, "we can no longer be friends. Our faith, our hope, our anchor on futurity is no longer the same."

"Deep is my sorrow that thou speakest truth. May God so judge me," said the Reformer, "as I would buy the conversion of a soul like thine with my dearest heart's blood."

"To thee, and with better reason, do I return the wish," replied the sub-prior; "it is such an arm as thine that should defend the bulwarks of the church, and it is now directing the battering-ram against them, and rendering practicable the breach through which all that is greedy, and all that is base, and all that is mutable and hot-headed in this innovating age already hope to advance to destruction and to spoil. But since such is our fate, that we can no longer fight side by side as friends, let us at least act as generous enemies. You cannot have forgotten,

O gran bontà dei cavalieri antiqui !
Erano nemici, eran' de fede diversa——

Although, perhaps," he added, stopping short in his quotation, "your new faith forbids you to reserve a place in your memory even for what high poets have recorded of loyal faith and generous sentiment."

"The faith of Buchanan," replied the preacher—"the faith of Buchanan and of Beza cannot be unfriendly to literature. But the poet you have quoted affords strains fitter for a dissolute court than for a convent."

"I might retort on your Theodore Beza," said the sub-prior, smiling; "but I hate the judgment that, like the flesh-fly, skims over whatever is sound, to detect and settle upon some spot which is tainted. But to the purpose. If I conduct thee or send thee a prisoner to St. Mary's, thou art to-night a tenant of the dungeon, to-morrow a burden to the gibbet-tree. If I were to let thee go hence at large, I were thereby wronging the Holy Church, and breaking mine own solemn vow. Other resolutions may be adopted in the capital, or better times may speedily ensue. Wilt thou remain a true prisoner upon thy parole, rescue or no rescue, as is the phrase amongst the warriors of this country? Wilt thou solemnly promise that thou wilt do so, and that at my summons thou wilt present thyself before the abbot and chapter of St. Mary's, and that thou wilt not stir from this house above a quarter of a mile in any direction? Wilt thou, I say, engage me thy word for this? and such is the sure trust which I repose in thy good faith, that thou shalt remain here unharmed and unsecured, a prisoner at large, subject only to appear before our court when called upon."

The preacher paused. "I am unwilling," he said, "to fetter my native liberty by any self-adopted engagement. But I am already in your power, and you may bind me to my answer. By such promise, to abide within a certain limit and to appear when called upon, I renounce not any liberty which I at present possess and am free to exercise; but, on the contrary, being in bonds, and at your mercy, I acquire thereby a liberty which I at present possess not. I will therefore accept of thy proffer, as what is courteously offered on thy part, and may be honourably accepted on mine."

"Stay yet," said the sub-prior, "one important part of thy engagement is forgotten: thou art farther to promise that, while thus left at liberty, thou wilt not preach or teach, directly or indirectly, any of those pestilent heresies by which so many souls have been in this our day won over from the kingdom of light to the kingdom of darkness."

"There we break off our treaty," said Warden, firmly. "Woe unto me if I preach not the Gospel!"

The sub-prior's countenance became clouded, and he again paced the apartment, and muttered, "A plague upon the self-willed fool!" then stopped short in his walk, and proceeded in his argument. "Why, by thine own reasoning, Henry, thy refusal here is but peevish obstinacy. It is in my power to place you where your preaching can reach no human ear; in promising therefore to abstain from it, you grant nothing which you have it in your power to refuse."

"I know not that," replied Henry Warden; "thou mayst indeed cast me into a dungeon, but can I foretell that my Master hath not task-work for me to perform even in that dreary mansion? The chains of saints have, ere now, been the means of breaking the bonds of Satan. In a prison, holy Paul found the jailor whom he brought to believe the word of salvation, he and all his house."

"Nay," said the sub-prior, in a tone betwixt anger and scorn, "if you match yourself with the blessed Apostle, it were time we had done; prepare to endure what thy folly, as well as thy heresy, deserves. Bind him, soldier."

With proud submission to his fate, and regarding the sub-prior with something which almost amounted to a smile of superiority, the preacher placed his arms so that the bonds could be again fastened round him.

"Spare me not," he said to Christie; for even that ruffian hesitated to draw the cord straitly.

The sub-prior, meanwhile, looked at him from under his cowl, which he had drawn over his head, and partly over his face, as if he wished to shade his own emotions. They were those of a huntsman within point-blank shot of a noble stag, who is yet too much struck with his majesty of front and of antler to take aim at him. They were those of a fowler, who, levelling his gun at a magnificent eagle, is yet reluctant to use his advantage when he sees the noble sovereign of the birds pruning himself in proud defiance of whatever may be attempted against him. The heart of the sub-prior, bigoted as he was, relented, and he doubted if he ought to purchase, by a rigorous discharge of what he deemed his duty, the remorse he might afterwards feel for the death of one so nobly independent in thought and character, the friend, besides, of his own happiest years, during which they had, side by side, striven in the noble race of knowledge, and indulged their intervals of repose in the lighter studies of classical and general letters.

The sub-prior's hand pressed his half-o'ershadowed cheek, and his eye, more completely obscured, was bent on the ground, as if to hide the workings of his relenting nature.

"Were but Edward safe from the infection," he thought to himself—"Edward, whose eager and enthusiastic mind presses forward in the chase of all that hath even the shadow of knowledge, I might trust this enthusiast with the women, after due caution to them that they cannot, without guilt, attend to his reveries."

As the sub-prior revolved these thoughts, and delayed the definitive order which was to determine the fate of the prisoner, a sudden noise at the entrance of the tower diverted his attention for an instant; and, his cheek and brow inflamed with all the glow of heat and determination, Edward Glendinning rushed into the room.

CHAPTER XXXII.

Then in my gown of sober grey
  Along the mountain path I'll wander,
And wind my solitary way
  To the sad shrine that courts me yonder.

There, in the calm monastic shade,
  All injuries may be forgiven,
And there for thee, obdurate maid,
  My orisons shall rise to heaven.
                        The Cruel Lady of the Mountain.

THE first words which Edward uttered were: "My brother is safe, reverend father—he is safe, thank God, and lives! There is not in Corrie-nan-Shian a grave, nor a vestige of a grave. The turf around the fountain has neither been disturbed by pick-axe, spade, or mattock since the deer's-hair first sprang there. He lives as surely as I live!"

The earnestness of the youth—the vivacity with which he looked and moved—the springy step, outstretched hand, and ardent eye, reminded Henry Warden of Halbert, so lately his guide. The brothers had indeed a strong family resemblance, though Halbert was far more athletic and active in his person, taller and better knit in the limbs, and though Edward had, on ordinary occasions, a look of more habitual acuteness and more profound reflection. The preacher was interested as well as the sub-prior.

"Of whom do you speak, my son?" he said, in a tone as unconcerned as if his own fate had not been at the same instant trembling in the balance, and as if a dungeon and death did not appear to be his instant doom—"of whom, I say, speak you? If of a youth somewhat older than you seem to be, brown-haired, open-featured, taller and stronger than you appear, yet having much of the same air, and of the same tone of voice—if such a one is the brother whom you seek, it may be I can tell you news of him."

"Speak, then, for Heaven's sake," said Edward; "life or death lies on thy tongue."

The sub-prior joined eagerly in the same request, and, without waiting to be urged, the preacher gave a minute account of the circumstances under which he met the elder Glendinning, with so exact a description of his person that there remained no doubt as to his identity. When he mentioned that Halbert Glendinning had conducted him to the dell, in which they found the grass bloody, and a grave newly closed, and told how the youth accused himself of the slaughter of Sir Piercie Shafton, the sub-prior looked on Edward with astonishment.

"Didst thou not say, even now," he said, "that there was no vestige of a grave in that spot?"

"No more vestige of the earth having been removed than if the turf had grown there since the days of Adam," replied Edward Glendinning. "It is true," he added, "that the adjacent grass was trampled and bloody."

"These are delusions of the Enemy," said the sub-prior, crossing himself. "Christian men may no longer doubt of it."

"But an it be so," said Warden, "Christian men might better guard themselves by the sword of prayer than by the idle form of a cabalistical spell."

"The badge of our salvation," said the sub-prior, "cannot be so termed: the sign of the cross disarmeth all evil spirits."

"Ay," answered Henry Warden, apt and armed for controversy, "but it should be borne in the heart, not scored with the fingers in the air. That very impassive air, through which your hand passes, shall as soon bear the imprint of your action as the external action shall avail the fond bigot who substitutes vain motions of the body, idle genuflections and signs of the cross, for the living and heart-born duties of faith and good works."

"I pity thee," said the sub-prior, as actively ready for polemics as himself—"I pity thee, Henry, and reply not to thee. Thou mayst as well winnow forth and measure the ocean with a sieve as mete out the power of holy words, deeds, and signs by the erring gage of thine own reason."

"Not by mine own reason would I mete them," said Warden; "but by His Holy Word, that unfading and unerring lamp of our paths, compared to which human reason is but as a glimmering and fading taper, and your boasted tradition only a misleading wild-fire. Show me your Scripture warrant for ascribing virtue to such vain signs and motions."

"I offered thee a fair field of debate," said the sub-prior, "which thou didst refuse. I will not at present resume the controversy."

"Were these my last accents," said the Reformer, "and were they uttered at the stake, half-choked with smoke, and as the fagots kindled into a blaze around me, with that last utterance I would testify against the superstitious devices of Rome."

The sub-prior suppressed with pain the controversial answer which arose to his lips, and turning to Edward Glendinning, he said: "There could be now no doubt that his mother ought presently to be informed that her son lived."

"I told you that two hours since," said Christie of the Clinthill, "an you would have believed me. But it seems you are more willing to take the word of an old grey sorner, whose life has been spent in pattering heresy, than mine, though I never rode a foray in my life without duly saying my paternoster."

"Go, then," said Father Eustace to Edward; "let thy sorrowing mother know that her son is restored to her from the grave, like the child of the widow of Zarephath; at the intercession," he added, looking at Henry Warden, "of the blessed saint whom I invoked in his behalf."

"Deceived thyself," said Warden, instantly, "thou art a deceiver of others. It was no dead man, no creature of clay, whom the blessed Tishbite invoked, when, stung by the reproach of the Shunamite woman, he prayed that her son's soul might come into him again."

"It was by his intercession, however," repeated the sub-prior; "for what says the Vulgate? Thus is it written: "*Et exaudivit Dominus vocem Helie; et reversa est anima pueri intra eum, et revixit*"; and thinkest thou the intercession of a glorified saint is more feeble than when he walks or earth, shrouded in a tabernacle of clay, and seeing but with the eye of flesh?"

During this controversy, Edward Glendinning appeared restless and impatient, agitated by some strong internal feeling, but whether of joy, grief, or expectation his countenance did not expressly declare. He took now the unusual freedom to break in upon the discourse of the sub-prior, who, notwithstanding his resolution to the contrary, was obviously kindling in the spirit of controversy, which Edward diverted by conjuring his reverence to allow him to speak a few words with him in private.

"Remove the prisoner," said the sub-prior to Christie; "look to him carefully that he escape not; but for thy life do him no injury."

His commands being obeyed, Edward and the monk were left alone, when the sub-prior thus addressed him:

"What hath come over thee, Edward, that thy eye kindles so wildly, and thy cheek is thus changing from scarlet to pale? Why didst thou break in so hastily and unadvisedly upon the argument with which I was prostrating yonder heretic? And wherefore dost thou not tell thy mother that her son is restored to her by the intercession, as Holy Church well warrants us to believe, of blessed St. Benedict, the patron of our order? For if ever my prayers were put forth to him with zeal, it hath been in behalf of this house, and thine eyes have seen the result; go tell it to thy mother."

"I must tell her then," said Edward, "that if she has regained one son, another is lost to her."

"What meanest thou, Edward? what language is this?" said the sub-prior.

"Father," said the youth, kneeling down to him, "my sin and my shame shall be told thee, and thou shalt witness my penance with thine own eyes."

"I comprehend thee not," said the sub-prior. "What canst thou have done to deserve such self-accusation? Hast thou too listened," he added, knitting his brows, "to the demon of heresy, ever most effectual tempter of those who, like yonder unhappy man, are distinguished by their love of knowledge?"

"I am guiltless in that matter," answered Glendinning, "nor have presumed to think otherwise than thou, my kind father, hast taught me, and than the church allows."

"And what is it then, my son," said the sub-prior, kindly, "which thus afflicts thy conscience? Speak it to me, that I may answer thee in the words of comfort; for the church's mercy is great to those obedient children who doubt not her power."

"My confession will require her mercy," replied Edward. "My brother Halbert, so kind, so grave, so gentle, who spoke not, thought not, acted not but in love to me, whose hand had aided me in every difficulty, whose eye watched over me like the eagle's over her nestlings, when they proved their first flight from the eyrie—this brother, so kind, so gentle, so affectionate—I heard of his sudden—his bloody—his violent death, and I rejoiced; I heard of his unexpected restoration, and I sorrowed!"

"Edward," said the father, "thou art beside thyself; what could urge thee to such odious ingratitude? In your hurry of spirits you have mistaken the confused tenor of your feelings. Go, my son, pray and compose thy mind; we will speak of this another time."

"No, father—no," said Edward, vehemently, "now or never! I will find the means to tame this rebellious heart of mine, or I will tear it out of my bosom. Mistake its passions! No, father, grief can ill be mistaken for joy. All wept, all shrieked around me—my mother—the menials—she too, the cause of my crime—all wept; and I—I could hardly disguise my brutal and insane joy under the appearance of revenge. 'Brother,' I said, 'I cannot give thee tears, but I will give thee blood.' Yes, father, as I counted hour after hour, while I kept watch upon the English prisoner, and said, 'I am an hour nearer to hope and to happiness——' "

"I understand thee not, Edward," said the monk, "nor can I conceive in what way thy brother's supposed murder should have affected thee with such unnatural joy. Surely the sordid desire to succeed him in his small possessions——"

"Perish the paltry trash!" said Edward, with the same

emotion. "No, father, it was rivalry—it was jealous rage—it was the love of Mary Avenel, that rendered me the unnatural wretch I confess myself!"

"Of Mary Avenel!" said the priest—"of a lady so high above either of you in name and in rank? How dared Halbert—how dared you, presume to lift your eye to her but in honour and respect, as to a superior of another degree from yours?"

"When did love wait for the sanction of heraldry?" replied Edward; "and in what but a line of dead ancestors was Mary our mother's guest and foster-child, different from us, with whom she was brought up? Enough, we loved—we both loved her! But the passion of Halbert was requited. He knew it not, he saw it not; but I was sharper-eyed. I saw that, even when I was more approved, Halbert was more beloved. With me she would sit for hours at our common task, with the cold simplicity and indifference of a sister, but with Halbert she trusted not herself. She changed colour, she was fluttered when he approached her; and when he left her she was sad, pensive, and solitary. I bore all this—I saw my rival's advancing progress in her affections—I bore it, father, and yet I hated him not—I could not hate him!"

"And well for thee that thou didst not," said the father; "wild and headstrong as thou art, wouldst thou hate thy brother for partaking in thine own folly?"

"Father," replied Edward, "the world esteems thee wise, and holds thy knowledge of mankind high; but thy question shows that thou hast never loved. It was by an effort that I saved myself from hating my kind and affectionate brother, who, all unsuspicious of my rivalry, was perpetually loading me with kindness. Nay, there were moods of my mind in which I could return that kindness for a time with energetic enthusiasm. Never did I feel this so strongly as on the night which parted us. But I could not help rejoicing when he was swept from my track; could not help sorrowing when he was again restored to be a stumbling-block in my paths."

"May God be gracious to thee, my son!" said the monk; "this is an awful state of mind. Even in such evil mood did the first murderer rise up against his brother, because Abel's was the more acceptable sacrifice."

"I will wrestle with the demon which has haunted me, father," replied the youth, firmly—"I will wrestle with him, and I will subdue him. But first I must remove from the scenes which are to follow here. I cannot endure that I should see Mary Avenel's eyes again flash with joy at the restoration of her lover. It were a sight to make indeed a second Cain of me! My fierce, turbid, and transitory joy discharged itself in a thirst to commit homicide, and how can I estimate the frenzy of my despair?"

"Madman!" said the sub-prior, "at what dreadful crime does thy fury drive?"

"My lot is determined, father," said Edward, in a resolute tone; "I will embrace the spiritual state which you have so oft recommended. It is my purpose to return with you to St. Mary's, and, with the permission of the Holy Virgin and of St. Benedict, to offer my profession to the abbot."

"Not now, my son," said the sub-prior—"not in this distemperature of mind. The wise and good accept not gifts which are made in heat of blood, and which may be after repented of; and shall we make our offerings to wisdom and to goodness itself with less of solemn resolution and deep devotion of mind than is necessary to make them acceptable to our own frail companions in this valley of darkness? This I say to thee, my son, not as meaning to deter thee from the good path thou art now inclined to prefer, but that thou mayst make thy vocation and thine election sure."

"There are actions, father," returned Edward, "which brook no delay, and this is one. It must be done this very *now*, or it may never be done. Let me go with you; let me not behold the return of Halbert into this house. Shame, and the sense of the injustice I have already done him, will join with these dreadful passions which urged me to do him yet farther wrong. Let me then go with you."

"With me, my son," said the sub-prior, "thou shalt surely go; but our rule, as well as reason and good order, require that you should dwell a space with us as a probationer, or

novice, before taking upon thee those final vows which, seques-
tering thee for ever from the world, dedicate thee to the service
of Heaven."

"And when shall we set forth, father?" said the youth, as
eagerly as if the journey which he was now undertaking led
to the pleasures of a summer holiday.

"Even now, if thou wilt," said the sub-prior, yielding to
his impetuosity; "go, then, and command them to prepare
for our departure. Yet stay," he said, as Edward, with all
the awakened enthusiasm of his character, hastened from his
presence, "come hither, my son, and kneel down."

Edward obeyed, and kneeled down before him. Notwithstanding his slight figure and thin features, the sub-prior
could, from the energy of his tone and the earnestness of his
devotional manner, impress his pupils and his penitents with
no ordinary feelings of personal reverence. His heart always
was, as well as seemed to be, in the duty which he was immediately performing; and the spiritual guide who thus shows
a deep conviction of the importance of his office seldom fails
to impress a similar feeling upon his hearers. Upon such occasions as the present his puny body seemed to assume more
majestic stature; his spare and emaciated countenance bore a
bolder, loftier, and more commanding port; his voice, always
beautiful, trembled as labouring under the immediate impulse
of the Divinity; and his whole demeanour seemed to bespeak,
not the mere ordinary man, but the organ of the church, in
which she had vested her high power for delivering sinners
from their load of iniquity.

"Hast thou, my fair son," said he, "faithfully recounted
the circumstances which have thus suddenly determined thee
to a religious life?"

"The sins I have confessed, my father," answered Edward;
"but I have not yet told of a strange appearance which, acting on my mind, hath, I think, aided to determine my resolution."

"Tell it, then, now," returned the sub-prior; "it is thy
duty to leave me uninstructed in nought, so that thereby I
may understand the temptation that besets thee."

"I tell it with unwillingness," said Edward; "for although, God wot, I speak but the mere truth, yet even while my tongue speaks it as truth, my own ears receive it as fable."

"Yet say the whole," said Father Eustace; "neither fear rebuke from me, seeing I may know reasons for receiving as true that which others might regard as fabulous."

"Know, then, father," replied Edward, "that betwixt hope and despair—and, Heavens! what a hope!—the hope to find the corpse mangled and crushed hastily in amongst the bloody clay which the foot of the scornful victor had trod down upon my good, my gentle, my courageous brother—I sped to the glen called Corrie-nan-Shian; but, as your reverence has been already informed, neither the grave, which my unhallowed wishes had, in spite of my better self, longed to see, nor any appearance of the earth having been opened, was visible in the solitary spot where Martin had, at morning yesterday, seen the fatal hillock. You know our dalesmen, father. The place hath an evil name, and this deception of the sight inclined them to leave it. My companions became affrighted, and hastened down the glen as men caught in trespass. My hopes were too much blighted, my mind too much agitated, to fear either the living or the dead. I descended the glen more slowly than they, often looking back, and not ill pleased with the poltroonery of my companions, which left me to my own perplexed and moody humour, and induced them to hasten into the broader dale. They were already out of sight and lost amongst the windings of the glen, when, looking back, I saw a female form standing beside the fountain——"

"How, my fair son?" said the sub-prior, "beware you jest not with your present situation!"

"I jest not, father," answered the youth; "it may be I shall never jest again—surely not for many a day. I saw, I say, the form of a female clad in white, such—such as the spirit which haunts the house of Avenel is supposed to be. Believe me, my father, for, by Heaven and earth, I say nought but what I saw with these eyes!"

"I believe thee, my son," said the monk; "proceed in thy strange story."

"The apparition," said Edward Glendinning, "sung, and thus ran her lay; for, strange as it may seem to you, her words abide by my remembrance as if they had been sung to me from infancy upward:

'Thou who seek'st my fountain lone,
With thoughts and hopes thou darest not own;
Whose heart within leap'd wildly glad
When most his brow seem'd dark and sad;
Hie thee back, thou find'st not here
Corpse or coffin, grave or bier.
The dead alive is gone and fled;
Go thou, and join the living dead!

The living dead, whose sober brow
Oft shrouds such thoughts as thou hast now,
Whose hearts within are seldom cured
Of passions by their vows abjured;
Where, under sad and solemn show,
Vain hopes are nursed, wild wishes glow.
Seek the convent's vaulted room,
Prayer and vigil be thy doom;
Doff the green, and don the grey,
To the cloister hence away!'"

"'Tis a wild lay," said the sub-prior, "and chanted, I fear me, with no good end. But we have power to turn the machinations of Satan to his shame. Edward, thou shalt go with me as thou desirest; thou shalt prove the life for which I have long thought thee best fitted: thou shalt aid, my son, this trembling hand of mine to sustain the Holy Ark, which bold unhallowed men press rashly forward to touch and to profane. Wilt thou not first see thy mother?"

"I will see no one," said Edward, hastily; "I will risk nothing that may shake the purpose of my heart. From St. Mary's they shall learn my destination—all of them shall learn it. My mother—Mary Avenel—my restored and happy brother—they shall all know that Edward lives no longer to the world to be a clog on their happiness. Mary shall no longer need to constrain her looks and expressions to coldness because am I nigh. She shall no longer——"

"My son," said the sub-prior, interrupting him, "it is not by looking back on the vanities and vexations of this world that we fit ourselves for the discharge of duties which are not of it. Go, get our horses ready, and, as we descend the glen together, I will teach thee the truths through which the fathers and wise men of old had that precious alchemy which can convert suffering into happiness."

CHAPTER XXXIII.

Now, on my faith, this gear is all entangled,
Like to the yarn-clue of the drowsy knitter,
Dragg'd by the frolic kitten through the cabin,
While the good dame sits nodding o'er the fire!
Masters, attend ; 'twill crave some skill to clear it.
                                        Old Play.

EDWARD, with the speed of one who doubts the steadiness of his own resolution, hastened to prepare the horses for their departure, and at the same time thanked and dismissed the neighbours who had come to his assistance, and who were not a little surprised both at the suddenness of his proposed departure and at the turn affairs had taken.

"Here's cold hospitality," quoth Dan of the Howlethirst to his comrades; "I trow the Glendinnings may die and come alive right oft ere I put foot in stirrup again for the matter."

Martin soothed them by placing food and liquor before them. They ate sullenly, however, and departed in bad humour.

The joyful news that Halbert Glendinning lived was quickly communicated through the sorrowing family. The mother wept and thanked Heaven alternately; until, her habits of domestic economy awakening as her feelings became calmer, she observed : "It would be an unco task to mend the yetts, and what were they to do while they were broken in that fashion? At open doors dogs come in."

Tibb remarked : "She aye thought Halbert was ower gleg at his weapon to be killed sae easily by ony Sir Piercie of them a'. They might say of these Southrons as they liked; but they had not the pith and wind of a canny Scot when it came to close grips."

On Mary Avenel the impression was inconceivably deeper.
She had but newly learned to pray, and it seemed to her that
her prayers had been instantly answered: that the compassion
of Heaven, which she had learned to implore in the words of
Scripture, had descended upon her after a manner almost
miraculous, and recalled the dead from the grave at the sound
of her lamentations. There was a dangerous degree of enthusiasm in this strain of feeling, but it originated in the purest
devotion.

A silken and embroidered muffler, one of the few articles of
more costly attire which she possessed, was devoted to the
purpose of wrapping up and concealing the sacred volume,
which henceforth she was to regard as her chiefest treasure,
lamenting only that, for want of a fitting interpreter, much
must remain to her a book closed and a fountain sealed. She
was unaware of the yet greater danger she incurred, of putting
an imperfect or even false sense upon some of the doctrines
which appeared most comprehensible. But Heaven had provided against both these hazards.

While Edward was preparing the horses, Christie of the
Clinthill again solicited his orders respecting the Reformed
preacher, Henry Warden, and again the worthy monk laboured to reconcile in his own mind the compassion and esteem which, almost in spite of him, he could not help feeling
for his former companion with the duty which he owed to the
church. The unexpected resolution of Edward had removed,
he thought, the chief objection to his being left at Glendearg.

" If I carry this Wellwood, or Warden, to the monastery,"
he thought, " he must die—die in his heresy—perish body
and soul. And though such a measure was once thought ad-
visable, to strike terror into the heretics, yet such is now
their daily-increasing strength that it may rather rouse them
to fury and to revenge. True, he refuses to pledge himself
to abstain from sowing his tares among the wheat; but the
ground here is too barren to receive them. I fear not his
making impression on these poor women, the vassals of the
church, and bred up in due obedience to her behests. The
keen, searching, inquiring, and bold disposition of Edward

might have afforded fuel to the fire; but that is removed, and there is nothing left which the flame may catch to. Thus shall he have no power to spread his evil doctrines abroad, and yet his life shall be preserved, and it may be his soul rescued as a prey from the fowler's net. I will myself contend with him in argument; for when we studied in common I yielded not to him, and surely the cause for which I struggle will support me, were I yet more weak than I deem myself. Were this man reclaimed from his errors, an hundredfold more advantage would arise to the church from his spiritual regeneration than from his temporal death."

Having finished these meditations, in which there was at once goodness of disposition and narrowness of principle, a considerable portion of self-opinion, and no small degree of self-delusion, the sub-prior commanded the prisoner to be brought into his presence.

"Henry," he said, "whatever a rigid sense of duty may demand of me, ancient friendship and Christian compassion forbid me to lead thee to assured death. Thou wert wont to be generous, though stern and stubborn in thy resolves; let not thy sense of what thine own thoughts term duty draw thee farther than mine have done. Remember, that every sheep whom thou shalt here lead astray from the fold will be demanded in time and through eternity of him who hath left thee the liberty of doing such evil. I ask no engagement of thee, save that thou remain a prisoner on thy word at this tower, and wilt appear when summoned."

"Thou hast found an invention to bind my hands," replied the preacher, "more sure than would have been the heaviest shackles in the prison of thy convent. I will not rashly do what may endanger thee with thy unhappy superiors, and I will be the more cautious because, if we had farther opportunity of conference, I trust thine own soul may yet be rescued as a brand from the burning, and that, casting from thee the livery of Anti-Christ, that trader in human sins and human souls, I may yet assist thee to lay hold on the Rock of Ages."

The sub-prior heard the sentiment, so similar to that which had occurred to himself, with the same kindling feelings with which the game-cock hears and replies to the challenge of his rival.

"I bless God and Our Lady," said he, drawing himself up, "that my faith is already anchored on that Rock on which St. Peter founded his church."

"It is a perversion of the text," said the eager Henry Warden, "grounded on a vain play upon words—a most idle paronomasia."

The controversy would have been rekindled, and in all probability—for what can ensure the good temper and moderation of polemics?—might have ended in the preacher's being transported a captive to the monastery, had not Christie of the Clinthill observed that it was growing late, and that he, having to descend the glen, which had no good reputation, cared not greatly for travelling there after sunset. The sub-prior, therefore, stifled his desire of argument, and again telling the preacher that he trusted to his gratitude and generosity, he bade him farewell.

"Be assured, mine old friend," replied Warden, "that no willing act of mine shall be to thy prejudice. But if my Master shall place work before me, I must obey God rather than man."

These two men, both excellent from natural disposition and acquired knowledge, had more points of similarity than they themselves would have admitted. In truth, the chief distinction betwixt them was that the Catholic, defending a religion which afforded little interest to the feelings, had, in his devotion to the cause he espoused, more of the head than of the heart, and was politic, cautious, and artful; while the Protestant, acting under the strong impulse of more lately adopted conviction, and feeling, as he justly might, a more animated confidence in his cause, was enthusiastic, eager, and precipitate in his desire to advance it. The priest would have been contented to defend, the preacher aspired to conquer; and, of course, the impulse by which the latter was governed was more active and more decisive. They could not part from each other without a second pressure of hands, and each looked in the face of his old companion, as he bade him adieu, with a countenance strongly expressive of sorrow, affection, and pity.

Father Eustace then explained briefly to Dame Glendinning that this person was to be her guest for some days, forbidding her and her whole household, under high spiritual censures, to hold any conversation with him on religious subjects, but commanding her to attend to his wants in all other particulars.

"May Our Lady forgive me, reverend father," said Dame Glendinning, somewhat dismayed at this intelligence, "but I must needs say that ower mony guests have been the ruin of mony a house, and I trow they will bring down Glendearg. First came the Lady of Avenel—her soul be at rest!—she meant nae ill, but she brought with her as mony bogles and fairies as hae kept the house in care ever since, sae that we hae been living as it were in a dream. And then came that English knight, if it please you, and if he hasna killed my son outright, he has chased him aff the gate, and it may be lang eneugh ere I see him again—forbye the damage done to outer door and inner door. And now your reverence has given me the charge of a heretic, who, it is like, may bring the great horned devil himself down upon us all; and they say that it is neither door nor window will serve him, but he will take away the side of the auld tower along with him. Nevertheless, reverend father, your pleasure is doubtless to be done to our power."

"Go to, woman," said the sub-prior; "send for workmen from the clachan, and let them charge the expense of their repairs to the community, and I will give the treasurer warrant to allow them. Moreover, in settling the rental-mails and feu-duties, thou shalt have allowance for the trouble and charges to which thou art now put; and I will cause strict search to be made after thy son."

The dame courtesied deep and low at each favourable expression; and when the sub-prior had done speaking, she added her farther hope, that the sub-prior would hold some communing with her gossip the miller concerning the fate of his daughter, and expound to him that the chance had by no means happened through any negligence on her part.

"I sair doubt me, father," she said, "whether Mysie finds her way back to the mill in a hurry; but it was all her father's own fault that let her run lamping about the country, riding on bare-backed naigs, and never settling to do a turn of wark within doors, unless it were to dress dainties at dinner-time for his ain kyte."

"You remind me, dame, of another matter of urgency," said Father Eustace; "and, God knows, too many of them press on me at this moment. This English knight must be sought out, and explanation given to him of these most strange chances. The giddy girl must also be recovered. If she hath suffered in reputation by this unhappy mistake, I will not hold myself innocent of the disgrace. Yet how to find them out I know not."

"So please you," said Christie of the Clinthill, "I am willing to take the chase, and bring them back by fair means or foul; for though you have always looked as black as night at me, whenever we have forgathered, yet I have not forgotten that, had it not been for you, 'my neck would have kenn'd the weight of my four quarters.' If any man can track the tread of them, I will say in the face of both Merse and Teviotdale, and take the Forest to boot, I am that man. But first I have matters to treat of on my master's score, if you will permit me to ride down the glen with you."

"Nay, but, my friend," said the sub-prior, "thou shouldst remember I have but slender cause to trust thee for a companion through a place so solitary."

"Tush! tush!" said the jack-man, "fear me not; I had the worst too surely to begin that sport again. Besides, have I not said a dozen of times I owe you a life? and when I owe a man either a good turn or a bad I never fail to pay it sooner or later. Moreover, beshrew me if I care to go alone down the glen, or even with my troopers, who are, every loon of them, as much devil's bairns as myself; whereas, if your reverence, since that is the word, take beads and psalter, and I come along with jack and spear, you will make the devils take the air, and I will make all human enemies take the earth."

Edward here entered, and told his reverence that his horse

was prepared. At this instant his eye caught his mother's, and the resolution which he had so strongly formed was staggered when he recollected the necessity of bidding her farewell. The sub-prior saw his embarrassment, and came to his relief.

"Dame," said he, "I forgot to mention that your son Edward goes with me to St. Mary's, and will not return for two or three days."

"You'll be wishing to help him to recover his brother? May the saints reward your kindness!"

The sub-prior returned the benediction, which, in this instance, he had not very well deserved, and he and Edward set forth on their route. They were presently followed by Christie, who came up with his followers at such a speedy pace as intimated sufficiently that his wish to obtain spiritual convoy through the glen was extremely sincere. He had, however, other matters to stimulate his speed, for he was desirous to communicate to the sub-prior a message from his master Julian, connected with the delivery of the prisoner Warden; and having requested the sub-prior to ride with him a few yards before Edward and the troopers of his own party, he thus addressed him, sometimes interrupting his discourse in a manner testifying that his fear of supernatural beings was not altogether lulled to rest by his confidence in the sanctity of his fellow-traveller.

"My master," said the rider, "deemed he had sent you an acceptable gift in that old heretic preacher; but it seems, from the slight care you have taken of him, that you make small account of the boon."

"Nay," said the sub-prior, "do not thus judge of it. The community must account highly of the service, and will reward it to thy master in goodly fashion. But this man and I are old friends, and I trust to bring him back from the paths of perdition."

"Nay," said the moss-trooper, "when I saw you shake hands at the beginning, I counted that you would fight it all out in love and honour, and that there would be no extreme dealings betwixt ye; however, it is all one to my master. St. Mary! what call you yon, sir monk?"

"The branch of a willow streaming across the path betwixt us and the sky."

"Beshrew me," said Christie, "if it looked not like a man's hand holding a sword. But touching my master, he, like a prudent man, hath kept himself aloof in these broken times, until he could see with precision what footing he was to stand upon. Right tempting offers he hath had from the Lords of Congregation, whom you call heretics; and at one time he was minded, to be plain with you, to have taken their way; for he was assured that the Lord James was coming this road at the head of a round body of cavalry. And accordingly Lord James did so far reckon upon him that he sent this man Warden, or whatsoever be his name, to my master's protection, as an assured friend; and, moreover, with tidings that he himself was marching hitherward at the head of a strong body of horse."

"Now, Our Lady forefend!" said the sub-prior.

"Amen!" answered Christie, in some trepidation, "did your reverence see aught?"

"Nothing whatever," replied the monk; "it was thy tale which wrested from me that exclamation."

"And it was some cause," replied he of the Clinthill, "for if Lord James should come hither, your halidome would smoke for it. But be of good cheer, that expedition is ended before it was begun. The Baron of Avenel had sure news that Lord James has been fain to march westward with his merry men, to protect Lord Semple against Cassilis and the Kennedies. By my faith, it will cost him a brush; for wot ye what they say of that name:

> 'Twixt Wigton and the town of Ayr,
> Portpatrick and the cruives of Cree,
> No man need think for to bide there,
> Unless he court St. Kennedie."

"Then," said the sub-prior, "the Lord James's purpose of coming southwards being broken cost this person, Henry Warden, a cold reception at Avenel Castle."

"It would not have been altogether so rough a one," said the moss-trooper, "for my master was in heavy thought what

to do in these unsettled times, and would scarce have hazarded
misusing a man sent to him by so terrible a leader as the Lord
James; but, to speak the truth, some busy devil tempted the
old man to meddle with my master's Christian liberty of
hand-fasting with Catherine of Newport.   So that broke the
wand of peace between them, and now ye may have my
master, and all the force he can make, at your devotion, for
Lord James never forgave wrong done to him; and if he come
by the upper hand he will have Julian's head if there were
never another of the name, as it is like there is not, excepting
the bit slip of a lassie yonder.   And now I have told you
more of my master's affairs than he would thank me for; but
you have done me a frank turn once, and I may need one at
your hands again."

"Thy frankness," said the sub-prior, "shall surely advantage thee; for much it concerns the church in these broken
times to know the purposes and motives of those around us.
But what is it that thy master expects from us in reward of
good service; for I esteem him one of those who are not willing to work without their hire?"

"Nay, that I can tell you flatly; for Lord James had
promised him, in case he would be of his faction in these
parts, an easy tack of the teind-sheaves of his own barony of
Avenel, together with the lands of Cranberry Moor, which lie
intersected with his own.   And he will look for no less at
your hand."

"But there is Old Gilbert of Cranberry Moor," said the
sub-prior, "what are we to make of him?   The heretic Lord
James may take on him to dispone upon the goods and lands
of the halidome at his pleasure, because, doubtless, but for
the protection of God, and the baronage which yet remain
faithful to their creed, he may despoil us of them by force;
but while they are the property of the community we may
not take steadings from ancient and faithful vassals to gratify
the covetousness of those who serve God only from the lucre
of gain."

"By the mass," said Christie, "it is well talking, sir priest;
but when ye consider that Gilbert has but two half-starved

cowardly peasants to follow him, and only an auld jaded aver to ride upon, fitter for the plough than for manly service; and that the Baron of Avenel never rides with fewer than ten jack-men at his back, and oftener with fifty, bodin in all that effeirs to war as if they were to do battle for a kingdom, and mounted on nags that nicker at the clash of a sword as if it were the clank of the lid of a corn-chest—I say, when ye have computed all this, you may guess which course will best serve your monastery."

"Friend," said the monk, "I would willingly purchase thy master's assistance on his own terms, since times leave us no better means of defence against the sacrilegious spoliation of heresy; but to take from a poor man his patrimony——"

"For that matter," said the rider, "his seat would scarce be a soft one if my master thought that Gilbert's interests stood betwixt him and what he wishes. The halidome has land enough, and Gilbert may be quartered elsewhere."

"We will consider the possibility of so disposing the matter," said the monk, "and will expect in consequence your master's most active assistance, with all the followers he can make, to join in the defence of the halidome against any force by which it may be threatened."

"A man's hand and a mailed glove on that,"[1] said the jack-man. "They call us marauders, thieves, and what not; but the side we take we hold by. And I will be blythe when my Baron comes to a point which side he will take, for the castle is a kind of hell—Our Lady forgive me for naming such a word in this place!—while he is in his mood, studying how he may best advantage himself. And now, Heaven be praised! we are in the open valley, and I may swear a round oath, should aught happen to provoke it."

"My friend," said the sub-prior, "thou hast little merit in abstaining from oaths or blasphemy if it be only out of fear of evil spirits."

"Nay, I am not quite a church vassal yet," said the jack-man, "and if you link the curb too tight on a young horse, I

[1] See Good Faith of the Borderers. Note 21.

promise you he will rear. Why, it is much for me to forbear old customs on any account whatever."

The night being fine, they forded the river at the spot where the sacristan met with his unhappy encounter with the spirit. As soon as they arrived at the gate of the monastery, the porter in waiting eagerly exclaimed: "Reverend father, the lord abbot is most anxious for your presence."

"Let these strangers be carried to the great hall," said the sub-prior, "and be treated with the best by the cellarer; reminding them, however, of that modesty and decency of conduct which becometh guests in a house like this."

"But the lord abbot demands you instantly, my venerable brother," said Father Philip, arriving in great haste. "I have not seen him more discouraged or desolate of counsel since the field of Pinkie Cleuch was stricken."

"I come, my good brother—I come," said Father Eustace. "I pray thee, good brother, let this youth, Edward Glendinning, be conveyed to the chamber of the novices, and placed under their instructor. God hath touched his heart, and he proposeth laying aside the vanities of the world to become a brother of our holy order; which, if his good parts be matched with fitting docility and humility, he may one day live to adorn."

"My very venerable brother," exclaimed old Father Nicolas, who came hobbling with a third summons to the sub-prior, "I pray thee to hasten to our worshipful lord abbot. The holy patroness be with us! never saw I abbot of the house of St. Mary's in such consternation; and yet I remember me well when Father Ingelram had the news of Flodden field."

"I come—I come, venerable brother," said Father Eustace. And having repeatedly ejaculated, "I come!" he at last went to the abbot in good earnest.

CHAPTER XXXIV.

It is not texts will do it. Church artillery
Are silenced soon by real ordnance,
And canons are but vain opposed to cannon.
Go, coin your crosier, melt your church plate down,
Bid the starved soldier banquet in your halls,
And quaff your long-saved hogsheads. Turn them out
Thus primed with your good cheer, to guard your wall,
And they will venture for't.

Old Play.

THE abbot received his counsellor with a tremulous eagerness of welcome which announced to the sub-prior an extreme
agitation of spirits and the utmost need of good counsel.
There was neither mazer-dish nor standing-cup upon the little
table at the elbow of his huge chair of state; his beads alone
lay there, and it seemed as if he had been telling them in
his extremity of distress. Beside the beads was placed the
mitre of the abbot, of an antique form and blazing with precious stones, and the rich and highly-embossed crosier rested
against the same table.

The sacristan and old Father Nicolas had followed the
sub-prior into the abbot's apartment, perhaps with the
hope of learning something of the important matter which
seemed to be in hand. They were not mistaken; for,
after having ushered in the sub-prior, and being themselves
in the act of retiring, the abbot made them a signal to
remain.

"My brethren," he said, "it is well known to you with
what painful zeal we have overseen the weighty affairs of
this house committed to our unworthy hand; your bread hath
been given to you, and your water hath been sure; I have not
wasted the revenues of the convent on vain pleasures, as hunting or hawking, or in change of rich cope or alb, or in feasting
idle bards and jesters, saving those who, according to old
wont, were received in time of Christmas and Easter. Neither have I enriched either mine own relations nor strange
women at the expense of the patrimony."

"There hath not been such a lord abbot," said Father
Nicolas, "to my knowledge, since the days of Abbot Ingelram,
who——"

At that portentous word, which always preluded a long
story, the abbot broke in.

"May God have mercy on his soul!—we talk not of him
now. What I would know of ye, my brethren, is, whether
I have, in your mind, faithfully discharged the duties of mine
office?"

"There has never been subject of complaint," answered the
sub-prior.

The sacristan, more diffuse, enumerated the various acts of
indulgence and kindness which the mild government of Abbot
Boniface had conferred on the brotherhood of St. Mary's—the
indulgentiæ, the *gratias*, the *biberes*, the weekly mess of boiled
almonds, the enlarged accommodation of the refectory, the
better arrangement of the cellarage, the improvement of the
revenue of the monastery, the diminution of the privations of
the brethren."

"You might have added, my brother," said the abbot, listening with melancholy acquiescence to the detail of his own
merits, "that I caused to be built that curious screen which
secureth the cloisters from the northeast wind. But all these
things avail nothing. As we read in holy Maccabee, *Capta
est civitas per voluntatem Dei*. It hath cost me no little
thought, no common toil, to keep these weighty matters in
such order as you have seen them; there was both barn and
binn to be kept full; infirmary, dormitory, guest-hall, and
refectory to be looked to; processions to be made, confessions
to be heard, strangers to be entertained, *veniæ* to be granted
or refused; and I warrant me, when every one of you was
asleep in your cell, the abbot hath lain awake for a full hour
by the bell, thinking how these matters might be ordered
seemly and suitably."

"May we ask, reverend my lord," said the sub-prior, "what
additional care has now been thrown upon you, since your discourse seems to point that way?"

"Marry, this it is," said the abbot. "The talk is not now

of *biberes* or of *caritas,* or of boiled almonds,[1] but of an English band coming against us from Hexham, commanded by Sir John Foster; nor is it of the screening us from the east wind, but how to escape Lord James Stuart, who cometh to lay waste and destroy with his heretic soldiers."

"I thought that purpose had been broken by the feud between Semple and the Kennedies," said the sub-prior, hastily.

"They have accorded that matter at the expense of the church as usual," said the abbot: "the Earl of Cassilis is to have the teind-sheaves of his lands, which were given to the house of Crossraguel, and he has stricken hands with Stuart, who is now called Murray. *Principes convenerunt in unum adversus Dominum.* There are the letters."

The sub-prior took the letters, which had come by an express messenger from the Primate of Scotland, who still laboured to uphold the tottering fabric of the system under which he was at length buried, and, stepping towards the lamp, read them with an air of deep and settled attention; the sacristan and Father Nicolas looked as helplessly at each other as the denizens of the poultry-yard when the hawk soars over it. The abbot seemed bowed down with the extremity of sorrowful apprehension, but kept his eye timorously fixed on the sub-prior, as if striving to catch some comfort from the expression of his countenance. When at length he beheld that, after a second intent perusal of the letters, he remained still silent and full of thought, he asked him in an anxious tone: "What is to be done?"

"Our duty must be done," answered the sub-prior, "and the rest is in the hands of God."

"Our duty—our duty!" answered the abbot, impatiently; "doubtless we are to do our duty; but what is that duty? or how will it serve us? Will bell, book, and candle drive back the English heretics? or will Murray care for psalms and antiphonars? or can I fight for the halidome like Judas Maccabeus against those profane Nicanors? or send the sacristan against this new Holofernes, to bring back his head in a basket?"

[1] See Indulgences of the Monks. Note 22.

"True, my lord abbot," said the sub-prior, "we cannot fight with carnal weapons, it is alike contrary to our habit and vow; but we can die for our convent and for our order. Besides, we can arm those who will and can fight. The English are but few in number, trusting, as it would seem, that they will be joined by Murray, whose march has been interrupted. If Foster, with his Cumberland and Hexham bandits, ventures to march into Scotland to pillage and despoil our house, we will levy our vassals, and, I trust, shall be found strong enough to give him battle."

"In the blessed name of Our Lady," said the abbot, "think you that I am Petrus Eremita, to go forth the leader of an host?"

"Nay," said the sub-prior, "let some man skilled in war lead our people: there is Julian Avenel, an approved soldier."

"But a scoffer, a debauched person, and, in brief, a man of Belial," quoth the abbot.

"Still," said the monk, "we must use his ministry in that to which he has been brought up. We can guerdon him richly, and indeed I already know the price of his service. The English, it is expected, will presently set forth, hoping here to seize upon Piercie Shafton, whose refuge being taken with us, they make the pretext of this unheard-of inroad."

"Is it even so?" said the abbot; "I never judged that his body of satin and his brain of feathers boded us much good."

"Yet we must have his assistance, if possible," said the sub-prior; "he may interest in our behalf the great Piercie, of whose friendship he boasts, and that good and faithful lord may break Foster's purpose. I will despatch the jack-man after him with all speed. Chiefly, however, I trust to the military spirit of the land, which will not suffer peace to be easily broken on the frontier. Credit me, my lord, it will bring to our side the hands of many whose hearts may have gone astray after strange doctrines. The great chiefs and barons will be ashamed to let the vassals of peaceful monks fight unaided against the old enemies of Scotland."

"It may be," said the abbot, "that Foster will wait for

Murray, whose purpose hitherward is but delayed for a short space."

"By the rood, he will not," said the sub-prior; "we know this Sir John Foster—a pestilent heretic, he will long to destroy the church; born a Borderer, he will thirst to plunder her of her wealth; a Border warden, he will be eager to ride in Scotland. There are too many causes to urge him on. If he joins with Murray, he will have at best but an auxiliary's share of the spoil; if he comes hither before him, he will reckon on the whole harvest of depredation as his own. Julian Avenel also has, as I have heard, some spite against Sir John Foster; they will fight, when they meet, with double determination. Sacristan, send for our bailiff. Where is the roll of fencible men liable to do suit and service to the halidome? Send off to the Baron of Meigallot; he can raise three-score horse and better. Say to him the monastery will compound with him for the customs of his bridge, which have been in controversy, if he will show himself a friend at such a point. And now, my lord, let us compute our possible numbers and those of the enemy, that human blood be not spilled in vain. Let us therefore calculate——"

"My brain is dizzied with the emergency," said the poor abbot. "I am not, I think, more a coward than others, so far as my own person is concerned; but speak to me of marching and collecting soldiers, and calculating forces, and you may as well tell of it to the youngest novice of a nunnery. But my resolution is taken. Brethren," he said, rising up, and coming forward with that dignity which his comely person enabled him to assume, "hear for the last time the voice of your Abbot Boniface. I have done for you the best that I could; in quieter times I had perhaps done better, for it was for quiet that I sought the cloister, which has been to me a place of turmoil, as much as if I had sate in the receipt of custom, or ridden forth as leader of an armed host. But now matters turn worse and worse, and I, as I grow old, am less able to struggle with them. Also, it becomes me not to hold a place whereof the duties, through my default or misfortune, may be but imperfectly filled by me. Wherefore I have resolved to demit this mine high office, so that the order of these matters may presently devolve upon Father Eustatius here present, our well-beloved sub-prior; and I now rejoice that he hath not been provided according to his merits elsewhere, seeing that I well hope he will succeed to the mitre and staff which it is my present purpose to lay down."

"In the name of Our Lady, do nothing hastily, my lord!" said Father Nicolas. "I do remember that when the worthy Abbot Ingelram, being in his ninetieth year—for I warrant you he could remember when Benedict the Thirteenth was deposed—and being ill at ease and bed-rid, the brethren rounded in his ear that he were better resign his office. And what said he, being a pleasant man? marry, that while he could crook his little finger he would keep hold of the crosier with it."

The sacristan also strongly remonstrated against the resolution of his superior, and set down the insufficiency he pleaded to the native modesty of his disposition. The abbot listened in downcast silence; even flattery could not win his ear.

Father Eustace took a nobler tone with his disconcerted and dejected superior. "My lord abbot," he said, "if I have been silent concerning the virtues with which you have governed this house, do not think that I am unaware of them. I know that no man ever brought to your high office a more sincere wish to do well to all mankind; and if your rule has not been marked with the bold lines which sometimes distinguished your spiritual predecessors, their faults have equally been strangers to your character."

"I did not believe," said the abbot, turning his looks to Father Eustace with some surprise, "that you, father, of all men, would have done me this justice."

"In your absence," said the sub-prior, "I have even done it more fully. Do not lose the good opinion which all men entertain of you by renouncing your office when your care is most needed."

"But, my brother," said the abbot, "I leave a more able in my place."

"That you do not," said Eustace; "because it is not neces-

sary you should resign in order to possess the use of whatever
experience or talent I may be accounted master of. I have
been long enough in this profession to know that the individual
qualities which any of us may have are not his own, but the
property of the community, and only so far useful when they
promote the general advantage. If you care not in person,
my lord, to deal with this troublesome matter, let me implore
you to go instantly to Edinburgh, and make what friends you
can in our behalf, while I in your absence will, as sub-prior,
do my duty in defence of the halidome. If I succeed, may
the honour and praise be yours, and if I fail, let the disgrace
and shame be mine own."

The abbot mused for a space, and then replied: "No, Father
Eustatius, you shall not conquer me by your generosity. In
times like these, this house must have a stronger pilotage
than my weak hands afford; and he who steers the vessel must
be chief of the crew. Shame were it to accept the praise of
other men's labours; and, in my poor mind, all the praise
which can be bestowed on him who undertakes a task so
perilous and perplexing is a meed beneath his merits. Misfortune to him would deprive him of an iota of it! Assume,
therefore, your authority to-night, and proceed in the preparations you judge necessary. Let the chapter be summoned to-
morrow after we have heard mass, and all shall be ordered as
I have told you. *Benedicite*, my brethren!—peace be with
you! May the new abbot-expectant sleep as sound as he who
is about to resign his mitre."

They retired, affected even to tears. The good abbot had
shown a point of his character to which they were strangers.
Even Father Eustace had held his spiritual superior hitherto as a good-humoured, indolent, self-indulgent man, whose
chief merit was the absence of gross faults; so that this sacrifice of power to a sense of duty, even if a little alloyed by the
meaner motives of fear and apprehended difficulties, raised
him considerably in the sub-prior's estimation. He even felt
an aversion to profit by the resignation of the Abbot Boniface, and in a manner to rise on his ruins; but this sentiment
did not long contend with those which led him to recollect

higher considerations. It could not be denied that Boniface was entirely unfit for his situation in the present crisis; and the sub-prior felt that he himself, acting merely as a delegate, could not well take the decisive measures which the time required; the weal of the community therefore demanded his elevation. If, besides, there crept in a feeling of an high dignity obtained, and the native exultation of a haughty spirit called to contend with the imminent dangers attached to a post of such distinction, these sentiments were so cunningly blended and amalgamated with others of a more disinterested nature that, as the sub-prior himself was unconscious of their agency, we, who have a regard for him, are not solicitous to detect it.

The abbot elect carried himself with more dignity than formerly, when giving such directions as the pressing circumstances of the times required; and those who approached him could perceive an unusual kindling of his falcon eye and an unusual flush upon his pale and faded cheek. With briefness and precision he wrote and dictated various letters to different barons, acquainting them with the meditated invasion of the halidome by the English, and conjuring them to lend aid and assistance as in a common cause. The temptation of advantage was held out to those whom he judged less sensible of the cause of honour, and all were urged by the motives of patriotism and ancient animosity to the English. The time had been when no such exhortations would have been necessary. But so essential was Elizabeth's aid to the Reformed party in Scotland, and so strong was that party almost everywhere, that there was reason to believe a great many would observe neutrality on the present occasion, even if they did not go the length of uniting with the English against the Catholics.

When Father Eustace considered the number of the immediate vassals of the church whose aid he might legally command, his heart sunk at the thoughts of ranking them under the banner of the fierce and profligate Julian Avenel.

"Were the young enthusiast Halbert Glendinning to be found," thought Father Eustace in his anxiety, "I would have risked the battle under his leading, young as he is, and with better hope of God's blessing. But the bailiff is now too infirm, nor know I a chief of name whom I might trust in this important matter better than this Avenel." He touched a bell which stood on the table, and commanded Christie of the Clinthill to be brought before him. "Thou owest me a life," said he to that person on his entrance, "and I may do thee another good turn if thou be'st sincere with me."

Christie had already drained two standing-cups of wine, which would, on another occasion, have added to the insolence of his familiarity. But at present there was something in the augmented dignity of manner of Father Eustace which imposed a restraint on him. Yet his answers partook of his usual character of undaunted assurance. He professed himself willing to return a true answer to all inquiries.

"Has the Baron, so styled, of Avenel any friendship with Sir John Foster, warden of the West Marches of England?"

"Such friendship as is between the wild-cat and the terrier," replied the rider.

"Will he do battle with him should they meet?"

"As surely," answered Christie, "as ever cock fought on Shrovetide even."

"And would he fight with Foster in the church's quarrel?"

"On any quarrel, or upon no quarrel whatever," replied the jack-man.

"We will then write to him, letting him know that if, upon occasion of an apprehended incursion by Sir John Foster, he will agree to join his force with ours, he shall lead our men, and be gratified for doing so to the extent of his wish. Yet one word more. Thou didst say thou couldst find out where the English knight Piercie Shafton has this day fled to?"

"That I can, and bring him back too, by fair means or force, as best likes your reverence."

"No force must be used upon him. Within what time wilt thou find him out?"

"Within thirty hours, so he have not crossed the Lothian firth. If it is to do you a pleasure, I will set off directly, and wind him as a sleuth-dog tracks the moss-trooper," answered Christie.

27

"Bring him hither, then, and thou wilt deserve good at our hands, which I may soon have free means of bestowing on thee."

"Thanks to your reverence, I put myself in your reverence's hands. We of the spear and snaffle walk something recklessly through life; but if a man were worse than he is, your reverence knows he must live, and that's not to be done without shifting, I trow."

"Peace, sir, and begone on thine errand; thou shalt have a letter from us to Sir Piercie."

Christie made two steps towards the door; then turning back and hesitating, like one who would make an impertinent pleasantry if he dared, he asked what he was to do with the wench, Mysie Happer, whom the Southron knight had carried off with him.

"Am I to bring her hither, please your reverence?"

"Hither, you malapert knave?" said the churchman; "remember you to whom you speak?"

"No offence meant," replied Christie; "but if such is not your will, I would carry her to Avenel Castle, where a well-favoured wench was never unwelcome."

"Bring the unfortunate girl to her father's, and break no scurril jests here," said the sub-prior. "See that thou guide her in all safety and honour."

"In safety, surely," said the rider, "and in such honour as her outbreak has left her. I bid your reverence farewell, I must be on horse before cock-crow."

"What, in the dark! how knowest thou which way to go?"

"I tracked the knight's horse-tread as far as near to the ford, as we rode along together," said Christie, "and I observed the track turn to the northward. He is for Edinburgh, I will warrant you; so soon as daylight comes I will be on the road again. It is a kenspeckle hoof-mark, for the shoe was made by old Eckie of Canonbie—I would swear to the curve of the cawker." So saying, he departed.

"Hateful necessity," said Father Eustace, looking after him, "that obliges us to use such implements as these! But, assailed as we are on all sides, and by all conditions of men, what alternative is left us? But now let me to my most needful task."

The abbot elect accordingly sate down to write letters, arrange orders, and take upon him the whole charge of an institution which tottered to its fall, with the same spirit of proud and devoted fortitude wherewith the commander of a fortress, reduced nearly to the last extremity, calculates what means remain to him to protract the fatal hour of successful storm. In the mean while Abbot Boniface, having given a few natural sighs to the downfall of the pre-eminence he had so long enjoyed amongst his brethren, fell fast asleep, leaving the whole cares and toils of office to his assistant and successor.

CHAPTER XXXV.

And when he came to broken briggs,
　He slack'd his bow and swam ;
And when he came to grass growing,
　Set down his feet and ran.
Gil Morrice.

WE return to Halbert Glendinning, who, as our readers may remember, took the highroad to Edinburgh. His intercourse with the preacher, Henry Warden, from whom he received a letter at the moment of his deliverance, had been so brief that he had not even learned the name of the nobleman to whose care he was recommended. Something like a name had been spoken indeed, but he had only comprehended that he was to meet the chief advancing towards the south, at the head of a party of horse. When day dawned on his journey, he was in the same uncertainty. A better scholar would have been informed by the address of the letter, but Halbert had not so far profited by Father Eustace's lessons as to be able to decipher it. His mother-wit taught him that he must not, in such uncertain times, be too hasty in asking information of any one; and when, after a long day's journey, night surprised him near a little village, he began to be dubious and anxious concerning the issue of his journey.

In a poor country, hospitality is generally exercised freely, and Halbert, when he requested a night's quarters, did nothing either degrading or extraordinary. The old woman to whom he made this request granted it the more readily that she thought she saw some resemblance between Halbert and her son Saunders, who had been killed in one of the frays so common in the time. It is true, Saunders was a short, square-made fellow, with red hair and a freckled face, and somewhat bandy-legged, whereas the stranger was of a brown complexion, tall, and remarkably well made. Nevertheless, the widow was clear that there existed a general resemblance betwixt her guest and Saunders, and kindly pressed him to share of her evening cheer. A pedlar, a man of about forty years old, was also her guest, who talked with great feeling of the misery of pursuing such a profession as his in the time of war and tumult.

"We think much of knights and soldiers," said he; "but the pedder-coffe who travels the land has need of more courage than them all. I am sure he maun face mair risk, God help him. Here have I come this length, trusting the godly Earl of Murray would be on his march to the Borders, for he was to have guestened with the Baron of Avenel; and instead of that comes news that he has gone westlandways about some tuilzie in Ayrshire. And what to do I wot not; for if I go to the south without a safeguard, the next bonny rider I meet might ease me of sack and pack, and maybe of my life to boot; and then, if I try to strike across the moors, I may be as ill off before I can join myself to that good lord's company."

No one was quicker at catching a hint than Halbert Glendinning. He said he himself had a desire to go westward. The pedlar looked at him with a very doubtful air, when the old dame, who perhaps thought her young guest resembled the umquhile Saunders not only in his looks, but in a certain pretty turn to slight-of-hand, which the defunct was supposed to have possessed, tipped him the wink, and assured the pedlar he need have no doubt that her young cousin was a true man.

"Cousin!" said the pedlar, "I thought you said this youth had been a stranger."

"Ill hearing makes ill rehearsing," said the landlady; "he is a stranger to me by eyesight, but that does not make him a stranger to me by blood, more especially seeing his likeness to my son Saunders, poor bairn."

The pedlar's scruples and jealousies being thus removed, or at least silenced, the travellers agreed that they would proceed in company together the next morning by daybreak, the pedlar acting as a guide to Glendinning, and the youth as a guard to the pedlar, until they should fall in with Murray's detachment of horse. It would appear that the landlady never doubted what was to be the event of this compact, for, taking Glendinning aside, she charged him "to be moderate with the puir body, but at all events not to forget to take a piece of black say, to make the auld wife a new rokelay." Halbert laughed, and took his leave.

It did not a little appal the pedlar, when, in the midst of a black heath, the young man told him the nature of the commission with which their hostess had charged him. He took heart, however, upon seeing the open, frank, and friendly demeanour of the youth, and vented his exclamations on the ungrateful old traitress. "I gave her," he said, "yestere'en, nae farther gane, a yard of that very black say, to make her a *couvre-chef;* but I see it is ill done to teach the cat the way to the kirn."

Thus set at ease on the intentions of his companion (for in those happy days the worst was always to be expected from a stranger), the pedlar acted as Halbert's guide over moss and moor, over hill and many a dale, in such a direction as might best lead them towards the route of Murray's party. At length they arrived upon the side of an eminence, which commanded a distant prospect over a tract of savage and desolate moorland, marshy and waste—an alternate change of shingly hill and level morass, only varied by blue stagnant pools of water. A road scarcely marked winded like a serpent through this wilderness, and the pedlar, pointing to it, said: "The road from Edinburgh to Glasgow. Here we must wait, and if Mur-

ray and his train be not already passed by, we shall soon see
trace of them, unless some new purpose shall have altered
their resolution; for in these blessed days no man, were he
the nearest the throne, as the Earl of Murray may be, knows
when he lays his head on his pillow at night where it is to lie
upon the following even."

They paused accordingly, and sat down, the pedlar cautious-
ly using for a seat the box which contained his treasures, and
not concealing from his companion that he wore under his
cloak a pistolet hanging at his belt in case of need.   He was
courteous, however, and offered Halbert a share of the provisions which he carried about him for refreshment.   They were
of the coarsest kind—oat-bread baked into cakes, oatmeal
slaked with cold water, an onion or two, and a morsel of
smoked ham, completed the feast.   But such as it was, no
Scotsman of the time, had his rank been much higher than
that of Glendinning, would have refused to share in it, especially as the pedlar produced, with a mysterious air, a tup's
horn, which he carried slung from his shoulders, and which,
when its contents were examined, produced to each party a
clam-shellful of excellent usquebaugh—a liquor strange to
Halbert, for the strong waters known in the south of Scotland
came from France, and in fact such were but rarely used.
The pedlar recommended it as excellent, said he had procured
it in his last visit to the braes of Doune, where he had securely
traded under the safe-conduct of the Laird of Buchanan.   He
also set an example to Halbert, by devoutly emptying the cup
"to the speedy downfall of Anti-Christ."

Their conviviality was scarce ended ere a rising dust was
seen on the road of which they commanded the prospect, and
half a score of horsemen were dimly descried advancing at
considerable speed, their casques glancing, and the points of
their spears twinkling, as they caught a glimpse of the sun.

"These," said the pedlar, "must be the outscourers of Murray's party; let us lie down in the peat-hag and keep ourselves out of sight."

"And why so?" said Halbert; "let us rather go down and
make a signal to them."

"God forbid!" replied the pedlar; "do you ken so ill the customs of our Scottish nation? That plump of spears that are spurring on so fast are doubtless commanded by some wild kinsman of Morton, or some such daring fear-nothing as neither regards God nor man. It is their business, if they meet with any enemies, to pick quarrels and clear the way of them; and the chief knows nothing of what happens, coming up with his more discreet and moderate friends, it may be a full mile in the rear. Were we to go near these lads of the laird's belt, your letter would do you little good, and my pack would do me muckle black ill; they would tirl every steek of claithes from our backs, fling us into a moss-hag with a stone at our heels, naked as the hour that brought us into this cumbered and sinful world, and neither Murray nor any other man ever the wiser. But if he did come to ken of it, what might he help it?—it would be accounted a mere mistake, and there were all the moan made. Oh, credit me, youth, that, when men draw cold steel on each other in their native country, they neither can nor may dwell deeply on the offences of those whose swords are useful to them."

They suffered, therefore, the vanguard, as it might be termed, of the Earl of Murray's host to pass forward; and it was not long until a denser cloud of dust began to arise to the northward.

"Now," said the pedlar, "let us hurry down the hill; for to tell the truth," said he, dragging Halbert along earnestly, "a Scottish noble's march is like a serpent: the head is furnished with fangs, and the tail hath its sting; the only harmless point of access is the main body."

"I will hasten as fast as you," said the youth; "but tell me why the rearward of such an army should be as dangerous as the van?"

"Because, as the vanguard consists of their picked wild desperates, resolute for mischief, such as neither fear God nor regard their fellow-creatures, but understand themselves bound to hurry from the road whatever is displeasing to themselves, so the rear-guard consists of misproud serving-men, who, being in charge of the baggage, take care to amend by their exactions upon travelling-merchants and others their own thefts on their master's property. You will hear the advanced *enfans perdus*, as the French call them, and so they are indeed, namely, children of the fall, singing unclean and fulsome ballads of sin and harlotrie. And then will come on the middle-ward, when you will hear the canticles and psalms sung by the Reforming nobles, and the gentry, and honest and pious clergy, by whom they are accompanied. And last of all, you will find in the rear a legion of godless lackeys, and palfreniers, and horse-boys, talking of nothing but dicing, drinking, and drabbing."

As the pedlar spoke, they had reached the side of the high-road, and Murray's main body was in sight, consisting of about three hundred horse, marching with great regularity, and in a closely compacted body. Some of the troopers wore the liveries of their masters, but this was not common. Most of them were dressed in such colours as chance dictated. But the majority being clad in blue cloth, and the whole armed with cuirass and back-plate, with sleeves of mail, gauntlets, and poldroons, and either mailed hose or strong jack-boots, they had something of a uniform appearance. Many of the leaders were clad in complete armour, and all in a certain half-military dress, which no man of quality in those disturbed times ever felt himself sufficiently safe to abandon.

The foremost of this party immediately rode up to the pedlar and to Halbert Glendinning, and demanded of them who they were. The pedlar told his story, the young Glendinning exhibited his letter, which a gentleman carried to Murray. In an instant after the word "Halt!" was given through the squadron, and at once the onward heavy tramp, which seemed the most distinctive attribute of the body, ceased, and was heard no more. The command was announced that the troop should halt here for an hour to refresh themselves and their horses. The pedlar was assured of safe protection, and accommodated with the use of a baggage horse. But at the same time he was ordered into the rear—a command which he reluctantly obeyed, and not without wringing pathetically the hand of Halbert as he separated from him.

The young heir of Glendearg was in the mean while conducted to a plot of ground more raised, and therefore drier, than the rest of the moor. Here a carpet was flung on the ground by way of tablecloth, and around it sat the leaders of the party, partaking of an entertainment as coarse, with relation to their rank, as that which Glendinning had so lately shared. Murray himself rose as he came forward, and advanced a step to meet him.

This celebrated person had in his appearance, as well as in his mind, much of the admirable qualities of James V., his father. Had not the stain of illegitimacy rested upon his birth, he would have filled the Scottish throne with as much honour as any of the Stuart race. But history, while she acknowledges his high talents, and much that was princely, nay, royal, in his conduct, cannot forget that ambition led him farther than honour or loyalty warranted. Brave amongst the bravest, fair in presence and in favour, skilful to manage the most intricate affairs, to attach to himself those who were doubtful, to stun and overwhelm, by the suddenness and intrepidity of his enterprises, those who were resolute in resistance, he attained, and as to personal merit certainly deserved, the highest place in the kingdom. But he abused, under the influence of strong temptation, the opportunities which his sister Mary's misfortunes and imprudence threw in his way: he supplanted his sovereign and benefactress in her power, and his history affords us one of those mixed characters in which principle was so often sacrificed to policy that we must condemn the statesman while we pity and regret the individual. Many events in his life give likelihood to the charge that he himself aimed at the crown; and it is too true that he countenanced the fatal expedient of establishing an English, that is, a foreign and a hostile, interest in the councils of Scotland. But his death may be received as an atonement for his offences, and may serve to show how much more safe is the person of a real patriot than that of the mere head of a faction, who is accounted answerable for the offences of his meanest attendants.

When Murray approached, the young rustic was naturally

abashed at the dignity of his presence. The commanding form, and the countenance to which high and important thoughts were familiar, the features which bore the resemblance of Scotland's long line of kings, were well calculated to impress awe and reverence. His dress had little to distinguish him from the high-born nobles and barons by whom he was attended. A buff-coat, richly embroidered with silken lace, supplied the place of armour; and a massive gold chain, with its medal, hung round his neck. His black velvet bonnet was decorated with a string of large and fair pearls, and with a small tufted feather; a long heavy sword was girt to his side, as the familiar companion of his hand. He wore gilded spurs on his boots, and these completed his equipment.

"This letter," he said, "is from the godly preacher of the Word, Henry Warden, young man, is it not so?" Halbert answered in the affirmative. "And he writes to us, it would seem, in some strait, and refers us to you for the circumstances. Let us know, I pray you, how things stand with him."

In some perturbation Halbert Glendinning gave an account of the circumstances which had accompanied the preacher's imprisonment. When he came to the discussion of the handfasting engagement, he was struck with the ominous and displeased expression of Murray's brows, and, contrary to all prudential and politic rule, seeing something was wrong, yet not well aware what that something was, had almost stopped short in his narrative.

"What ails the fool?" said the Earl, drawing his dark-red eyebrows together, while the same dusky glow kindled on his brow. "Hast thou not learned to tell a true tale without stammering?"

"So please you," answered Halbert, with considerable address, "I have never before spoken in such a presence."

"He seems a modest youth," said Murray, turning to his next attendant, "and yet one who in a good cause will neither fear friend nor foe. Speak on, friend, and speak freely."

Halbert then gave an account of the quarrel betwixt Julian Avenel and the preacher, which the Earl, biting his lip the while, compelled himself to listen to as a thing of indifference. At first he appeared even to take the part of the Baron.

"Henry Warden," he said, "is too hot in his zeal. The law both of God and man maketh allowance for certain alliances, though not strictly formal, and the issue of such may succeed."

This general declaration he expressed, accompanying it with a glance around upon the few followers who were present at this interview. The most of them answered: "There is no contravening that"; but one or two looked on the ground, and were silent. Murray then turned again to Glendinning, commanding him to say what next chanced, and not to omit any particular. When he mentioned the manner in which Julian had cast from him his concubine, Murray drew a deep breath, set his teeth hard, and laid his hand on the hilt of his dagger. Casting his eyes once more around the circle, which was now augmented by one or two of the Reformed preachers, he seemed to devour his rage in silence, and again commanded Halbert to proceed. When he came to describe how Warden had been dragged to a dungeon, the Earl seemed to have found the point at which he might give vent to his own resentment, secure of the sympathy and approbation of all who were present. "Judge you," he said, looking to those around him— "judge you, my peers and noble gentlemen of Scotland, betwixt me and this Julian Avenel—he hath broken his own word, and hath violated my safe-conduct; and judge you also, my reverend brethren—he hath put his hand forth upon a preacher of the Gospel, and perchance may sell his blood to the worshippers of Anti-Christ!"

"Let him die the death of a traitor," said the secular chiefs, "and let his tongue be struck through with the hangman's fiery iron, to avenge his perjury!"

"Let him go down to his place with Baal's priests," said the preachers, "and be his ashes cast into Tophet."

Murray heard them with the smile of expected revenge; yet it is probable that the brutal treatment of the female, whose circumstances somewhat resembled those of the Earl's own mother, had its share in the grim smile which curled his sunburnt cheek and his haughty lip. To Halbert Glendinning, when his narrative was finished, he spoke with great kindness.

"He is a bold and gallant youth," said he to those around, "and formed of the stuff which becomes a bustling time. There are periods when men's spirits shine bravely through them. I will know something more of him."

He questioned him more particularly concerning the Baron of Avenel's probable forces, the strength of his castle, the dispositions of his next heir, and this brought necessarily forward the sad history of his brother's daughter, Mary Avenel, which was told with an embarrassment that did not escape Murray.

"Ha! Julian Avenel," he said, "and do you provoke my resentment, when you have so much more reason to deprecate my justice! I knew Walter Avenel, a true Scotsman and a good soldier. Our sister, the Queen, must right his daughter; and were her land restored, she would be a fitting bride to some brave man who may better merit our favour than the traitor Julian." Then looking at Halbert, he said: "Art thou of gentle blood, young man?"

Halbert, with a faltering and uncertain voice, began to speak of his distant pretensions to claim a descent from the ancient Glendonwynes of Galloway, when Murray interrupted him with a smile.

"Nay—nay, leave pedigrees to bards and heralds. In our days, each man is the son of his own deeds. The glorious light of Reformation hath shone alike on prince and peasant; and peasant as well as prince may be illustrated by fighting in its defence. It is a stirring world, where all may advance themselves who have stout hearts and strong arms. Tell me frankly why thou hast left thy father's house."

Halbert Glendinning made a frank confession of his duel with Piercie Shafton, and mentioned his supposed death.

"By my hand," said Murray, "thou art a bold sparrowhawk, to match thee so early with such a kite as Piercie Shafton. Queen Elizabeth would give her glove filled with gold crowns to know that meddling coxcomb to be under the sod. Would she not, Morton?"

Ay, by my word, and esteem her glove a better gift than tne crowns," replied Morton, "which few Border lads like this fellow well esteem just valuation."

"But what shall we do with this young homicide?" said Murray; "what will our preachers say?"

"Tell them of Moses and of Benaiah," said Morton; "it is but the smiting of an Egyptian when all is said out."

"Let it be so," said Murray, laughing; "but we will bury the tale, as the prophet did the body, in the sand. I will take care of this swankie. Be near to us, Glendinning, since that is thy name. We retain thee as a squire of our household. The master of our horse will see thee fully equipped and armed."

During the expedition which he was now engaged in, Murray found several opportunities of putting Glendinning's courage and presence of mind to the test, and he began to rise so rapidly in his esteem that those who knew the Earl considered the youth's fortune as certain. One step only was wanting to raise him to a still higher degree of confidence and favour: it was the abjuration of the Popish religion. The ministers who attended upon Murray, and formed his chief support amongst the people, found an easy convert in Halbert Glendinning, who, from his earliest days, had never felt much devotion towards the Catholic faith, and who listened eagerly to more reasonable views of religion. By thus adopting the faith of his master, he rose higher in his favour, and was constantly about his person during his prolonged stay in the west of Scotland, which the intractability of those whom the Earl had to deal with protracted from day to day and week to week.

CHAPTER XXXVI

Faint the din of battle bray'd
   Distant down the hollow wind;
War and terror fled before,
   Wounds and death were left behind.
               PENROSE.

THE autumn of the year was well advanced, when the Earl of Morton one morning rather unexpectedly entered the antechamber of Murray, in which Halbert Glendinning was in waiting.

"Call your master, Halbert," said the Earl; "I have news for him from Teviotdale; and for you too, Glendinning. News!—news! my Lord of Murray!" he exclaimed at the door of the Earl's bedroom; "come forth instantly."

The Earl appeared, and greeted his ally, demanding eagerly his tidings.

"I have had a sure friend with me from the south," said Morton; "he has been at St. Mary's Monastery, and brings important tidings."

"Of what complexion?" said Murray, "and can you trust the bearer?"

"He is faithful, on my life," said Morton; "I wish all around your lordship may prove equally so."

"At what, and whom, do you point?" demanded Murray.

"Here is the Egyptian of trusty Halbert Glendinning, our Southland Moses, come alive again, and flourishing, gay and bright as ever, in that Teviotdale Goshen, the halidome of Kennaquhair."

"What mean you, my lord?" said Murray.

"Only that your new henchman has put a false tale upon you. Piercie Shafton is alive and well; by the same token that the gull is thought to be detained there by love to a miller's daughter, who roamed the country with him in disguise."

"Glendinning," said Murray, bending his brow into his

darkest frown, "thou hast not, I trust, dared to bring me a lie in thy mouth, in order to win my confidence!"

"My lord," said Halbert, "I am incapable of a lie. I should choke on one were my life to require that I pronounced it. I say, that this sword of my father was through the body: the point came out behind his back, the hilt pressed upon his breastbone. And I will plunge it as deep in the body of any one who shall dare to charge me with falsehood."

"How, fellow!" said Morton, "wouldst thou beard a nobleman?"

"Be silent, Halbert," said Murray, "and you, my Lord of Morton, forbear him. I see truth written on his brow."

"I wish the inside of the manuscript may correspond with the superscription," replied his more suspicious ally. "Look to it, my lord, you will one day lose your life by too much confidence."

"And you will lose your friends by being too readily suspicious," answered Murray. "Enough of this—let me hear thy tidings."

"Sir John Foster," said Morton, "is about to send a party into Scotland to waste the halidome."

"How! without waiting my presence and permission?" said Murray; "he is mad. Will he come as an enemy into the Queen's country?"

"He has Elizabeth's express orders," answered Morton, "and they are not to be trifled with. Indeed, his march has been more than once projected and laid aside during the time we have been here, and has caused much alarm at Kennaquhair. Boniface, the old abbot, has resigned, and whom think you they have chosen in his place?"

"No one surely," said Murray; "they would presume to hold no election until the Queen's pleasure and mine were known?"

Morton shrugged his shoulders. "They have chosen the pupil of old Cardinal Batoun, that wily, determined champion of Rome, the bosom-friend of our busy Primate of St. Andrews. Eustace, late the sub-prior of Kennaquhair, is now its abbot, and, like a second Pope Julius, is levying men and making musters to fight with Foster if he comes forward."

"We must prevent that meeting," said Murray, hastily; "whichever party wins the day, it were a fatal encounter for us. Who commands the troop of the abbot?"

"Our faithful old friend, Julian Avenel, nothing less," answered Morton.

"Glendinning," said Murray, "sound trumpets to horse directly, and let all who love us get on horseback without delay. Yes, my lord, this were indeed a fatal dilemma. If we take part with our English friends, the country will cry shame on us—the very old wives will attack us with their rocks and spindles—the very stones of the street will rise up against us; we cannot set our face to such a deed of infamy. And my sister, whose confidence I already have such difficulty in preserving, will altogether withdraw it from me. Then, were we to oppose the English warden, Elizabeth would call it a protecting of her enemies and wot not, and we should lose her."

"The she-dragon," said Morton, "is the best card in our pack; and yet I would not willingly stand still and see English blades carve Scots' flesh. What say you to loitering by the way, marching fair and easy for fear of spoiling our horses? They might then fight dog fight bull, fight abbot fight archer, and no one could blame us for what chanced when we were not present."

"All would blame us, James Douglas," replied Murray; "we should lose both sides. We had better advance with the utmost celerity, and do what we can to keep the peace betwixt them. I would the nag that brought Piercie Shafton hither had broken his neck over the highest heuch in Northumberland! He is a proper coxcomb to make all this bustle about, and to occasion perhaps a national war!"

"Had we known in time," said Douglas, "we might have had him privily waited upon as he entered the Borders; there are strapping lads enough would have rid us of him for the lucre of his spur-whang. But to the saddle, James Stuart, since so the phrase goes. I hear your trumpets sound to horse and away; we shall soon see which nag is best breathed."

Followed by a train of about three hundred well-mounted men-at-arms, these two powerful barons directed their course to Dumíries, and from thence eastward to Teviotdale, marching at a rate which, as Morton had foretold, soon disabled a good many of their horses, so that, when they approached the scene of expected action, there were not above two hundred of their train remaining in a body, and of these most were mounted on steeds which had been sorely jaded.

They had hitherto been amused and agitated by various reports concerning the advance of the English soldiers, and the degree of resistance which the abbot was able to oppose to them. But when they were six or seven miles from St. Mary's of Kennaquhair, a gentleman of the country, whom Murray had summoned to attend him, and on whose intelligence he knew he could rely, arrived at the head of two or three servants, "bloody with spurring, fiery red with haste." According to his report, Sir John Foster, after several times announcing, and as often delaying, his intended incursion, had at last been so stung with the news that Piercie Shafton was openly residing within the halidome that he determined to execute the commands of his mistress, which directed him, at every risk, to make himself master of the Euphuist's person. The abbot's unceasing exertions had collected a body of men almost equal in number to those of the English warden, but less practised in arms. They were united under the command of Julian Avenel, and it was apprehended they would join battle upon the banks of a small stream which forms the verge of the halidome.

"Who knows the place?" said Murray.

"I do, my lord," answered Glendinning.

"'Tis well," said the Earl; "take a score of the best-mounted horse; make what haste thou canst, and announce to them that I am coming up instantly with a strong power, and will cut to pieces, without mercy, whichever party strikes the first blow. Davidson," said he to the gentleman who brought the intelligence. "thou shalt be my guide. Hie thee

28

on, Glendinning. Say to Foster, I conjure him, as he respects his mistress's service, that he will leave the matter in my hands. Say to the abbot, I will burn the monastery over his head, if he strikes a stroke till I come. Tell the dog, Julian Avenel, that he hath already one deep score to settle with me, I will set his head on the top of the highest pinnacle of St. Mary's if he presume to open another. Make haste, and spare not the spur for fear of spoiling horse-flesh."

"Your bidding shall be obeyed, my lord," said Glendinning; and choosing those whose horses were in best plight to be his attendants, he went off as fast as the jaded state of their cavalry permitted. Hill and hollow vanished from under the feet of the chargers.

They had not ridden above half the way when they met stragglers coming off from the field, whose appearance announced that the conflict was begun. Two supported in their arms a third, their elder brother, who was pierced with an arrow through the body. Halbert, who knew them to belong to the halidome, called them by their names, and questioned them of the state of the affray; but just then, in spite of their efforts to retain him in the saddle, their brother dropped from the horse, and they dismounted in haste to receive his last breath. From men thus engaged no information was to be obtained. Glendinning, therefore, pushed on with his little troop, the more anxiously as he perceived other stragglers, bearing St. Andrew's cross upon their caps and corslets, flying apparently from the field of battle. Most of these, when they were aware of a body of horsemen approaching on the road, held to the one hand or the other, at such a distance as precluded coming to speech of them. Others, whose fear was more intense, kept the onward road, galloping wildly as fast as their horses could carry them, and when questioned, only glared without reply on those who spoke to them, and rode on without drawing bridle. Several of these were also known to Halbert, who had therefore no doubt, from the circumstances in which he met them, that the men of the halidome were defeated. He became now unspeakably anxious concerning the fate of his brother, who, he could not doubt, must have been engaged in the affray. He therefore increased the speed of his horse, so that not above five or six of his followers could keep up with him. At length he reached a little hill, at the descent of which, surrounded by a semicircular sweep of a small stream, lay the plain which had been the scene of the skirmish.

It was a melancholy spectacle. War and terror, to use the expression of the poet, had rushed on to the field, and left only wounds and death behind them. The battle had been stoutly contested, as was almost always the case with these Border skirmishes, where ancient hatred and mutual injuries made men stubborn in maintaining the cause of their conflict. Towards the middle of the plain there lay the bodies of several men who had fallen in the very act of grappling with the enemy; and there were seen countenances which still bore the stern expression of unextinguishable hate and defiance, hands which clasped the hilt of the broken falchion, or strove in vain to pluck the deadly arrow from the wound. Some were wounded, and, cowed of the courage they had lately shown, were begging aid and craving water in a tone of melancholy depression, while others tried to teach the faltering tongue to pronounce some half-forgotten prayer, which, even when first learned, they had but half-understood. Halbert, uncertain what course he was next to pursue, rode through the plain to see if, among the dead or wounded, he could discover any traces of his brother Edward. He experienced no interruption from the English. A distant cloud of dust announced that they were still pursuing the scattered fugitives, and he guessed that to approach them with his followers, until they were again under some command, would be to throw away his own life and that of his men, whom the victors would instantly confound with the Scots against whom they had been successful. He resolved, therefore, to pause until Murray came up with his forces, to which he was the more readily moved as he heard the trumpets of the English warden sounding the retreat, and recalling from the pursuit. He drew his men together, and made a stand in an advantageous spot of ground, which had been occupied by the Scots in the beginning of the action, and most fiercely disputed while the skirmish lasted.

While he stood here, Halbert's ear was assailed by the feeble moan of a woman, which he had not expected to hear amid that scene, until the retreat of the foes had permitted the relations of the slain to approach, for the purpose of paying them the last duties. He looked with anxiety, and at length observed that by the body of a knight in bright armour, whose crest, though soiled and broken, still showed the marks of rank and birth, there sat a female, wrapt in a horseman's cloak, and holding something pressed against her bosom, which he soon discovered to be a child. He glanced towards the English. They advanced not, and the continued and prolonged sound of their trumpets, with the shouts of the leaders, announced that their powers would not be instantly reassembled. He had, therefore, a moment to look after this unfortunate woman. He gave his horse to a spearman as he dismounted, and approaching the unhappy female, asked her, in the most soothing tone he could assume, whether he could assist her in her distress. The mourner made him no direct answer; but endeavouring, with a trembling and unskilful hand, to undo the springs of the visor and gorget, said, in a tone of impatient grief: "Oh, he would recover instantly could I but give him air—land and living, life and honour, would I give for the power of undoing these cruel iron platings that suffocate him!" He that would soothe sorrow must not argue on the vanity of the most deceitful hopes. The body lay as that of one whose last draught of vital air had been drawn, and who must never more have concern with the nether sky. But Halbert Glendinning failed not to raise the visor and cast loose the gorget, when, to his great surprise, he recognised the pale face of Julian Avenel. His last fight was over: the fierce and turbid spirit had departed in the strife in which it had so long delighted.

"Alas! he is gone," said Halbert, speaking to the young woman, in whom he had now no difficulty of knowing the unhappy Catherine.

"Oh, no, no, no!" she reiterated, "do not say so; he is not

dead, he is but in a swoon. I have lain as long in one my-self; and then his voice would rouse me, when he spoke kind-ly, and said, 'Catherine, look up for my sake.' And look up, Julian, for mine!" she said, addressing the senseless corpse. "I know you do but counterfeit to frighten me, but I am not frightened," she added, with an hysterical attempt to laugh; and then instantly changing her tone, entreated him to "Speak, were it but to curse my folly. Oh, the rudest word you ever said to me would now sound like the dearest you wasted on me before I gave you all. Lift him up," she said—"lift him up, for God's sake!—have you no compassion? He promised to wed me if I bore him a boy, and this child is so like to its father! How shall he keep his word, if you do not help me to awaken him? Christie of the Clinthill—Rowley—Hutch-eon! ye were constant at his feast, but ye fled from him at the fray, false villains as ye are!"

"Not I, by Heaven!" said a dying man, who made some shift to raise himself on his elbow, and discovered to Halbert the well-known features of Christie; "I fled not a foot, and a man can but fight while his breath lasts: mine is going fast. So, youngster," said he, looking at Glendinning, and seeing his military dress, "thou hast ta'en the basnet at last? It is a better cap to live in than die in. I would chance had sent thy brother here instead, there was good in him; but thou art as wild, and wilt soon be as wicked, as myself."

"God forbid!" said Halbert, hastily.

"Marry, and amen, with all my heart," said the wounded man; "there will be company enow without thee where I am going. But God be praised I had no hand in that wicked-ness," said he, looking to poor Catherine; and with some exclamation in his mouth that sounded betwixt a prayer and a curse, the soul of Christie of the Clinthill took wing to the last account.

Deeply wrapt in the painful interest which these shocking events had excited, Glendinning forgot for a moment his own situation and duties, and was first recalled to them by a tram-pling of horse, and the cry of "St. George for England," which the English soldiers still continued to use. His handful of men, for most of the stragglers had waited for Murray's coming up, remained on horseback, holding their lances upright, having no command either to submit or resist.

"There stands our captain," said one of them, as a strong party of English came up, the vanguard of Foster's troop.

"Your captain! with his sword sheathed, and on foot in the presence of his enemy? a raw soldier, I warrant him," said the English leader. "So ho! young man, is your dream out, and will you now answer me if you will fight or fly?"

"Neither," answered Halbert Glendinning, with great tranquillity.

"Then throw down thy sword and yield thee," answered the Englishman.

"Not till I can help myself no otherwise," said Halbert, with the same moderation of tone and manner.

"Art thou for thine own hand, friend, or to whom dost thou owe service?" demanded the English captain.

"To the noble Earl of Murray."

"Then thou servest," said the Southron, "the most disloyal nobleman who breathes—false both to England and Scotland."

"Thou liest!" said Glendinning, regardless of all consequences.

"Ha! art thou so hot now, and wert so cold but a minute since? I lie, do I? Wilt thou do battle with me on that quarrel?"

"With one to one—one to two—or two to five, as you list," said Halbert Glendinning; "grant me but a fair field."

"That thou shalt have. Stand back, my mates," said the brave Englishman. "If I fall, give him fair play, and let him go off free with his people."

"Long life to the noble captain!" cried the soldiers, as impatient to see the duel as if it had been a bull-baiting.

"He will have a short life of it, though," said the sergeant, "if he, an old man of sixty, is to fight for any reason, or for no reason, with every man he·meets, and especially the young fellows he might be father to. And here comes the warden besides, to see the sword-play."

In fact, Sir John Foster came up with a considerable body

of his horsemen, just as his captain, whose age rendered him unequal to the combat with so strong and active a youth as Glendinning, was deprived of his sword.

"Take it up for shame, old Stawarth Bolton," said the English warden; "and thou, young man, tell me who and what thou art?"

"A follower of the Earl of Murray, who bore his will to your honour," answered Glendinning; "but here he comes to say it himself, I see the van of his horsemen come over the hills."

"Get into order, my masters," said Sir John Foster to his followers; "you that have broken your spears, draw your swords We are something unprovided for a second field, but if yonder dark cloud on the hill-edge bring us foul weather we must bear as bravely as our broken cloaks will bide it. Meanwhile, Stawarth, we have got the deer we have hunted for: here is Piercie Shafton hard and fast betwixt two troopers."

"Who, that lad?" said Bolton; "he is no more Piercie Shafton than I am. He hath his gay cloak indeed; but Piercie Shafton is a round dozen of years older than that slip of roguery. I have known him since he was thus high. Did you never see him in the tiltyard or in the presence?"

"To the devil with such vanities!" said Sir John Foster; "when had I leisure for them or anything else? During my whole life has she kept me to this hangman's office, chasing thieves one day and traitors another, in daily fear of my life; the lance never hung up in the hall, the foot never out of the stirrup, the saddles never off my nags' backs; and now, because I have been mistaken in the person of a man I never saw, I warrant me the next letters from the privy council will rate me as I were a dog. A man were better dead than thus slaved and harassed!"

A trumpet interrupted Foster's complaints, and a Scottish pursuivant who attended declared, "That the noble Earl of Murray desired, in all honour and safety, a personal conference with Sir John Foster, midway between their parties, with six of company in each, and ten free minutes to come and go."

"And now," said the Englishman, "comes another plague. I must go speak with yonder false Scot, and he knows how to frame his devices, to cast dust in the eyes of a plain man, as well as ever a knave in the north. I am no match for him in words, and for hard blows we are but too ill provided. Pursuivant, we grant the conference; and you, sir swordsman (speaking to young Glendinning), draw off with your troopers to your own party—march—attend your Earl's trumpet. Stawarth Bolton, put our troop in order, and be ready to move forward at the wagging of a finger. Get you gone to your own friends, I tell you, sir squire, and loiter not here."

Notwithstanding this peremptory order, Halbert Glendinning could not help stopping to cast a look upon the unfortunate Catherine, who lay insensible of the danger and of the trampling of so many horses around her—insensible, as the second glance assured him, of all and for ever. Glendinning almost rejoiced when he saw that the last misery of life was over, and that the hoofs of the war-horses, amongst which he was compelled to leave her, could only injure and deface a senseless corpse. He caught the infant from her arms, half-ashamed of the shout of laughter which rose on all sides at seeing an armed man in such a situation assume such an unwonted and inconvenient burden.

"Shoulder your infant!" cried a harquebusier.

"Port your infant!" said a pikeman.

"Peace, ye brutes," said Stawarth Bolton, "and respect humanity in others, if you have none yourselves. I pardon the lad having done some discredit to my grey hairs, when I see him take care of that helpless creature, which ye would have trampled upon as if ye had been littered of bitch-wolves, not born of women."

While this passed, the leaders on either side met in the neutral space betwixt the forces of either, and the Earl accosted the English warden: "Is this fair or honest usage, Sir John, or for whom do you hold the Earl of Morton and myself, that you ride in Scotland with arrayed banner, fight, slay, and make prisoners at your own pleasure? Is it well done, think you, to spoil our land and shed our blood, after the many proofs we have given to your mistress of our devotion due to her will, saving always the allegiance due to our own sovereign?"

"My Lord of Murray," answered Foster, "all the world knows you to be a man of quick ingine and deep wisdom, and these several weeks have you held me in hand with promising to arrest my sovereign mistress's rebel, this Piercie Shafton of Wilverton, and you have never kept your word, alleging turmoils in the west, and I wot not what other causes of hinderance. Now, since he has had the insolence to return hither, and live openly within ten miles of England, I could no longer, in plain duty to my mistress and queen, tarry upon your successive delays, and therefore I have used her force to take her rebel, by the strong hand, wherever I can find him."

"And is Piercie Shafton in your hands, then?" said the Earl of Murray. "Be aware that I may not, without my own great shame, suffer you to remove him hence without doing battle."

"Will you, Lord Earl, after all the advantages you have received at the hands of the Queen of England, do battle in the cause of her rebel?" said Sir John Foster.

"Not so, Sir John," answered the Earl, "but I will fight to the death in defence of the liberties of our free kingdom of Scotland."

"By my faith," said Sir John Foster, "I am well content; my sword is not blunted with all it has done yet this day."

"By my honour, Sir John," said Sir George Heron of Chipchase, "there is but little reason we should fight these Scottish lords e'en now, for I hold opinion with old Stawarth Bolton, and believe yonder prisoner to be no more Piercie Shafton than he is the Earl of Northumberland; and you were but ill advised to break the peace betwixt the countries for a prisoner of less consequence than that gay mischief-maker."

"Sir George," replied Foster, "I have often heard you herons are afraid of hawks. Nay, lay not hand on sword, man—I did but jest; and for this prisoner, let him be brought up hither, that we may see who or what he is—always under assurance, my lords," he continued, addressing the Scots.

"Upon our word and honour," said Morton, "we will offer no violence."

The laugh turned against Sir John Foster considerably when the prisoner, being brought up, proved not only a different person from Sir Piercie Shafton, but a female in man's attire.

"Pluck the mantle from the quean's face, and cast her to the horse-boys," said Foster; "she has kept such company ere now, I warrant."

Even Murray was moved to laughter, no common thing with him, at the disappointment of the English warden; but he would not permit any violence to be offered to the fair Molinara, who had thus a second time rescued Sir Piercie Shafton at her own personal risk.

"You have already done more mischief than you can well answer," said the Earl to the English warden, "and it were dishonour to me should I permit you to harm a hair of this young woman's head."

"My lord," said Morton, "if Sir John will ride apart with me but for one moment, I will show him such reasons as shall make him content to depart, and to refer this unhappy day's work to the judgment of the commissioners nominated to try offences on the Border."

He then led Sir John Foster aside, and spoke to him in this manner: "Sir John Foster, I much marvel that a man who knows your Queen Elizabeth as you do should not know that, if you hope anything from her, it must be for doing her useful service, not for involving her in quarrels with her neighbours without any advantage. Sir knight, I will speak frankly what I know to be true. Had you seized the true Piercie Shafton by this ill-advised inroad; and had your deed threatened, as most likely it might, a breach betwixt the countries, your politic princess and her politic council would rather have disgraced Sir John Foster than entered into war in his behalf. But now that you have stricken short of your aim, you may rely on it you will have little thanks for carrying the matter farther. I will work thus far on the Earl of Murray that he will undertake to dismiss Sir Piercie Shafton from the realm of Scotland. Be well advised, and let the matter now pass off; you will gain nothing by farther violence, for if we fight, you, as the fewer and the weaker through your former action, will needs have the worse."

Sir John Foster listened with his head declining on his breast-plate.

"It is a cursed chance," he said, "and I shall have little thanks for my day's work."

He then rode up to Murray, and said that, in deference to his lordship's presence and that of my Lord of Morton, he had come to the resolution of withdrawing himself, with his power, without farther proceedings.

"Stop there, Sir John Foster," said Murray, "I cannot permit you to retire in safety, unless you leave some one who may be surety to Scotland that the injuries you have at present done us may be fully accounted for; you will reflect that, by permitting your retreat, I become accountable to my Sovereign, who will demand a reckoning of me for the blood of her subjects, if I suffer those who shed it to depart so easily."

"It shall never be told in England," said the warden, "that John Foster gave pledges like a subdued man, and that on the very field on which he stands victorious. But," he added, after a moment's pause, "if Stawarth Bolton wills to abide with you on his own free choice, I will say nothing against it; and, as I bethink me, it were better he should stay to see the dismissal of this same Piercie Shafton."

"I receive him as your hostage, nevertheless, and shall treat him as such," said the Earl of Murray. But Foster, turning away as if to give directions to Bolton and his men, affected not to hear this observation.

"There rides a faithful servant of his most beautiful and sovereign lady," said Murray aside to Morton. "Happy man! he knows not whether the execution of her commands may not cost him his head; and yet he is most certain that to leave them unexecuted will bring disgrace and death without reprieve. Happy are they who are not only subjected to the caprices of Dame Fortune, but held bound to account and be responsible for them, and that to a sovereign as moody and fickle as her humorous ladyship herself!"

"We also have a female sovereign, my lord," said Morton.

"We have so, Douglas," said the Earl, with a suppressed sigh; "but it remains to be seen how long a female hand can hold the reins of power in a realm so wild as ours. We will now go on to St. Mary's, and see ourselves after the state of that house. Glendinning, look to that woman, and protect her. What the fiend, man, hast thou got in thine arms? An infant, as I live! Where couldst thou find such a charge, at such a place and moment?"

Halbert Glendinning briefly told the story. The Earl rode forward to the place were the body of Julian Avenel lay, with his unhappy companion's arms wrapt around him, like the trunk of an uprooted oak borne down by the tempest with all its ivy garlands. Both were cold dead. Murray was touched in an unwonted degree, remembering, perhaps, his own birth. "What have they to answer for, Douglas," he said, "who thus abuse the sweetest gifts of affection?"

The Earl of Morton, unhappy in his marriage, was a libertine in his amours.

"You must ask that question of Henry Warden, my lord, or of John Knox: I am but a wild counsellor in women's matters."

"Forward to St. Mary's," said the Earl; "pass the word on. Glendinning, give the infant to this same female cavalier, and let it be taken charge of. Let no dishonour be done to the dead bodies, and call on the country to bury or remove them. Forward, I say, my masters!"

CHAPTER XXXVII.

Gone to be married ?—Gone to swear a peace.
King John.

THE news of the lost battle, so quickly carried by the fugitives to the village and convent, had spread the greatest alarm among the inhabitants. The sacristan and other monks counselled flight; the treasurer recommended that the church plate should be offered as a tribute to bribe the English officer; the abbot alone was unmoved and undaunted.

"My brethren," he said, "since God has not given our people victory in the combat, it must be because He requires of us, His spiritual soldiers, to fight the good fight of martyrdom—a conflict in which nothing but our own faint-hearted cowardice can make us fail of victory. Let us assume, then, the armour of faith, and prepare, if it be necessary, to die under the ruin of these shrines, to the service of which we have devoted ourselves. Highly honoured are we all in this distinguished summons, from our dear brother Nicolas, whose grey hairs have been preserved until they should be surrounded by the crown of martyrdom, down to my beloved son Edward, who, arriving at the vineyard at the latest hour of the day, is yet permitted to share its toils with those who have laboured from the morning. Be of good courage, my children. I dare not, like my sainted predecessors, promise to you that you shall be preserved by miracle; I and you are alike unworthy of that especial interposition, which, in earlier times, turned the sword of sacrilege against the bosom of tyrants by whom it was wielded, daunted the hardened hearts of heretics with prodigies, and called down hosts of angels to defend the shrine of God and of the Virgin. Yet, by Heavenly aid, you shall this day see that your father and abbot will not disgrace the mitre which sits upon his brow. Go to your cells, my children, and exercise your private devotions. Array yourselves also in alb and cope, as for our most solemn festivals, and be ready, when the tolling of the largest bell announces the approach of the enemy, to march forth to meet them in solemn procession. Let the church be opened to afford such refuge as may be to those of our vassals who, from their exertion in this day's unhappy battle or other cause, are particularly apprehensive of the rage of the enemy. Tell Sir Piercie Shafton, if he has escaped the fight——"

"I am here, most venerable abbot," replied Sir Piercie; "and if it so seemeth meet to you, I will presently assemble such of the men as have escaped this escaramouche, and will renew the resistance, even unto the death. Certes, you will learn from all that I did my part in this unhappy matter. Had it pleased Julian Avenel to have attended to my counsel, specially in somewhat withdrawing of his main battle, even as you may have marked the heron eschew the stoop of the falcon, receiving him rather upon his beak than upon his wing, affairs, as I do conceive, might have had a different face, and we might then, in a more bellicose manner, have maintained that affray. Nevertheless, I would not be understood to speak anything in disregard of Julian Avenel, whom I saw fall fighting manfully with his face to his enemy, which hath banished from my memory the unseemly term of 'meddling coxcomb,' with which it pleased him something rashly to qualify my advice, and for which, had it pleased Heaven and the saints to have prolonged the life of that excellent person, I had it bound upon my soul to have put him to death with my own hand."

"Sir Piercie," said the abbot, at length interrupting him, "our time allows brief leisure to speak what might have been."

"You are right, most venerable lord and father," replied the incorrigible Euphuist; "the preterite, as grammarians have it, concerns frail mortality less than the future mood, and indeed our cogitations respect chiefly the present. In a word, I am willing to head all who will follow me, and offer such opposition as manhood and mortality may permit to the advance of the English, though they be my own countrymen; and be assured, Piercie Shafton will measure his length, being five feet ten inches, on the ground as he stands, rather than give two yards in retreat, according to the usual motion in which we retrograde."

"I thank you, sir knight," said the abbot, "and I doubt not that you would make your words good; but it is not the will of Heaven that carnal weapons should rescue us. We are called to endure, not to resist, and may not waste the blood of our innocent commons in vain. Fruitless opposition becomes not men of our profession: they have my commands to resign the sword and the spear. God and Our Lady have not blessed our banner."

"Bethink you, reverend lord," said Piercie Shafton, very

eagerly, "ere you resign the defence that is in your power. There are many posts near the entry of this village where brave men might live or die to the advantage; and I have this additional motive to make defence—the safety, namely, of a fair friend, who, I hope, hath escaped the hands of the heretics."

"I understand you, Sir Piercie," said the abbot; "you mean the daughter of our convent's miller?"

"Reverend my lord," said Sir Piercie, not without hesitation, "the fair Mysinda is, as may be in some sort alleged, the daughter of one who mechanically prepareth corn to be manipulated into bread, without which we could not exist, and which is therefore an employment in itself honourable, nay, necessary. Nevertheless, if the purest sentiments of a generous mind, streaming forth like the rays of the sun reflected by a diamond, may ennoble one who is in some sort the daughter of a molendinary mechanic——"

"I have no time for all this, sir knight," said the abbot; "be it enough to answer, that with our will we war no longer with carnal weapons. We of the spirituality will teach you of the temporality how to die in cold blood, our hands not clenched for resistance, but folded for prayer; our minds not filled with jealous hatred, but with Christian meekness and forgiveness; our ears not deafened, nor our senses confused, by the sound of clamorous instruments of war; but, on the contrary, our voices composed to Halleluiah, Kyrie Eleison, and Salve Regina, and our blood temperate and cold, as those who think upon reconciling themselves with God, not of avenging themselves of their fellow-mortals."

"Lord abbot," said Sir Piercie, "this is nothing to the fate of my Molinara, whom, I beseech you to observe, I will not abandon, while golden hilt and steel blade bide together on my falchion. I commanded her not to follow us to the field, and yet methought I saw her in her page's attire amongst the rear of the combatants."

"You must seek elsewhere for the person in whose fate you are so deeply interested," said the abbot; "and at present I will pray of your knighthood to inquire concerning her at the church, in which all our more defenceless vassals have taken refuge. It is my advice to you, that you also abide by the horns of the altar; and, Sir Piercie Shafton," he added, " be of one thing secure, that if you come to harm, it will involve the whole of this brotherhood; for never, I trust, will the meanest of us buy safety at the expense of surrendering a friend or a guest. Leave us, my son, and may God be your aid !"

When Sir Piercie Shafton had departed, and the abbot was about to betake himself to his own cell, he was surprised by an unknown person anxiously requiring a conference, who, being admitted, proved to be no other than Henry Warden. The abbot started as he entered, and exclaimed angrily : " Ha! are the few hours that fate allows him who may last wear the mitre of this house not to be excused from the intrusion of heresy? Dost thou come," he said, " to enjoy the hopes which fate holds out to thy demented and accursed sect, to see the besom of destruction sweep away the pride of old religion—to deface our shrines—to mutilate and lay waste the bodies of our benefactors, as well as their sepulchres—to destroy the pinnacles and carved work of God's house and Our Lady's?"

" Peace, William Allan!" said the Protestant preacher, with dignified composure; " for none of these purposes do I come. I would have these stately shrines deprived of the idols which, no longer simply regarded as the effigies of the good and the wise, have become the objects of foul idolatry. I would otherwise have its ornaments subsist, unless as they are, or may be, a snare to the souls of men; and especially do I condemn those ravages which have been made by the heady fury of the people, stung into zeal against will-worship by bloody persecution. Against such wanton devastations I lift my testimony."

" Idle distinguisher that thou art!" said the Abbot Eustace, interrupting him; " what signifies the pretext under which thou dost despoil the house of God? and why at this present emergence wilt thou insult the master of it by thy ill-omened presence?"

" Thou art unjust, William Allan," said Warden; " but I

am not the less settled in my resolution. Thou hast protected me some time since at the hazard of thy rank, and what I know thou holdest still dearer, at the risk of thy reputation with thine own sect. Our party is now uppermost, and, believe me, I have come down the valley, in which thou didst quarter me for sequestration's sake, simply with the wish to keep my engagements to thee."

"Ay," answered the abbot, "and it may be that my listening to that worldly and infirm compassion which pleaded with me for thy life is now avenged by this impending judgment. Heaven hath smitten, it may be, the erring shepherd and scattered the flock."

"Think better of the Divine judgments," said Warden. "Not for thy sins, which are those of thy blinded education and circumstances—not for thine own sins, William Allan, art thou stricken, but for the accumulated guilt which thy misnamed church hath accumulated on her head, and those of her votaries, by the errors and corruptions of ages."

"Now, by my sure belief in the Rock of Peter," said the abbot, "thou dost rekindle the last spark of human indignation for which my bosom has fuel! I thought I might not again have felt the impulse of earthly passion, and it is thy voice which once more calls me to the expression of human anger!—yes, it is thy voice that comest to insult me in my hour of sorrow, with these blasphemous accusations of that church which hath kept the light of Christianity alive from the times of the Apostles till now."

"From the times of the Apostles?" said the preacher, eagerly. "*Negatur, Gulielme Allan,* the primitive church differed as much from that of Rome as did light from darkness, which, did time permit, I should speedily prove. And worse dost thou judge in saying I come to insult thee in thy hour of affliction, being here, God wot, with the Christian wish of fulfilling an engagement I had made to my host, and of rendering myself to thy will while it had yet power to exercise aught upon me, and, if it might so be, to mitigate in thy behalf the rage of the victors whom God hath sent as a scourge to thy obstinacy."

29

"I will none of thy intercession," said the abbot, sternly; "the dignity to which the church has exalted me never should have swelled my bosom more proudly in the time of the highest prosperity than it doth at this crisis. I ask nothing of thee, but the assurance that my lenity to thee hath been the means of perverting no soul to Satan—that I have not given to the wolf any of the stray lambs whom the Great Shepherd of souls had entrusted to my charge."

"William Allan," answered the Protestant, "I will be sincere with thee. What I promised I have kept: I have withheld my voice from speaking even good things. But it has pleased Heaven to call the maiden Mary Avenel to a better sense of faith than thou and all the disciples of Rome can teach. Her I have aided with my humble power: I have extricated her from the machinations of evil spirits, to which she and her house were exposed during the blindness of their Romish superstition, and, praise be to my Master! I have not reason to fear she will again be caught in thy snares."

"Wretched man!" said the abbot, unable to suppress his rising indignation, "is it to the abbot of St. Mary's that you boast having misled the soul of a dweller in Our Lady's halidome into the paths of foul error and damning heresy? Thou dost urge me, Wellwood, beyond what it becomes me to bear, and movest me to employ the few moments of power I may yet possess in removing from the face of the earth one whose qualities, given by God, have been so utterly perverted as thine to the service of Satan."

"Do thy pleasure," said the preacher; "thy vain wrath shall not prevent my doing my duty to advantage thee, where it may be done without neglecting my higher call. I go to the Earl of Murray."

Their conference, which was advancing fast into bitter disputation, was here interrupted by the deep and sullen toll of the largest and heaviest bell of the convent—a sound famous in the chronicles of the community for dispelling of tempests and putting to flight demons, but which now only announced danger, without affording any means of warding against it. Hastily repeating his orders that all the brethren should attend in the choir, arrayed for solemn procession, the abbot ascended to the battlements of the lofty monastery by his own private staircase, and there met the sacristan, who had been in the act of directing the tolling of the huge bell, which fell under his duty.

"It is the last time I shall discharge mine office, most venerable father and lord," said he to the abbot, "for yonder come the Philistines; but I would not that the large bell of St. Mary's should sound for the last time otherwise than in true and full tone. I have been a sinful man for one of our holy profession," added he, looking upward, "yet may I presume to say, not a bell hath sounded out of tune from the tower of the house while Father Philip had the superintendence of the chime and the belfry."

The abbot, without reply, cast his eyes towards the path which, winding around the mountain, descends upon Kennaquhair from the southeast. He beheld at a distance a cloud of dust, and heard the neighing of many horses, while the occasional sparkle of the long line of spears, as they came downwards into the valley, announced that the band came thither in arms.

"Shame on my weakness!" said Abbot Eustace, dashing the tears from his eyes; "my sight is too much dimmed to observe their motions. Look, my son Edward," for his favourite novice had again joined him, "and tell me what ensigns they bear."

"They are Scottish men when all is done," exclaimed Edward. "I see the white crosses: it may be the Western Borderers, or Fernieherst and his clan."

"Look at the banner," said the abbot; "tell me what are the blazonries?"

"The arms of Scotland," said Edward—"the lion and its tressure, quartered, as I think, with three cushions. Can it be the royal standard?"

"Alas! no," said the abbot, "it is that of the Earl of Murray. He hath assumed with his new conquest the badge of the valiant Randolph, and hath dropped from his hereditary coat the bend which indicates his own base birth: would to

God he may not have blotted it also from his memory, and aim as well at possessing the name as the power of a king!"

"At least, my father," said Edward, "he will secure us from the violence of the Southron."

"Ay, my son, as the shepherd secures a silly lamb from the wolf, which he destines in due time to his own banquet.   Oh, my son, evil days are on us!   A breach has been made in the walls of our sanctuary : thy brother hath fallen from the faith. Such news brought my last secret intelligence.   Murray has already spoken of rewarding his services with the hand of Mary Avenel."

"Of Mary Avenel!" said the novice, tottering towards and grasping hold of one of the carved pinnacles which adorned the proud battlement.

"Ay, of Mary Avenel, my son, who has also abjured the faith of her fathers.   Weep not, my Edward—weep not, my beloved son! or weep for their apostasy, and not for their union.   Bless God, who hath called thee to Himself out of the tents of wickedness; but for the grace of Our Lady and St. Benedict, thou also hadst been a castaway."

"I endeavour, my father," said Edward—"I endeavour to forget; but what I would now blot from my memory has been the thought of all my former life.   Murray dare not forward a match so unequal in birth."

"He dares do what suits his purpose.   The Castle of Avenel is strong, and needs a good castellan, devoted to his service; as for the difference of their birth, he will mind it no more than he would mind defacing the natural regularity of the ground, were it necessary he should erect upon it military lines and intrenchments.   But do not droop for that : awaken thy soul within thee, my son.   Think you part with a vain vision, an idle dream, nursed in solitude and inaction.   I weep not, yet what am I now like to lose?   Look at these towers, where saints dwelt, and where heroes have been buried.   Think that I, so briefly called to preside over the pious flock, which has dwelt here since the first light of Christianity, may be this day written down the last father of this holy community. Come, let us descend and meet our fate. I see them approach near to the village."

The abbot descended. The novice cast a glance around him; yet the sense of the danger impending over the stately structure, with which he was now united, was unable to banish the recollection of Mary Avenel. "His brother's bride!" he pulled the cowl over his face, and followed his superior.

The whole bells of the abbey now added their peal to the death-toll of the largest, which had so long sounded. The monks wept and prayed as they got themselves into the order of their procession for the last time, as seemed but too probable.

"It is well our Father Boniface hath retired to the inland," said Father Philip; "he could never have put over this day, it would have broken his heart!"

"God be with the soul of Abbot Ingelram!" said old Father Nicolas, "there were no such doings in his days. They say we are to be put forth of the cloisters; and how I am to live anywhere else than where I have lived for these seventy years, I wot not: the best is, that I have not long to live anywhere."

A few moments after this the great gate of the abbey was flung open, and the procession moved slowly forward from beneath its huge and richly adorned gateway. Cross and banner, pix and chalice, shrines containing relics, and censers steaming with incense, preceded and were intermingled with the long and solemn array of the brotherhood, in their long black gowns and cowls, with their white scapularies hanging over them, the various officers of the convent each displaying his proper badge of office. In the centre of the procession came the abbot, surrounded and supported by his chief assistants. He was dressed in his habit of high solemnity, and appeared as much unconcerned as if he had been taking his usual part in some ordinary ceremony. After him came the inferior persons of the convent—the novices in their albs or white dresses, and the lay brethren distinguished by their beards, which were seldom worn by the fathers. Women and children, mixed with a few men, came in the rear, bewailing the apprehended desolation of their ancient sanctuary. They moved, however, in order, and restrained the marks of their sorrow to a low wailing sound, which rather mingled with than interrupted the measured chant of the monks.

In this order the procession entered the market-place of the village of Kennaquhair, which was then, as now, distinguished by an ancient cross of curious workmanship, the gift of some former monarch of Scotland. Close by the cross, of much greater antiquity, and scarcely less honoured, was an immensely large oak-tree,[1] which perhaps had witnessed the worship of the Druids, ere the stately monastery to which it adjoined had raised its spires in honour of the Christian faith. Like the bentang-tree of the African villages, or the Plaistow oak mentioned in White's *Natural History of Selborne*, this tree was the rendezvous of the villagers, and regarded with peculiar veneration; a feeling common to most nations, and which perhaps may be traced up to the remote period when the patriarch feasted the angels under the oak at Mamre.

The monks formed themselves each in their due place around the cross, while under the ruins of the aged tree crowded the old and the feeble, with others who felt the common alarm. When they had thus arranged themselves, there was a deep and solemn pause. The monks stilled their chant, the lay populace hushed their lamentations, and all awaited in terror and silence the arrival of those heretical forces whom they had been so long taught to regard with fear and trembling.

A distant trampling was at length heard, and the glance of spears was seen to shine through the trees above the village. The sounds increased, and became more thick, one close continuous rushing sound, in which the tread of hoofs was mingled with the ringing of armour. The horsemen soon appeared at the principal entrance which leads into the irregular square or market-place which forms the centre of the village. They entered two by two, slowly, and in the greatest order. The

---

[1] It is scarcely necessary to say that in Melrose, the prototype of Kennaquhair, no such oak ever existed.

van continued to move on, riding round the open space, until they had attained the utmost point, and then turning their horses' heads to the street, stood fast; their companions followed in the same order, until the whole market-place was closely surrounded with soldiers; and the files who followed, making the same manœuvre, formed an inner line within those who had first arrived, until the place was begirt with a quaddruple file of horsemen closely drawn up. There was now a pause, of which the abbot availed himself, by commanding the brotherhood to raise the solemn chant *De profundis clamavi.* He looked around the armed ranks, to see what impression the solemn sounds made on them. All were silent; but the brows of some had an expression of contempt, and almost all the rest bore a look of indifference: their course had been too long decided to permit past feelings of enthusiasm to be anew awakened by a procession or by a hymn.

"Their hearts are hardened," said the abbot to himself in dejection, but not in despair; "it remains to see whether those of their leaders are equally obdurate."

The leaders, in the mean while, were advancing slowly, and Murray, with Morton, rode in deep conversation before a chosen band of their most distinguished followers, amongst whom came Halbert Glendinning. But the preacher, Henry Warden, who, upon leaving the monastery, had instantly joined them, was the only person admitted to their conference.

"You are determined then," said Morton to Murray, "to give the heiress of Avenel, with all her pretensions, to this nameless and obscure young man?"

"Hath not Warden told you," said Murray, "that they have been bred together, and are lovers from their youth upward?"

"And that they are both," said Warden, "by means which may be almost termed miraculous, rescued from the delusions of Rome, and brought within the pale of the true church. My residence at Glendearg hath made me well acquainted with these things. Ill would it beseem my habit and my calling to thrust myself into match-making and giving in marriage, but worse were it in me to see your lordships do needless wrong to the feelings which are proper to our nature, and which, being indulged honestly and under the restraints of religion, become a pledge of domestic quiet here and future happiness in a better world. I say, that you will do ill to rend those ties asunder, and to give this maiden to the kinsman of Lord Morton, though Lord Morton's kinsman he be."

"These are fair reasons, my Lord of Murray," said Morton, "why you should refuse me so simple a boon as to bestow this silly damsel upon young Bennygask. Speak out plainly, my lord: say you would rather see the Castle of Avenel in the hands of one who owes his name and existence solely to your favour than in the power of a Douglas, and of my kinsman."

"My Lord of Morton," said Murray, "I have done nothing in this matter which should aggrieve you. This young man Glendinning has done me good service, and may do me more. My promise was in some degree passed to him, and that while Julian Avenel was alive, when aught beside the maiden's lily hand would have been hard to come by; whereas you never thought of such an alliance for your kinsman till you saw Julian lie dead yonder on the field, and knew his land to be a waif free to the first who could seize it. Come—come, my lord, you do less than justice to your gallant kinsman in wishing him a bride bred up under the milk-pail; for this girl is a peasant wench in all but the accident of birth. I thought you had more deep respect for the honour of the Douglasses."

"The honour of the Douglasses is safe in my keeping," answered Morton, haughtily; "that of other ancient families may suffer as well as the name of Avenel if rustics are to be matched with the blood of our ancient barons."

"This is but idle talking," answered Lord Murray; "in times like these we must look to men and not to pedigrees. Hay was but a rustic before the battle of Luncarty: the bloody yoke actually dragged the plough ere it was blazoned on a crest by the herald. Times of action make princes into peasants, and boors into barons. All families have sprung from some one mean man; and it is well if they have never degenerated from his virtue who raised them first from obscurity."

"My Lord of Murray will please to except the house of

Douglas," said Morton, haughtily: "men have seen it in the tree, but never in the sapling; have seen it in the stream, but never in the fountain.[1] In the earliest of our Scottish annals, the Black Douglas was powerful and distinguished as now."

"I bend to the honours of the house of Douglas," said Murray, somewhat ironically; "I am conscious we of the royal house have little right to compete with them in dignity. What though we have worn crowns and carried sceptres for a few generations, if our genealogy moves no farther back than to the humble *Alanus Dapifer!*"[2]

Morton's cheek reddened as he was about to reply; but Henry Warden availed himself of the liberty which the Protestant clergy long possessed, and exerted it to interrupt a discussion which was becoming too eager and personal to be friendly.

"My lords," he said, "I must be bold in discharging the duty of my Master. It is a shame and scandal to hear two nobles, whose hands have been so forward in the work of reformation, fall into discord about such vain follies as now occupy your thoughts. Bethink you how long you have thought with one mind, seen with one eye, heard with one ear, confirmed by your union the congregation of the church, appalled by your joint authority the congregation of Anti-Christ; and will you now fall into discord about an old decayed castle and a few barren hills, about the loves and likings of a humble spearsman and a damsel bred in the same obscurity, or about the still vainer questions of idle genealogy?"

"The good man hath spoken right, noble Douglas," said Murray, reaching him his hand, "our union is too essential to the good cause to be broken off upon such idle terms of dissension. I am fixed to gratify Glendinning in this matter: my promise is passed. The wars, in which I have had my share, have made many a family miserable; I will at least try if I may not make one happy. There are maids and manors enow in Scotland: I promise you, my noble ally, that young Bennygask shall be richly wived."

---

[1] See Pedigree of the Douglas Family.   Note 23.
[2] See Pedigree of the Stuart Family.   Note 24.

"My lord," said Warden, "you speak nobly, and like a Christian. Alas! this is a land of hatred and bloodshed; let us not chase from thence the few traces that remain of gentle and domestic love. And be not too eager for wealth to thy noble kinsman, my Lord of Morton, seeing contentment in the marriage state no way depends on it."

"If you allude to my family misfortune," said Morton, whose countess, wedded by him for her estate and honours, was insane in her mind, "the habit you wear, and the liberty, or rather license, of your profession, protect you from my resentment."

"Alas! my lord," replied Warden, "how quick and sensitive is our self-love! When, pressing forward in our high calling, we point out the errors of the sovereign, who praises our boldness more than the noble Morton? But touch we upon his own sore, which most needs lancing, and he shrinks from the faithful chirurgeon in fear and impatient anger!"

"Enough of this, good and reverend sir," said Murray; "you transgress the prudence yourself recommended even now. We are now close upon the village, and the proud abbot is come forth at the head of his hive. Thou hast pleaded well for him, Warden, otherwise I had taken this occasion to pull down the nest and chase away the rooks."

"Nay, but do not so," said Warden; "this William Allan, whom they call the Abbot Eustatius, is a man whose misfortunes would more prejudice our cause than his prosperity. You cannot inflict more than he will endure; and the more that he is made to bear, the higher will be the influence of his talents and his courage. In his conventual throne he will be but coldly looked on—disliked, it may be, and envied. But turn his crucifix of gold into a crucifix of wood; let him travel through the land, an oppressed and impoverished man, and his patience, his eloquence, and learning will win more hearts from the good cause than all the mitred abbots of Scotland have been able to make prey of during the last hundred years."

"Tush!—tush! man," said Morton, "the revenues of the halidome will bring more men, spears, and horses into the field in one day than his preaching in a whole lifetime.

These are not the days of Peter the Hermit, when monks could march armies from England to Jerusalem; but gold and good deeds will still do as much or more than ever. Had Julian Avenel had but a score or two more men this morning, Sir John Foster had not missed a worse welcome. I say, confiscating the monk's revenues is drawing his fang-teeth."

"We will surely lay him under contribution," said Murray; "and, moreover, if he desires to remain in his abbey, he will do well to produce Piercie Shafton."

As he thus spoke, they entered the market-place, distinguished by their complete armour and their lofty plumes, as well as by the number of followers bearing their colours and badges. Both these powerful nobles, but more especially Murray, so nearly allied to the crown, had at that time a retinue and household not much inferior to that of Scottish royalty. As they advanced into the market-place, a pursuivant, passing forward from their train, addressed the monks in these words: "The abbot of St. Mary's is commanded to appear before the Earl of Murray."

"The abbot of St. Mary's," said Eustace, "is, in the patrimony of his convent, superior to every temporal lord. Let the Earl of Murray, if he seeks him, come himself to his presence."

On receiving this answer, Murray smiled scornfully, and dismounting from his lofty saddle, he advanced, accompanied by Morton, and followed by others, to the body of monks assembled around the cross. There was an appearance of shrinking among them at the approach of the heretic lord, so dreaded and so powerful. But the abbot, casting on them a glance of rebuke and encouragement, stepped forth from their ranks like a courageous leader, when he sees that his personal valour must be displayed to revive the drooping courage of his followers. "Lord James Stuart," he said, "or Earl of Murray, if that be thy title, I, Eustatius, abbot of St. Mary's, demand by what right you have filled our peaceful village, and surrounded our brethren, with these bands of armed men? If hospitality is sought, we have never refused it to courteous asking; if violence be meant against peaceful churchmen, let us know at once the pretext and the object?"

"Sir abbot," said Murray, "your language would better have become another age, and a presence inferior to ours. We come not here to reply to your interrogations, but to demand of you why you have broken the peace, collecting your vassals in arms, and convocating the Queen's lieges, whereby many men have been slain, and much trouble, perchance breach of amity with England, is likely to arise?"

"*Lupus in fabula,*" answered the abbot, scornfully. "The wolf accused the sheep of muddying the stream when he drank in it above her; but it served as a pretext for devouring her. Convocate the Queen's lieges? I did so to defend the Queen's land against foreigners. I did but my duty; and I regret I had not the means to do it more effectually."

"And was it also a part of your duty to receive and harbour the Queen of England's rebel and traitor; and to inflame a war betwixt England and Scotland?" said Murray.

"In my younger days, my lord," answered the abbot, with the same intrepidity, "a war with England was no such dreaded matter; and not merely a mitred abbot, bound by his rule to show hospitality and afford sanctuary to all, but the poorest Scottish peasant, would have been ashamed to have pleaded fear of England as the reason for shutting his door against a persecuted exile. But in those olden days the English seldom saw the face of a Scottish nobleman, save through the bars of his visor."

"Monk!" said the Earl of Morton, sternly, "this insolence will little avail thee; the days are gone by when Rome's priests were permitted to brave noblemen with impunity. Give us up this Piercie Shafton, or by my father's crest I will set thy abbey in a bright flame!"

"And if thou dost, Lord of Morton, its ruins will tumble above the tombs of thine own ancestors. Be the issue as God wills, the abbot of St. Mary's gives up no one whom he hath promised to protect."

"Abbot," said Murray, "bethink thee ere we are driven to deal roughly. The hands of these men," he said, pointing to the soldiers, "will make wild work among shrines and cells, if we are compelled to undertake a search for this Englishman."

"Ye shall not need," said a voice from the crowd; and, advancing gracefully before the earls, the Euphuist flung from him the mantle in which he was muffled.

"*Via* the cloud that shadowed Shafton!" said he: "behold, my lords, the knight of Wilverton, who spares you the guilt of violence and sacrilege."

"I protest before God and man against any infraction of the privileges of this house," said the abbot, "by an attempt to impose violent hands upon the person of this noble knight. If there be yet spirit in a Scottish Parliament, we will make you hear of this elsewhere, my lords!"

"Spare your threats," said Murray; "it may be my purpose with Sir Piercie Shafton is not such as thou dost suppose. Attach him, pursuivant, as our prisoner, rescue or no rescue."

"I yield myself," said the Euphuist, "reserving my right to defy my Lord of Murray and my Lord of Morton to single duel, even as one gentleman may demand satisfaction of another."

"You shall not want those who will answer your challenge, sir knight," replied Morton, "without aspiring to men above thine own degree."

"And where am I to find these superlative champions," said the English knight, "whose blood runs more pure than that of Piercie Shafton?"

"Here is a flight for you, my lord!" said Murray.

"As ever was flown by a wild goose," said Stawarth Bolton, who had now approached to the front of the party.

"Who dared to say that word?" said the Euphuist, his face crimson with rage.

"Tut! man," said Bolton, "make the best of it, thy mother's father was but a tailor, old Overstitch of Holderness. Why, what! because thou art a misproud bird, and despisest thine own natural lineage, and rufflest in unpaid silks and velvets, and keepest company with gallants and cutters, must we lose our memory for that? Thy mother, Moll Overstitch, was the prettiest wench in those parts; she was wedded by wild Shafton of Wilverton, who, men say, was akin to the Piercie on the wrong side of the blanket."

"Help the knight to some strong waters," said Morton; "he hath fallen from such a height that he is stunned with the tumble."

In fact, Sir Piercie Shafton looked like a man stricken by a thunderbolt, while, notwithstanding the seriousness of the scene hitherto, no one of those present, not even the abbot himself, could refrain from laughing at the rueful and mortified expression of his face.

"Laugh on," he said at length—"laugh on, my masters," shrugging his shoulders; "it is not for me to be offended; yet would I know full fain from that squire who is laughing with the loudest how he had discovered this unhappy blot in an otherwise spotless lineage, and for what purpose he hath made it known?"

"_I_ make it known?" said Halbert Glendinning, in astonishment, for to him this pathetic appeal was made. "I never heard the thing till this moment." [1]

"Why, did not that old rude soldier learn it from thee?" said the knight, in increasing amazement.

"Not I, by Heaven!" said Bolton; "I never saw the youth in my life before."

"But you _have_ seen him ere now, my worthy master," said Dame Glendinning, bursting in her turn from the crowd. "My son, this is Stawarth Bolton, he to whom we owe life and the means of preserving it; if he be prisoner, as seems most likely, use thine interest with these noble lords to be kind to the widow's friend."

"What, my Dame of the Glen!" said Bolton, "thy brow is more withered, as well as mine, since we met last, but thy tongue holds the touch better than my arm. This boy of thine gave me the foil sorely this morning. The brown varlet has turned as stout a trooper as I prophesied; and where is white head?"

[1] See The White Spirit. Note 25.

"Alas!" said the mother, looking down, "Edward has taken orders, and become a monk of this abbey."

"A monk and a soldier! Evil trades both, my good dame. Better have made one a good master fashioner, like old Overstitch of Holderness. I sighed when I envied you the two bonny children, but I sigh not now to call either the monk or the soldier mine own. The soldier dies in the field; the monk scarce lives in the cloister."

"My dearest mother," said Halbert, "where is Edward? Can I not speak with him?"

"He has just left us for the present," said Father Philip, "upon a message from the lord abbot."

"And Mary, my dearest mother?" said Halbert. Mary Avenel was not far distant, and the three were soon withdrawn from the crowd, to hear and relate their various chances of fortune.

While the subordinate personages thus disposed of themselves, the abbot held serious discussion with the two earls, and, partly yielding to their demands, partly defending himself with skill and eloquence, was enabled to make a composition for his convent, which left it provisionally in no worse situation than before. The earls were the more reluctant to drive matters to extremity, since he protested that, if urged beyond what his conscience would comply with, he would throw the whole lands of the monastery into the Queen of Scotland's hands, to be disposed of at her pleasure. This would not have answered the views of the earls, who were contented, for the time, with a moderate sacrifice of money and lands. Matters being so far settled, the abbot became anxious for the fate of Sir Piercie Shafton, and implored mercy in his behalf.

"He is a coxcomb," he said, "my lords, but he is a generous, though a vain, fool; and it is my firm belief you have this day done him more pain than if you had run a poniard into him."

"Run a needle into him you mean, abbot," said the Earl of Morton; "by mine honour, I thought this grandson of a fashioner of doublets was descended from a crowned head at least!"

"I hold with the abbot," said Murray; "there were little honour in surrendering him to Elizabeth, but he shall be sent where he can do her no injury. Our pursuivant and Bolton shall escort him to Dunbar, and ship him off for Flanders. But soft, here he comes, and leading a female, as I think."

"Lords and others," said the English knight, with great solemnity, "make way for the lady of Piercie Shafton—a secret which I listed not to make known, till fate, which hath betrayed what I vainly strove to conceal, makes me less desirous to hide that which I now announce to you."

"It is Mysie Happer, the miller's daughter, on my life!" said Tibb Tacket. "I thought the pride of these Piercies would have a fa'."

"It is indeed the lovely Mysinda," said the knight, "whose merits towards her devoted servant deserved higher rank than he had to bestow."

"I suspect, though," said Murray, "that we should not have heard of the miller's daughter being made a lady had not the knight proved to be the grandson of a tailor."

"My lord," said Sir Piercie Shafton, "it is poor valour to strike him that cannot smite again; and I hope you will consider what is due to a prisoner by the law of arms, and say nothing more on this odious subject. When I am once more mine own man, I will find a new road to dignity."

"*Shape* one, I presume," said the Earl of Morton.

"Nay, Douglas, you will drive him mad," said Murray; "besides, we have other matter in hand. I must see Warden wed Glendinning with Mary Avenel, and put him in possession of his wife's castle without delay. It will be best done ere our forces leave these parts."

"And I," said the miller, "have the like grist to grind; for I hope some one of the good fathers will wed my wench with her gay bridegroom."

"It needs not," said Shafton; "the ceremonial hath been solemnly performed."

"It will not be the worse of another bolting," said the miller; "it is always best to be sure, as I say when I chance to take multure twice from the same meal-sack."

"Stave the miller off him," said Murray, "or he will worry him dead. The abbot, my lord, offers us the hospitality of the convent; I move we should repair hither, Sir Piercie and all of us. I must learn to know the Maid of Avenel; to-morrow I must act as her father. All Scotland shall see how Murray can reward a faithful servant."

Mary Avenel and her lover avoided meeting the abbot, and took up their temporary abode in a house of the village, where next day their hands were united by the Protestant preacher in presence of the two earls. On the same day Piercie Shafton and his bride departed, under an escort which was to conduct him to the seaside, and see him embark for the Low Countries. Early on the following morning the bands of the earls were under march to the Castle of Avenel, to invest the young bridegroom with the property of his wife, which was surrendered to them without opposition.

But not without those omens which seemed to mark every remarkable event which befell the fated family did Mary take possession of the ancient castle of her forefathers. The same warlike form which had appeared more than once at Glendearg was seen by Tibb Tacket and Martin, who returned with their young mistress to partake her altered fortunes. It glided before the cavalcade as they advanced upon the long causeway, paused at each drawbridge, and flourished its hand, as in triumph, as it disappeared under the gloomy archway, which was surmounted by the insignia of the house of Avenel. The two trusty servants made their vision only known to Dame Glendinning, who, with much pride of heart, had accompanied her son to see him take his rank among the barons of the land. "Oh, my dear bairn!" she exclaimed, when she heard the tale, "the castle is a grand place to be sure, but I wish ye dinna a' desire to be back in the quiet braes of Glendearg before the play be played out." But this natural reflection, springing from maternal anxiety, was soon forgotten amid the busy and pleasing task of examining and admiring the new habitation of her son.

While these affairs were passing, Edward had hidden himself and his sorrows in the paternal Tower of Glendearg, where

30

every object was full of matter for bitter reflection. The abbot's kindness had despatched him thither upon pretence of placing some papers belonging to the abbey in safety and secrecy; but in reality to prevent his witnessing the triumph of his brother. Through the deserted apartments, the scene of so many bitter reflections, the unhappy youth stalked like a discontented ghost, conjuring up around him at every step new subjects for sorrow and for self-torment. Impatient at length of the state of irritation and agonised recollection in which he found himself, he rushed out and walked hastily up the glen, as if to shake off the load which hung upon his mind. The sun was setting when he reached the entrance of Corrie-nan-Shian, and the recollection of what he had seen when he last visited that haunted ravine burst on his mind. He was in a humour, however, rather to seek out danger than to avoid it.

"I will face this mystic being," he said; "she foretold the fate which has wrapped me in this dress; I will know whether she has aught else to tell me of a life which cannot but be miserable."

He failed not to see the White Spirit seated by her accustomed haunt, and singing in her usual low and sweet tone. While she sung she seemed to look with sorrow on her golden zone, which was now diminished to the fineness of a silken thread.

> " Fare thee well, thou holly green!
> Thou shalt seldom now be seen,
> With all thy glittering garlands bending
> As to greet my slow descending,
> Startling the bewilder'd hind,
> Who sees thee wave without a wind.
>
> Farewell, fountain! now not long
> Shalt thou murmur to my song,
> While thy crystal bubbles, glancing,
> Keep the time in mystic dancing,
> Rise and swell, are burst and lost,
> Like mortal schemes by fortune crost.
>
> The knot of fate at length is tied,
> The churl is lord, the maid is bride.
> Vainly did my magic sleight
> Send the lover from her sight;
> Wither bush, and perish well,
> Fall'n is lofty Avenel!"

The Vision seemed to weep while she sung; and the words impressed on Edward a melancholy belief that the alliance of Mary with his brother might be fatal to them both.

Here terminates the First Part of the Benedictine's Manu-(script. I have in vain endeavoured to ascertain the precise period of the story, as the dates cannot be exactly reconciled with those of the most accredited histories. But it is astonishing how careless the writers of Utopia are upon these important subjects. I observe that the learned Mr. Laurence Templeton, in his late publication, entitled *Ivanhoe*, has not only blessed the bed of Edward the Confessor with an offspring unknown to history, with sundry other solecisms of the same kind, but has inverted the order of nature, and feasted his swine with acorns in the midst of summer. All that can be alleged by the warmest admirer of this Author amounts to this, that the circumstances objected to are just as true as the rest of the story; which appears to me, more especially in the matter of the acorns, to be a very imperfect defence, and that the Author will do well to profit by Captain Absolute's advice to his servant, and never tell him more lies than are indispensably necessary.